The Mysterious Hermit
of the Tomb

The Mysterious Hermit of the Tomb;
Or, The Phantom of the Old Château

by
Étienne-Léon de Lamothe-Langon

Translated, annotated and introduced by
Brian Stableford

A Black Coat Press Book

ISBN 978-1-61227-734-9. First Printing. May 2018. Published by Black Coat Press, an imprint of Hollywood Comics.com, LLC, P.O. Box 17270, Encino, CA 91416.
Printed in the United States of America.

TABLE OF CONTENTS

Introduction

(by the Translator)

L'Hermite de la tombe mystérieuse, ou Le Fantôme du vieux château, anecdote extraite des annales du treizième siè-cle, "par Mme Anne Radcliffe, et traduite sur le manuscript anglais par M. E. L. D. L. Baron de Langon" was first published in three volumes in Paris by Ménard et Desenne fils in 1816; it was reprinted in 1822 by Lecointe et Durey with the slight variation that the initial H was removed from the first word of the title, and from the word *hermite* wherever it appears in the text. A German translation, presumable pirated and issued anonymously, appeared in 1817. It is here translated as *The Mysterious Hermit of the Tomb* (the original title is ambiguous, but the text makes it abundantly clear that that is the fashion in which it should be construed). The novel is not, in fact, a translation of a work by the celebrated English author of Gothic novels Anne Radcliffe, and its attribution to her is an imposture, its real author being the alleged translator

The initials of that translator rendered in the by-line of the novel stand for "Monsieur Étienne-Léon de Lamothe" and the *Biographie toulousaine* that the same author published in 1822 revealed that the person in question was a much-decorated Imperial administrator, a "maintaineur" of the Jeux Floraux (an annual Toulousan literary competition) and a member of the Académie des Sciences de Toulouse. He is recorded there, in a relatively brief note, as the elder of the two sons of Joseph de Lamothe (1750-1794), a member of the Parlement de Toulouse who had been executed during the Revolution following the suppression of that parlement, on allegedly-spurious charges. Other articles dealing with the members of the family note that Étienne's father, his uncle, also named Étienne, and his grandfather, Christophe, were

7

also notable for literary and heroic endeavors and that they had significant associations with the town of Saint-Félix de Caraman (now Saint-Félix de Lauragais), which plays a key role in the novel.

Although that information might well be accurate, the shape of Lamothe-Langon's subsequent career does cast a shadow of suspicion over everything he wrote, as he became a prolific faker of memoirs and embellisher of history. The breakthrough work that boosted Lamothe-Langon's career to sudden and enormous success, and which remains in print to this day, was published under several different variants of its title during the author's lifetime; it consists of six volumes, first issued in 1829-30, of the supposed memoirs of one of King Louis XV's mistresses, the Comtesse Du Barry. The Comtesse, who eventually perished on the guillotine during the Terror at the age of fifty, had neglected to write her memoirs herself, although she had been the victim of scabrous and slanderous fictitious accounts of her life while she was the King's favorite, on which Lamothe-Langon drew, and which he elaborated considerably in their salacious detail.

Following the success of that enterprise, Lamothe-Langon made every effort to capitalize on it, and spent the next decade churning out fake memoirs by the dozen, many of which similarly featured royal mistresses and other "ladies of quality," but whose range extended to take in many other famous individuals, ranging from the Duc de Richelieu through various kings to Talleyrand and Napoléon Bonaparte (three times), as well as the notorious charlatans Cagliostro and the Comte de Saint-Germain. He had, however, had a rich and somewhat checkered career before obtaining that success, and had already written several works seeking to establish himself as a serious and scrupulous historian, climaxing with his *Histoire de l'Inquisition en France* [History of the Inquisition in France] (1829). That volume had numerous references to the Annales de Toulouse, of which three versions had been published, but when the references were checked in the 1960s they were found to be mostly false, the lists of names in the published Annales having been extensively embellished by fictitious details.

Prior to that discovery being made, many of the "facts" recorded in the *Histoire de l'Inquisition* had been widely repeated, especially in histories of witchcraft and Catharism, initiating a pattern of fantasization of Toulousan history that was to be further elaborated, in spectacular fashion by the three-volume *Histoire des Albigeois: Les Albigeois et l'Inquisition* (1870-1872) written by Napoléon Peyrat (1809-1881). Lamothe-Langon had earlier written 459 articles for the *Biographie toulousaine*, of which he was the principal compiler, and he had published a *Biographie des préfets des 87 départements de la France, par un sous-préfet* (1826), as well as contributing articles to several other reference books, but the extent to which that work might be polluted by invention is still unknown, because no one has carried out a thorough investigation.

The full extent of the author's literary work is unknown; some of his pseudonyms probably remain untraced, and it seems likely that some fake memoirs by other hands have been wrongly attributed to him—he certainly worked in collaboration with numerous other writers during his prolific phase—and nobody has ever made a thorough attempted to sort out the bibliographical nightmare to which the Bibliothèque Nationale's catalogue provides numerous hints, although a tentative beginning was made in Richard Switzer's *Etienne-Leon Lamothe-Langon and the French Popular Novel* (1955). Even his biography is somewhat confused. In contrast to the brief account he provided himself, cited above, one contemporary bibliographical encyclopedia asserts that his original name was Langon, the "Lamothe" having been added belatedly, and that he was probably not of aristocratic descent. He certainly obtained his barony by loyal service to the Empire, as a civil servant (although he did claim to have distinguished himself in battle in Italy while in administrative service there, and to have earned his ennoblement that way). If he owed his early success in life to his loyalty to the Napoleonic cause rather than his early literary endeavors, however, he owed his eventual literary career to the ruination that followed the Empire's collapse, when old Bonapartists fell out of fashion as instruments of state.

The future Baron de Lamothe-Langon was born in Toulouse in 1786 and remained there until he was twenty, when he went to Paris, hoping to make his fortune. His own accounts of his youth allege that he was a brilliant student who had already embarked on prolific literary endeavors before leaving his home town, but it was not until he reached Paris that he first reached print, initially trying to make his name as a poet. In that capacity he published a number of Odes dedicated to various highly-placed personages, including members of Napoléon's family and the painter Jacques-Louis David, as well as a 130-verse account of *Louis XVI dans sa prison* (1808). He called himself Léon de La Motte for a while, and is mistakenly described as a "*poète de Montpellier*" in the *Martyrologie littéraire* of 1816, which not only assumes that he is dead but prints his self-penned epitaph: "*Ci git un fou de qualité/Méchant poëte [sic], amant fidelle/Qui fit mille vers pour sa belle/Et pas un seul pour la posterité.*" [Here lies a noble fool/A bad poet but faithful lover/Who wrote a thousand verses for his lady-love/But not a single one for posterity].

The *Martyrologie littéraire* does note that the fictitious poet wrote prose as well, naming two works, but does not take the trouble to record the fact that he did so under a modified pseudonym, Léon de La Motte-Houdancourt—a blatant attempt to link his supposed descent to the famous Maréchal de France, Philippe de La Mothe-Houdancourt (1605-1657). Contemporary bibliographies credit him with three prose works published during the first phase of his career—*Cinq chapitres de mon roman, ou les Rêves de ma cousine* [Five Chapters of my Novel; or, My Cousin's Dreams](1808); *Clémence Isaure et les troubadours, précédé d'un Précis historique sur les troubadours et les jeux floraux* [Clémence Isaure and the Troubadours, preceded by a Historical Summary of the Troubadours and the Floral Games] (1808); and

10

Gabriel, ou le Fanatisme [Gabriel; or, Fanaticism] (1809)—without giving any further indication of what they contain. The Toulousian *Académie des Jeux Floraux* is the oldest literary society in the world, founded in 1323 by the *Consistori del Gay Saber* [The Society of the Gay Science, in Occitan, then the language of Provençal]. Clémence Isaure was its legendary figurehead, frequently depicted in paintings and statues as a lady holding a flower—the ideal object of desire in the chivalric mythology of the troubadours. The "jeux floraux" were, and still are, annual competitions in which prizes were awarded for poetry. "Léon de La Motte" appears to have considered himself to be, or at least represented himself as, a modern troubadour.

That brief initial phase of Lamothe-Langon's literary activity was, however, cut short when he began his administrative career, initially as a *sous-préfet*, in which capacity he returned to Toulouse in 1811, and then as *préfet* of the same city, before being transferred to various other locations. He was apparently still in possession of an administrative office in Carcassonne during the Hundred Days, having remained in his post during the first phase of the Restoration, but following the debacle of 1815 he was thrown out, at which point he went back home to Toulouse, and set out determinedly to make a living from his pen.

L'Hermite de la tombe mystérieuse, ou le Fantôme du vieux château was the first substantial fruit of that new determination. It was followed by the four-volume *Tête de mort, ou la Croix du Cimetière de Saint-Adrien* [The Death's-Head; or, The Cross of St. Adrian's Cemetery] (1817), which is credited him in bibliographies but the title-page of which is unavailable for inspection. The same is true of his next novel, *Les Mystères de la tour de Saint-Jean ou Les Chevaliers du Temple* [The Mysteries of St. John's Tower; or, The Knights Templar] (1819) although one World-Cat annotation also lists Ann Radcliffe and Matthew Gregory Lewis as "co-authors," so that too might have been published as a fake translation.

The author published another novel in 1819 under the Lamotte-Houdancourt pseudonym, *Maître Étienne, ou Les Fermiers et les chatelains* [Maître Étienne; or, Farmers and Chatelains]; it bears no subtitle, but might well have been the first of a series of novels whose later inclusions are mostly advertised as *romans de moeurs* [novels of manners]—which is to say, stories of contemporary life supposedly illustrative of customs and folkways. Such novels were to become the author's major specialism during the 1820s, although their displacement of Gothic thrillers was gradual.

The list of previous works included in the 1825 novel *La Vampire* (tr. as *The Virgin Vampire*)[1] does not include *Le Spectre de la galerie du château d'Estalens, ou le Sauveur mystérieux* [The Specter of the Gallery of the Château d'Estalens; or, The Mysterious Rescuer] (1820, described falsely as a translation from the English "by Baron G***) or *Les Apparitions du château de Tarabel, ou le Protecteur invisible* [The Ghosts of the Château de Tarabel; or, The Invisible Protector] (1822, signed M. le baron de L.), and although both are credited to Lamothe-Langon in the BN catalogue they are probably not his. The list does include, however, *Jean de Procida, ou les Vêpres Siciliennes, roman historique* [Jean de Procida; or, The Sicilian Vespers] (1821, signed Baron de Lamothe-Langon) and another similarly-signed historical novel *Le Monastère des Frères noirs, ou l'Étendard de la mort* [The Monastery of the Black Friars; or, The Standard of Death] (1825, four volumes).

La Vampire and *Le Monastère des Frères noirs* seem to have been Lamothe-Langon's final works in the Gothic vein for some while. The other books that he published in 1825 were *Le 21 janvier, ou la Malédiction d'un père* [The Twenty-First of January; or, A Father's Curse], *Monsieur le préfet* [The Prefect] and *La Province à Paris, ou les Caquets d'une grande ville* [Provincialism in Paris, or Big City Gossip], all of which seem to be *romans de moeurs*, perhaps autobiograph-

---

[1] Black Coat Press, ISBN 978-1-61227-032-6.

ically-influenced. He did incorporate some Gothic elements into the much later *Souvenirs d'un fantôme, chroniques d'un cimetière* [A Phantom's Memories; Chronicles of a Cemetery] (1838), which consists of fake memoirs in a more satirical vein, and *La Cloche du trépassé, ou Les Mystères du château de Beauvoir* [The Funeral Bell; or, The Mysteries of the Château de Beauvoir] (1839), but he seems to have set that phase of his work firmly aside for many years after 1825.

Most of the novels Lamothe-Langon published in the late 1820s were subtitled *romans de moeurs*, but one thus advertised might be reckoned something of an anomaly, being *L'Espion de police* [The Police Spy] (1826). Although not a fake memoir itself, despite its pretensions to realism, it might have helped to inspire one of the most famous of all the fake memoirs of the period, Eugène Vidocq's *Mémoires* (1828), the author of which made extravagant claims regarding his founding of the Sûreté—and thus became the godfather of the entire genre of crime fiction, cited by Edgar Allan Poe, Honoré de Balzac, Paul Féval and many other pioneers of honest fiction in that vein. It is possible that seeing his explicit work of fiction ripped off in that way helped to prompt Lamothe-Langon to demonstrate that he could play a similar game in a broader arena, having already begun to prepare the stage in *La Cour d'un prince régnant ou Les Deux maîtresses* [The Court of a Reigning Prince; or The Two Mistresses] (1827) and *Le Chancelier et les censeurs* [The Chancellor and the Censors] (1828). The latter novel features Madame Du Barry as a central character, and contributed several incidents to her fake memoirs.

The other labeled *romans de moeurs* of this period were *Le Grand seigneur et la pauvre fille* [The Nobleman and the Poor Girl] (1829), *Le Ventru, ou Comme ils étaient naguère* [The Obese Man; or, How Things Were Before] (1829), *Le Fournisseur et la Provençale* [The Tradesman and the Provençal Girl] (1830) and *Le Duc et le page* [The Duke and the Page-Boy] (1831). The sequence of titles presumably offers a fair indication of the direction the work in question followed, and the manner in which its interest in salacious material was developed. Given that Lamothe-Langon was also working on reference books and supposedly serious historical works during that period, the intensity of his production was remarkable even before he stepped it up by a further gear in the 1830s.

How many prose works Lamothe-Langon produced in total is difficult to estimate, partly because he cited figures himself that are probably exaggerated, but there were at least a hundred. He also claimed to have written many more that remained unpublished, although that too might well have been an exaggeration. What is certain, however—and perhaps odd—is that his production tailed off abruptly after 1840 and soon stopped entirely, even though he did not die until 1864. He therefore took no part in the spectacular boom in popular fiction that followed the *feuilleton*-based newspaper circulation wars of the later 1840s, although he would seem to have been ideally qualified to do so. Nor did he return to any conspicuous activity of any kind after Napoléon III's *coup d'état* in 1851, when old Bonapartists finally came back into fashion (although he was in his sixties by then, and might have blotted his copybook somewhat with his three faked memoirs of the first Emperor).

What became of Lamothe-Langon after 1840 remains something of a mystery; although he published a few more books, they might have been written earlier; if he really had written numerous unpublished novels when he claimed to have done so; late publications like *L'Homme de la nuit, ou les mystères* [The Nocturnal Man; or, The Mysteries] (1842) and *La Dame du comptoir, ou une Princesse incognito* [The Lady at the Counter; or, The Princess in Disguise] (1844) might have been leftovers rather than nostalgic revisitations of youthful pastures. He might simply have figured that he had made enough money by 1840, and could throw away his quills, but it might also be the case that his health had deteriorated. There is an inevitable temptation to suspect something more exotically fitting to a life of sustained deception, but there was always a prosaic figure behind the poseur, and it would not be inappropriate if he had reverted to mere ordinariness long before his demise.

 L'Hermite de la tombe mystérieuse is an interesting novel in several ways, including the fact that it seems to have helped pave the way for his history of the Inquisition, not merely because it s preface is a kind of preliminary sketch for the first volume of the latter work, which offers a detailed account of the Albigensian crusade as the event that paved the way for the founding of the Inquisition, although it carefully leaves out of account the actual founder of the Inquisition, Dominic Guzman, inserting a fictitious character in his stead.

 That aspect of the work is thus connected, via Napoléon Peyrat's elaborations, to Maurice Magre's novel *Le Sang du Toulouse* (1931; tr. as *The Blood of Toulouse*),[2] which makes an interesting contrast with it. Although the only element of Magre's novel that might have derived indirectly from Lamothe-Langon is the role allegedly played by subterranean tunnels in the siege of Carcassonne, it is notable that two minor elements of Lamothe-Langon's novel are echoed, in greatly elaborated fashion, in another Magre novel, *Le Trésor des Albigeois* (1938; tr. as *The Albigensian Treasure*),[3] which reproduces the legend of the sunken lake underneath the Church of Saint-Sernin and also makes much—as many of Magre's works do—of a secret society of custodians on an esoteric wisdom very similar to the one that Bérenger de Saint-Félix encounters in Toledo.

 The relationship of *L'Hermite de la tombe mystérieuse* to the work of the English Gothic novelist Ann Radcliffe is also interesting, although its claim to be her work is distinctly tongue-in-cheek and the story does not make any serious attempt at imitation. Translations of Ann Radcliffe's novels, especially *The Mysteries of Udolpho* (1794) and *The Italian* (1797), had been extremely popular in France, and had estab-

---

[2] Black Coat Press, ISBN 978-1-61227-677-9.
[3] Black Coat Press, ISBN 978-1-61227-686-1.

15

lished an important stereotype imitated in numerous *romans noir*. They had given rise to one previous fake, which is referenced by Lamothe-Langon in the final line of his novel, *Le Tombeau* [The Tomb] (1799), the "translation" of which was initially attributed to "Hector-Chaussier et Bizet," although a later edition is credited to André Morellet,[4] the *philosophe* who had translated *L'Italien* in 1797. That novel had been reprinted in 1821 by Lecointe et Durey, who also reprinted *L'Ermite de la tombe mystérieuse* a year later.

It seems probable that the success of *Le Tombeau* promoted Lamothe-Langon to employ a similar disguise for *L'Hermite de la tombe*, but the principal result of that imposture seems to have been a stark demonstration of the incompatibility of elements of Gothic horror fiction and elements of the hybrid genre of courtly and chivalric romance allegedly developed of the troubadours of Occitan in the twelfth century. Lamothe Langon introduces Baron Arembert de Saint-Félix as a stock Gothic villain, parodic in the sufferings afflicted upon him by seemingly supernatural apparitions, but immediately contrasts him with his ward Adémar, a knight *poursuivant* whose literary pedigree goes back to Chrétien de Troyes, rapidly supplementing him with a troubadour from the same stable.

The resultant collision of those two genres would be awkward enough, but the clash is further complicated by the attempt to graft both genres on to the actual history of the late twelfth and early thirteenth centuries, which makes for a truly bizarre chimera. The whole point of twelfth-century romance

---

[4] If Morellet really was the author of *Le Tombeau*, that opens up the possibility that he was also the author of *Les Diableries*, signed "Hector Chaussiet et Pizet" [sic], although that work only seems to be known via a single secondary reference of 1799. The Bibliothèque Nationale, on the other hand, conflates "Hector Chaussiet" with the playwright Hector Chaussier, who might have written vaudevilles supplied with a music-master from Caen named Pizet.

16

was that it was utterly fantastic, referring back to mytholo-gized periods of history (Carolingian France and Arthurian England) as a kind of admonition to contemporary barons and knights, who bore no resemblance whatsoever to the likes of Roland, Lancelot and Percival, being vicious thugs for whom pillage, mass-murder and rape were a way of life. The attempt to represent the genocidal participants in the Albigensian cru-sade and their adversaries as if they were knights of romance is grotesque in itself, even without the supplementation of lubricious Gothic villains whose castles, replete with incredi-ble subterrains and garish hauntings, offer a metaphorical model of the guilt-stricken mind that is as distant from twelfth-century romantic illusion as it is from brutal twelfth-century reality. The resultant confusion does, however, have a surreal charm that transcends the limits of the ludicrous.

In 1922 the Romantic Movement was just getting under way in Paris, and had yet to produce very much in the way of prose fiction, although Charles Nodier had just begin to lead the way, with fiction influenced by both Gothic and folkloris-tic material. Lamothe-Langon was not alone, therefore in the schematics of his experimentation, and it must be remembered that he really was an experimental writer, boldly pioneering untrodden literary territory. If his creativity was a profligate, and the resultant smorgasbord a slightly indigestible, it also had a bold defiance of conventions and hoary expectation that displays an admirably zestful iconoclasm. As a member of the *avant garde* of French Romanticism, Lamothe-Langon was something of a berserker, but he was not without effect, and he did set up valuable signposts for the practitioners of feuilleton fiction, of which *L'Hermite de la tombe mystérieuse* was a significant one, and those writers found it easier to become giants because his were among the sturdy shoulders they had to stand on.

The following translation was made from the copy of the 1822 edition reproduced on the Bibliothèque Nationale's *gallica* website. The first edition, available for consultation on

Google Books, appear to be identical save for the alteration of the spelling of *Hermite/Ermite*.

Brian Stableford

Preface

(by the Author posing as a Translator)

On seeing the frontispiece of their romance the name of Madame Anne Radcliffe I am convinced that the reader will exclaim: "Yet another work attributed to that woman celebrated in her genre! Are there not enough visions of the château of the Pyrenees, the Forest of Montalbano, the Convent of Saint Catherine, etc., without a Mysterious Hermit of the Tomb coming to put our credulity to another proof and weary our patience? May God give Madame Radcliffe peace in her tomb, for we are pursued in her name sufficiently in his world."

Reader, of either sex, please hear us out before condemning us. Perhaps we are acting in good faith; perhaps we believed that were translating a production of the creator of the genre of terror. Listen to the story that we are going to tell, read the book that we are offering you. Our frankness will disarm you, in all appearance, and if this book is read without ennui, to tell you the truth, we shall have been able to help you relax for a few hours.

I was living in Toulouse in the early days of the month of April 1814. Like a great many residents of the surrounding area I had come to seek refuge in the city from the fury of the war. Maréchal Soult,[5] whose great feats of arms and victorious retreat recall the memory of the greatest captains, counterbalanced with a small army of twenty-five thousand men, harassed by fatigue, lacking everything and having hope only in

---

[5] Nicolas Jean-de-Dieu Soult (1769-1851) was Napoléon's chief-of-staff during the Waterloo campaign and is blamed by some historians for losing the crucial battle by giving misleading orders to Maréchal Grouchy that led to his removal from the battlefield.

their courage, the eighty thousand soldiers that Lord Wellington commanded.

The English army, provisioned beyond its needs, was traveling through peaceful regions that did not treat it as an enemy; it had all the advantages, and its general obtained from circumstances that were favorable a marvelous assistance for his military knowledge. After having hesitated for nearly a month to attack Toulouse, leaving that time to the intrepid Maréchal Duc de Dalmatie to fortify his defensive line, he decided to force the French position.

The attack took place on 10 April, Easter Day. The battle lasted from daybreak until nightfall. Prodigies of valor were performed by the French troops; they made fifteen thousand enemies bite the dust before ceding the formidable redoubts they were defending, and one can say with pride that if the course of political events had not forced the Maréchal to withdraw, Lord Wellington would have bought the city of Toulouse more dearly and would have taken longer to take possession of it. The losses of his army were so considerable that he could not recommence the combat the following day.

In the end, the French general evacuated the city, but his enemy dared not trouble him in his retreat. He seemed then to be similar to a lion that one dares not pursue when one has been fortunate enough to abandon the prey of which it had taken possession. Maréchal Soult was to take up new positions further away, and, ever more redoubtable, made preparations with the debris of his army to oppose new barriers to the enemy, who pushed toward him but who did not have the glory of vanquishing him.

The English officers wounded in that bloody battle were divided between the houses of Toulouse after Wellington had made his entry there. I had the satisfaction of being able to give my cares to a young Scotsman, who wanted to show me some gratitude for the services that I was fortunate enough to render him. He could not walk and I took pleasure in keeping him company.

After having talked politics for a long time, and argued politely enough on a point on which we could not fall into accord—for it was a matter of the preeminence that each of us claimed for his nation—we changed the subject and fell back on literature. A new subject of dissent: he praised Shakespeare, I cited Corneille; he named Pope, quickly I recited a song from *Le Lutrin*;[6] to Bacon I opposed Montesquieu, to Fielding the author of *Gil Blas*; I believed Madame de Sévigné superior to Lady Montague; in sum, we were in less accord in that that matter than the other.

The moment for us to separate arrived; I quit Toulouse, he left for Paris. Then he wanted to recognize worthily the little that I had done for him.

"Monsieur," he said to me one day, "you like letters; you have, you say, written a few novels; permit me to offer you one that belongs to me, which was given to me by one of my relatives, Mrs. Anne Radcliffe."

At that well-known name I shivered; I asked my young officer whether the novel of which he was speaking was by that illustrious lady. He certified that to me, and handed me the manuscript, which I had a great deal of difficulty reading. After having deciphered it, I had less doubt about the name of its author, but I have permitted myself to suppress long descriptions, I have retouched the geographical part that was not in conformity with the locales, and I have reestablished the exactitude of historical facts to which the author had paid scant attention. I have added a few ballads and put at the head, for general information, a "Historical Summary of the Albigensian War," which will serve to allow the novel to be read more fruitfully. This is the result of my labor. I shall deem myself happy if you do not find that I would have done better to suppress the translation entirely.

---

[6] *Le Lutrin* (1672-84) is a parody of epic poetry by Nicolas Boileau, which antedated Pope's *Dunciad* by some decades.

Historical Summary of the Albigensian War

The heresy of the Albigensians owed its birth to a certain Pierre de Bruys, a Provençal who was the first to spread that reprehensible error in the Languedoc.[7] First he attacked the baptism of children, the sacrament of the Eucharist, the prayer for the dead and the cult of images. It was nevertheless seen subsequently that his disciples recognized two gods.

The most considerable of his partisans was the monk Henri, a heresiarch all the more dangerous because his manners were more insinuating than his master's. He quit the habit of his order, but he conserved its modesty. His eloquence was seductive, and it was difficult to defend oneself against the impressions he wanted to give. In particular, he subjugated Alphonse Jourdain, Comte de Toulouse, who considered him blessed; and Saint Bernard himself admitted, in his letters that it was not surprising that the cleverest individuals allowed themselves to be blinded by such a rogue.[8]

---

[7] Pierre de Bruys (?-c.1131) was a popular preacher who was murdered by a mob, whose existence and opinions are only known via an attack launched against them by Pierre de Montboisier (1092-1156), the Abbot of Cluny. The notion that his ideas influenced the Albigensians a century later is pure speculation, although he might have influenced a later popular preacher, Henri de Lausanne (?-1148), about whom very little is reliably known, although he appears to have had some success attracting adherents in Toulouse before his ideas were opposed there by Saint Bernard, and it is not impossible that Henrician ideas were handed down subversively to the Albigensians.

[8] Alphonse Jourdain (1103-1148) became Comte de Toulouse in 1109; after his death he was succeeded by Raymond V, the father of Raymond VI; the story of the mysterious hermit

The heresy made considerable progress during the twelfth century; the south of France, and the Languedoc in particular, were inundated by it. The Church did not take long to be alarmed by the impetus those dangerous errors acquired. Several councils anathematized them; that of Lombers, a small village in the Albigeois, not the former Episcopal seat of that name on the banks of the Save, was the one in which the heresiarchs were condemned with the greatest solemnity.[9]

The leader of the Albigensians was named Olivier; he combined a persuasive eloquence with profound knowledge. He had no hesitation in going to the council and arguing against the priests who composed it. He was opposed by the Archbishop of Narbonne, the Bishop of Nîmes, and the Abbots of Cendrus and Froidefront. The appointed judges were the Bishop of Albi, Arnauld de Bé, and the Abbots of Castres, Undereil and Candeille.

The novelty of the spectacle, and the interest of the cause that was to be treated there, attracted the most considerable individuals. Seen coming to Lombers were Constance, Comtesse de Toulouse and sister of Louis-le-Jeune, the Vicomtes de Béziers and de Lautrec, the Bishops of Toulouse, Agde, Béziers and Lodève, the Abbots of Gaillac, Saint-Pons, etc.

---

eliminates Raymond V, thus contributing to the confusion of the story's chronology.

[9] Lombers is said to have been the scene of a debate between the rival Catholic and Cathar Bishops of Albi in the 1180s, but the historical evidence is based on a single chronicle by Guillaume de Puylaurens; it does not feature the elaborate cast of characters cited in the following paragraphs, although a few of the names are cited by other sources with reference to an earlier debate that allegedly took place in 1165, for which it is difficult to find any citation prior to Lamothe-Langon. Some other works allege that a "Cathar Council" was held in 1167 in the Château de Saint-Félix, but the authenticity of the 17th century source document for that assertion is highly dubious.

The heretics were condemned on all points, convicted of bad faith, and constrained to submit to the penances that the Church imposed on them.

Guillaume Trencavel, Comte de Carcassonne, Vicomte de Béziers, d'Albi and de Castres, whose presence, firmness and good intentions had contributed a great deal to the result of the conference, claimed the honor of exterminating the heresy, but he was deceived in his desires, for, a short time afterwards, the inhabitants of Béziers, having risen up against him, killed him in the cathedral of that city, to which he had gone to hear their demands, and wounded the Archbishop, who tried to defend him. His son, Roger Trencavel, avenged that cruel death, but could not prevent the heresy from infesting the city.[10]

The heresy continued to acquired new strength, no matter what was to be done to overturn it; it was dominant in the lands submissive to the Comtes de Toulouse, so Raymond VI, nicknamed the Old, who then reigned, was accused of secretly favoring it. Pope Innocent III, placed on the pontifical throne in that era, sent legates to combat the enemies of the Church in 1198, 1202 and 1204. They confounded them, but could not vanquish their stubbornness.

Pierre de Castelnauld was the most energetic of the Holy Father's envoys. Raymond VI always found him in his path. He sought to seduce him and soften him toward the unfortunates whose father he considered himself to be, since he was their sovereign, but without success. Pierre de Castelnauld did not take long to attach him. In order to conclude the disputes,

---

[10] Almost all sources cite the name of the father of the Roger Trencavel featured in Lamothe-Langon's story as Roger, and his grandfather's name as Raymond. Raymond Trencavel was murdered in the cathedral, but for reasons that had no obvious connection with the Albigensian heresy. Footnoting all the distortions in the remainder of the essay would become tedious, but the notes so far given offer an impression of its reliability.

Raymond promised to go to Saint-Gilles, where there were a few conferences, which, far from soothing them reciprocally, animated them further. The Comte threatened the legate with his wrath; the latter attempted to leave, but as he was about to board a boat to cross the Rhône, two men approached him and assassinated him.

Castelnauld was said to have died forgiving his murderers, and Comte Raymond was suspected of having armed their sacrilegious hands; he could not, however, be convicted of such a crime. We prefer to think that vile courtiers believed that they were satisfying his vengeance by immolating the man who had insulted him.[11] Perhaps he ought to have extracted a striking justice from it, and his negligence in that regard served as a pretext for those who wanted to doom him.

Innocent III, on learning the news of Pierre de Castelnauld's assassination, had a crusade published, directed less against the heretics than against the Comte de Toulouse. In the meantime, Foulques, the Bishop of Toulouse, abused and denounced to the heavens a prince he called sacrilegious. His enthusiastic zeal merited him the honor of being delegated to the Pope by the new legates. He ran to Rome to embitter minds.

Foulques, or Folquet, was the son of a Genoese merchant named Alphonse established in Marseille. The latter, when he died, left an immense fortune to young Foulques, who, disdaining the peaceful life of a merchant, preferred to put on the costume of a troubadour, which was to open the doors of princely palaces to him. Richard of England, Alphonse II, King of Aragon, and Raymond V, Comte de Toulouse, heaped him with favors, but he attached himself preferentially to Barral, Vicomte de Marseille.

Azalaïs de Roquemartine, the Vicomte's wife, who was celebrated for her charms, her intelligence and her urbanity,

---

[11] Maurice Magre bases the plot of *Le Sang de Toulouse* (q.v.) on that supposition, with the exception that he deems the courtiers in question to be heroic rather than vile,

saw the most famous troubadours attached to her carriage. Foulques augmented their number, but he wanted to please her and chose the means that he permitted himself to employ poorly. The irritated Vicomtesse expelled him from the court.

He traveled through several regions and stopped for a long time in Montpellier, where Guillaume VIII reigned, who had married a daughter of Manuel, the Emperor of Constantinople. Finally, weary of society, he became a monk of the Order of Cîteaux; his wife—for he was married—and his two sons followed his example. But the peace of the cloister did not calm the impetuosity of his character; he emerged from the obscurity of the monastery and, from the gallant troubadour and libertine he had been before, he became an insolent and rebellious fanatic. As soon as he was on the Episcopal throne, he signaled himself by means of a host of enterprises both bold and culpable; he excited the wrath of the Holy See against its sovereign, the Comte de Toulouse, at a time when it was redoubtable.

Raymond, who loved his people, refused the executions that were demanded of him. However, the storm was approaching; the crusade preached against the Albigensians had had the greatest success. Rightly frightened by the multitude that was about to fall upon him, Raymond VI asked for a new absolution from the excommunications launched against him. He consented to surrender to the legat Milon seven fortified places. A council assembled at Saint-Gilles; Raymond was summoned there, he was judged, and he reentered the Church, after having submitted to the most humiliating of ceremonies.

An altar was set up under the vestibule of the abbey, on which the holy sacrament was exposed, as well as the relics of holy martyrs. A large number of Archbishops, prelates and noble barons were present. Raymond was taken to that place stripped of his garments and naked to the waist; he promised new obedience to the Pope, submission to the penances imposed on him, and eternal hatred of the heretics. Following those honorable amends, the legate Milon passed his stole around his neck and, holding it by the two ends, he introduced him into the church while whipping him with and handful of rods. The absolution followed that chastisement.

After the ceremony, Raymond, unable to go back, so great was the crowd, was constrained to traverse one of the aisles, to which the tomb of Pierre de Castelnauld had been transported, with the consequence that several people cried that the prince had made honorable amends to him after his death.

While these things were happening in the Languedoc, the cross was taken in all the cities of France. Soon, a formidable army was assembled in the summer of 1207 on the banks of the Rhône. At its head were seen Odon, Duc de Bourgogne; Pierre de Courtenay, Comte d'Auxerre; Simon de Montfort, Comte de Lincestre;[12] le Comte de Nevers,[13] Guy de Levis and a host of illustrious persons who believed that they were serving God in immolating the heretics.

Philippe-Auguste, King of France, left the enemies of the Comte de Toulouse to occupy themselves with his ruination. He was unable to forgive him for having recognized the supremacy of the Emperor of Germany, and that fatal condescension on Raymond's part was the thing that contribution most to his doom. The legate demanded that he lead the crusaders himself, and that he was with them to combat his unfortunate subjects.

The operations of the campaign were opened by the siege of Béziers, a populous city placed on a hill, the foot of which was irrigated by the river Orbe: a frightful siege marked in history in letters of blood. Eighty thousand people were put to the sword there. It is said that before the carnage commenced, the crusaders asked the Abbot of Cîteaux how they were to

---

[12] This title is amended in the story to "Comte de Leycestre," which I have there corrected to "Earl of Leicester," but I have left it as it is given in this prefatory essay.

[13] The Comte de Nevers who took part in the Albigensian crusade was Hervé IV de Donzy; in the story the title is given to an entirely fictitious character.

recognize the Catholics among the Albigensians. "Kill them all; God will know his own," that monster replied, who preferred to see the blood of the innocent shed rather than let a single guilty individual escape.

From Béziers they went to Carcassonne, defended by young Roger Trencavel, Comte Raymond's nephew. Means of accommodation were attempted in his favor. Pierre, King of Aragon, who wanted to take a hand in that, could not succeed. The city was constrained to surrender; the inhabitants were expelled, and all those successfully convicted of heresy hanged or burned.[14] The Vicomte was arrested, and died a few days later, not without suspicion of poison.

It was then that Simon de Montfort, Comte de Lincestre, succeeded in being chosen as the leader of the enterprise, after the refusal of the Duc de Bourgogne and the Duc de Nevers.[15] Covering his ambitious pretentions with the veil of religion, he pushed the Comte de Toulouse to the end by all sorts of underhanded methods. Raymond, excommunicated for the third time, went to Rome to defend himself. In vain, the legate Milon and Comte de Montfort united their skill to appease the Comte de Toulouse; they could not deflect him from the journey.

He arrived in Rome in January 1210. The Pope received him with distinction, welcomed his complaints, dressed him in a rich cloak, gave him a precious ring, and granted him a brief that prohibited the disposal of his lands, given that he had been judged innocent of the murder of Pierre de Castelnauld.

During his absence, Montfort invaded the greater part of his estates. Raymond returned diligently in order to defend them. The two rivals declared war on one another. Simon had

---

[14] Author's note: "The historical part that is found in the romance concerning the siege of Carcassonne is in conformity with the most scrupulous verity." That is a bare-faced lie.

[15] This allegation comes from the story; in fact, Montfort was always in command.

a fourth excommunication launched against him by a legate who was misled and disobeyed the Pope.

Foulques, ever fanatical, roused the people against Raymond, and pushed insolence so far as to tell the prince that he had to quit Toulouse while he was making ordinations, because the legates had thrown a prohibition over the places where Raymond was. Raymond, insulted by such a demand, sent Foulques in his turn an order to quit his estates.

"It is not the Comte who made me Bishop," Foulques replied. "I was elected by ecclesiastical law, not intruded by violence or by his authority, so I will not leave because of him. Let him come if he dares; I am ready to die in order to arrive at glory by the chalice of the passion; let him come, the tyrant, accompanied by his satellites; he will find me alone and unarmed; I wait the recompense and I have no fear of what men can do to me."

He continued to stand up to Raymond thus, and it was only three weeks later that he left Toulouse of his own will. He went to take refuge in Montfort's camp; from there he excited to Toulousans to revolt. Not having been able to succeed in that, he ordered the clergy to leave the city, which they did immediately, marching barefoot and taking the holy sacrament with them.

Montfort, animated by Foulques' advice, applied himself to the conquest of several cities in the environs of Toulouse. Lavaur was delivered to the flames; the greater number of its inhabitants were thrown into them, and Giraude, who was its lady, was thrown alive into a well, which was covered in stones all the way to its mouth.

Raymond, who perceived Montfort's project, hastened to fortify Toulouse. It was not long before his preparations became necessary, for the crusaders laid siege to it in 1211. Unable to invest the city walls entirely they attempted an attack from the direction of the outlying districts, but the Comte, aided by the princes of Foix and Comminges, was fortunate enough to repel his enemies' efforts, and even to lift the siege.

As he withdrew, Simon took possession by treason of the Château de Montferrand, defended by Baudouin, the brother of the Comte de Toulouse; that warrior, betraying the interests of his family, made a treaty with Montfort, but he was cruelly punished for it. Having fallen into the hands of Raymond's partisans some time later, he was hanged without mercy, and his brother was present at the expedition.

Knowing that the crusaders' leader was enclosed in Castelnaudary with few troops, Raymond hastened there in order to surprise hm. His attempt was not crowned with success; he was repelled, with losses. Finally, after much negotiation, the two armies met under the walls of Muret. The army of the Comte de Toulouse, swelled by that of the King of Aragon, who was commanding it personally, amounted to sixty thousand combatants. Montfort dared to attack it with scarcely three thousand men. In the first collision the King of Aragon was killed; disorder followed his death, the rout became complete and the Comte de Lincestre—if the historians of the time can be believed—caused twenty thousand of his enemies to bite the dust, and only had to regret the loss of three men.

The battle of Muret dealt the final blow to Raymond. The Council of Latran, in 1215, stripped him of his estates; only a pension of four thousand marcs was awarded to him, and his son, Raymond the Younger, only obtained from the vast provinces that the sovereignty of his family composed, the Marquisat of Provence. Montfort was solemnly recognized as Comte de Toulouse.

Raymond's subjects did not take long to want to shake off the usurper's yoke; the war recommenced. Toulouse finally declared in favor of its legitimate masters, Montfort came to besiege it, entered it as victor, put it to pillage, delivered it to the flames on the advice of Bishop Foulques and massacred its principal inhabitants pitilessly. His barbarity did not subjugate the Toulousans. Scarcely had he gone away than they rebelled again, summoning Raymond the Younger, who returned in haste, and was aided by the most distinguished Barons and Seigneurs of the surrounding areas, among whose number the historians of the Languedoc list Gaspard de Labarthe, Roger de Comminges, Bertrand, Jourdain de Lille, Gérard de Gourdon, Seigneur de Caraman, Bertrand de Montaigu and his brother Gaillard Bertrand, and Guitard de Marmande, Étienne and Agravic de la Valète, Huc and Gérard de Lamothe, Bertrand de Pestillac, Gérard d'Amanieu and Pierre de Castelnauld.[16]

Montfort came running with an army of more than a hundred thousand men, but the term of his days had arrived. He found death under the walls of the city; he was killed by a stone launched by a machine; some said that a woman bore him the mortal blow. His death annihilated his family's hopes, his army was constrained to withdraw and lift the siege of Toulouse. Soon, even Amaury, Montfort's son, ceded all his rights to Louis VIII. King of France, who continued the war.

Finally, a peace treaty put an end to that bloody struggle. Raymond VII, who had succeeded his father, recovered a substantial part of his estates, and, having married his daughter Jeanne to Alphonse, Comte de Poitiers, the brother of Saint Louis, he was able to contrive the happiness of his subjects. After Jeanne's death, the comté de Toulouse passed to the French crown.

Such was the outcome of that war, in which arms were taken up less to punish the heretics than to ruin a prince whose grandeur had become redoubtable to his neighbors, and in which the pretext of avenging the cause of Heaven served as a veil for earthly ambitions.

---

[16] Author's reference: "Dom Vaissete, *Histoire du Languedoc*, p. 416, year 1217." The specific reference is mistaken but the list of names is probably accurate. The name Gérard de Lamothe, which echoes the author's affected name, is also cited in his subsequent novel *Souvenirs d'un fantôme* (1838); a troubadour of that name is known to have assisted Raymond VI in the defense of Toulouse in 1217, along with two of his brothers, Huc and Arnaud.

THE MYSTERIOUS HERMIT OF THE TOMB; or, THE PHANTOM OF THE OLD CHÂTEAU

PART ONE

Chapter I: The Storm

Come, O Muses of Occitania, come to me, either dancing to the sound of the joyful tambourine or sighing a plaintive ballad on the amorous harp. I want to sing the praises of your children; I want to recall those fortunate epochs when the triple alliance as formed of songs, combats and sweet tenderness, when beauty inspired both the warrior flying to his victory and the minstrel lover of the pleasant triumphs that do not cost the vanquished tears. Alas, they have disappeared, those days of glory and gallantry. Today, disenchanted amour has lost its happiest charms; it no longer blushes, it has ceased to merit the worship that our sensible ancestors had devoted to it...

O Muses, unroll for me the tableau of centuries past; and you, troubadours, pour into my soul a portion of your amiable genius. All my wishes will be fulfilled if I can obtain a few flowers of your crown, and if ever beauty grants me a smile, O troubadours, I shall owe it to you!

It was night; black clouds charged with hail and lightning were advancing from the south, driven by the impetuous sirocco. The trees, violently agitated, collided with one another, groaning; the fields, covered with gilded ears of wheat, were on the brink of seeing their rich hope annihilated; and in the long galleries of the fortified château of Saint-Félix, whistling sounds were heard that imported fear into all souls.

Even Arembert, in spite of his bravery, was prey to the most baneful terrors. The storm that was about to burst over the town reminded him vividly of the one that passion had ignited in his heart.

In the midst of his principal vassals, Arembert was pacing back and forth in the large audience hall of his noble dwelling, Sometimes, stopping dead, he attached his gaze to the stained glass of the windows, seemingly searching through them to ascertain the progress of the storm; sometimes, marching with precipitate strides, he seemed to indicate by his abrupt movement that he might be trying to escape disastrous thoughts. Unhappy Arembert! At what price have you bought the pomp that surrounds you!

Meanwhile, the clouds were rising over the horizon, the thunder was rumbling forcefully, and frequent lightning flashes shone over the countryside, carrying into the hall a fugitive clarity that illuminated its extent momentarily. Several minutes ago, Arembert had run to sit down under the elevated awning, the mark of his power; he hid his head in his hands; he did not speak, but frequent sighs were heard, exhaled from a breast oppressed by a thousand painful memories.

Standing around him, in a respectful silence, his officers were contemplating him with pity when a terrible thunderclap appeared to wake him, and the page who was closest to him thought he heard these words emerge from his mouth:

"Well, what are you waiting for? Strike, then, vengeful heaven."

After a few moments, Arembert, proudly raising his somber forehead, asked in an altered voice whether young Adémar had returned to the château.

"Nor, Sire Baron," replied Roberto, his man of confidence, "the youth, who left at the fourth hour of the day, only accompanied by a squire, has not reappeared within our ramparts."

"Why, when the tempest is rumbling, does he stay away?"

"Perhaps, surprised by the storm, he has sought shelter in a vassal's cottage."

"As soon as he appears, do not forget to tell him that I want to speak to him without delay. What an evening, Roberto! The air has never seemed to me to be inflamed to such a point!"

"You ought to be accustomed to storms, Monseigneur; our country has been their arena for a long time."

"How feeble man is! I shiver in spite of myself when the flashes of lightning announce its fall."

"Arembert ought to fear it," pronounced a voice.

Arembert rose to his feet precipitately and angrily. "What insolent person dares to insult his master? Guards, search for him; seize him and let him be precipitated into the dungeon of the great tower!"

He had spoken, and people ran to carry out his orders, but no one had spoken; all those who were in the hall, devoured by an inexpressible terror, were only able to tremble and remain silent.

"Roberto! Roberto!" cried Arembert.

"Sire Baron?"

"It is time this ended; I want to know the audacious individual who has been playing with me for so many years. What docs he want with me? What does he seek?"

"Vengeance!" said the voice.

"Again!" said Arembert and his officers.

And again the lightning, falling with an indescribable din, penetrates into the hall, strikes Arembert's escutcheon, pulverizes it, smashes his armor and, exiting again in a column of fire, runs to bury itself in a tree in the garden, to which it sets fire.

Terror, brought to its peak, becomes general. Everyone, by virtue of a spontaneous movement, places one knee on the ground, and the Eternal is the object of their prayer.

Arembert has not shared in the general devotion; his eyes do not roll beneath their lids; his mouth is agape and his entire body remains in a frightful immobility. Several seconds go by thus.

Finally, Arembert, coming round, addresses himself to Roberto, and in a voice that he tries to render tranquil, he commands him to go and inform the pilgrim who arrived two hours ago that he is ready to grant him the audience that the latter wishes so dearly.

After having bowed, Roberto draws away. Valets arrive, bringing wax candles; they distribute them around the hall. During that occupation, the pilgrim, conducted by Roberto, presents himself. Then Arembert makes a sign, and everyone retires, leaving him alone with the newcomer.

"Approach, man of God; I am disposed to listen to what you have to say to me."

"Sire Baron, it is not about myself that I want to talk to you; God forbid that I occupy your time with such an unimportant object."

"What do you want, then?"

"The interest of the Church alone has brought me to you."

"Explain yourself."

"Can I do so in surety?"

"Trust in my word."

"I am tranquil henceforth. A political tempest is about to burst over the neighboring lands. Far from expelling the heretics from his estates, Comte Raymond de Toulouse is lending them a support whose consequences can only be disastrous for Christianity. The Albigensians are raising their impious heads, their number is increasing; they are threatening our holy religion; everywhere the cry of the just is making itself heard, everywhere people are asking the Lord to put an end to an abomination that is making Toulouse a second Babylon.

"The cry of the just has been heard; already, coming from all directions, ardent defenders of the faith are taking up arms in order to annihilate a perverse race; but success will not crown their efforts so long as Raymond reigns in the Languedoc; their house has been secretly polluted for a long time with the venom of heresy. Raymond VI grants an evident protection to those whom Rome has condemned; it is necessary, in order to obtain the chastisement of his audacity, that he fall with those who have rendered his doom necessary. Already, everything is prepared for that attempt; the Comtes de Bourgogne, de Nevers and de Montfort have taken up arms the cause of the Church is already triumphant; Béziers, that superb city, has fallen to the crusaders' arms, and its blazing walls already announce the fate reserved for the Lord's enemies."

"Can it be! What, Béziers…?"

"Has disappeared in the ashes. Its towers, which the flames devoured, its fugitive inhabitants, everything announces that the Albigensians will only oppose an impotent resistance to us. And you, whom the Comte de Toulouse has long misunderstood, whose services he has only recompensed with ingratitude, will you be obstinate in burying yourself under his ruins, while, while a prosperous fate might shine for you? Informed of our valor, the leaders of the crusaders wants to conserve you, and even augment your possessions; will you refuse their generous offers? Will you stick to a fidelity that can only be prejudicial to you? Believe me, hasten to accept the propositions that I am charged with making to you…"

"But the name of traitor…," said Arembert.

"Are you one, in fighting for God's cause?"

"My oath of obedience…"

"Only the heretics can reproach you for it."

"What guarantee do I have of the promises made to me?"

"Come to treat with the crusaders in person," said the pilgrim. "They will be at the gates of Carcassonne at dawn tomorrow. They will speak to you."

"Is Raymond not among them?"

"What does a prince who will soon cease to be one matter to you? Sire Arembert, will you permit me to speak to you in all confidence?"

"I beg you to do so."

"Your name has reached me, as well as the renown of secret pains that are rending your soul."

"Is that possible?" said Arembert, involuntarily.

"Whatever the cause of your chagrins might be, it depends on you to put an end to them. Throw yourself into the arms of the Church, embrace its defense; it will protect you, it will forgive you, it can sanction everything that men might do, and that which men cannot do. It can assure you the peace of your conscience."

"If I thought that...!"

"I assure you of it."

"No," said the voice, "there are sins for which Heaven refuses its pardon; its ministers do not have the power to undo them."

"Great God!" cried the pilgrim.

"Do you hear it, that voice, which pursues me incessantly," said Arembert, "which assails me at all hours and which, when I deliver myself to sleep, wakes me up by lavishing threats upon me? What am I saying, sleep? There is none for me; if fatigue weighs upon my eyes, my imagination retraces for me...no, it cannot retrace anything for me!"

With those words, Arembert falls silent; a clap of thunder is heard; thus the conscience of the Baron de Saint-Félix is rumbling dully.

In spite of his apparent piety, even the pilgrim was gripped by fear; he leaned on his staff; his head inclined toward the ground and he seemed to reflect. Finally, after an interval of silence, he addressed himself to Arembert:

"Will you give me a response, Sire Baron?"

"I intend to take it myself," said Arembert.

Bowing, the pilgrim was about to withdraw when a page, opening the door to the hall, announced young Adémar. The latter came in slowly; his expression was somber, and, far from running to the Baron in order to kiss his hand, as he was accustomed to do, he contented himself with bowing respectfully. Arembert, too distressed to pay any heed to the youth's new conduct, asked him where he had passed the time of the storm.

"Not far from your château," said Adémar, "is the forest of Caillavel; at one of the crossroads of that wood, the hermit Étienne has established his dwelling, next to a tomb that he seems to be guarding carefully. It is there that I sought a refuge against the waters of heaven, which were falling in torrents."

"The hermit Étienne!" said the pilgrim. "It seems to me that the legate Milon has ordered me to visit his modest dwelling."[17]

"I don't know whether it will be easy for you to penetrate as far as him," said Arembert. "People rarely approach him, and his hermitage appears to be guarded by beings of a superior essence. He has settled in my domains however; one evening, I wanted to enter his habitation, but a sight that still troubles me at the moment when I am speaking to you, constrained me to recoil involuntarily. Since that time I have not attempted again to approach a bizarre being who takes pleasure in surrounding himself with magic and mysteries."

"It's said that his influence is all-powerful over the people of the region," said the pilgrim.

"He alone preserves my vassals from the poison of heresy, which had made immense progress in the surrounding area. But Adémar, go and get ready to accompany me."

Adémar went pale. "You're leaving?"

---

[17] A papal legate named Milon is mentioned by the chronicler who accompanied the crusaders, Pierre de Vaux-de-Cernay, as having been in conflict with Raymond when the latter was trying to reconcile himself with the church, but is said to have died soon afterwards, and certainly did not take the leading role in the crusade attributed to him in the story.

"The interest of my barony demands that I go to Carcassonne promptly."

"I was counting on obtaining permission from you to go to Toulouse tomorrow."

"What design can take you there?"

Adémar hesitated. "I am going there to satisfy the designs of the saintly hermit Étienne."

"Has he put his confidence in your hands so rapidly?"

"It is a secret, at least, of which he has made me the depositary."

"Monseigneur Arembert," said the pilgrim, "let the noble Adémar fulfill the promise he has made to the venerable Étienne; perhaps he is sending this fine knight to Bishop Foulques, whose zeal for the good cause is well known."

Adémar bowed without making any reply, although the pilgrim's glance seemed to be inviting him to do so. He addressed the Baron de Saint-Félix, and, in a timid voice, he asked him whether he would permit him to keep the promise he had made.

"Yes," Arembert replied. "You can leave tomorrow; take care not to prolong your absence, and come back when you can to my château, where you will carry out my orders if they have arrived ahead of you, or at least await them."

He had finished. Adémar saluted him and withdrew, followed by the pilgrim, while the Baron, preceded by his squires, went to his apartments.

Chapter II: The Hermit

By virtue of a secret presentiment, Adémar had not wanted to inform Arembert of the cause that was to take him to the capital of Raymond's estates the following day.

Rising before dawn, guided by his love of hunting, Adémar had quit the Château de Saint-Félix with the intention of roaming the wood of Caillavel, the retreat of wild beasts and game less redoubtable to combat. Followed by Aubin, his principal squire, he had hastened his destrier's pace, and he had been in the forest for some time when the sun rose over the horizon. Then, fatigued by a difficult course, he dismounted and approached a stream that gave freshness to the noble oaks and, while contemplating the fugitive water, he sang a ballad that the celebrated troubadour Pierre Vidal had once composed:[18]

Flower of spring shines at dawn,
For the pleasures she receives that day;
Her fresh bud opens and colors
In the pure breath of Zephyr and Amour.

Flower of spring, with her charmed beauty
Lavishes her attractions on the butterfly.
She is happy, she believed that she is loved!
Transports of amour make regrets fall silent.

Flower of spring, on her weakened stem
Cedes to the rigors of the mutinous aquilon.
No more happiness, your youth is past;
Evening destroys the dreams of the morn.

---

[18] Author's note: "Music by Momigui."

While Adémar was singing, a hermit, attracted by his melodious voice, had emerged from the density of the forest and drawn nearer in order to listen to him. The hermit was named Étienne; he had appeared in the region a long time ago, like one of those superior beings who sometimes descend from the ethereal spheres in order to bring happiness to the part of the globe on which they have cast a sympathetic gaze. No one knew where Étienne had been born; nothing certain could be said when people spoke about him, but the peasants called him "the hermit of the tomb."

That name originated from a vast mausoleum of black marble that stood beside his hermitage; that tomb, devoid of an inscription, was placed on four steps of white marble; its form was pyramidal. In the middle of one of its faces there was a bronze door that had no lock; a sword fixed in two grooves was its only defense, but that simple rampart was a thousand times more difficult to overcome than the high crenellations of warrior towns; no man would have dared conceive the idea of approaching a place that the vulgar believed to be destined to profound mysteries and guarded by invisible powers.

There were no marvelous tales to which the hermit Étienne did not lend himself. Here it was claimed that blinding flames guarded the approaches to his dwelling by night; there others asserted that when the chariot of darkness descended from the black mountains, he had been seen, clad in a bizarre costume, being carried through the air on luminous clouds; sometimes his voice had retained hail ready to escape in the night; sometimes he had summoned the obedient lightning down upon a brigand ready to slay an unfortunate individual. Father Étienne's retired life furnished aliments to the avid curiosity of the villagers; it was rare for anyone to succeed in talking to him, and even rarer for anyone to be introduced into his hermitage, but every time he left it, it was only to do good; he had never returned from his excursions without bringing back the blessings of the unfortunate.

If there were numerous difficulties in reaching him, there were even greater ones in contemplating his face; no one could boast of having glimpsed it, so careful was he hermit to hide it; a vast hood covered it incessantly, and it was only at intervals that one sometimes saw two sparkling eyes shining within it.

Étienne's stature surpassed that of the tallest men; he was six feet and several inches tall, either because he was thus formed or because his costume or the boots that he wore increased his immeasurable stature considerably. In his hands he held a black and knotty staff on which he leaned; his black beard fell in waves over his breast, and a long red robe enveloped his entire body. It was in that apparel that he presented himself before Adémar.

The latter, surprised by his appearance, hesitated momentarily as to whether he ought not to take him for a vision, but, remembering the hermit Étienne, he had no doubt that it was him.

If the hermit had astonished Adémar, Adémar had interested the hermit. Few knights possessed the amiable youth's charms; on seeing him, one experienced a need to love him. His black hair, curly by nature, fell over his shoulders and played around his eyes, which sometimes shone with fiery courage and sometimes displayed an attractive melancholy. Nothing equaled Adémar's smile; by turns proud or gracious, it expressed bravery or tenderness. Born with a soul on fire, the ward of Baron de Saint-Félix idolized the fair sex that heaven has created for our happiness; to him, nothing equaled a woman; he considered her the peer of the angels; Adémar would have done anything for her; his valor would protect her, his wit would seduce her.

When he saw the hermit, far from fleeing, he advanced, prostrated himself and, ready to request his blessing, he said: "Father, impose your hands on a knight."

"Get up, Monseigneur," said the hermit. "Such a posture does not befit a noble Baron before a poor monk."

"Thus youth ought to act," said Adémar, "in order to be respected in its turn when age has curbed its superb forehead."

"Those words charm me, Knight. Whence comes so much wisdom combined with so much beauty?"

"Raised by Baron de Saint-Félix."

"Those are not lessons that he can give you."

"I do not think you have any complaint against him?" Adémar queried.

Without responding to the question the hermit said: "Dare I ask you the story of your life? My request might astonish you, but your features recall memories."

"I have nothing to hide from you, Man of God," he said.

And both of them sat down on a tree felled by a wood-cutter's ax, one preparing to inform, and the other to listen with avid attention.

"A few leagues from the ancient fatherland of the Tectosages, the town of Saint-Félix stands on a high hill, over-looking all the neighboring land. The town is proud of its position and the power of the Baron to whom it is attributed. Its suzerain is no longer in the days of his spring; in the summer of his life he does not seem sensible to that tranquility, the adornment of a man whose memories are not bitter.

"For a long time Arembert has not known the calm of re-pose; it is necessary that the agitation of the body incessantly stuns a heart that dreads reflection. At forty, the somber Arembert has not yet felt the pleasures of amour; always fly-ing to where war is rumbling, he seems to have refused a sen-timent that embellishes existence; he seeks combats avidly, and, redoubtable by virtue of his bravery, the Comte de Tou-louse sees him as one of his firmest supports.

"For seventeen years Arembert has possessed the barony that was transmitted to him by his ancestors; his father, the noble Amanieu, was found dead in his bed without anything having caused the expectation of that sinister death. After the loss of that benevolent lord, the barony belonged to Arembert's brother, who had incontestable right of birth over him. Bérenger succeeded his father, but scarcely two months had gone by when the pious desire to go and liberate the Holy Sepulcher drew him toward the fields of Idumea; that was for his misfortune. He embarked at Marseille; since then, no one has had any news of him, and it was only after a few years that it became certain that he had perished, a victim of the rage of the sea.

"Arembert, having seen all of his family disappear in a short time, remained plunged in a profound melancholy for some time. He fled the presence of his vassals; even his dearest friends did not have the right to penetrate the solitude he had chosen. Not far from Saint-Félix he had château a built into which he went in order to deliver himself to his morosity. Sometimes, however, he ran through the apartments that separated him from his guards, uttering horrible cries and bathed in cold sweat that brought frissons to his weakened body.

"At those times, Arembert only respired war. He ran to make incursions into the domains of lords against whom he thought he had some complaint. He fought pitilessly, and victory almost always crowned his audacious enterprises. On returning to his possessions he summoned his friends and troubadours. Brilliant fêtes were held, and pleasures, for some time, troubled the profound silence of the vaults of the Château de Saint-Félix; but soon, further dolors came to lay siege of Arembert's heart, and the combats did not take long to recommence.

"One day, tranquil in the new dwelling that he had built on the heights of Saint-Julia, when he seemed less unhappy, a squire presents himself to his eyes; his armor is covered in dust, his voice is tremulous, he seems very emotional. Arembert, surprised, hastens to interrogate him: 'What is your name, vassal, and how do you dare to appear before Baron de Saint-Félix without having been announced by his pages?'

"'Oh, Sire Arembert, says the squire, 'pardon my negligence in favor of the chagrin that is devouring me; I have lost my master—your, friend, in a word—the Seigneur de Saint-Pons is no more.'

"Arembert gets up precipitately. 'Wretch! What are you telling me? Who is he audacious person who has dared to attack a man I cherished as much as myself? Speak; in naming him to me, you will ensure your master's vengeance and the punishment of is murderer.'

"'Alas, Sire Baron," said the squire, 'the man who has caused my sovereign to perish is certain of impunity by virtue of his power.'

"'Name him, I tell you,' says Arembert. 'Whoever he is, even if he is as powerful as the Comte de Toulouse himself, I shall not hesitate to challenge him.'

"'No, Sire Baron, the noble Raymond is too great to attack in a cowardly fashion; perfidy is unknown in that ancient family.'

"'Leave the eulogy there and tell me about my friend.'

"'Well, his murderer is the Vicomte de Carcassonne.'

"'Tremble, audacious warrior,' says Arembert, "your doom is assured. Hola! Guards! Sound the horn immediately; let the bells be heard from the summit of the battlements; summon my men-at-arms; let my standard be deployed. Pages, prepare my armor!'

"Thus the impetuous knight expresses himself; he shivers with impatience. He calls for vengeance with loud cries, or rather, he is glad to have found a pretext that will furnish an apparent justification for the new war that he is burning to undertake.

"His orders are executed; the surrounding areas assemble their soldiers. Montgeai sends twenty archers, twenty cavaliers and sixty lancers; Aureac furnishes the suzerain a troop of two hundred men; Roumens, Cadenac and Craissens send as many; a number twice as great assembles in the valleys and on the hills of Saint-Paulet, Mourville, the Vaux, Balègue and Belesta, and those various corps, combined with the troops on watch in Saint-Félix, form an army of nearly two thousand men.

"It was with that detachment that the proud Baron, reinforced by the troops of his friend, the Sire de Saint-Pons, marched against Vicomte Roger Trencavel. Hugues de Saint-Pons, Arembert's friend, combined an uncommon bravery with an unparalleled ferocity; the excursions that he never ceased, even in times of peace, to make against Vicomte Roger's vassals, had wearied the patience of that prince; he had set himself at the head of his troops and, having drawn Hugues into an ambush, had massacred him pitilessly. Knowing the amity that linked his enemy with Baron Arembert, he had no doubt that the latter would seek to avenge his death, and, far from scorning such an adversary, he did not send his squadrons away, and held himself ready to fight.

"Scarcely four days had gone by, and dawn was opening its doors in the radiant Orient, when the dwarf placed constantly at the top of the keep of the principal tower of Carcassonne hastened to give the alarm signal. He had perceived Arembert's soldiers rapidly descending the hills that formed the ring of the horizon. Trencavel, leaping out of bed, hastily put on his armor, gave his orders and sent two heralds, bearers of pacific words.

"Arembert, hearing the bells sounding the tocsin and seeing the archers covering the ramparts, no longer thought of surprising his adversary. He had his troop stop, and, wanting to allow them to take a few hours of repose, he commanded that the tents be erected. While he was delivering himself to his concern, the drawbridge was seen to be lowered; two heralds, their tunics blazoned with Roger's enamels, advanced holding the staffs marking their mission.

"Arembert ordered that they be brought to him. They saluted him by taking off their fur hats and the older of the two said: 'Sire Arembert, Baron de Saint-Félix, what do you want to do? Has not peace been declared between Raymond de Toulouse and Roger de Carcassonne? Can a vassal start a war by his own will? Does he not need the assistance of is suzerain prince? What is your ambition pretending? For what cause have you come to attack my Vicomte without a preliminary declaration? Your heralds have not appeared in Carcassonne;

47

we only learned that we were your enemies when your pennants appeared within sight of our ramparts?'

"Arembert replied: 'Herald of the title of Carcassonne, it ill befits your Vicomte to speak to me about the truce he has concluded with my feudal lord, having broken it every time that he thought that it could no longer be convenient for him, and who always excites the princes of Narbonne, Foix, Montpellier and Nîmes to arm themselves against the house of Toulouse. Believe me, Herald, it is not for the Trencavels to speak about the oaths they have made. You ask me for what cause I have armed my vassals? It is for the most just vengeance, to punish the murderer of my friend, and to ravage the lands of the proud Vicomte. Herald, take him my response, and accept this as a mark of my esteem for the august function in which you are clad.'

"So saying, he took from his finger a rich sapphire, which had once been given to him by the Duc d'Aquitaine, and he constrained the herald to accept it; he had the second given a purse of gold, and sent them away with words of war.

"Trencavel had not hoped for a fortunate success to the attempt he had made, but he wanted to put the forms of justice on his side and prejudice the Comte de Toulouse against the Baron de Saint-Félix. The latter, not suspecting the ruse, only saw the Vicomte de Carcassonne's step as evidence of his weakness. He thought that the victory awaited him and, without waiting any longer, he sounded the charge.

Chapter III: The Lady and the Troubadour

"Trencavel, too courageous to shut himself away in his walls when he could fight his enemy in the plain, had brought his troops down from the ramparts on to the banks of the rapid Aude, and was preparing to dispute the river crossing with his rival. Far from being stopped by that obstacle, the impetuous Arembert, after having harangued his soldiers briefly, pushed his horse into the water and began swimming, carrying his sword in one hand and his banner in the other, on which was painted a silver bell on a field of azure, the arms of his barony.

"The colossal stature of Arembert, his rich helmet sur-rounded by the Baron's circle, the ornaments that covered him, his breastplate and his destrier all announced him as the leader of the assailants. Trencavel, surprised by his audacity, calling his men-at-arms to him, ran to meet him, in the hope of overturning him in the river; but it was not easy to vanquish Arembert.

"That superb warrior, impatient to signal himself, attacks and slays with his first blow the knight Léonard, who saw the town of Penautier under his law; four other warriors share his fate. The Carcassonnian troops, struck with astonishment, re-coil, and by that movement give Arembert's soldiers time to emerge from the Aude, which is bathing them, and hurl themselves over its bank.

"In vain, Trencavel tries to rally his squadrons; even his noble courage is constrained to cede, but his retreat is not a flight; he retires fighting, and passing over the drawbridge, he enters the city, ashamed of having recoiled.

"Arembert, intoxicated by that first success, would like to do more; his hope is to take possession of Carcassonne; but it is easier to reduce a few squadrons to disarray in flat country than to scale walls defended by their position as much as the courage of their inhabitants.

"While Arembert was seeking in his head for some means to bring the design he was meditating to a conclusion, night veiled the sky. He had retired his tent when the squire who had come to announce the death of his friend asked to be introduced to his presence. 'Seigneur,' he said to him, approaching, 'Forcing Trencavel in his ramparts presents great difficulties; his army is numerous; his vassals cannot take long to send him powerful aid. Perhaps even the Comte de Toulouse, who has become his brother-in-law, would not want to suffer your generous enterprise. I offer you a quicker fashion of ensuring your vengeance. The Vicomtesse de Carcassonne is with her son in the Château de Lezignan; it is impossible to imagine that anyone would attempt an attack in that direction. Do what your enemies cannot foresee. At the head of your men-at-arms, depart without delay; daylight will not have shown yet when you have already reached your objective; attack them abruptly. Seize the Vicomtesse and her son, take them back to your domains, and do not break their irons until a ransom has been granted to you that will indemnify you for all your expenses.'

"The squire's speech made a strong impression on Arembert, who did not doubt the success of that enterprise and put it into execution. At the head of four hundred men-at-arms he departed promptly There was no way of being able to defend the Château de Lezignan; only a few crossbowmen were placed as sentinels on the turrets and the crenellations; they were attacked with so much celerity that the princess only learned of the arrival of the besiegers when they appeared in her apartment. She had just got up to go to the seigneurial chapel in order to offer God the tribute of her prayers.

"I leave you to imagine, venerable hermit, what her despair was when she found herself in the hands of her husband's enemies. 'Madame,' Arembert said to her, imperiously. 'It is necessary to follow me without resistance. You are my prisoner, and the fate of arms has put you in my power.' The princess tried to make a few protests, but they were unsuccessful; Arembert was too joyful at the success of his attempt. He took with him not only young Roger Trencavel and his mother but also two children who had been the companions of the Vicomte's son since his earliest years; the first was named Odon; the other was me."

The Hermit interrupted the story. "You! Great God! Can you be Adémar?"

"You have pronounced my name," said Adémar.

"My son…yes, Chevalier, for is permissible for me to give you that sweet name." The hermit sighed. "I knew your father well."

"What are you saying? My birth is not unknown to you? Alas, until his day, I thought myself an unfortunate individual abandoned in infancy, perhaps the issue of the basest blood."

"No, you do not owe the light of day to an obscure vassal. Hold up your head with pride; those who put you into this agitated world never knew anything but commanding their fellows."

"Are you obstinate in keeping silent regarding their name and rank?" demanded Adémar.

"It is impossible for me to satisfy you on that point."

"Is my mother still alive?"

The hermit uttered a profound sigh. "She has ended her career; she is no longer suffering."

"O dolor!" cried Adémar. "What! I can no longer receive her kisses! Does my father remain to me, at least?"

"The night of the tomb envelops his destiny."

"So I learn of their existence only to mourn their loss. For what reason do you refuse to satisfy my curiosity?"

"The hour of revelations has not yet arrived," said the hermit.

"May it not be long in sounding!"

"Continue your story, please, and tell me how you remained in the power of a…of Arembert."

"The Baron de Saint-Félix," Adémar continued, "proud of his conquest, was taking the Vicomtesse away when, at a turning in the woods, a numerous troop barred his way. They were the soldiers of the Vicomte de Carcassonne who, informed by a traitor of Arembert's march, were waiting for his return. Arembert, rendered desperate by that new check, employed all of his courage to vanquish them, but without success; the number of his enemies was increasing with every moment, which his men-at-arms were biting the dust.

"It was finally necessary to think of effecting his retreat, but he did not want to draw away without leaving a mark of his vengeance. Deceived by my rich garments , he thought he saw in me the son of Roger; he hastened to seize me, and cleaving rapidly through the phalanges of his adversaries, he succeeded in escaping with a few cavaliers reanimate by his courage. Such was the result of his enterprise; his life was in danger; he had lost the elite of his soldiers therein—and since then, he has conserved in his heart a powerful hatred against the Vicomte de Carcassonne.

"The latter, doubtless to please his wife, who appeared to attach a great price to having me with her, solicited Baron Arembert for a long time to replace me in his possession. He offered a considerable ransom, but it was refused; Arembert did not want to release his prey. I was raised by him with the greatest care; he had me taught everything that a knight ought to know, and as soon as I had reached the required age, I was admitted into the noble society that King Arthur imagined for the wellbeing of the earth. I did not think then that my origin was as illustrious as you have just made me understand."

"Noble Chevalier," said the Hermit, "your story has interested me keenly. I sense with pleasure that my amity ought to follow the esteem that I have for you already. It is true, then that Arembert still possesses a shadow of virtue? But since the time when reason has illuminated its torch within you, have you learned to know him?"

"As I have already told you," said Adémar, "it seems to me that a secret chagrin is lacerating him. He is often seen hiding the tears that escape him involuntarily; by night he gets up from his bed and, uttering lamentable cries, he goes through the rooms of his château as if he were being pursued by a sinister and menacing apparition."

"Adémar," said the hermit, "there is a remunerative God who watches incessantly over the recompenses that he has promised to virtue, as to the chastisements that he owes to vice. I cannot tell you any more, but a time will come when you will be able to pierce the mysteries that cover my existence. In the meantime, young man, if the conversation of an old man like me does not appear to you to be wearisome, come to the hermitage of the tomb sometimes; I will always welcome you with pleasure, even with tenderness; but do not appear there after the moment when the sun has plunged its sparkling crown into the ocean; when darkness surrounds me I adore the Creator, and woe betide the man who seeks to introduce himself into a place guarded by the angel of death!"

With those words, the hermit stood up, making a sign of amity to Adémar, and drew away without waiting for a response, leaving the young knight more astonished by his encounter than by his bizarre speeches.

What does he mean? he said to himself. *What! Should I form suspicions regarding the Baron's honesty because a man that I do not know dares to accuse him before me? Who is he, this mysterious hermit, and how does he know my family? Why does he insist on not telling me what I have such a great interest in knowing? Might he be one of those cunning tricksters? No, nothing in the hermit announces the mortal deceiver. He seems too grand to be culpable; I can scarcely believe that a lie could poison his discourse. But what is his goal in piquing my curiosity thus? Perhaps he wishes...*

A piercing scream that made itself heard attracted Adémar's attention and suspended the course of his reflections. A second scream reached his ears; without further delay, the knight drew his sword and, followed by his squire, he ran in the direction from which the sound seemed to be coming.

He had passed a dense thicket when, on entering a clearing in the wood, he perceived two squires at grips with seven brigands, one of whom had already seized a demoiselle of tall stature and a proud and majestic gaze. With a rapidity akin to that of an eagle, Adémar hurled himself at the aggressors, and the first stroke of his blade severed the head of the assassin placed nearest to him. He plunged the point of his sword into the breast of the second; his varlet struck a third. Frightened, the others fled, abandoning their prey.

The gallant Adémar, victorious, brought the rescued beauty to her feet and, setting one knee on the ground, he said: "Lady, what else can I do for your service?"

The unknown woman, replacing with a vivid blush the pallor that covered her face, replied: "Sire Chevalier, you are worthy of your title."

"Was I not recommended," said Adémar, "when the accolade was given to me, to fear God, to respect my prince and to love ladies?"

"You are French, Chevalier?" said the stranger.

"I take glory from it, noble demoiselle."

While they were chatting thus, the brave Adémar made the following reflections privately, congratulating himself that such a beautiful person had not fallen into the hands of brigands. He wondered silently what unfamiliar disturbance was rising in his heart; he did not know yet that amour, sometimes slow to be born, often ignites with the rapidity of the spark that catches fire by virtue of the impact of two stones. With a respectful admiration he contemplated the woman who was henceforth to command as sovereign in his soul.

The magnificence of the young woman's garments, the long veil that hung down to the ground, the haughtiness of her smile, the two squires that were following her and the three women escorting her all announced that her rank as the highest of all. Intimidated, Adémar asked her, stammering, whether she believed that his presence might be useful to her.

"Chevalier," she said to him, "I ought not to be far away from the goal of my journey; if you can indicate it to me, you will complete the acquisition of just rights to my gratitude; I am going to see the hermit of the tomb."

"Can it be, Madame," said Adémar, "that the respectable monk in question is fortunate enough to draw you to him?"

"Do you know him?" asked the stranger.

"Absent for a long time from this region, it is only today that I have been able to encounter him; he treated me with a marked distinction, and I confess that what he said has given me the desire to talk to him at greater length."

"My liberator can be certain that the hermit Father will always see him with pleasure," said the unknown woman. "Please lead me to him, and I will talk to him about all that I owe you."

At those words, Adémar, leaping lightly on to his horse, which Aubin had bought to him, placed himself beside the stranger, holding his hat in his hand; he rode alongside her thus to reach the hermitage. From the place where they were, it was necessary to traverse a rather profound valley, at the bottom of which the stream ran beside which Adémar had previously reposed. They followed that route and, after a few minutes, the trees became more widely spaced, allowing the travelers to perceive the hermitage of the tomb.

Having heard the hoof-beats of the horses, the hermit approached the simple barrier that closed his dwelling; he opened it and, having looked at the young woman, he fell to his knees.

"Get up, Father," she said to him. "Such a posture is inappropriate for you."

"O daughter of my sovereign," said the hermit, "is it not the posture that a modest hermit ought to adopt before the noble Aliénor, who received the light of day from Raymond VI, Comte de Toulouse?"[19]

On hearing the imposing name of Aliénor, Adémar felt his heart become constricted again, and it was with difficulty

---

[19] The historical Raymond VI had three surviving children, one daughter by his second wife (the sister of Roger II Trencavel, the father of the one featured in the story), named Constance, and a son and a daughter, Raymond VII and Joan, by his third wife, Joan Plantagenet (the daughter of Henry II of England and Eleanor of Aquitaine). Aliénor [Eleanor in English], is fictitious.

that he imitated the hermit. The latter asked him what event had brought him back to him immediately.

Aliénor spoke, and told the hermit what Adémar had done for her.

The old man, listening to such a story, raised his hands toward the heavens and cried, as if involuntarily: "Oh my God, I thank you. He is worthy of his family!"

Adémar threw himself upon the hermit's hands. "Please," he said, "tell me what you are keeping quiet; let me know the name of my parents."

"Have I not told you already? It is not yet time for me to explain."

"Does a mystery cover the birth of this valiant chevalier?" asked Aliénor.

"He will shiver when he knows who he is."

"What are you saying to me?" said Adémar.

"More than I ought to have told you," said the hermit, "but between us, Adémar, you are not a stranger to us; be a witness to the confidence that the beautiful Aliénor is about to make to me."

Only too glad to be permitted not to quit her, Adémar accepted that proposal eagerly. As he entered the hermit's dwelling he could not help directing a curious gaze in all directions. After having passed the barrier, he perceived the tomb of which we have already given a description; that aspect drew an involuntary frisson from him, and he followed Étienne. The room in which he found himself had for an ornament a complete suit of armor; on a crude table there was a sand-glass next to a skull, and on the wall someone had written in three places, in bloody characters, the frightful word: VENGEANCE.

Surprised by all that he saw, and charmed by the presence of Aliénor, Adémar maintained a profound silence. The tall demoiselle by his side did not speak while the hermit occupied himself in garnishing his table with a few fruits and dairy products.

When Aliénor had appeased her hunger, she got ready to inform the holy personage of the motive that had brought her to him. He sat down on a large stone, and Adémar followed his example, Aliénor began thus:

"You have anticipated it, hermit; my father's power has finally armed the anxiety of his superiors. Raymond is going to be immolated, not to the religion that he reveres but to the ambition of those who envy his estates. A numerous crusade has gathered, not so much against the Albigensians as against him. Already, Béziers has fallen to the effort of that devastating army; Carcassonne is under threat and its fall will be followed by that of Toulouse.

"Among the crusader princes, one above all is distinguished by his bravery as by his projects; still adroit in dissimulation, he is hiding a scheme that he is meditating; he only speaks of the cause of Heaven, when it is for his own that he is fighting; he pretends a zeal that he would not have if it did not serve his purposes. Accustomed to sacrifice everything to them, he laughs at the holiest oaths, deceives incessantly and employs his bravery for his aggrandizement. Blindly submissive to the church in the eyes of the vulgar, in secret he is able to thwart its designs; the Holy Father has no more ardent servant or redoubtable adversary. Ferocious by nature and knavish in character, such is Simon de Montfort, as he is known in France.

"Two lords share power with him; one is the Duc de Bourgogne, a loyal knight, honest and full of honor, who seeks, in attacking the heretics, not the increase of his domains but a augmentation of glory; there are no perfidious secrets to fear from him; he only fights on the battlefield, it is only there that he is to be feared. The Comte de Nevers is his worthy rival: the same valor, the same generosity. While the Comte de Montfort only wants to enrich himself, those two sovereigns only desire renown.

"A hundred times more dangerous than Montfort, the impetuous legate Milon detests my father personally; in addition to the interests of the Church he has his own cause to sustain; he cannot pardon Comte Raymond's noble frankness and he has sworn his doom.

"Another priest is also our adversary; that is the Bishop of Toulouse, Foulques, once known for his amorous enthusiasm, now famous for his unparalleled fanaticism. He only dreams of heresy, he only desires to see the fall of his sovereign's throne. Always united with Milon, they will succeed in seeing their culpable designs through to the end.

"In order to deflect the storm raised against him, the Comte de Toulouse has taken the cross in vain; his submission has been taken for weakness. Doubtless, in order to crush him, they are only waiting for a favorable moment. In that dangerous position he thinks that it is appropriate to use all the resources of prudence. He knows, hermit, your attachment to his cause; he has sent me to you in order to engage you to employ all the influence that your virtues give you over the inhabitants of this region to prevent them from being seduced by the emissaries that the crusaders will not fail to distribute everywhere."

"The Comte's confidence honors me," said the hermit. "I dare say that it was unnecessary; I knew already what my duty commanded."

"The Comte, who is threatened, would not fear anything," said Aliénor, "if he had a large number of servants as faithful as you."

"Madame," said Adémar, "I dispute with the venerable hermit the honor of being one of your magnanimous father's defenders."

"Follow the inspiration of your heart, young man," said the hermit. "It will lead you along the brilliant road of honor, as well as that of renown. Go to Toulouse, offer your services to Raymond, merit his praise, render yourself worthy of one day being dearer to him. Here, Adémar, accept this sword. It was your father's."

Adémar kissed the blade. "My father, a Seigneur?"

"He only made use of it for just causes; it never oppressed the weak, but it was the terror of the wicked. Let its employment not change in your hands; and you, princess, buckle it around the waist of your new defender."

Moved by that speech, flattered by Aliénor's attention and the hermit's action, Adémar felt burning tears flowing from his eyes. "By the Mother of God," he cried, "I swear never to abandon the cause that engages me without return; guide me, Princesse, to the place where my blood ought to flow for your defense."

"How I love such devotion!" said Aliénor. "Knight, you will be invincible."

"I surely will be if you deign to admit my enterprise."

"My father alone has the right to name my chevaliers, but you can proclaim yourself his."

"When the mystery can have its conclusion," said the hermit, "the Comte de Toulouse will not disavow Adémar; it is nevertheless necessary, young man, that you keep silent about the resolution you have just made. It is necessary that the foreigners do not learn that this modest hermitage has received the daughter of the powerful Comte Raymond; it is appropriate above all not to tell Baron Arembert; it is equally necessary that the sword I have given you does not strike his sight; a time will come when we will be constrained to present it to him. So, Adémar, content yourself with telling him that the hermit of the tomb is sending you to Toulouse; I don't doubt that he will consent to that, but above all, say nothing that could give rise in his mind to dangerous suspicions."

Thus spoke the hermit. He engaged Adémar not to go away for the rest of the day; he took pleasure in conversing with him. He questioned him about his religious principles, for in those days there was a merit in belief, and impiety was in horror everywhere.

It was then that the clouds, being too dense, burst with a frightful din. The storm lasted for a long time, and had already lasted for an hour when they heard someone knocking on the external door of the hermitage. Étienne, only trusting himself, went to open it.

He did not take long to reappear, followed by a young man whose costume announced a troubadour, clad in a light chamois cloak embroidered with silver; a white velvet doublet and elegant boots with curled toes completed his adornment. He had slung his nacre-encrusted guitar over his shoulder; the plumes of his hat were dripping, soaked by rainwater, but the disorder of his garments had not altered his gaiety. He had a charming face; his eyes were dark, his face colored, his teeth dazzlingly white; his entire person expressed confidence and frankness.

"Salutations," he said, as he came in, "to the amiable hosts who have been kind enough to offer a refuge to a child of the gay science."[20]

"Minstrel," said Aliénor, "you can pay for your welcome with some light tenson or a melancholy ballad."

"It is not to beauty that we would refuse to make ourselves heard, but it will be necessary for the thunderclaps not to want to accompany my voice, which would then be difficult to hear."

The troubadour's response summoned smiles to the lips of his listeners.

"Your name cannot be unknown, Troubadour," said the hermit.

"It has sometimes resounded on the banks of the Garonne. The château of the marquis my father, is named Mauléon, and my name is Savary."[21]

"Yes, certainly, genteel minstrel," said Aliénor, "your name has reached me. At the court of Toulouse no one men-

---

[20] The musical art of the troubadours was known in Occitan as the *gai saber* [gay science].

[21] The historical Savary de Mauléon (1181-1233) was an important Poictevin warrior and troubadour, as the author points out in one of his own footnotes, blaming the misappropriation of the name here in the author of the manuscript he is pretending to translate.

tions Pierre Vidal without also citing the brilliant Savary de Mauléon."

"How great your indulgence is, Madame!" said the troubadour. "That is to unite the name of the nightingale with that of a mere hedge-sparrow. Oh, if some renown crowns me, it is to the lady who inspires me that I owe it."

"Your songs have informed the world of that," said Aliénor. "Fortunate the beauty that gives birth to such writings! However, satisfy our impatience by tuning your instrument."

"To refuse would be pride; I shall sing out of modesty. May my ballad please you and interest you in the fate of the amours whose adventures I shall relate."

With those words, after a short prelude, he sang a long complainte, such as people loved in those days, but the fashionability of which has long passed.

Savary's song charmed his listeners. Adémar, a witness to the enthusiasm that the minstrel inspired in the young Comtesse, promised himself that he too would merit it one day.

In the end, the storm ceased. The hermit, while engaging Savary to spend the night in his hermitage, asked Adémar to be prompt in returning before the first light of dawn. Adémar went away, sighing, and, left alone, he dared to cast a glance into his heart.

What new sentiment is agitating me? he said to himself. *Has the sight of a woman ignited the subtle flame that is devouring me? Can I be in love already? You, in love, Adémar? Is she your equal? Is she an orphan? No, insensate; your amour is more than blind; it dares to address itself to the daughter of your powerful sovereign. My amour! Can I give that name to this sudden delirium? Is it not a child of my imagination, which will dissipate when night folds away its veils? No, Aliénor, no; the fire that you have ignited will not be consumed with such promptitude; doubtless, I shall never inform you of the harm that you have been able to do me; but by my actions, I will constrain you to cast your gaze upon me,*

and if I do not obtain tenderness. I shall force you to agree
that I was worthy of aspiring to it, or meriting it.

It was in thinking thus that he went back up to the Châ-teau de Saint-Félix, after having instructed his squire to maintain a strict silence regarding all the day's events.

As he went into his apartment, one of the Baron's pages came to tell him that the latter was waiting for him; he hastened to go to Arembert, and the resultant conversation they had was recorded in a previous chapter. Entirely occupied with Aliénor, seeing her image everywhere, even in the midst of darkness, it took him a long time to find the sleep that fled him. Finally, his eyelids became heavy, and his soul, exempt from remorse, did not take long to savor the necessary repose.

Chapter IV: The Hermit Begins to Show Himself

Midnight had just sounded on the clock of the château and silence reigned everywhere when Arembert, after having struggled against his memories for a long time, began to feel drowsy. But divine justice was watching over him. Scarcely had his eyelids closed than he seemed to see, rising at the foot of his bed, a lead coffin that, opening violently, released a black smoke from its interior. It spread throughout the room, but then, gathering together, it formed a solid body and took on human features.

Whose were they? Those of Arembert's father! At that redoubtable sight, the knight, although asleep, shivers and trembles. Without speaking, the shade gazes at him relentlessly; soon, its features turn pale and are disfigured, becoming similar to those of a cadaver.

At that moment the menacing phantom puts its hand to its cranium, and, wrenching its mortal shell away forcefully, it presents to the eyes of the culpable Arembert the aspect of a hideous skeleton. At that sight, the terrified Baron wakes up with horror; his entire being in chilled by a cruel frisson; he tries to scream, but cannot; and what becomes of him, either because God permits it or because his imagination takes pleasure in tormented him, when he sees that frightful vision that he believed to be a game of his slumber?

His cries and howls fill the entire château; he summons his officers, he commands his guards. What is his design? What does he want to do against a power before which all the powers of the earth ought to be annihilated? Arembert's vassals surround him in vain; they cannot distract him. His shocked soul constantly represents to him that which he seeks to escape.

"Go away, frightful phantom!" he cries, dolorously. "Why do you incessantly inflict me with your fatal aspect? Why not strike me once and for all; I would rather die than be menaced incessantly. But can I not disarm you? Is there not a power superior to you? Until now I have rejected the aid that the Church offers me. Come on; it's necessary to appeal to it; it's necessary to implore divine mercy at the foot of the altar, if it can exist for me."

Having said that, full of impatience, he suddenly forms the project of going to interrogate the hermit of the tomb; but people try to retain him, they engage him to return to his abandoned bed. He refuses obstinately to do that; it is not in repose that he can hope for anything. In his impatience, he wants to have the pilgrim woken up, and he wants someone to fetch Adémar.

Scarcely has he given an order than he withdraws it immediately; he does not know what he wants, and the whitening dawn surprises him in his irresolution. Scarcely has he seen the first rays of daylight shine than, putting on his armor, he emerges from his château, traverses the town and goes down toward the hermitage, alone, after having forbidden his officers to follow him.

A thousand thoughts besiege him as he approaches the place that he fears; he does not know whether the hermit will want to speak to him this time; he dreads new visions; everything wearies him; everything torments him; he is in the painful situation that lacerates criminals when sins appear in all their horror and dread lays siege to their soul.

Oh well! The man who seeks to reestablish peace in his agitated senses must commit the blackest deeds, so slippery is the slope that draws the vicious individual, but at the bottom is the precipice, and punishment follows the crime closely.

The hermit was far from expecting Arembert's arrival. Only awake for a few moments, he had opened the door of his cell with the intention of offering his first thoughts to God. Buried under his hood, clad in his red robe, he was approaching the tomb when a confused noise audible through the foliage attracted his attention. He turned round, and how many thoughts rose up in his mind when he recognized the Baron!

Involuntarily, he blurted: "Arembert! Him, here!"

Troubled by that exclamation, Arembert said: "Can it be that the sight of me inspires such horror?"

"It is for you to be your own judge," said the hermit.

"Will you condemn me before having heard me?"

"What can you tell me that I do not know?"

"No, you don't know everything that I can tell you," said Arembert. "My confessions are innumerable; but will they procure me pardon?"

"Have you forgotten the mountains of Narbonne?"

"What! You know…?"

"Arembert, you had a father.

Going pale, Arembert repeated "A father!"

"A brother."

"A brother!"

"Well, do I not know?"

Trying to pull himself together, Arembert said: "What are you trying to imply with your insidious questions? Yes, of course, I had a family that was very dear to me."

"Arembert!"

"Fate stole them from me. Is it necessary for you, who are unknown to me, to take pleasure in reminding me of those painful memories? By what right have you come to establish yourself in my domains? Do you think, if I have had the kindness to leave you in peace, that you ought, for my recompense, to seek to trouble me? Should you not fear…?"

"Is it to threaten me that Arembert has come to me? Last night, when his dejected soul only presented frightful images to him, did he think about banishing me from the retreat I occupy in the heart of the woods? Arembert, there is no longer any wellbeing for you until your father's ashes repose in the sepulcher of his ancestors."

"What lie are you reporting to me? Since his death, the remains of the author of my days have been placed in the depths of the crypts where my ancestors lie."

"Dare you go down there to make sure of that?"

Arembert recoiled. "Me, descend into those obscure vaults! Pass through their tenebrous detours! No, never."

"The man whose soul is tranquil," said the hermit, "does not fear the shades of those who are no more."

"Do you know whether my soul knows fear?"

"What sentiment agitated you, then, during the night that has just gone by?"

"A victim of my feeble imagination, I might have felt insensate terrors, but today..."

"For what reason did you want to see me?"

"I hoped to discover a consoler in you; I could not have believed that this place contained one of my most intractable enemies."

"I am only the enemy of the wicked; decide now whether I ought to welcome you or repel you."

"Man, whoever you might be, appease my torment, crush me, or make yourself known."

"Well," said the hermit, "if you want to know who I am, if you want your fate to change, go in a year to the mountains of Narbonne."

"Again! Yes, I'll go there; yes, I want to put an end to all the evils to which I am prey."

"If you want to abridge them, it only depends on your own will; why not break the irons…?"

"Hermit, you know too much."

"I would have preferred to have known nothing," said the hermit. "But adieu, any further conversation between us is henceforth futile; we will take this up again in a year."

Having said that, he withdrew, and constrained Arembert to do likewise.

The latter, slowly going back along the paths that led from the wood to his vassal town, reflected on what he had heard. He lost himself in vain conjectures; he promised himself to raise an obstacle to the liaison that appeared to be forming between the hermit of the tomb and young Adémar.

No, he said to himself, *I cannot permit that young man to link himself with my enemy; for that person, who hides his name and his fortune, can only detest me. Oh, if possible, let*

us warn Adémar against him; his age will render him suscep-
tible to acquire the impressions I want to give him.

So he said; but there was no longer time. Rising as early as the Baron, the vigilant Adémar, awakened by his amour, had followed his suzerain at a distance. Respecting their secrets, he had kept far enough away from the two individuals to be unable to hear their conversation, and, as soon as he had seen Arembert withdraw, bearing the imprint of consternation on his brow, he had approached the hermit.

The latter, on seeing him, congratulated him on his diligence and introduced him to the interior of his dwelling without delay.

Aliénor had just got up. A vivid blush, which she could not control, revealed the pleasure she experienced in seeing her liberator again. He advanced toward her eagerly. They were already conversing when the silvery sounds of a guitar announced Savary de Mauléon, wearing his joy on his face. The amiable troubadour appeared; he kissed the hem of Aliénor's robe, saluted the hermit respectfully and placed his hand cordially in Adémar's.

"How many attractions the awakening of nature offers to those who know how to enjoy it!" cried the child of the Muses. "And how they are augmented when one can admire them with individuals in whom one is interested!" Addressing Aliénor, he went on: "Princesse, deign to accept the homage of my guitar and my sword. What am I saying? No, I cannot sing your praises. Bélisène de Foix alone demands my songs; I cannot praise another beauty than hers—but I can fight to defend your rights."

"Genteel troubadour," said Aliénor, "God forbid that I should want to steal you from your friend! I know how sacred the oaths of amorous servitude are."

"Could I, noble lady, break those that I have promised to keep so many times, for which I have made the Virgin Mother and the Savior of the Word the guarantors?"

The minutes were going by. The hermit, impatient to see his guests leave, fearing that Arembert might raise some obstacle to Adémar's departure, engaged Aliénor not to wait any longer. The latter, desirous of conducting the two valiant defenders to her brother, thanked Étienne warmly, and, leaping on to her palfrey, departed escorted by Mauléon and her liberator.

The scant security of the roads, then infested by brigands who were becoming more audacious at the approach of civil war, constrained the knights to take a much longer route, so much did their modesty force them to mistrust their valor. They went up the steep hill of Pastourie, traversed the dense woods and, leaving Falga to the left, they descended into the valley of Auriac. That small town is remarkable by virtue of the singularity of its position, and for the Gothic steeple that serves as its adornment.

Not far from Auriac, on a hill defended by ramparts and solid fortifications, stands the town of Caraman, which enjoys an immense view of rare beauty. After Caraman, the ancient barony of Lanta appears, which, throughout the epochs of intestinal wars that desolated France, always furnished intrepid soldiers. Our travelers rested there for a while in order to avoid the excessive heat of the day, and when the star of light leaned toward its decline they departed rapidly, saluting the village of Montauriol, placed to the left of the road, Flourens, remarkable for its artificial grotto, Fonssegrive, one fortified, and Lasbordes, situated on the Lers, the waters of which fertilize the neighboring fields.

Finally, climbing the hills that surround Toulouse, they saluted that great city, where fanaticism would soon mark its victims. Adémar had never visited the capital of the Tectosages; his heart was stirred by the thought that he was about to be introduced to a court that was renowned for its urbanity and for its love of the fine arts.

On returning to his château, Arembert sent for Adémar. It was not without a true displeasure that he learned that he had already gone. His first impulse was to send a squire to call him back, but, having reflected, he renounced a project that would put him at odds with the hermit of the forest. He summoned the concierge Roberto and, having drawn him into a secret chamber he said to him: "Well, Roberto, is everything in the same state?"

"Yes, Sire Baron."

"Never any complaint on his part?"

"He does not proffer a single word."

"Perhaps he is no more."

"Only his scorn prevents him from replying to me."

"It's seventeen years since he was free. Oh, why is he not still?"

"Are you repenting of it?" asked Roberto.

"There are moments when, vanquished by the weakness of his essence, a man no longer recognizes himself; it's necessary that I succeed in at least extracting a word from him."

"Are you going to descend into the subterrains?" Roberto asked, alarmed.

"What could prevent me from doing so?"

"Have you forgotten the apparition?"

"Roberto!" said Arembert, furiously. "Why are you reminding me? Pick up that lamp, open the secret door, and march. I'll follow you."

The Baron's menacing expression constrained the vassal to obey. The latter pressed lightly on a panel of the woodwork that decorated the apartment, triggered a mechanism that opened a carefully hidden door, and revealed an exceedingly narrow corridor leading to a steep spiral stairway, which the two individuals descended with precaution. The last steps, covered with a dense damp, ended in a long gallery

"It has been a long time," said Arembert, "since I passed through these somber dwellings. What silence! What mourning! What horror! And yet, it is here that I have confined..."

Roberto stopped and seized Arembert's arm. "Can you not see anything, Monseigneur?"

"Coward! What can you have to fear? And why would you, when you have to come down here every day?"

"In the name of God, Monseigneur, tell me whether any object strikes you gaze?"

Terrified, Arembert replied: "O Heaven! What vision is coming to afflict my sight again!"

Numbed by fear, his feet seemingly enchained to the ground, his eyes extinct, by what horror does he not feel overwhelmed when he discovers, in the depths of the gallery and in front of the door of the dungeon into which he wants to penetrate, the gigantic hermit of the tomb, armed with wrath and displaying a cup that he is holding in his hand!

But he does not speak; he contents himself with frightening Arembert.

The later, emerging from his state of stupor, far from seeking to advance toward the phantom, recoils, and, climbing the stairway again with an extreme celerity, returns to his room. He orders Roberto to close the panel again carefully, and, falling into an armchair, remains for a long time as if deprived of consciousness.

Chapter V: The Old Troubadour

No troublesome encounter having arrested our travelers, they entered Toulouse at the moment when the shadow was descending from the summit of the Pyrenees, which were outlined in the distance. Throwing her veil over her face in order not to be perceived by the Toulousans, who would have made the air resound with their acclamations if they had recognized the cherished daughter of their valorous Comte, Aliénor hastened her palfrey's pace, and soon arrived outside the gates of the superb Château Narbonnais, the abode of the sovereigns of Toulouse.

The guards who constantly watched over the gates, having perceived Aliénor, lowered the tips of their javelins as a sign of respect. Squires and pages came running. It was not long before she was surrounded by her court, and it was in the midst of that cortege that she reached her brother.

Young Raymond[22] had not gone with his father to the crusaders' camp; he had remained in Toulouse to prepare the plans and means of defense that he judged indispensable, for he could not believe that the army the legate Milon commanded was not destined to act against his father and him.

It was with a true joy that Raymond saw his sister again; he ran to her and embraced her tenderly. Then Aliénor, taking Adémar by the hand, introduced him to the young Comte, and, naming him her liberator, recounted the bravery with which he had come to her aid when she was attacked by brigands in the forest. In brief, she praised the service that he had rendered her so highly that Raymond, taking him aside, thanked him warmly.

---

[22] Author's note: "The two Comtes de Toulouse had the same name; henceforth we shall call Raymond VI the Comte de Toulouse and his son Raymond."

71

"Chevalier," he said, "whatever the recompense that you want to claim, I swear by Saint Sernin[23] not to refuse it to you."

"Yes, Monseigneur, I do have a favor to ask of you."

"Speak; it will be granted."

"Do me the honor of permitting me always to fight by your side."

"With you, Chevalier, one cannot hope to defeat you in grandeur of soul."

In order to change the subject of a conversation that was painful for his modesty, Adémar had Savary come forward. The latter was preparing to pay his compliment to the prince when, having looked at him intently, he uttered a cry and fell to his knees. "Comte Raymond, is it to you that I owe my life?"

Nobly, Raymond replied: "Can the brave and gallant Savary appreciate a slight service to that extent? Would he not have done the same?"

"Oh, Comte," said Savary, "it is fine to be generous, but is there is anything to equal the service that one is glad to render one's rival?"

"To his fortunate rival, also," said Raymond, cheerfully.

---

[23] Author's note: "Saint Sernin was the first Bishop of Toulouse and the object of a particular veneration by the inhabitants of that great city. Saint Exupéry, one of his successors to the Episcopal throne, erected a church remarkable in its Gothic magnificence. That immense temple, built in the form of a Latin cross, has five ranks of naves; in addition to the superior church there is a subterrain in which the bodies of martyrs are deposited, which are found there in great number. Tradition asserts that the edifice is built over a lake and is sustained by thousands of piles. People of distinguished merit have believed that assertion and Monsieur de Montaigu, in an esteemed work on the antiquities of Toulouse, recounts a most singular story on that subject." The work by "Monsieur de Montaigu" is elusive.

"Permit me to proclaim your magnanimity, Prince."

"Well, while I go write to my father, entertain my sister and this worthy night."

Thus, removing himself from the eulogies he merited, Raymond left Aliénor, Savary and Adémar together. The troubadour then spoke to them in these terms:

The story of the Troubadour Savary de Mauléon[24]

From my earliest youth, the love of poetry inflamed my seething imagination; I only sighed after literary palms, and already, in my essays, I sought to conquer the applause that I sensed was necessary to me. My sirventes depicted the corruption of our mores, which have degenerated so much; my tensons celebrated the spring and the beauties of nature.[25] But

---

[24] Author's note: "The author is mistaken in making the troubadour Savary an heir of the house of Gascony. He was a Poictevin, and took his name from the town of Mauléon in Poitou. It might be the case, however, that particular memoirs also place a Savary de Mauléon among the Gascon poets. We only thought that we ought to point out the error in order to prove that the author has not followed history exactly. (The translator)." The likelihood is that the author had already written this story, featuring the Poictevin Savary de Mauléon, before co-opting it into the present story and making the adjustment of this footnote.

[25] Author's note: "*Sirventes* was the name given to the genre of poetry in which the troubadours made use for their historical works. They were speeches in verse of a sort in which praise, blame or invective were set at the poet's whim. Almost all the troubadours writing in that fashion showed a liberty of sprit and independence that earned the praise of princes, who tolerated their speaking thus. Then, sovereigns protected without oppressing, and one could think and speak without fear of displeasing a monarch or his favorite. Everything was submitted to the severe censure of sirventes: the Church, the great

I toiled in vain; my poetry was cold, nothing animated it. In despair at the scant success of my constant enterprises, I soon formed he project of quitting the harp permanently; then, gripped again by the sonorous instrument, I tried to do better; all was futile, the genius was captive, my efforts only ended in giving birth to cold compositions.

I do not know what I had become, when, one day, weary of my superfluous efforts, I went out of the Château de Mauléon with despair in my heart and headed for the country.

Dawn was just breaking in all its matinal pomp; clouds tinted with gold and crimson were grouped in sumptuous columns around the point where the sun was about to appear; mists, still darkened, were retreating toward the summits of the mountains, and in spite of their thickness, allowing the highest peaks of the Pyrenees to be seen shining with the first rays of the star whose presence vivifies the world. A thousand birds were chirping in the branches of the fir trees and the old oaks; the waves of the stream of Gaverni were flowing rapidly amid the flowers, each petal of which supported a diamantine drop of morning dew.

In brief, never had nature appeared to me with so much pomp. I felt my heart beating rapidly; tears were forming in my eyes; I was agitated by an anxiety that had its charms.

---

and the beautiful; nothing was spared. They attacked vices, of which they were the terror. In sirventes, whether a jongleur, a knight, a demoiselle had asked the advice of a troubadour, he responded wisely and virtue spoke through his mouth.

"*Novelles* or *nouvelles* offered pretty details; they were piquant tales whose charm resided in their naivety; *pastourelles* were distinguished by the same simplicity. That genre was a species of drama in which shepherds and shepherdesses conversed with tenderness and innocence, and without pretention. A *tenson* was an ordinary song sung by two interlocutors, for instance between a chevalier and a troubadour."

"Oh!" I exclaimed, with transport. "Yes, this is the moment to engender works that the troubadours would not disavow, that the jongleurs would be glad to perform, either in the home of the King of Aragon, the halls of the palace of Toulouse, or in a tournament of amour presided over by the beautiful Vicomtesse de Marseille."

Having said that, prompt to profit from my enthusiasm, I took up my guitar, and strove to extract a few sounds from it; I searched for verses.

Alas, everything still refused to serve my desire; I remained mute.

Despair took possession of my soul, and, in a fit of anger, I threw the useless instrument away; tears soothed me.

"That is it!" I cried. "I renounce forever an art that has become my torture. No more singing, no more desire for renown. Let glory alone replace all my sentiments."

I was speaking thus when I noticed a respectable old man nearby. His beard and hair were white; his body was covered by a green tunic; a sword reposed by his side. He was leaning on a knotty staff, while over his shoulders hung a light harp.

"Pardon an old minstrel," he said, approaching me, "for interrogating a young one, but I cannot resist the desire to learn the cause of the chagrin that is devouring you. Perhaps I can dissipate it."

"No, Father," I said, "you cannot deliver me from it."

"Old age is the age of experience; it has seen a great deal, it can give useful advice."

"Oh, what can you tell me that could teach me the art of verses?"

"So you're complaining of your verve. Perhaps you don't know the means of igniting it."

"What have I not tried in order to succeed in that, Troubadour?"

"It's necessary, my son, to renounce that beautiful art if amour cannot inspire gracious or tender ballads in you."

Astonished, I said: "Amour, Father! I've never known it."

"What are you thinking, young man? You want to find[26] and you have not loved? I'm not astonished that your head is disenchanted. Poor fellow! No, without doubt, you'll never be able to sing. Not to love! Can one be a poet without amour? Look at all the minstrels that Europe honors; they have all loved. The greatest kings and he greatest captains have known that sweet and beautiful sentiment. It is by virtue of it that the soul is purified; it is at the feet of ladies that one forms the most sublime songs; it is the hope of pleasing them that gives birth to heroes. Hasten to love, young man. Let's see: the celebrated Pierre Vidal[27] sighed at the knees of Adélaïde,

---

[26] The author inserts a note here to the effect that it is from the word *trouver* [to find], "which is to say, to invent, that the word *troubadour* comes." He subsequently adds a modification: "Different etymologies are given to the word. Petrarch thought it came from *trompatori*, meaning trumpeter in Italian, because troubadours sometimes made use of a trumpet to attract attention before commencing their sings." He notes however, that those deriving it from *trouver* are in the majority.

[27] Author's note: "Such a bizarre mixture of wit and absurdity, wisdom and folly, characterize the minstrel Pierre Vidal that one might call him the Don Quixote of troubadours. He was the son of a Toulousan furrier, possessed agreeable talents, a superior genius, a fine voice and had such a high opinion of himself that it rendered him the plaything of lades and noblemen. Although they laughed at his follies, his verses were welcomed. They inspired love for their author in a lady of Saint-Gilles, whose husband, a disobliging chevalier, took revenge on him by having his tongue split. Far from being corrected by that adventure, he dared to bear his pleas to the beautiful Adélaïde de Roques Martine, the wife of the Vicomte de Marseille. The Sire de Barral, who was not jealous, accorded him familiar entries. The Vicomtesse, who sang under the name Audierna, was diverted by him, and gave him reason to think that she loved him. Deceived by such fine appearances, he sighed, lamented and gave rise to reproaches.

Vicomtesse de Marseille; the impetuous Bertrand de Born[28] sang the praises of Maenz de Montagnac, daughter of the Vicomte de Turenne; Albert de Sisteron[29] was inspired by the beautiful and illustrious Marquise de Malasina; Hugues du

---

There were quarrels but the Vicomte restored peace by engaging his wife to promise anything. One day, Vidal approached when she was asleep and kissed her; she woke up laughing, thinking that he was her husband, but on seeing the troubadour she screamed and forced Vidal to flee Marseille. He went to Palestine, where he signaled himself by his exploits, and then married a Greek princess in Cyprus, and thought that he had acquired rights to the Empire of the Orient; he took the title of Emperor, dressed with the marks of that dignity and prepared to conquer Constantinople. He died after having giving the memory of his sovereign, Raymond VI, Comte de Toulouse, proofs of an inviolable attachment, leaving the renown of a man of genius and unparalleled extravagance."

[28] Author's note: "The troubadour Bertrand de Born, Vicomte d'Hautefort, was one of the heroes of the twelfth century. A passion for arms and glory, arrogance combined with suppleness and gallantry with poetic talent, an ardent imagination and a quick wit, much activity and courage, with a distinguished rank, enabled him to signal himself in several careers. Maenz de Montagnac inspired a vivid and stormy tenderness in him but jealousy troubled his amour; Maenz suspected him of having written verses for a rival and dismissed him in her wrath. Such rigor inspired touching ballads; finally, tenderness prevailed and Bertrand reentered the lady's good graces. After fighting valiantly and leading a very active life he ended his career as a monk of Cîteaux."

[29] Author's note: "Albert de Sisteron loved the Marquise de Malaspina, one of the most beautiful and most illustrious ladies of Provence. He was loved in return, and they could not live without one another. Their union gave rise to evil talk; finally the Marquise asked him to go away; he did, and nothing more was heard of him."

Penna,[30] lowly-born, contrived, thanks to his genius to become the husband of the noble Mabille de Simiane. Imitate those genteel troubadours; then, perhaps, you will feel in your soul the noble impulses that will render you worthy of the palms of renown."

"Yes, old man, I sense that I ought to love; but too much pride agitates me to sigh at the feet of a common beauty."

"Above all, refrain from placing your affections badly. It is appropriate only to cherish a noble lady; the more highly-placed the object of your amour is, the higher the sentiments rise. Listen: not far from Mauléon the powerful Comte de Foix has established his dwelling; a daughter assembles all his affections. The divine Bélisène sees her charms adored by all the knights, barons and troubadours in the land; they burn for her, but her heart is still insensible to their cares. Go; sigh after her; let her inspire you, and your guitar will soon accompany songs that beauties will love to repeat."

Charmed by the words of the old minstrel, in despair to have been devoid of amour for so long, I sensed that a new life was animating my being. My ideas were magnified; but everywhere I saw the image of Bélisène, and I already felt that I loved her idolatrously. I hastened to pick up my abandoned guitar, and a ballad that I composed appeared to me to be worthy of being retained:[31]

---

[30] Author's note: "Hugues de Penna, born in Messac in Agenois, was the son of a merchant. A fine voice and a taste for singing decided him on a career as a jongleur. At first he sang the songs of others, and then composed his own. He knew the genealogies of the great seigneurs of the region very well; that as a merit in the courts. He had a passion for gambling and taverns. Eventually, he married Mabille de Simiane."

[31] Author's note: "The music for this ballad was composed by the Comte de Toulouse-Lautrec."

Ah, this is truly the time for amour,
The flower is reborn in the boscage,
The wood will once again contain
The beautiful voice of the nightingale.

It says to us: all must be animated
Amour reigns over the orchard.
Ah, this is truly the time for amour,
Spring is the season of the love-song.

The sentinel on the tower
Thinks of the inhumane damsel;
The noble youth loves in his turn
His young and noble chatelaine.
The world appears to catch fire,
In nature ever repeating
Ah, this is truly the time for amour
Spring is the season of the love-song.

The butterfly loves the flower,
The stream its fresh bank,
The vine the victorious oak
And the zephyr the wild rose.
Sweet pleasure seems to animate
Everything that breathes or grows;
Ah, this is truly the time for amour
Spring is the season of the love-song.

The old troubadour encouraged me, applauding my progress; I was soon unable to separate from him; he became my master, he made me repeat my verses and, never ceasing to talk to me about Bélisène, he always nourished my amour. Impatient to see that beauty, I formed the project of quitting the Château de Mauléon, but the fear of displeasing my mother retained me.

"I also feared the cunning of Sigisbart, a knight whose origin was similar to mine, and whose ambition was known to me; I knew that my domains had long been the object of his envy; I could not doubt that he had spread the most frightful calumnies regarding my mother. Married very young to the Marquis my father, Adélaïde was never able to inspire amour in him; the marquis, uniquely occupied with combats, neglected tenderness. He perished in battle two years after his marriage to Adélaïde. She regretted him, but the sweetest affections soon came to replace her husband in her heart.

Antoine d'Urgel, famous for his bravery, felt the most virtuous of passions for Adélaïde; my mother did not take long to surrender, believing that she was giving me a support against the enterprises of Sigisbart; ceding to her penchant, she formed ties of which I could only approve once age had ripened my reason.

It was then that Sigisbart deployed all his blackness; a rumor soon circulated in Mauléon; it said that in order to crown her amour, Adélaïde had not hesitated to steep her hands in the blood of the Marquis de Mauléon. The people, extreme in everything, delivered themselves to insolent murmurs. My mother, too generous, was scornful of those outrageous rumors; Antoine d'Urgel wanted to punish them, but, far from destroying them, his imprudence only gave them further growth.

Finally, I advised that noble friend to leave his spouse for a time and go to the Court of Rome, assuring him that his absence, slowing the efforts of malevolence, would render him his innocence. D'Urgel believed me; he left after making us the most tender adieux, and I remained to console my mother. It was then that my bizarre amour was born. What was my despair at having advised d'Urgel to leave! If he had stayed in Mauléon, I would not have feared abandoning my mother to fly to where tenderness summoned me.

News that reached me, however, determined me to run to the divine Bélisène. In order to celebrate the peace treaty that had just been concluded with the Comte de Toulouse, the Comte de Foix had a tournament proclaimed that was to be linked to singing games. I could not resist my desire to signal myself in those fêtes, whether by breaking a lance or agitating the silvery strings of the amorous harp; but I did not want my name to be known; I would have died of shame if I had been defeated before Bélisène. Then, only confiding in the troubadour that I have already mentioned, I asked him what I ought to do.

"Sire," he said to me, "leave secretly; take two varlets and two squires with you; do not affect a pomp that would add nothing to your triumph, and would augment your humiliation."

I resolved to follow his advice; I thus committed an imprudence that would have had the most disastrous results if Heaven had not taken the conduct of my destiny in hand. I left during the night, without leaving behind any mark that could reassure my mother as to my destiny. Alas, I still deplore my conduct on that occasion every day.

Chapter VI: The Ballad and the Jousts

When I arrived in the city of Foix, I found a numerous host of knights, minstrels and curiosity-seekers everywhere, who had been attracted by the Comte's proclamations. It was not without difficulty that I succeeded in finding lodgings; all the houses were already occupied. Finally, a good burger was kind enough to take me in.

"Troubadour," he said to me, "is it simple curiosity that brings you within our walls, of have you come to dispute the prize for poetry?"

"I don't want to be confounded with the crowd," I told him, "and I hope for recompense in songs and arms."

"You will be fortunate if you obtain them, for the charming Bélisène, our sovereign's daughter, will distribute them with her white hand."

"What are you saying? Oh, doubtless the most famous troubadours and knights will come running from all parts to conquer them."

"I wish them, as well as you, a complete success, but I fear that none of the competitors will be able to please our young Comtesse."

"Is her heart insensible, then?"

"The troubadours only celebrate her beauty; no one can boast of having obtained a sigh from that exceedingly proud princesse."

Far from discouraging me, the man's words lent me new strength. I know not what presentiment made me hope that I would be fortunate, but it was with an extreme patience that I waited for the next day. The sound of bells and military instruments announced its arrival. I hastened to put on an elegant costume and, followed by my two varlets, I went to the prepared place.

Outside the gates of the city, lists had been constructed, surrounded by amphitheaters in which the nobility, the ladies and the demoiselles were placed, ornamented by their charms and assisted by brilliant attire. I searched among them for Bélisène, but she had not yet arrived; I recognized that by the calmness of my heart, which would have beaten rapidly if it had been near the lady of its amorous thoughts.

Soon, a sound of clarions and trumpets was heard. Preceded by the officers of his house, the Comte de Foix advanced, surrounded by the magnificence that befit his rank. Behind him marched, not a mortal but an angel, and until today, Madame (Savary addressed himself to Aliénor) I had thought that the earth did not contain her equal. I did not see her adornment; only her charming face attracted my gaze.

Shall I describe her attractions for you? No, I could only speak of them imperfectly, and besides, it's impossible that you have not seen her more than once. Oh, if I had loved Bélisène before having known her, with what sentiment was I not animated when I could contemplate her supernatural beauty! I wanted to intoxicate myself with the pleasure of seeing her; immobile before her, considering hr with an unparalleled admiration, I no longer sought expressions; I sensed that she would supply me with them.

Meanwhile, the whole assembly was in place; it had been settled that the troubadours would dispute the prize for a ballad or a poem. We were six competitors, all the others bearing a known name, for every time the judges pronounced one, cries and applause went up on all sides. Only I was unknown, to such an extent that when Savary was named, and all eyes turned toward me, my rivals could not help allowing disdainful smiles to wander over their harmonious lips. But I saw Bélisène looking at me with interest, and from then on, I thought myself more favored than my adversaries.

We were ordered to begin; I was to sing sixth. The first two recited long sirventes, in which they dared maladroitly to speak ill of women; a general clamor rose up against them, which constrained them to withdraw shameful. The third, Guilhem d'Anduse, voiced a warrior song, which he designated by the name of a song of return.

Amédée de la Broquère,[32] who succeeded him, sang about the exploits and inconstancy of a celebrated paladin of Charlemagne's court, Renaud de Montauban:[33]

Lance at the ready, helmet firm,
Marched one of the knights of France;
Sometimes by tenderness inflamed
Sometimes conducted by valor;
Cousin of the paladin Roland,
Ever dear to more than one beauty
And redoubted for infidelity;
He was Renaud de Montauban.

Then in a somber manor
A victim of jealousy
Under the yoke of a cruel guard
A demoiselle was weeping
To snatch her from her tyrant
Had a noble knight appeared?
He could not be mistaken;
He was Renaud de Montauban.

If talk was sometimes heard
Of a flighty chevalier,
Skilled in varying his choice.
In the town and in the village;
Enterprising in amorous games,
Friend of a tearful beauty
Feared by the local husbands;
It was Renaud de Montauban.

One day the damsel Alix,
Walking in a boscage,

---

[32] Literary histories of France include mention of Hameus or Amédée de La Broquière [sic] but the song quoted is not his,
[33] Author's note: "Music composed by M. Dalvimare."

84

Perceived in the dense thicket
A knight of high descent.
He spoke to her so gallantly
That he charmed the timid beauty;
Nine months later...the knave!
It was Renaud de Montauban.

Oh, those were the good old times!
A proud and sensible knight
Loved damsels and battled Moors;
For French knights all was possible.
One above all, braver and greater,
Made for amour and for war,
Populated and depopulated the earth;
It was Renaud de Montauban.

My turn finally arrived. Advancing toward the platform where the Comtesse de Foix was seated, I sought to fix her attention on me by means of a remarkable ballad.[34]

Amorously to love is the sovereign good;
Because in loving one forgets everything.
Believe me, the man who loves no one
Does not know the charm of life.

That glad charm is imprinted in a kiss,
In a gaze it is revealed again;
And happiness seems to be refused
To the icy heart that flees or ignores it.

Charm of amour! Delightful allure!
By a sigh you reveal you presence;
In sweet words if the lover paints well,
You can also speak in his silence.

---

[34] Author's note: "The music to this ballad is yet to be written."

All is embellished for momentary joy;
For you the heart ignites and sighs.
Vague desire! Unquiet sentiment!
How happy is he who inspires you!

Thus I sang, and with one voice, the prize was awarded to me. I do not know whether the subject lent itself to my genius, or whether the weakness of my rivals... Forgive me, Madame for that movement of vanity; it is quite natural to the man who owes his victory to the tenderness of his love. I was taken before Bélisène, who, placing the crown of myrtle on my young head personally, delighted me with the soft words that she pronounced. I received a rich bracelet from her hand, in which the fires of rubies and a superb diamond were combined, but greater still was my desire not to be content with a single success.

While the lists were being prepared for the jousts that were about to take place, I returned to my host's house, and there, taking of my troubadour's mantle, I put on my armor, which was all white, that of a young poursuivant.[35] My helmet, devoid of ornamentation, supported a crest of white plumes. I had erased the family escutcheon painted on my buckler and in its place I had engraved an emblem that I shall describe to you. In the middle of an illuminated cloud was placed an anchor, on which an amour was leaning, holding a harp; a banner allowed the words IN HOPE to be read.

The singularity of my accoutrement and my motto piqued curiosity. No one guessed that I might be the minstrel who had just won the singing prize, but they did not doubt that

---

[35] Author's note: "The name of *poursuivant* was given in that era to a young knight who, newly received, was seeking adventures for the first time. Ordinary, he set forth in quest of them mounted on a white horse and clad in white armor. His buckler bore no emblem; the knight had to wait, before choosing one, until he had merited it by some striking deed."

I was an adolescent who wanted to furnish his first career. Was it another idea of my self-esteem? It seemed to me that the Comtesse's gaze settled on me preferentially. *Let's go*, I said to myself; *let's merit that new honor*.

The lists were prepared; the Comte de Foix made a sign to the judges and the maréchal de camp to give the signal. They hastened to obey; the trumpets sounded the charge, and we took up an attacking posture. Instructed by masters skilled in the art of tourneys, I understood that it was necessary for me to employ all their lessons.

Alone, a knight named Ranichilde-le-Hardi sustained the impact of eight combatants. I was the ninth. We ran at one another at the top speed of our chargers, but my adversary's lance went astray, while mine, striking him in the middle of his body, tipped him into the arena. He got up, in despair at his fall. For myself, I finished my course and, holding firm in my stirrups, prepared to face the impact of a new assailant.

The man who replaced Ranichilde was a Portuguese, vain by virtue of his birth and proud of his strength, and so presumptuous that he could not believe it possible that he might be beaten. Scarcely saluting the ladies, he set off impetuously; his horse, although vigorous, was buckling under the weight of the gigantic warrior. I saw the extent of the danger that I was about to confront, but I thought of Bélisène and I felt a new ardor. We reached on another in the middle of the list; the blow that we delivered mutually was terrible; our lances broke into shards and we were each thrown back on to the rump of our chargers. More fortunate than the Portuguese, I did not lose my equilibrium, whereas he, in spite of his efforts, vacated the saddle. Long and noisy applause signaled that joust.

No other competitor having presented himself to dispute the victory, the honor of the day was accorded to me. The Comtesse summoned me a second time; I flew rather than ran in order to go to her, Before speaking to her, the heralds of arms asked my name in order to proclaim it; I hastened to tell them and, continuing on my way, advanced toward Bélisène.

At the moment when I took off my helmet in order to make myself known, the heralds raised my buckler, crying "Savary the Troubadour!"

The entire numerous assembly congratulated me on my double success with unanimous acclamation. I saw Bélisène's forehead ornamented by a slight blush. "Chevalier," she said to me, "what can have inspired you to sustain yourself in the two combats you have undertaken?"

"Lady," I said, in a low voice, "the desire to be crowned by your hand."

Those words redoubled the young comtesse's embarrassment; feigning to take them for a gallantry, like those with which the French are not miserly, she welcomed them with a gracious smile.

The jousts had just concluded when a knight of tall stature equipped with brilliant arms, presented himself at the barrier. The sound of the horn announced that he was requesting combat. I sensed in my soul the need to punish his audacity and the irregularity of his request, for I have no doubt that the noble Aliénor and the brave Adémar know that custom does not permit challenges once the lists are closed.

"Monseigneur," I said to the Comte, "If you will permit, I will respond to the appeal of that idle chevalier."

"Valiant troubadour," he prince replied, "I am reluctant to see you fight at the moment when victory belongs to you; however, if you feel that your strength is not overly exhausted, I consent to your adding a further leaf to your laurels."

Having said that, he made a sign to one of his pages, and ordered that a fresh horse be brought for me. A magnificent Andalusian was brought.

"Chevalier," said the Comte, "accept this as a testimony of my esteem."

The barriers were therefore closed again, the trumpets sounded the signal, and I departed, followed by the good wishes of the entire audience. My charger, faster than that of my adversary, reached a third of its course; the points of our lances struck our shields, and by a bizarre hazard, we were both thrown on to the sand. We got up nimbly and abandoned our lances to draw our swords; the combat recommenced, more terrible than all those I had already sustained. While I attacked or sought to defend myself, I could not help admiring the courage of the unknown knight, and frankly, I cursed the point of honor that had brought me to undertake that new assault.

While I was reflecting thus, the chevalier struck me rude blows. I returned a few, but the combat still remained equal when the stump of a lance, catching in the legs of my adversary, caused him to stumble and constrained him to kiss the dust. I ran forward to hold out my hand in order that he got get up again; he accepted my help. Then I proposed that we continue the combat.

"No, Chevalier," he said. "I don't want to dispute victory with you any longer. I admit myself vanquished."

Charmed by his resolution, I thanked him warmly, and, linking arms, we returned to the Comte's balcony. He pressed the knight to make himself known, but he still refused to do so, drawing away after saluting the count and his daughter profoundly.

No other accident came to trouble the ceremony; I was crowned a second time, and I sensed my amour redoubling again. Bélisène took my arm to return to her palace. The rest of the day was spent in games. I was intoxicated by the pleasure of seeing my beloved. The idea of my mother, the dread she might feel in being ignorant of my destiny, did not present itself to me at all. Blinded by the bandage that tenderness had put over my eyes, I was insensible to any other sentiment; but, assiduous in regard to Bélisène, my songs and my speech soon told that beauty the secret of my heart.

She refused for a long time to let me read hers, but finally, the sweet confession escaped her lips, and in an instant, I was able to believe myself the happiest of men. I confided the secret of my birth to her. She saw with delight that I was not of blood inferior to hers. That confidence charmed her, and from that day on the future seemed embellished to her gaze.

That felicity could not always be stable; it was necessary that frightful catastrophes would throw some poison into the happiness that we enjoyed.

Chapter VII: The Rival

Don Juan d'Astorga, Admiral of Léon, summoned by his taste to the court of the Comte de Foix, could not see Bélisène without experiencing an imperious amour for her. Don Juan, at the age when the passions are developed with the most violence, had never learned to contain them. Accustomed to seeing everything yield before him, it could not enter his mind that it was possible for him to be refused. The splendor of the sovereign power with which Bélisène was clad did not impose itself upon him; he resolved to take advantage of the first favorable opportunity to express his fervor. Not being able to produce one thereafter, he obsessed Bélisène.

I was furious with him; that superb Spaniard had the gift of displeasing me greatly. Believing me to be only a simple minstrel, he treated me with the insulting familiarity that displeases an elevated heart so greatly. Soon, he thought he perceived that my sight had dared to be raised as far as Bélisène; he quivered with rage in consequence, and if he did not insult me immediately, it was because he could not believe that my tenderness was even tolerated.

For several days, abundant rain had put obstacles in the way of the frequent walks that it was customary to take in the immense gardens of the palace.[36] Finally, the sun, having struggled against the clouds, dissipated them, and one morning, allowing us to see its shining face, it promised us a fine evening. As soon as the heat had eased everyone hastened to stroll in the park.

---

[36] Author's note: "The author of the romance had never been to Foix; otherwise, she would have known that the château of the Comtes was situated on a high crag, and that there was no room for the immense gardens of which she speaks. (The translator.)"

The Comte followed us; wanting to speak to me about a fête that he intended to give, he retained me and chatted with me. Don Juan saw the favorable opportunity that such a moment offered; he did not want to lose it, and, offering his hand to Bélisène, he drew away with her

"How charming these places are," he said, uttering a profound sigh, "and how painful it will be to separate from them!"

"Are you intending to quit us soon?" asked Bélisène.

"Yes, Madame; not as immediately as I should have."

Bélisène smiled. "Remember, Chevalier, that that is a remark I could not have expected."

"Can it be that it was made to you by all those who went away from you? Oh, Madame, would it not have been a hundred times better never to have known you than perpetually to deplore the day that gave birth..."

"It seems to me that my father is a long way from us."

"I can see, Madame, that you are trying to escape me; you do not want to hear the confession of a sentiment..."

"I want to return to the Comte."

"No, Madame, you shall not go away before I have told you about the flame to which you have given birth."

"Chevalier!"

"If I believed that the love of the Admiral of Léon offended you, I would have been able to enclose it in total silence, but whatever the splendor of your rank, I do not think that my cares can seem to you unworthy of being offered to you."

"Do you believe, Seigneur, that a title is sufficient to please?"

"No, Madame, and I'm beginning to perceive that."

"What do you mean?"

"That which you cannot hide from me. I presumed too much of the nobility of your inclinations to want to form the idea that that obscure troubadour, the sight of whom fatigues me, could interest you; but everything convinces me today..."

"What does it matter to you, Seigneur, what my attachment might be, since you cannot flatter yourself on conquering it? And as for that chevalier, whom you affect to scorn, he is of a blood to which perhaps the Admirals of Castile and Léon..."

"That's enough, Madame—but tremble for your loyal chevalier."

Having said that, furious at the affront he had suffered, perhaps for the first time, the presumptuous Spaniard drew away abruptly. Bélisène, favored by his flight, returned to her father and me, promising herself not to inform me of the admiral's threats.

The Come de Foix, weary of a stroll that as fatiguing him, went back to his palace, while his court took pleasure in enjoying the charms of a beautiful evening. We went to a pond surrounded by white marble seats backed up against orange trees whose sweet odor perfumed the air. There, troubadours were singing their tensons and knights were relating the great feats of arms of barons and heroes.

Scarcely had the Comte de Foix retired when Don Juan presented himself before him. The cowardly rival, pouring the poisons of calumny upon me, represented me as a vile schemer devoid of birth and fortune, skillful only in the art of seduction. He warned him about the amour that Bélisène had for me. In the end, he did it so effectively that the alarmed Comte sent one of his pages to look for me on his behalf.

The messenger fulfilled his master's orders and, without suspecting Don Juan's perfidy, I rendered to the Comte's request.

"Savary," he said, "until now I have not permitted myself to interrogate you about your parents and your rank, but I can no longer welcome in my court an individual who does not want to be known."

"Monseigneur, I am a knight, like you, and a troubadour or the glory of ladies."

"Listen to me, young man. Are you treated without regard?"

"It would ill behoove me to complain."

"Have I not been an honest and good Seigneur for you?"

"Monseigneur, nowhere have I received better nourishment."[37]

"Well, why is it that you only recognize everything I have done for you by your ingratitude?"

Vehemently, I replied: "The man lies in his throat who has been able to say such things to you, and, weapons in hand, I am ready to support what I say."

You can rehabilitate yourself in my mind with a word," said the Comte. "Make yourself known; one is always suspicious of the man who hides; a virtuous man shows himself uncovered."

"Yes, Sire Comte, I have been wrong not to tell you who I am; it is time you learned the name of which I am proud. The man who is known in your court as the minstrel Savary is known elsewhere by the title of the Marquis of Mauléon."

"Can that be true?" aid the Comte, with satisfaction.

I placed my hand on the guard of my sword. "I affirm it, word of a chevalier."

"What bizarre thought led you to keep silent regarding your birth?"

"Only my entire frankness can excuse my fault."

Then, revealing my entire history, I told him about the amour that his daughter inspired in me, and I also told him about the tender reciprocity that she accorded me; I made him sense that my alliance could not displease him. What more can I tell you? I did it so well that before we separated, the Comte embraced me tenderly and permitted me to ask for the hand of Bélisène.

My delirium was extreme. In the transports of my joy, I did not think of asking him who the person was who, by his reports, had tried to harm me in his eyes; I only thought of having my beloved summoned. She came running; my delight

---

[37] Author's note: "This phrase means a distinguished reception, or a good education."

became hers. Her father repeated he promise that he had made me, but he demanded that I leave promptly in order to go and inform my mother, as impatient as him to fix the epoch of my happiness.

It was decided that I would leave the following day to return to Mauléon. We agreed to keep our agreement secret. I only communicated my departure to the courtiers. Dissimulating his joy, Don Juan flattered himself that I was only going away because I had been banished by the Comte, but, far from making me aware of his conspiracy, it was with a penetrating expression that he received my adieux.

He did not appear the following day. We were told that, accompanied by some of his domestics, he had departed at daybreak to make a journey that might retain him all week. Just as it was of no importance to me whether he was with me, as his presence displeased Bélisène, no one was pained by his disappearance.

The hour that was about to separate me from my beloved was about to sound when cries resounded in the château; I heard my name pronounced. I ran to inform myself as to the cause of the rumor, but I was not given the time. A varlet came to tell me that an old troubadour, weeping bitter tears, was asking to speak to me without delay. The Comte de Foix ordered that he be brought in.

He advanced, and I recognized him as the man who had ignited in my soul the desire to know amour.

"Oh, Monseigneur," he cried, "What enemy demon can have brought you to quit your seigncury? Mourning, crime and death inhabit it now."

"Troubadour, what do you mean? Hasten to speak in order to render calm to my frightened heart."

"Alas, Sire Marquis, your illustrious mother, the victim of a clever scoundrel, is in irons, and the fourth day hence will be that of her execution."

"Troubadour, what are you telling me? What fable is this? My mother, my virtuous mother, has been accused?"

"More than that; she has been condemned!"

"For what is she reproached? Who are the reckless individuals who, without redoubting me…?"

"Your death is imputed to her, and her accuser is the Chevalier Sigisbart."

"Please, Troubadour, recount the events that have taken place in my absence."

Chapter VIII: The Calumny

"A fortnight had gone by since your departure; the reason for your sudden flight was unknown. Only I was able to provide the key to it, but, engaged by the promise that I had made to you, not only did I not want to say anything on your account, but I also left Mauléon in order that my presence would not give anyone the desire to interrogate me.

"The people, avid for the marvelous, claimed at first that, instructed by a vision that had appeared to you, you had gone to bury yourself in a Spanish monastery; others affirmed that you had gone to the Holy Land. In sum, everyone made up a story to which they brought imaginary proofs.

"Soon, a muffled rumor began to spread, which asserted that you had perished, that Comte d'Urgel had only pretended to go to Italy in order to conceal his crime. It was said that, in collaboration with your mother, he had gone to that extremity in order to make the marquisat pass into his family. That calumny, rejected at first, was accredited and welcomed; the Chevalier Sigisbart pretended to scorn it; he spoke to the Marquise about it himself. Frightened and desperate, she wanted to purge herself on oath; she was told that, strong in her innocence, she ought not to lower herself to that point. She had the weakness to listen to those perfidious insinuations; that was the cause of her doom.

"Another week went by; weeping for our fate and her misfortunes in the silence of the château, the noble Adélaïde did not think of treason. Suddenly, the people assembled under the balcony overlooking the main square; the words *homicide, vengeance* and *justice* were pronounced.

"The Marquise, indignant at the insolence of your subjects, got up, summoned her gentlemen and her guards and ordered them to charge the multitude in order to disperse them. They were about to obey her when the door of the palace was forced.

"Sigisbart penetrates into his sovereign lady's abode with weapons in hand. Two individuals laden with chains, bearing in all their features the imprint of assassins are following him, escorted by a mutinous crowd. The Marquise, unintimidated by their audacity, advances toward them and in an irritated voice asks Sigisbart what motive has brought him to rebel.

"Without replying to that question, Sigisbart says: 'Marquise, the subjects of Marquis Savary, your son, anxious about his absence, want to know what important interest retains him far from Mauléon. We have no doubt that you cannot be ignorant of the place to which he has gone; we are convinced that it is easy to tell us.'

"'Sigisbart,' says the Marquise, 'I do not know whether I ought to reply to you; you come into my palace with all the appearances of sedition; however, as I want to please those you have blinded, forgiving them their aberration, I declare before Heaven that my son's fate is unknown to me.'

"'That is enough, Madame,' says Sigisbart. 'If you know nothing about your son's fate, these two wretches I have brought can tell us more.'

"Then the two chained men fall to their knees, protesting and swearing in the name of God that they have murdered young Savary in obedience to the orders of the Marquise and the Comte, her husband.

"At that horrible accusation, your mother utters a cry of despair. She tries to protest her innocence, but they do not want to listen; her most faithful partisans are the first to heap her with reproaches. A sovereign an instant before, she becomes the prisoner of her own subjects: a great example of the games of Fortune, who sometimes takes pleasure in destroying and sometimes raising the great to the summit of her wheel.

"You mother, in spite of her plaints, is arrested on the depositions of the two false witnesses; she is given her apartment for a prison; guards are placed on all the avenues. Foreign troops hired by Sigisbart enter the town, doubtless destined to oppose any enterprises that might be made by the few friends who, having recovered from their initial error, have no doubt that the Marquise is the victim of a clever scoundrel.

"The next day the council assembled, presided by Sigisbart, as a member of your family. The unfortunate Adélaïde is brought before it, suffering more from the suspicion that is weighing upon her than the torture that awaits her. The two assassins are summoned, but they are dead. A violent poison had been given to them; they died in frightful convulsions, but before expiring, they had renewed their accusation, and protested in addition that their death was also the work of the Marquise.

"Her noble and precise justification, and the victorious arguments that she brought forward in her favor were utterly unheeded by the judges, prejudiced or bought. Violating the rights of princes, they dared to pronounce the sentence that condemned their sovereign to execution by fire, if no chevalier could prove her innocence with weapons in hand, as ancient usage prescribed.

"The Marquise was accorded a week to present her defender; at the same time, by virtue of a refined barbarity, great care was taken to distance from her all those who might have fought in her favor, and Sigisbart, redoubtable for his valor, declared himself her adversary.

"It was then that rumor of the story reached me in my retreat. Fearful of the danger your mother was running, my first impulse was to hasten to disabuse the judges, but a reflection stopped me: an old and obscure troubadour, could I hope that my feeble voice could counterbalance the determination of Sigisbart? Would I not be arrested myself before I could speak? What can veracity do without strength against powerful perversity, which is constrained always to accumulate further crimes in order not to lose the fruits of those already committed?

"Then I made the decision to come and find you, not doubting that you were still at this court; my hope has not been disappointed; I have found you, and now I am no longer anxious either for your mother's days or for the punishment that her enemy warrants."

"Let's go, Troubadour!" I cried. "Let the man who has committed the fault repair it. Let us go and slay Sigisbart with my blade and my presence. By my inconsiderate flight I have caused my mother's misfortune; let my return avenge her on the villain who has dared to attack her."

The Comte de Foix shared my indignation. He offered to assemble troops and place himself at their head in order to come with me to free the Marquise.

"No, Monseigneur," I said to him, "let me have the sole honor of that enterprise. Whatever its outcome might be, my mother is bound to be justified; I only want to share with myself the glory of avenging her."

Without losing a minute, I had my destrier prepared. After having promised the Comte and his charming daughter to inform them of the success of the endeavor that I was about to undertake, I left, followed by my two squires, my two pages and the old troubadour.

We rode until nightfall. The veil of evening was already enveloping the mountains when, as we were passing through a narrow defile I saw a dwarf coming toward me who seemed desolate.

"Oh, Monseigneur," he cried, as soon as he as within earshot, "if appearance is not deceptive, you must be a noble knight. Oh, if it is for honor and for ladies that you are in quest of adventure, follow me; I can procure you the pleasure of being useful to the most beautiful person in the world, but at the same time the most unfortunate."

"Friend," I replied, "I am ready to follow you, provided that I can be free to resume my journey tomorrow morning."

"Monseigneur," said the dwarf, "only come to speak to the beautiful Comtesse Indie; her château is the one that you can see over there on that rock. It is there that she is mourning the loss of her son, stolen from her by a disloyal knight."

"What can I do for her I that circumstance?"

"Fight the felon. My mistress has proposed that to a large number of knights in vain; all of them, when they learned the name of the villain that it was necessary to punish, would not dare to measure their words against his."

"What is the name of this redoubtable knight, then?"

"His name is Don Juan d'Astorga."

"Friend, I know him; he is undoubtedly brave and strong, but if I were fighting for a just cause, I would not hesitate to attack him. In the meantime, take me to the Vicomtesse Indie."

Without replying, he dwarf led me along a narrow road. It was necessary to cross a bridge. Scarcely had we set foot on it to cross than it tilted and we fell into a profound ditch.

I understood immediately that I was the victim of a trap, but who could I accuse? Only the name of Sigisbart came to mind.

In the situation I which I found myself, however, I had a slight movement of joy, because I did not see the old troubadour sharing my captivity. More fortunate than us, perhaps he had avoided the trap into which I had fallen, and I could expect my deliverance from him. My vassals, consternated by their situation, deplored it bitterly.

Chapter IX: Vengeance

We were left in that sad place for some time. Finally, the trapdoor opened again. A rope was thrown down to us to help us climb up. As each of my companions reached the height of the hole, he was seized and tied up. I preferred death to the indignity that awaited me and I shouted to the men-at-arms that I did not want to render myself their prisoner. Without paying any attention to what I said, they hastened to descend on all sides; I defended myself in vain; vanquished by numbers, I was knocked down.

When they had rendered it impossible for me to resist any longer, they dragged me to the fatal château. As I passed over the drawbridge I thought that it was closing forever. How bitter my reflections were! How my heart was breaking at the thought that my mother would perhaps perish by my fault, without my being able to help her. I abandoned myself then to all the impetuosity of my character; I made the walls of the chamber to which I had been taken resound with my clamors; I implored the pity of my jailers; I begged them to render me a liberty that was so necessary to me.

They made no reply; wearied by my pleas they went away, closing the heavy iron door that oppose my exit. Left alone, I suffered even more. The entire night went by in that state; I could not sleep for an instant, and, leaning sadly on the thick bars of my widow, I abandoned myself to all my dolor.

At that moment, the bolts of my prison were violently withdrawn, and I turned round. The door opened and I saw appear before me, not Sigisbart, whom I expected, but Don Juan. At the sight of him, a cry of surprise escaped me.

"Sire Marquis," the cruel Spaniard said, ironically, "you see that it is easier to disguise your true name than to escape my vengeance. So long as I thought that Savary was only an obscure troubadour, I did not deign to punish him for the tenderness that he had been able to make the beautiful Bélisène share; now that, better informed, I know that his rivalry might be redoubtable to me, I judge it appropriate to make sure of him."

"Don Juan," I said, "you conduct belies that of the generous nation to which you belong. Have the loyal Spaniards not taught you that one avenges oneself on a rival weapons in hand, and that it is only cowards who employ treason? You say that you love Bélisène; were there not other means to assure yourself of her possession? Do you think I would have refused to meet you on the field of honor?"

"I don't doubt your bravery," said Don Juan, "but I think it unnecessary to employ mine when other means can ensure the success of my projects. If I had been defeated by you, Bélisène would have been lost to me irrevocably. Now I can be certain of stealing her from you forever. I know what motive is causing you to return to Mauléon; you want to go to the aid of a cherished mother to whom the slightest delay might be fatal. Well, you shall not save her and will cause her death twice over, for I will only return your liberty if you agree to the proposition that I am going to make to you."

"Do me the honor of telling me what it is."

"You can save your mother; I consent to that; but cede Bélisène to me."

"What do you mean?"

"You will give me your word as a knight that you will not return to the court of the Comte de Foix; that, without informing him of the veritable reason for your conduct, you will break with him and his daughter; that you will flee her; in a word, that you will appear inconstant in her eyes."

"Detestable monster! Who can have furnished your soul with such detestable counsel? What! I must renounce the happiness that awaits me! I must release Bélisène and abandon her to a villain like you! No, no, a hundred times no. Go away, traitor, and leave me alone."

Coldly, Don Juan said: "Let amour prevail over nature; let your mother be the victim of your passion."

"My mother, you say! What! My mother might die?"

"If no knight presents himself, she will suffer the ultimate penalty."

"Frightful image! Oh, Don Juan, be generous; let me fulfill the holiest of duties, but don't ask me for something that will ensure my death."

"Your dolor is of no importance to me. It is not for you that I have pity; a rival inspires nothing in me but hatred. Meanwhile, time is being wasted in useless talk; pronounce your final resolution; if you accept what I propose, the doors will open before you; if you refuse, you will cause the death of your mother; I will leave you in this prison, from which you will have no more hope of emerging; I shall spread the rumor that you have perished, a victim of Sigisbart's ambition; no suspicion will be raised against me, and an impenetrable veil will cover your fate henceforth."

"Amour! Nature! Sentiments that lacerate me alternately! However, is it necessary that if I satisfy one, the other will cost me eternal tears? Bélisène, can I renounce you forever? My mother, can I pronounce your death sentence? No, virtue will prevail over tenderness, I will be worthy of the blood of which I am the issue. Yes, Don Juan, I swear to you..."

"Seigneur Chevalier!" cried a varlet, irrupting into the chamber and addressing my rival. "Hasten to defend yourself, or, rather, think about saving yourself; a troop of armed men is scaling your château."

"Let my vengeance not be disappointed!" said Don Juan, drawing his sword in order to strike me.

At the moment when that new crime was about to be consummated, however, a fully-armed knight appeared, leapt upon the Spaniard and felled him to the floor with a thrust of his sharpened blade.

I advanced toward my liberator; and with what astonishment was I struck when I recognized the warrior against whom I had fought in the recent tourney, at the moment when I was victorious.

"Generous stranger," I said to him, "Oh, it is me who is vanquished today by your grandeur of soul!"

"Noble Savary," he replied, taking off his helmet and allowing me to admire his majestic face, "I am fulfilling the conditions that honor imposed on me when I was armed as a knight."

"May I not know your name?"

"Allow me to keep silent; let it suffice for you to know that, like you, I am an admirer of the beautiful Comtesse de Foix."

Then the old troubadour appeared. "Oh, my dear master," he said, "how glad I am to have secured your deliverance! When you fell into the trap that had been set for you, hazard determined that I was a few paces behind. Suspecting treason, I rode away as far as my horse could carry me, and placed myself on the highway, in the hope of encountering there a loyal knight who would take care of extracting you from the peril that menaced you. No one came.

"Dawn was about to break when I heard hoof-beats that gave me reason to think that a numerous troop was approaching. I spoke to their leader, telling him of your danger; I did not hide your name from him. Immediately, he commanded his men-at-arms to follow him. We avoided the dangerous bridge and reached the walls of the château. Having found an accessible place, we scaled the wall abruptly. You know the rest. Your enemy has been punished, and I do not have to mourn your loss."

The knight, my liberator, advised me to leave the château. We departed immediately, after which Don Juan was carried to a bed, still unconscious. We thought he would die, but he survived, to my misfortune.

Having repeated my thanks to the knight, who was obstinate in remaining unknown, I prepared to separate from him. He quit me, and I did not see him again until today. Yes, beautiful Aliénor, that knight, who saved my life and honor, is Prince Raymond, your illustrious brother, who, ever great, commands his passions with as much facility as we abandon ourselves to them.

Fearing to encounter some new encounter that might raise obstacles in my path, I pressed the pace of my destrier urgently. Finally, I arrived in Mauléon on the eve of the execrable day that would see my death or my mother's virtue nobly avenged.

As we entered the town we saw a large crowd of people going toward the main square. Still maintaining the strictest incognito, I separated myself from my cortege and, accompanied by a single squire, I followed the curious crowd. We arrived some time before a herald dressed in black, mounted on a horse of the same color, appeared in the midst of the multitude; he was preceded by four pages carrying, on a rich black velvet cushion, Sigisbart's gauntlet, the challenge to combat.

The herald had the trumpets sounded even times, and said:

"To all knights, my lord and master, Sigisbart de Mauléon, makes it known that he will appear in the closed field tomorrow, fully armed, to sustain toward and against all, that Adélaïde, daughter of the Vicomte de Gimoes and Marquise de Mauléon, has treacherously murdered or had murdered, young Savary, sovereign Marquis de Mauléon, declaring in his soul and conscience that he believes his cause to be just, and repeats by my voice that he will sustain his word in the lists prepared at the hour of noon. Now, if there is any knight who wishes to fight against him, let him appear and pick up the gauntlet that I throw to him."

With those words, the herald did indeed pick up the gauntlet and throw it on the ground. There was a profound silence; no one offered himself to defend the unfortunate woman. Then, cleaving through the crowd I advanced toward the herald.

"Herald," I said to him, "go tell your master that a knight has presented himself who has picked up his pledge; that the knight accuses Sigisbart of being an execrable calumniator, protests that the latter has lied in his throat and that he hopes that the judgment of God, in justifying the Marquise Adélaïde, will punish the true guilty party. Herald, I will sustain my word tomorrow."

The people, who an instant before, had seen the insult delivered to their sovereign without being worthy, uttered cries of joy at the appearance of a defender. The herald and the officers were nonplussed; they had not thought that any knight would be reckless enough to confront Sigisbart; but since one had presented himself, they could only defend what the sacred law of chivalry demanded.

It was not without a secret terror that Sigisbart learned that an adversary had just pronounced against him, but, confident in his bravery, he believed himself to be invincible. The Marquise was informed that she had found a defender. She wanted to see me. In spite of the desire I had to throw myself into her arms, I refused her request; it would have been impossible for my heart to constrain itself in her presence.

The next day would illuminate the mortal combat that was to decide my life or that of my enemy. No cause more singular was ever submitted to the judgment of God: on one side, a knight accusing a mother of having caused the death of her son; on the other, that son, believed to be dead, fighting on because of an unjustly accused mother.

At daybreak, the bells, by their silvery sound, announced the duel that was about to take place. A large crowd filled the environs of the lists. The executioners arrived first, leading the horses dragging the stretcher destined to carry away whichever of the two assailants was vanquished; those men of blood built an immense pyre and placed themselves carefully around it.

The sound of a veiled drum announced the advent of the Marquise; she was walking in the midst of her maidservants, who sometimes dissolved in tears and sometimes invoked the justice of God. Holy monks surrounded my mother; they sustained and encouraged her. She was clad in black; long veils covered her face, hiding from us the tears of pride that escaped her eyes. She placed herself next to the pyre. Her guards moved away. She was to be regarded as free until the outcome of the combat.

It had been decided that we would not make use of our horses, so I appeared on foot, armed with an ax and a dagger. Sigisbart, escorted by all his pages, advanced pompously. He looked at me with scorn and, not deigning to salute me, took up his position. We renewed our challenges. Each of us having persisted in sustaining his word, the judges of the camp ordered us to proceed.

It was not a simple point of honor or a pass of arms that was at stake; it was life or death. Sigisbart and I measured one another with our eyes momentarily; soon we clashed; our axes collided, and peril menaced us by turns. Employing cunning, strength and skill, we balanced fortune; sometimes one of us recoiled, sometimes his adversary retreated in his turn; our blows were equally anticipated and parried.

However, anger rose in my breast as Sigisbart resisted me; I abandoned myself to my natural impetuosity; I pressed my enemy, and dazzled him with the speed of the blows I truck. Finally, seizing my ax more forcefully, deceiving Sigisbart with a feint, I plunged the dagger into his side. He fell on the sand.

"Disloyal knight," I cried, "confess your crimes."

"Yes," he said, in an expiring voice. "I am culpable, and Heaven is punishing me unjustly. It was me who instigated the two calumniators; it was me who caused them to perish when they became useless to me, instead of rewarding them as I had promised. I declare that Savary's fate is unknown to me."

"And I will make it known to everyone," I cried. "People, recognize your sovereign! My mother, see your son in your avenger!"

It would be in vain, Madame Aliénor, were I to try to depict for you the scene that succeeded the tableau of horror that I have traced for you. My mother's joy, my own, and that of my subjects, was unparalleled. Sigisbart expired with the regret of seeing us all happy. I delivered his body to the executioners, as I was obliged to do; I had his accomplices punished and I obtained my mother's consent for my marriage to Bélisène.

"I was not able to fly back to that noble friend as promptly as I would have wished. The cares of my marquisat retained me for a year. I employed that time either in occupying myself with my subjects' affairs or delivering myself to my penchant for poetry, a penchant that had earned me a faint renown. Antoine d'Urgel, my mother's husband, finally returned; I confided all my authority to him, and went to Foix.

There was no longer time to think of the marriage; war was rumbling in our homeland; the crusaders were threatening not only Raymond's estates but also those of the Comte de Foix. We had resolved to support the Comte de Toulouse. I went to see him at Castelnaudary, from which I was coming when the storm, having caused me to lose my way, took me to the dwelling of the hermit of the tomb. There, Madame, I had the pleasure of encountering you, that of uniting myself in amity with the valiant Adémar and, subsequently, rediscovering my liberator in your brother.

Thus Savary de Mauléon concluded his story.

PART TWO

Chapter I: The Visions in the Gallery

Insatiable desires of the grandeurs of the earth, how far will you take men in sin? Can you not stop them on the slope that draws them away? Can you not deflect them from the pernicious desire to sacrifice everything to their interest? And you, remorse of the heart, inexorable cry of conscience, you do not cease to thunder and make yourself heard; you sow terrors in the criminal's path; you always surround his bed with the most frightening illusions; repose for him is devoid of charms, pleasure always troubled by a few bitter memories; afflicting ideas pursue him without leaving him an instant of calm, and yet nothing changes his soul, he will still be as wicked, everything will only serve to harass him futilely; and to deliver him from his initial dreads he will not hesitate to commit further sins.

Behold Arembert, tormented relentlessly by a vengeful shade, finding the redoubtable hermit everywhere; he only occupies himself with odious thoughts; he begins to repent of the protection that he has thus far accorded to the young and virtuous Adémar. The sinister projects that he was rolling in his head, to which amour would soon give a new extension, will guide Arembert until nightfall.

The pilgrim had quit him and Adémar had departed for Toulouse, so the Baron found himself alone. When night had replaced day, in order to provide some distraction from the thoughts that had presented themselves in a host to his imagination, he was walking in the long gallery of his château. A skillful hand had painted on the stained glass widows the glorious history of Arembert's ancestors; on every side their victories and generous actions were depicted. Among those scenes, one in particular riveted Arembert's attention; scarcely had he examined it than a convulsive tremor gripped him. He tore himself away from the place in which he was standing and ran to the other extremity of the gallery. Soon, in fact, even more consternated, he returned to his chamber.

Scarcely had he closed the door than, blushing at his involuntary fear, he resolved to go back to the place where he had been so frightened. He opened the door that gave access to the gallery; he ran rather than walked; he turned an avid gaze toward the mysterious stained glass windows.

They had disappeared...

The Baron's astonishment was indescribable. *Can it be*, he said to himself, *that my imagination is taking pleasure in reminding me incessantly of a memory...? Insensate, I have only seen on those mute panes illusions that I had created. What being on earth could boast of knowing enough of the story of my life to dare to trace the most frightful event?*

"Me!" replied a sepulchral voice that he did not take long to recognize.

Overwhelmed by the most just fear, the terrified Arembert scarcely dared to tremble, but it was beyond his strength to be able to turn around to contemplate the person who had spoken. A profound groan was heard.

At that moment, the moon, disengaged from the clouds by which was surrounded caused the reflection on the wall before which Arembert was placed of a gigantic shadow whose form was that of an armed knight. Bewildered, the Baron gathered all the faculties of his soul and demanded: "Who are you, who take pleasure in pursuing me?"

There was no reply to his question. A second sigh was uttered.

At that moment, new clouds having enveloped the moon, the shadow of the knight disappeared, and silence reigned in the vast gallery. Placing his hand on his forehead, Arembert withdrew after a few minutes. He went to find his squires, and everyone was struck with astonishment on contemplating the discolored face of the suzerain.

The latter put off the hour of his retreat; he dreaded finding himself alone. A criminal does not like solitude; he needs noise to stifle the interior voice that reminds him of what he wants to forget. The night was advancing, however. At the moment when the courtiers hoped that he would order the retirement, Arembert ordered that candelabra of new wax candles be placed, and that wine should be brought originating from the rich vineyards of Guienne. He was obeyed promptly.

"Companions," he said to the knights, "I drink to the brave."

"And we," they replied in chorus, "drink to our Baron."

"And I," said a loud voice, "drink to Bérenger!"

A thunderbolt falling at Arembert's feet could not have produced as much effect on him as that sinister voice.

"Bérenger" he cried. "Who speaks of Bérenger?"

But the voice had fallen silent, while the vassals maintained silence in their consternation.

In the meantime, the dwarf on the keep was heard sounding the horn. A squire appeared. He told the Baron that a knight, escorted by four men-at-arms and conducting a lady, was requesting to be introduced into the château immediately. The reply had been given that it was past the time, and that the gate would not be opened again until daybreak. Then he had passed a ring through the postern and asked that it be taken to Arembert immediately.

The latter having taken it, he considered it attentively; then, showing some evidence of joy, he ordered that the knight be admitted without making him wait any longer.

Immediately, preceded by his pages, he went to meet the unknown.

After the drawbridge had been lowered, the cortege entered the courtyard of the château. The knight who was arriving and Arembert embraced one another reciprocally, and, followed by the travelers, he returned to the audience hall.

Scarcely had they entered when the lady that the knight was conducting took off the long veil that covered her and threw herself at the Baron's feet and asked him for support and protection against the enterprises of Don Juan d'Astorga.

Arembert had already sent his men away. "Lady," he said to the afflicted beauty, "my friend has not come to my château for me to betray the duties of hospitality."

Don Juan d'Astorga, for it was him, replied to the unfortunate Bélisène, whom you will already have divined on hearing the Castilian Admiral named: "Comtesse, lose henceforth any hope of removing yourself from my amour; if I have succeeded in stealing you from your father, I have the power to conserve you under my dependence. It is not Arembert who will betray me; we have been found ourselves together in such an occasion that we are forever bound to one another. Our interests are common."

"If this knight is your friend," said Bélisène, scornfully, "he must, like you, be culpable. Yes. I recognize my error; I ought not to have implored his generosity."

"I do not know, Madame," said Arembert, "for what reason you are insulting Don Juan, and why you are enveloping me in your hatred."

"Does a kidnapper and a murderer merit the regard of his victim?"

"Madame!" said Don Juan.

"What does your anger matter to me? I brave it; d'Astorga is too odious in my eyes to be able to inspire any dread."

"Think, Madame, that you are in my power here," said Don Juan, "and that I can punish your unjust aversion."

"Is it by inspiring dread that Don Juan thinks to give birth to love?" said Bélisène.

"Sentiment is immaterial to me; I can command you. It is sufficient to see my desires satisfied."

"What!" cried Bélisène. "Will no support be offered to me?"

"That of virtue," pronounced a voice.

"Arembert," said Don Juan, "what does this mean…?"

"Has Don Juan forgotten the mountains of Narbonne?" said the voice.

"Just Heaven!" exclaimed Don Juan.

"Oh, whoever you are," said Bélisène, "hasten to appear."

"Where crime acts," said the voice, "I shall not fail to render myself."

A profound silence followed that extraordinary conversation. Arembert, not wanting to prolong any further an evening already too far advanced, had an old woman summoned whose exterior announced nullity; he recommended Bélisène to her, and the beautiful young woman, without casting a glance at the two knights, drew away, preceded by her new guardian.

The latter, whose name was Germaine, looking at the young Comtesse curiously, could not help telling her that she pitied her for being constrained to inhabit the chamber to which she was being taken.

"What does the place matter," said Bélisène, "provided that I am away from my cruel persecutor?"

"It would have been a hundred times better not to quit the chevalier with whom you came."

"Is the chamber very redoubtable, then?"

"Oh, Madame," said Germaine, "if you knew everything that is said to have happened in that place! I will refrain from telling you; I would be sorry to frighten you."

"You have, in fact, succeeded in reassuring me," said Bélisène.

"Shall I tell you that the Baron's father died there; that since that day voices have been heard groaning, and that no one dares stay there?"

"And that is the place that has been chosen for my prison?"

"Undoubtedly, Madame," said Germaine, "the Sire Baron must have something against you, for he only sends people there that he wants to punish."

"Will you not be staying with me?"

"May the good Queen of the Angels, whom I revere, preserve me from spending the night in such a place! I would not be found alive the next day."

"Your fears, my good woman, have little foundation; Heaven is doubtless miserly with the prodigy with which you are pleased to entertain me."

It was then that they arrived at the door of the redoubtable rom. Germaine opened it tremulously; she placed the lamp on a richly decorated side-table and got ready to make up the bed.

Bélisène took advantage of that moment to examine her apartment. The dimensions of the room were immense; old tapestries of silk and gold decorated the walls, against which reposed suits of armor conquered by Baron Amanieu, Arembert's father, from the Comtes du Gévaudan. In the middle stood a huge bed in violet velvet embroidered in all its seams. It was surmounted by ostrich plumes and crowned by a heavy cornice sculpted with care; at intervals there were little mirrors such as were fabricated in those days, placed between the windows.

Bélisène looked to see whether it was possible for anyone to introduce themselves into the room. She only found one door, which opened into a small wood-paneled cabinet, from which there was no exit.

Germaine, having hastened to conclude her work, wished Bélisène good night and, without waiting for a response, promptly ran away.

Left alone, Bélisène, had no wish to undress. She threw herself on to the bed fully clothed, resolved to stay awake until daybreak, a moment that was not far off, for it as in the season of the shortest nights.

The Comtesse de Foix had been lying down for some time when the door of the little cabinet creaked as it turned on its hinges. Frightened, she sat up, and was gripped by terror when she perceived a phantom of enormous stature, clad in a ample red robe. At that sight she uttered a lamentable cry, but her fear was appeased when the individual said to her in a soft voice: "Calm yourself, Comtesse de Foix; if crime inhabits these walls, there is also a genius protective of innocence. Cease to fear the enterprises of Don Juan; he will not dare insult someone protected by the mysterious hermit of the tomb."

"Oh, whoever you are," said Bélisène, "if you are not a satellite of my persecutor, employ your cares to get me out of this odious dwelling."

"Elsewhere, I could not protect you; here you can remain without alarm."

Having spoken thus, the hermit went back into the cabinet and disappeared without him being able to hear the words that Bélisène addressed to him.

Somewhat reassured by what she had just seen, she delivered herself to sweet hopes. Soon, the first rays of daylight, penetrating as far as her, found her embraced by the charms of a reparative slumber.

Chapter II: Two Villains Reunited

Since the moment when Raymond had struck Don Juan in the château in the Pyrenees, the latter, delivered to the care of his domestics, had spent more than a year in state that made them despair of his life. Nature had prevailed, however; he recovered, and throughout the time of his forced repose he invented new perfidies to cause Savary to perish, as well as to assure himself of the possession of Bélisène; finally, he was able to devote himself to the execution of his projects.

He did not take long to return to the court of Foix; there, hidden in the crowd, he awaited a favorable moment. Savary did not quit Bélisène. The cowardly Juan, fearing the bravery of the noble knight, dared not attack him openly, nor abduct his lover.

Events constrained Savary to go to Toulouse. Juan thought that the war, which would not take long to catch fire, and which threatened the house of Foix, would furnish him with the means of retaining Bélisène irrevocably if he could succeed in kidnapping her. The same day when the Marquis de Mauléon quit his beautiful friend, Juan, having assembled his accomplices, penetrated into the gardens of the palace by night. A woman in Bélisène's retinue, whom he had taken care to buy, opened the interior door of the apartment for him.

After spending the evening with her father, reading him the chronicles of Archbishop Turpin, Bélisène, urged by the desire to think about her lover, retired at the usual hour. She sat in her room, strummed her guitar, and, inspired by amour, she composed songs of dolor and absence.

Her ballad concluded, she knelt down on her prie-dieu and, raising her thoughts toward the Creator, she was offering him her homage when she heard footsteps behind her. She tried to turn round but, without giving her the time, someone threw a thick veil over her face; she uttered a faint cry and fainted immediately.

Charmed by an incident that served him so well, Don Juan carried the unfortunate Bélisène away. He took her out of the palace and, taking her on to his horse, he drew away from a place that he was about to fill with trouble and confusion.

For a long time, the Castilian Admiral had been linked with Baron Saint-Félix by the amity that can exist between perverse souls when the same crimes have united them. Once, in the mountains of Narbonne, Don Juan had rendered a signal service to Arembert; the latter, out of gratitude, did not think he ought to refuse Don Juan the hospitality he requested.

After Bélisène's retirement, the two disloyal knights talked about the mysterious voice that had mingled in their conversation. Don Juan, a Spaniard and superstitious, did not disguise his fear.

"For so many years I have been the witness of such inconceivable adventures," Arembert told him, "that I ought at least to fear them; however, I cannot be exposed to contemplating those prodigies of nature without experiencing all the tortures of Hell. Oh, Don Juan, if only I could recommence my career! I know full well what reef I would avoid."

Don Juan asked him whether the prisoner was still in his power.

"Yes; he has not quit the subterrain in which he must spend his life; but I have not seen him again since the day when I precipitated him into it."

"Would his presence give birth to some regret in you?"

"Oh, it has not depended on me not to contemplate my victim again; the inhabitants of the other world, appearing to me in the most menacing forms, have forbidden me entry to his prison; he is invisible for me, whereas his guardian, Roberto, either shows more courage or is less subject to the anger of the invisible spirits."

"I did not know, Arembert, that your château was the theater of apparitions. What interest can Heaven take in a mortal who ought to be lost in the number?"

The day was beginning to dawn; Don Juan retired to his room and Arembert, unable to find an instant's slumber, decided to depart at noon for the crusaders' army, which ought by now to have arrived at Carcassonne.

The pilgrim, after having left Arembert, had been taken by a varlet to the hermitage. He questioned his guide with regard to the person he was going to see, and learned that, although constantly ready to talk to the unfortunate, the hermit almost always refused to visit noble barons.

When they were within sight of the hermitage the varlet abandoned the pilgrim. The later, covering his garments with dust in order to give himself the appearance of a poor traveler, advanced to the barrier and, striking it with his staff, he called to the hermit, who appeared immediately.

"Good hermit," said the pilgrim, "will you grant a few refreshments to a servant of Saint-Jacques de Compostelle?"

Making an angry gesture on recognizing the man who was speaking to him, he hermit said: "You're asking me for hospitality? Who are you?"

"My name is Paul; I'm Burgundian."

"You are going to fulfill a pious duty, you tell me, and you suffer a lie to profane our lips?"

"Why do you speak to me thus?"

"Why do you adopt a character that is not yours? Why do you hide under a name that does not belong to you?"

"Me?" said the pilgrim.

"Yes, you, Isarn de Boncombre, Abbot of Saint Exupéry. Is your name Paul? And are you Burgundian?"

"Can it be that I am known to you?" asked the pilgrim.

"A long time ago I appeared in the theater of society, and I have seen figuring therein men whose state summoned them to obscurity."

"I hear you, hermit; that reproach is addressed to me; but if I have emerged from the silence of the cloister, it was for the service of God."

"Do you call it serving God to breathe into the people the spirit of revolt and sedition? By what right do you come to this country? Of what do you accuse the Comte de Toulouse? And what design brings you to me? It is not to ask me for shelter but to win me to the army of the crusaders, to render me a satellite of the ambitious Comte de Montfort, who, for his own interest, wants to fill this rich land with blood and burnings. Isarn, it is not against the Albigensians that Montfort is directing himself; it is against Raymond's heritage, which he wants to invade. Don't hope that he will succeed; the love of the people assures the Comtes de Toulouse a certain triumph. Perhaps they will succumb to their enemies' first efforts, but when the political storms have rumbled for some time, you shall see the unjust foreigner dispossessed of the estates he intends to usurp."

"I divine without difficulty, Hermit, that the holy cause does not have a partisan in you."

"Religion sees in me one of the most submissive of its children," said the hermit, "but I know how to separate the cause of its ministers from its own. It is not by persecutions that one extirpates heresies; it is by persuasion that verity triumphs. Adieu; a longer conversation would be futile. Take my response to the legate Milon as well as the ambitious Montfort; tell them that they will find in me an irreconcilable enemy, and Comte Raymond a loyal and faithful subject."

At those words, confounded and furious, the pilgrim went away, muttering threats and imprecations, while the hermit, leaning against the tomb, pursued him with a scornful smile.

Chapter III: The Ballad of the Phantom

The sun had risen a long time ago when Arembert prepared to depart for the crusaders' camp. Before setting forth,
he assembled his varlets and men-at-arms and announced to
them that his journey might last for some time. He added that
during his absence he confided authority to Ferdinand, the
name that Dun Juan had adopted. With that care fulfilled, he
left, escorted by a numerous retinue, as his rank warranted.

After riding for some time, the extreme heat constrained
Arembert to stop on the edge of a little wood. While his domestics prepared the tents he wanted to walk in the wood and,
still occupied with his black ideas, he was only dreaming of
phantoms and sinister apparitions. Giving no thought to remaining close to his squadron, he continued his course; he had
already been walking for some time when the sounds of a guitar reached him.

He stopped; the lugubrious prelude played on the instrument caught his attention and he listened carefully. He saw the
singer through the branches; it was a young shepherd who,
while guarding his flock, was repeating this alarming ballad.

When over the towers of old châteaux
Nocturnal tempests rumble,
When the night veils its torches,
When the storm empties its urns,
From the redoubted depths of the coffin
Uttering funeral howls,
A phantom dressed in mourning
Launches forth into the darkness.

On its face where lightning shines
The fury that oppresses is painted;
It delights in showing the sword
That its vengeful hand is wielding;

Standing beside the murderer,
Who is devoured by frightful despair,
The phantom displays the breast
In which the wound is still fuming.

Then these redoubtable words
Emerge from that hideous mouth:
"Always to augment your woes,
I will come to sit down on your bed;
No longer hope that repose
Will ever suspend your alarms;
Always my sinister sobs
Will be able to steal its charms.

Frightful companion of your fate,
By day and by night in my fury
I shall ever offer you the death
That your barbarity gave to me.
You had no pity for my tears,
You had no pity for my soul,
And I laugh now at your dolors,
Vile brigand, infamous knight.

Do not think that a pious legacy
Will ever suspend my vengeance;
In vain the religious saints
Would want to embrace your defense.
Until the last moment I will
Announce heaven's justice to you,
And beyond the eternal monument
An eternal torture awaits you."

Motionless in the place where he was standing, Arembert could not command his astonishment, much less his dread. The words of the phantom in the young shepherd's ballad were the same ones that resounded incessantly in his ears at night.

Wanting clarification of such an inconceivable resemblance, he resolved to interrogate the villager. Having parted the branches that separated him from the other, Arembert appeared to the surprised eyes of the person from whom he wanted an explanation.

At the sight of the Baron, the richness of whose garments heightened his natural good looks, the inhabitant of huts got up respectfully and then, prostrating himself before him, asked what a noble seigneur could need from a simple vassal.

"Shepherd." Arembert said, "I heard the ballad that you have just sung; it pleased me, and I would like to know the name of the minstrel who composed it. Is it yours?"

"No, Monseigneur," said the shepherd, "it does not belong to a paltry vassal to find such a ballad; it was taught to me."

"Well, my friend, by whom? I am extremely interested to know."

"In the forest of Caillavel, whose oaks you can see from here, equaling the height of the hills, there is a devout hermit..."

"Might it be him from whom you got the ballad?"

"You are correct, Sire Chevalier."

To himself, Arembert murmured: "Inexplicable man!" To the shepherd, he said: "How has the hermit, who is said to be to reserved, familiarized himself with you to the point of permitting you to learn his songs?"

"The holy individual wanted to recompense by that means a small service I rendered him during the last grape harvest. 'André,' he said to me, 'I will teach you a long ballad; sing it every day when you know it, but above all, try to do so in such a way that Baron de Saint-Félix can hear it. He will listen to it with interest, and when he asks you the name of the author of the song, you can tell him that it is the hermit of the tomb. Be certain that he will reward you, especially if you tell him that I beg him to do so.'"

"Insolent fellow!" Arembert muttered. "He dares to play with me. Oh, that my vengeance...but alas, can it attain that mortal, who seems not to be one? Yes, rather that revolt against his yoke, let us rather seek to render him less irritated against me." To the other, he said: "Shepherd, come here; receive this gold that the Baron de Saint-Félix gives you, and don't forget to tell the hermit who has commanded you to trouble my repose."

Having said that, Arembert drew away rapidly and rejoined his men; he pressed them to depart and, as he hoped that his suffering might dissipate with distance, he spurred his destrier urgently. Its rapid gallop took him to Castelnaudary in a short time. There he learned that the crusaders were besieging Carcassonne, and that people were expecting to hear news at any moment of the taking of the city.

Wanting to signal himself in that siege, Arembert continued his route. It was not in the quarters of the Comte de Toulouse that Baron de Saint-Félix presented himself, as he should have done; he went directly to the tent of Simon de Montfort. Abbot Isarn de Boncombre was with the latter. As soon as he perceived Arembert he hastened to introduce him to Montfort as a zealous Catholic who had come to be a crusader and make common cause with those who were obedient to the Pontiff of Rome.

Montfort, charmed at being able to attract to his party as powerful a seigneur as Baron Arembert, made him all sorts of caresses, and treated him in a distinguished manner. Soon, through the intermediary of Isarn, a sort of familiarity was established between them, and Arembert was initiated into the conspiracies of which the Comte de Toulouse was to be the victim.

The city of Carcassonne, which the crusaders were then besieging, was entirely situated to the right of the Aude; the fortifications, which were its principal strength, were elevated on a rock at the base of which the river flowed; they were accompanied by two outlying districts each surrounded by ditches. In addition to its advantageous situation and its natural strength, Vicomte Raymond-Roger—the son of the man mentioned in the early pages of this story—who had hastened there to defend it, had been careful to equip it well and to augment its fortifications. For that, it was said, he had made use of the stones of the refectory and the choir-stalls of the regular canons of the cathedral. Finally, the garrison was numerous, and composed of the Vicomte's principal vassals who were enclosed in the place with him, along with the inhabitants of the city and all those from the surrounding area, who had withdrawn there with their best effects, as a place of safety.

The crusaders had no sooner camped outside the walls of Carcassonne than Vicomte Roger, having gone up to the top of a tower, had resolved to make a sortie the following night. In the prime of life, the likeable Roger had succeeded his father; a gallant knight and a faithful husband, marriage had previously united him with the seductive Agnès, daughter of the Seigneur de Montpellier. A fruit of their union had contributed to their happiness;[38] fortune seemed to be smiling on them when the most frightful catastrophe precipitated them into an abyss of woe.

Blind to the errors of the Albigensians, Vicomte Roger did not find them as culpable as Rome claimed; he saw them as faithful subjects and not fanatics in revolt; so, far from persecuting them, he protected them; he embraced their defense, even though, in his heart, he was a zealous Catholic. It was against him that the crusaders turned their first efforts; less powerful than the Comte de Toulouse, he was easier to overturn, so they wanted to try via him to defeat the most powerful of princely vassals of the crown of France.

Constrained by the imperious laws of necessity, the Comte de Toulouse, wanting to ward off the tempest that was menacing him, had been forced to join the crusaders in order

---

[38] The historical Raymond-Roger Trencavel was indeed married to Agnès de Montpellier, but there is no record of their having had a child; the year of her birth is recorded as 1195, so she could only have been fourteen years old during the siege of Carcassonne August 1209.

to crush his sister's son; he shuddered at that, but the interest of his throne and that of his son spoke to him even more loudly. In that position he hastened to send a courier to his son, who, at that moment—as we have already said—was preparing Toulouse for a necessary defense, to engage him to come, with his sister, to the camp outside Carcassonne.

Since the day when Savary de Mauléon had recounted his adventures to them, Aliénor, Adémar and Raymond had been resting, anticipating the new dangers that were about to fall upon them. For Adémar, forgetting glory, Arembert's orders and the hermit who had initially inspired such a vivid curiosity in him, he saw nothing but Aliénor; he only breathed for her. Respecting the object of his amour, considering the immense distance that separated them, he enclosed in his heart the sentiment by which he was devoured, but his cares were in vain; his flame pierced his words and his actions; at those moments he forgot everything and the prism of his love dazzled him.

The imposing Aliénor, proud of her high birth, previously a stranger to all tenderness, only took pleasure in the tumult of courts. Surrounded by the pomp appropriate to her rank, she did not think that a simple knight could ever merit her lowering her gaze toward him; but the bizarre child who liked reducing distances and confounding distinctions invented by human pride, struck her heart, and it was for Adémar's good fortune.

Far from letting him know the preference that she accorded him, she changed her conduct toward him; the most marked coldness succeeded the confidence that she had initially testified to him; she no longer permitted him to come to pay his court at times when the host of courtiers were not introduced; everywhere, she avoided him, without affectation but with the lightness that the grand employ toward those they see without interest.

Alas, Adémar, Aliénor's liberator, saw himself confounded among those who did not merit anything from the beautiful Comtesse. He poured his chagrin into Savary's heart. The genteel troubadour, too frank to suspect the dissimulation of Aliénor's conduct, sought to cure his friend by engaging him to fly to where glory summoned him. That advice was impossible to follow; Adémar would have sacrificed anything, except the pleasure of contemplating every day the lady to whom he had devoted his existence.

If Aliénor constrained her tenderness in his presence, however, in silence she let it burst forth. Indignant at what she called her weakness, she sought to cure herself of it, but the arrow launched by Amour had been too cleverly directed; nothing could deaden its pain and, apart from Amour, nothing can cure the wounds that he can inflict; that arrow was like the famous lance of the son of Peleus, which alone could scar the wounds that it had afflicted.

It was at that moment that the message from the Comte de Toulouse reached his daughter. Aliénor applauded with enthusiasm a journey that might offer some distraction to her suffering soul; she was in a hurry to quit the Tectosage city.

Her desire to go to Carcassonne was shared with her brother. He knew that the King of Aragon was to appear there, accompanied by his daughter, and for a long time the hearts of Sancia and Raymond had been united by the most tender knots.[39] Destined for one another since early childhood, they had learned to love one another while getting to know one another; alone, with their parents, they knew the secret of their

---

[39] Pedro II of Aragon (1178-1213) did go to Carcassonne in an attempt to intercede on Raymond-Roger's behalf before the crusaders attacked the city, but his only acknowledged child by Marie de Montpellier (Agnès' sister) was a son; some sources suggest that she did have a daughter named Sancia, but gave her date of birth as 1206 or 1208; one source alleges that she was betrothed to Raymond VII of Toulouse soon after her birth, but even if that were true, she could not have been a young woman in 1209.

union, and, delicate lovers, they delighted in covering with veils a mystery favorable to their sentiment.

Raymond had not seen Sancia for two years. Momentarily inconstant to his amour, he had been able to sigh for the beautiful Comtesse de Foix, but veritable amour had not taken long to make him blush at his infidelity. Raymond abjured the chains that might have rendered him culpable; he wanted, by the excess of his ardor, to have his slight inconstancy forgotten.

For Adémar, whatever the pleasure he experienced in following Aliénor, he could not think without pain that her rare beauty was about to be offered to the gaze of a host of princes who would all, he supposed, immediately yearn for the joy of possessing her. He also redoubted, without being able to explain why, reappearing before Arembert. He did not know to what he ought to attribute the distancing of which he sometimes accused himself, except the insinuations of the old hermit. However, he could not remain in Toulouse and, in spite of his scant desire to go to Carcassonne, he made his preparations for departure.

As they were about to set forth, a courier arrived, out of breath, and, hardly able to explain himself, he asked to speak to the Marquis de Mauléon. Savary, who was alerted without delay, hastened to go to the page, fearing a new misfortune. Alas, what a rude blow struck his amorous heart when he learned from a letter that the Comte de Foix had written to him, that he had lost his love, that Bélisène had been abducted. Astonishment, dolor and rage suspended the faculties of his soul momentarily; he swore that he would give himself no peace or respite until Bélisène had been recovered and the treacherous Don Juan had paid the price for his perfidy.

That despairing news changed his projects completely; instead of leaving immediately for Carcassonne he wanted to go to the Comte de Foix to confer with him regarding the steps they might take with the intention of recovering the unfortunate Bélisène. After having bid his friends adieu tenderly, he took the road to Pamiers, where the Comte de Foix was.

Chapter IV: The Arrival at the Camp

Meanwhile, Raymond, having assembled a numerous escort, as was necessary in those troubled times to ensure free progress, took the road that led to Carcassonne, accompanied by Aliénor and the brave Adémar. Before the end of the morning they had passed Ramonville, Castanet, Pompertusat, Deyme, Montgiscard and Baziège; they rested in Ville-Franche and then continued their journey. They left behind them Avignonet, and Monferrant, then fortified, and nightfall saw them entering the walls of Castelnaudary.

Adémar, finding himself so close to the places that had seen his childhood, could not help casting his eyes upon the town of Saint-Félix, which, situated on a high crag, was discovered to his gaze. He could not see the vast forest of Caillavel, but his vivid imagination immediately transported him to the hermitage, and a profound sigh escaped his oppressed heart when he recalled the hermit, as well as the fatal encounter that had enabled him to know the haughty Aliénor.

While he was buried in his reverie, surrendering himself to his amorous thoughts, his suzerain, young Raymond, found an old friend who was very dear to him. Famous since his adolescence for his courage as well as his songs, the honor of Toulouse, the troubadour Pierre Vidal, inflamed by the transports of a ardent genius, had extracted himself from the obscurity that must have been his initial lot; since then, welcomed by all the princes, meriting their protection by his noble qualities, he had become the object of envy, but also the love of ladies. At that moment he had returned from an expedition undertaken in the attempt to return to his wife the throne of Constantinople, to which she had rights. Joyous at seeing Raymond again, he took pleasure in recounting his adventures.

The following day having dawned under the celestial vault, the noble travelers, joined by Vidal, departed for Carcassonne; they arrived at the camp outside the city at the tenth hour of the day, and the Comte de Toulouse embraced his two children. After the first expansions of filial tenderness, Prince Raymond introduced Adémar to the Comte, his father, reporting to him the signal service that the knight had rendered the majestic Aliénor.

An appreciator of all fine actions, the Comte gave Adémar the welcome that he merited. "Generous knight," he said to him, "I have all the more need at the moment of great warriors like you because I see myself abandoned by my principal vassals. I deplore the infidelity of one in particular, because of his courage and power; I regret the Baron de Saint-Félix."

"Oh what are you saying to me, Prince?" said Adémar. "Is it possible that Arembert has forgotten the laws of honor?"

"Do you know him, Chevalier?"

"Monseigneur, I owe him the nourishment I have received; but if my gratitude speaks for him, it cannot make me consent to share his error; faithful to my legitimate sovereign, I can only regard as a weakness the condescension of a knight to a foreign authority."

"Always conserve those noble sentiments," said the Comte de Toulouse. "They are worthy of a great heart. Yes, young Adémar, a man is never truly great who is not able to submit to his legitimate sovereign; obedience is the first virtue of subjects."

"Sire Comte, permit me to speak to Arembert; perhaps my voice can recall him to the path of duty, or, at least, if I cannot change him, I shall have the glory of having tried to do so."

"I confide my interests to your wisdom without difficulty. At an age when one ordinarily only listens to the passions, Chevalier, you possess a reason that is the prerogative of maturity. Yes, I like to hear you; your features and the sound of your voice remind me of a memory that is very precious to me; I do not know by what accident of nature your face is the living portrait of a sister who was very dear to me, and whom death took away from me too soon."

As he spoke thus, the Comte de Toulouse covered his eyes with his hand, as if to veil his tears. Raymond and Aliénor, surprised by what they had just heard, withdrew without daring to distract their father. Adémar, as astonished as them, followed their example and, asking for directions to Arembert's tent, went there promptly.

When he arrived, Baron de Saint-Félix was alone, occupied in writing. Having not found a page to announce him, Adémar entered abruptly; the Baron did not hear him; entirely intent on his task, he did not perceive that he was no longer alone, and, without thinking about the imprudence he was about to commit, he read aloud what he had just written.

"Yes, Roberto, I demand it; it is necessary that, without losing any time, you go at the head of a company to the hermitage in the forest; it is necessary that you take possession of the person of the hermit, that you take him to my château and that you imprison him in the subterrains of the keep. Also watch without respite over the prisoner I have confided to you; make sure that he does not escape from the irons that he must retain until the end of his life. If he makes any attempt to escape, or if an unknown enemy should form any enterprise to secure his release, I hereby authorize you, stamped with my seal, to kill him immediately. Finally, I instruct you to obey Señor Ferdinand and to watch over his captive. In a few days I will be with you, accompanied by one of the leaders of the crusaders. Your master, Arembert."

Stupefied by what he had just heard, Adémar understood that he was in great danger if the Baron perceived that he had heard everything; trying to make as little noise as possible, he regained the door. Then, returning, he trod heavily.

On seeing him, Arembert shuddered; precipitately, he hid the letter that he had just written in his bosom and, standing up, came toward the knight.

"Is that you, Adémar? You have prolonged your absence; it appears that the hermit must have charged you with a matter of the utmost importance."

"He sent me to Comte Raymond, Monseigneur, to take him the assurance of his fidelity, and I have joined mine to it."

"You, Adémar! And since when, pray, do you think you have the right to make an oath to anyone other than me?"

"Monseigneur, the Comte de Toulouse is your suzerain; his cause ought to be yours; thus, I believed that I was doing what you would have ordered me to do."

"The Comte de Toulouse, since he is proscribed, has lost his suzerainty over his vassals; the legates have released us from our promises, and if the Raymonds do not submit entirely to the Church, our conscience obliges us to become their enemies."

"Pardon me, Sire Baron, if I dare not to think in that fashion; I do not know how far the power of priests might extent, but I know that there is no limit to fidelity. No power has the right to preach revolt, and those whom God has established in order to reconcile us with him, cannot order us to take up arms against those he has instituted to represent him on earth."

"Young man," said Arembert, "the company of the hermit, doubtless infested with heresy, has become pernicious to you; he has taught you to reason when you ought to obey. Vassal knight, march when I command you to do so and do not seek to inform yourself against whom I wish to do battle."

"Let serfs and slaves conduct themselves thus," said Adémar. "A noble knight only allows himself to be guided by the light of wisdom and the inspirations of honor."

"The more you talk the more you astonish your master. Who has raised you? Who has taken care of your education? Who was it who armed you as a knight?"

"It was you, Monseigneur, and do not think that I have lost the memory of it."

"You are, therefore, my work. So you belong to me."

"Yes, I am your work; but I only belong to those who gave me the light of day."

"Do you know your parents?" demanded Arembert, troubled.

"I do not know their name and their function. Stolen by you at an early age from the Vicomtesse de Carcassonne, who was raising me with her son and young Odon, the companion of our games, and taken to your château, I have been unable to obtain enlightenment as to my family. The Vicomtesse is dead, and my hope is buried in her tomb."

"Well then, Adémar," said Arembert, "do not seek to irritate your benefactor, the man who has taken the place of your father. Believe me, attach yourself to obeying me and you will be happier one day; leave this exaggerated heroism, which is not without danger for you; know how to yield to circumstances. Seduced by the name of the Comte de Toulouse, you have conceived the thought that honor constrains you to march under his flag; disabuse yourself, it is me who ought to direct your misunderstood bravery. Do not be obstinate in uniting yourself with a Prince who is menaced by the thunderbolts of the Church; you would be dragged into his ruination without being able to delay it for an instant."

"It will doubtless cost me, Monseigneur, to persist in what you call my obstinacy; and yet, I feel that it is impossible for me to act differently. Whether it is error on my part or sympathy for those overwhelmed by misfortune, I am ready to share Raymond's fate."

"That's enough, Adémar! Leave my presence, and remember that my heart is henceforth closed to you."

"Oh, Monseigneur, show more generosity; suffer that I follow the cause that summons me; excuse me in favor of the motive that directs me."

"Reply to me," demanded Arembert. "Will you embrace my party or that of Raymond, whose ingratitude in my regard has been only too well proven?"

"It will displease you, I but I cannot change my resolutions."

"Get out; do not let me see you again."

Thus terminated the conversation, in which the Baron did not deploy all the arrogance that was natural to him, and in which it was visible through his anger that he was ready to pardon Adémar. As for the latter, he needed all the courage of amour to resist the man he believed to be his benefactor. But could he take up arms against the father and brother of Aliénor? That effort was impossible for him, and even if the cause he was following had been blameworthy, he would not have been able to prevent himself from embracing it.

After having quit the Baron, he hastened to inform the hermit of the tomb, by means of a note, of the danger that he was in. It was the squire Aubin, who had always been with him, in Toulouse as in Carcassonne, that he sent to the hermit. The faithful confidant of his master, Aubin promised to deliver the letter with which he was charged with all diligence; he did not put off his journey for a second, and Adémar was more tranquil after he had seen him depart.

Adémar could not take account of the sentiment that bore him to cherish the hermit. That bizarre individual, surrounded by mystery, had succeeded in touching his heart singularly; he would not have seen him fall into Arembert's power without a sharp chagrin. Adémar had not forgotten that he had appeared to know the secret of his birth. In his conversation with the Baron he had not wanted to make him aware of that detail; he feared displeasing Arembert by proving to him that he had kept quiet about his conversation with the hermit.

Chapter V: The Two Princesses

Rumor of the arrival of young Raymond and his sister did not take long to spread through the camp. The principal crusaders, still led by the gallantry that had always been the prerogative of the French, brought them to the Comte de Toulouse's tent in order to present their homage to his beautiful daughter. Arembert was not the last to appear; disguising his projects, he conducted himself externally as he ought to have done toward his suzerain. He appeared before Aliénor, and a new sentiment suddenly appeared in his soul. It was not a virtuous amour—Arembert was incapable of that—but a frenzied desire to possess that beautiful individual.

The Baron forgot his age; he only saw his ardor; he burned to unite himself with Aliénor, but, at the same time, he saw a host of obstacles that were opposed to what he wanted to achieve. Nothing was capable of stopping him though, and, far from reconciling himself with the father of the object of his desire, he swore to bring him down, in the thought that it would be easier for him to obtain Aliénor after the Comte de Toulouse's fall.

Arembert's sentiments were shared by a large number of knights; all of them from that moment on, with a common thought, abandoned the cause of the crusaders to follow that of the Raymonds.

Among Adémar's rivals, one above all appeared to him to be the most redoubtable. That was the valiant Comte de Nevers, who combined the splendor of his birth with the most likeable qualities; Léogard was his name. A third rival also presented himself, less elevated than the others by his dignities, he ceded nothing to them in regard to his birth and his virtues; Gui de Lévis, *maréchal de la foi*, followed his friend Simon de Montfort, who glory he shared, while disapproving of his ambition. Young and brave, Gui could not see Aliénor without adoring her, but for the moment he imitated Adémar and kept silent regarding the state of his heart.

Aliénor, the object of so many desires, merited such lofty tenderness; her soul, formed on the model of all the virtues, fulfilled that fine task; sensitive, compassionate to tears of dolor, seeking the unfortunate in order to shield them with benefits from herself, adoring her father, cherishing her family, pious in her religion, she embellished that combination of perfections with a host of charms that surpassed all those with which nature had adorned other beauties; the elevation of her stature, the majesty of her stride, the arrogance of her gaze, dark eyes brilliant with the fire of her intelligence, long hair whose color matched that of her eyes, a charming and noble voice, a face whose perfect oval stimulated admiration, arms sculpted by perfection and seductive strength all united to make Aliénor the most beautiful as well as the most celestial individual. One might have thought, on seeing her, that she was a loan that the earth had made from Heaven.

Poor Adémar abandoned himself to the most profound sadness; he saw new obstacles around him that closed every path to happiness.

Alas, he said to himself, *how blind I am! Can I hope that fate will change for me? A poor knight, can I become a noble baron? Can I prevail against the seigneurs who are presenting themselves in a crowd to obtain Aliénor's hand? Oh, wretch, if you had perished in childhood, you would not be the target of the blows of misfortune. Was it necessary that Adémar should seek to seduce the daughter of a prince? Shall I deceive the amity that the two Raymonds have shown me? On all sides I see nothing but precipices; let's seek to avoid them; let's flee.*

Having said that, he headed for open country. He followed the route that led to Castelnaudary, and there, companying himself on his cherished guitar, he sang about his amour. The help of the Muses sometimes soothed our valiant knight; he suffered less when he could voice his tenderness.

While he was resting, leaning on his lance, he heard a slight rustle nearby caused by someone approaching. He

137

looked up, uttered a cry, and flew into the arms of the hermit of the forest.

"Dear Adémar," the other said to him. "I appreciate what you have done for me. Don't worry; it is beyond Arembert's power to make me his prisoner; when you sent your squire to me I had already quit my hermitage to come to Carcassonne; Aubin met me on the road; he gave me your letter, and it has served my projects marvelously."

"What are you going to do?" Adémar asked.

"I'm going to find Arembert."

"You'll expose yourself to his anger."

"I know how to put a brake on it."

"I don't know how the hatred that he has for you was engendered, but it seems to me that it might be difficult to extinguish."

"There are hearts that desire darkness," said the hermit, "and cannot tolerate a good man shining a light on what they have so much interest in hiding. Nevertheless, I do not want Arembert to find us together; it is necessary that I appear to him alone. He does not like to see me, and yet he would desire that I make myself known to him."

"Will it never be permissible for me to contemplate your face?"

"The time will come to lift the veil by which my face is covered."

While talking they arrived at the gates of the camp. Separating from the hermit, Adémar returned to the Comte de Toulouse's quarters, while his companion headed for those of the Baron de Saint-Félix.

The Comte received Adémar with his customary benevolence. They had already been conversing for some time when someone came to tell the Comte that a knight who had emerged from Carcassonne was asking to speak to him. The latter did not doubt that it was a message from his nephew, Vicomte Roger, so he invited the knight to appear before him.

Bearing on his face a gaiety tempered by dolor, exactly as tall as Adémar and just as handsome and brave, Odon appeared to the Comte de Toulouse's gaze. The latter, astonished by the resemblance that there was between the newcomer and Adémar, considered him for a few moments in silence.

As for Adémar, he sensed by the movements of his heart that the knight must be Odon, the companion of his childhood and perhaps his brother. Not daring, however, to burst forth before the Comte, he was waiting when the later addressed Odon and said: "Pardon me, Chevalier, if I am not receiving you with the regard that is your due, but your sight has renewed an emotion to which the warrior you see beside me has already given birth. Yes, I could have mistaken you for him if the color of your hair were not different. Move closer, Adémar."

"Adémar!" Odon exclaimed. "Oh, Seigneur, what name have you pronounced? I once had a friend, a brother, who bore that name. Fifteen years have gone by since war separated me from him."

Adémar threw himself into Odon's arms. "Do you recognize him, Odon?"

"Great God! It's him!"

"Yes, it's Adémar," said Adémar, "who has not seen his friend for such a long time, but who has never ceased to cherish him."

"Why, interesting knights," asked the Comte de Toulouse, "have you not thought of finding one another?"

"It is only a short while ago," Adémar replied, "that I obtained knowledge of the place where I was born."

"For a long time," said Odon, "Vicomte Roger and I believed that Adémar was dead."

"Let nothing separate us henceforth, my friend!" said Adémar. "Promise me not to quit me again."

"Adémar," said Odon, "I can promise that without difficulty, but it is necessary to promise me not to bear arms against Vicomte Roger. I owe everything to his benefits, and my gratitude to him is limitless, as is his amity. Sire Comte de Toulouse, your unfortunate nephew wants to obtain peace; tears and the tenderness he has for his wife, have softened his proud courage; he does not tremble for himself, he only fears the furies of war for his subjects and family; he is ready to subscribe to the conditions that are imposed on him, as long as they are worthy of him. Hasten to assemble the legates, the leaders of the army and obtain a suspension of arms from them; tell them that Roger is willing to come to them in order to sign a treaty that will render repose to his people."

"It required the evils of which I am the target to make me part of an army determined to cause the doom of my sister's son," said the Comte. You should not doubt, Chevalier, the paternal love that I have for Roger, but I cannot be useful to him; I have no influence. What I am saying? I am scarcely tolerated; people hide from me; I am kept away from councils; I am refused the regard to which my rank has a right to expect; of what help can I be to Roger? But a more powerful support, even having a marked preponderance, will arrive shortly. To speak thus is to assure you that the King of Aragon is coming. Under the specious pretext that he is suzerain of a part of the Vicomte's lands, he can impose himself on the crusaders. Let us put our hope in him; let him speak and act for Roger; I will support eagerly anything he can so in favor of my nephew."

After that speech, the Comte de Toulouse engaged Odon to rest, and, giving the pretext of a meeting with the legate, he left, leaving the two young knights together, charmed to see one another again after such a long separation.

Adémar told Odon about his adventures, while hiding the passion that the Comtesse Aliénor had inspired in him. The story piqued Odon's curiosity vividly; he was burning with desire to see the hermit and consult him as to his fate, and his joy was great when he learned that he too was close by,

"As for me," Odon said, "my life has been far less agitated. A friend rather than a subject of Roger, I have not quit him; we have always fought together since arms were put into our hands; I was the confidant of his love for the beautiful Agnès de Montpellier; and if I had a story to tell it would be his, and not that of my life, which has not been signaled by any extraordinary event."

Having withdrawn to his tent, Arembert was preparing to have the letter he had addressed to Roberto sent when, instead of the varlet he was expecting, he saw the hermit appear

"Him again!" he exclaimed.

"Is it because the sight of me fatigues you that you have destined a subterrain for my abode?" asked the hermit.

"What do you mean?"

"Are you pretending not to understand me? Will you deny that the letter placed next to your escutcheon does not contain an order addressed to your Roberto to seize my person and retain me in secret confinement?"

"Man or demon, whatever you are, make yourself known! You have been my despair for too long!"

"I do not want the sight of me to strike you dead; it will bring you down."

"Where have I encountered you? On what occasion was the hatred that I seem to inspire in you born?"

"Interrogate your heart, and it will tell you the day on which you ceased to be virtuous."

"You are not replying to me I speaking thus," Arembert complained

"I do not want to confound you," said the hermit, "but by what right did you think you were acting in pronouncing my arbitrary detention? Did you believe me to be devoid of resources? Did you hope to get rid of me, simply by virtue of your desire alone? Make no mistake, Arembert. I can only be made to do what I want, and if anyone issues commands, it will be me. Your dungeons already contain enough victims; there is one above all…you ought to understand me. You must know that their entry is not forbidden to me. Have I not already encountered you there?"

"Even if you punish my resolution immediately, it is necessary that I know you," Arembert said. "Do not hope to escape me in a camp where everyone is devoted to me. Show me your face, or my soldiers will take possession of your person."

"Well," said the hermit, "since it is necessary for me to appear to you as I am, let us see whether, after having contemplated my face, you want to call your men-at-arms to enable them to share your surprise."

So saying, he took off the long red mantle in which he was incessantly clad, throwing his hood back over his shoulders, and presented to Arembert's gaze a hideous and fleshless skeleton.

The horror of such a spectacle acted forcefully on the Baron's soul; he could not help uttering a groan, and he fell to the ground, unconscious...

At that time a great rumor was heard throughout the camp. The crusaders ran from all parts to see the King of Aragon, the brother-in-law of the Comte de Toulouse, who had arrived from Spain accompanied by his daughter Sancia.

The impatient Raymond had already run to met his future wife; his transports on seeing Sancia told her that she had never ceased to be loved by him, and her naïve blush told her lover that he too had always been dear.

Not as tall as Aliénor, perhaps slimmer, the blonde Sancia conceded nothing in beauty to the sister of the man she adored. Her beautiful hair, naturally curly, surrounded every part of her modest face, over which the dawn had lavished its roses, while tinting them with the brightest irony. Similar in color to a blue eglantine, Sancia's beautiful eyes seemed enveloped by her long eyelids, while the eyebrows crowning them formed perfect arcs. Her nose, formed in a straight line, her mouth, where alabaster stood out in the form of teeth, and her nascent breasts, embellished her youth with every splendor, adding further charms to Sancia's moral perfections. To the ingenuousness of her age she added restraint, the prerogative of her sex; but, incapable of dissimulation, she did not know how to conceal in her soul the sentiments by which she was animated. A beautiful flower, she merited fortune smiling on her virtues.

Chapter VI: The Crusaders' Council

By virtue of his arrival, the King of Castile disconcerted the projects of a few crusaders who were trembling before a prey ready to escape them. As the attachment of Pope Innocent III for the Prince in question was well known, however, no one dared treat him disrespectfully.

Crusaders, in whose number appeared the Duc de Bourgogne, the Comte de Nevers and Simon de Monfort, came to welcome him on his arrival. He testified to them the particular desire he had to be able to reconcile them with Comte Roger. Simon de Montfort hastened to respond that such a question could only be discussed before the Council, and that, out of regard for the King, it would be convened immediately.

After the crusaders had gone, Pedro—that was the King of Aragon's name—gave a secret audience to Odon. He promised the latter to do everything to bring Roger's enemies back to milder sentiments; he engaged the young knight to report those hopes to Roger. Joyful at the news with which he was charged, Odon did not want to put off taking the road to Carcassonne, and although he had not yet seen the hermit, he did not hesitate to sacrifice his desire to his master's interest. He separated from Adémar, renewing the protestations of an amity that would never weaken; and, after a mutual embrace, he extracted himself from the arms of the man he was pleased to call his brother.

Meanwhile, the Abbot of Cîteaux, having learned of the arrival of the King of Aragon, sent word that he was ready to receive him. Pardoning the impropriety of such a message, Pedro, who did not want to embitter the legate against the Vicomte de Carcassonne, went to his tent, accompanied by the Comte de Toulouse.

On approaching the abbot he requested mercy for Roger Trencavel, and begged him to enter into negotiations with him. He represented to him, in addition, that the crusaders ought to be satisfied with the enormous damage they had caused, in burning Béziers and ruining the outlying districts of Carcassonne.

Without responding to that speech, the Abbot asked him whether the Vicomte had charged him with proposing peace. The King replied in the negative, but said that if he were permitted to enter the city, he was convinced that Roger would not refuse his mediation. The legate, excited by Simon de Montfort, was inclined to reject the King's request, but the remainder of the Seigneurs testified that it would be inappropriate to refuse such a proposal. The King, therefore, obtained the permission that he wanted.

Leaving his daughter in the care of Aliénor, he went to Carcassonne. At the sight of him, the people, who were hoping to see in him a liberator, welcomed him with cries of joy. The Vicomte hastened come to meet him, and, after having kissed the monarch's hand respectfully, he embraced the King, who shed a few tears at the fate that might has await the young hero.

When they went to the palace, Agnès, Roger's wife, came in her turn to salute the Prince. The latter was extremely affected by the dolor spread over the face of that beautiful woman. "Madame," he said to her, "all is not yet desperate; the Vicomte has doubtless lost a great deal, but beautiful domain still remain to him; he cannot be despoiled of all his possessions—at least, I would like believe so. Charged with coming to ask what the conditions are to which he will agree to subscribe, I am convinced that I can reconcile him with the legate.

"Oh, Sire," Agnès replied, "I cannot distract myself; I still seem to see Death extending her sharpened scythe over my husband's head."

"Why afflict yourself so, Agnès?" said Roger. "Fortune has not yet deceived my courage. Repelled in all the assaults they have attempted, the crusaders are not are not as close to reducing me as they are pleased to think; I haven't yet lost everything."

"What can your valor do against that ever-renascent army?" Agnes said. "Against those knights who redouble their bravery with their religious fervor? Every assault takes away some of your soldiers, every day their army is augmented. All your efforts will be futile. Oh, my husband, accept peace if it is proposed to you!"

"I don't want to reject it," said Roger, "since I have solicited it myself; but I don't want it to be shameful. I would a hundred times rather be buried under the ruins of my capital."

"I admire and approve of the nobility of your sentiments, Vicomte," said the King. "You will agree with me, however, that such circumstances submit us to difficult conditions; Princes, like their subjects, often see their heads bowed under the hand of necessity; one does what it orders us to do; the clever man knows how to yield to momentary interest, and wait for better circumstances."

"I know as well as you do, Sire," said Roger, "what you have just explained to me; I am ready to make all the sacrifices that I believe I can accept, but don't ask any more of me."

Then entering into confidence with the King of Aragon, he dictated to him what he was to say to the crusaders. Agnès begged Pedro to intercede for her husband, and Odon went with the King, with orders to report the decision of the Council to the Vicomte. It was agreed that if Roger refused to submit to the conditions that might be imposed on him, he would hoist a red flag over the highest tower in the city.

After those agreements, the King of Aragon left in order to return to the camp. Agnès embraced her son, covering him with tears. Roger, far from wasting time in vain waiting, toured the ramparts, giving orders everywhere; for he did not believe in the success of the King of Aragon's negotiations. He knew only too well that the war was not directed against the Albigensians so much as against his own estates. Not wanting to increase his wife's chagrin, however, he hid that baneful conviction from her.

During the absence of the King of Aragon, Vicomte Roger's enemies neglected nothing to prejudice against him a party of the crusaders. When the King reappeared it was necessary to assemble the Council in order to hear what he had to say on Roger's behalf, but already, more than half the members that were to listen to the Vicomte's proposals had agreed not to grant them.

The legate, in his quality as the Holy Father's representative, placed himself on the highest seat, in order to preside over the deliberations that might be undertaken. To his right he had the Duc de Bourgogne, the Comte de Nevers, the Bishops of Limoges, Basas, Cahors and Agen, the Vicomte de Turenne, the Seigneur de Pardillan, etc. To his left were placed the Comte de Toulouse, Comte Raymond his son, the Archbishop of Bordeaux, the Comte d'Auvergne, Gui de Lévis, Bertrand de Cadaillac, Guillaume, Archbishop of Bourges, the Seigneur de Castelnau de Montratier, all zealous crusaders, but differing on the subject of the Vicomte de Carcassonne.

The King of Aragon was introduced into the Council. When he appeared everyone stood up in order to do him honor; then, making a sign that he was going to speak, he expressed himself in these terms:

"Ministers of the Lord, Comtes and noble Baron, I have come to implore you in favor of a young prince related to several of us by blood ties. Calumny accused him of being a supporter of the heresy, or at least not declaring his opposition to it. He has charged me to tell you that the Church has no child more faithful. He does not intend to deny that his estates are infested with heretics, but it is not him who ought to be punished for that; he has only held the reins of government for some time.

"During his stormy minority, his tutors and his officers granted their special protection to the Albigensians, whom he abhors. In the short time since he has reached his majority, he has striven to extirpate the heresy; his efforts were being crowned with success every day when the army of crusaders fell upon him, when he saw himself attacked without any declaration. You have done him enough harm; forty thousand of his subjects have been slaughtered in Béziers; the two suburbs

146

of Carcassonne are prey to flames. Do you not think that he has suffered enough? And if you still demand some reparation from him in conformity with the laws of justice, he is ready to grant it."

The King's speech made some impression; the legate hastened to engage him to leave the assembly in order not to appear to be hindering the deliberations. The King consented to that. He left. And when he was recalled, the legate's words assured him that the Vicomte's ruination was assured.

"Sire King," the legate said to him, "we have taken into consideration the speech that you have just made, but we cannot hide from you that we think that you have been deceived by Roger Trencavel. In spite of his vain protestations, his attachment to the cause of the Albigensians is too well known for anyone to think that he is abandoning it. No, that is not his secret intention; he wants to dissimulate, because danger is pressing him, and you will see him falling back into his perverse inclinations when the avengers of the faith have gone.

"Sire King, we do not want the death of the impious man, we only desire his conversion; while not wanting to crush the Vicomte de Carcassonne, our conscience forbids us to leave him a power that he will abuse sooner or later, for the doom of his subjects. It is necessary that, renouncing his domains, he abandon the city, one of thirteen, permitting him, by special grace to carry away arms and luggage; furthermore, we enjoin him to withdraw to the city that we dictate to him. King of Aragon, that is all we can do, and we are only doing that out of esteem for the Vicomte's intercessor."

"Such conditions," said the King of Aragon, "can only be imposed on an enemy at bay, not one capable of defending himself."

"His defense cannot be prolonged," said the legate. "Heaven and earth are fighting against him; he ought to deem himself fortunate in the indulgence with which we are treating him."

"My mission is fulfilled," said the King. "I shall withdraw; but I see that human passions sometimes profane the interests of God, which they pretend to embrace."

Irritated against the Council he went back to the tents of the Comte de Toulouse, where Odon was waiting impatiently. "Chevalier," he said to him, "there is no more hope of peace; they desire your master's fall; listen to the propositions that they dare to make for him."

After having hard them, Odon was very indignant. He took his leave of the King, whom he assured that the Vicomte would prefer death to submission. He embraced Adémar tenderly, saying "Oh, my friend, perhaps we shall not see one another again."

"Dear Odon," said Adémar, "what baneful thought occupies you? Might the war not be favorable to you?"

"Whatever the outcome of the war might be, my fate is linked to the Vicomte's; but I cannot foresee what destiny has in preparation for me."

He drew away with those words.

As soon as the inhabitants of Carcassonne had recognized him, the postern was opened and he marched toward the Vicomte's palace.

When the latter perceived him, he said: "What are you bringing me, friend?"

"Hoist the red flag, Monseigneur; the combats are about to recommence."

"What are you saying, Chevalier?" said Agnès. "Are the crusaders inexorable then?"

"They want the death or infamy of your husband."

"Have they proposed my dishonor?" asked the Vicomte.

"Prince, you are to abandon Carcassonne; you are to renounce your authority, and, escorted by a dozen chevaliers, you are to withdraw to the prison assigned to you."

"What! Is it knights who have been able to make such demands of me? Do they not know that if I acceded to them, I would be unworthy of my title? Faithful subjects, you have heard these debasing propositions—should I accept them?"

"No, no!" cried voices from all parts of the multitude. "Rather perish a thousand times!"

That said, they precipitated themselves once again toward the ramparts; new defenses were prepared, and, while the distraught Agnès retired to her oratory in order to weep there in silence, her spouse, seething with anger, swore to bury himself under the walls of his capital. He threw into the ditch personally the white flag that was the emblem of the peace for which they had hoped, and replaced it with the red flag, around which it seems that the phantom of Death was flying furiously.

Chapter VII: The Attack

At the sight of the sign announcing that the Vicomte wants to try the fortune of war again, the crusaders, for their part, utter homicidal cries; the soldiers demand with loud cries to fly to the assault; their leaders, sharing the same impatience, give the signal; the trumpets and the cymbals make themselves heard; the squadrons, marching under the orders of their captains, surround the pennants on which the armories of the families to which they belong are painted.

The Duc de Bourgogne, the Seigneur de Montratier, the Vicomte de Turenne, the Comte de Nevers, Simon de Montfort, his son Amaury, Gui de Lévis and Antoine de Voisin launch their men forward first, carrying immense ladders in strong hands. They threaten to reach the elevated crenellations. A warrior follows them; it is Arembert. Not seeing him appear at the council, Montfort had hastened to go to his tent; he had found him there, bearing on his pale face the imprint of an unparalleled fear.

"Baron," Montfort asked him, "what cause can have produced the fear that respires in all your features?"

"Noble Comte," said Arembert, "there are extraordinary events that do not permit us to doubt that Heaven sometimes suspends the course of the laws that its profound wisdom has given the universe."

"Have you witnessed some sinister apparition?" Montfort demanded.

"Death itself appeared to me."

"Death! What are you saying, Baron?"

"Can I name otherwise the phantom that came to afflict my gaze?"

Then he told Montfort about the coming of the hermit, his conversation with him, and what terror he had experienced when the mysterious individuals had shown him, by taking off its cloak, the most frightful skeleton.

Impressed by such a story, the Comte de Montfort could not help shivering. Arembert confessed to him that, not being able to command his terror, he had fainted, and did not know what might have become of the specter.

In order to distract the Baron, Montfort told him about the Council's decision, and the hope that there was that the Vicomte de Carcassonne would not submit. While they were talking, someone came to inform them that the red flag had been hoisted, and that the attacks were about to recommence.

Impatient to lose the memory of his vision, with arms in hand, Arembert was one of the first to plant his ladder against the walls of the city and to climb it rapidly. His gigantic stature and the blows he dealt announced to the besieged that the enemy who threatened them was one of the most redoubtable; they hastened around him, threatening him with their long pikes and launching enormous lumps of rock at him, but their efforts were in vain; Arembert resisted their bravery; his courage was not intimidated by anything,

Already he had reached the summit of the crenellations; nothing more remained for him to do but to enter into the place and open the way for the soldiers who were following him, when a new adversary appeared, relenting Arembert's zeal by his presence alone: it was the hermit!

Beneath his robe, the armor in which he was clad was visible; a steel helmet covered his head, but his hand was not carrying any weapon; he suddenly appeared to the Baron's eyes crossing a section of the wall; he stood before him and, without saying a word, made him a sign to go back. Still struck by the memory of his morning vision, Arembert felt his courage abandoning him, in spite of his determination; his arm grew heavy and, whatever his secret desire might have been, he felt constrained to obey the mysterious individual's imperious gesture.

The besieged, seeing that the knight whose blows they feared had stopped, without pursuing his enterprise, they rallied, and returned to him, striking at him with their lances. Only looking at the hermit, Arembert descended his ladder without thinking of defending himself; the hermit did not quit the rampart until he saw Arembert lose himself in the crowd of crusaders.

Meanwhile from all parts, the besiegers, in spite of their number, found themselves energetically repelled. The Vicomte de Carcassonne, Odon, the Seigneur de Malras and the Sire de Bellegarde sustained the attacks successfully; they were seen everywhere exciting the warriors by their example as well as their speech. Perceiving that the crusaders were beginning to get discouraged, they redoubled their efforts; victory condescended to crowned them.

Montfort, the Duc de Bourgogne and all the besieging Seigneurs, unable to vanquish an ever-increasing resistance, had the retreat sounded and they withdrew, leaving a considerable number of dead on the battlefield. The besieged, perceiving their triumph, uttered deafening clamors, which, reaching the ears of Agnès, told her that her husband still lived and reigned. Numb with joy, she ran to meet him, and they yielded themselves to the sweetest transports.

During these various events, the hermit had retired as soon as he had seen that his presence was no longer necessary. In the heat of combat the besieged had not noticed him at first, but, soon attracting their attention by his exploits, they wondered who the bizarrely clad knight who had fought with so much valor might be. After the victory, they wanted to introduce him to Comte Roger, who asked to see him; he could no longer be found. His advent and his mysterious flight gave birth to a host of rumors; credulity and exaggeration giving birth, the inhabitants of Carcassonne were convinced that a superior genius had fought for them; their clever leader did not dissuade them from that idea.

The beautiful Sancia did not take long to share Aliénor's conquests; several knights attempted to attract her gaze; one of them presented himself in the prime of life and beauty. The son of a father who already announced what he was to be,

Amaury de Montfort, proud of his birth and his qualities, dared to aspire to the hand of the King of Aragon.

As brave as his father, the young knight did not possess his adroit politics or fertile resources; he only know how to please and to fight; his presumption was unparalleled; inflated by his successes which the beauties who ornamented the court in the days of Philippe Auguste, it never entered his head that Occitan would not also be the theater of his amorous exploits.[40]

At the sight of Sancia he sensed that it was more than a lover that he desired her to be; he wanted her for a wife—but it was not easy to supplant the noble Raymond; he would have suffered it with difficulty, and Sancia seemed to share his amour. Those obstacles, which would have deterred any other knight, did not appear insurmountable to Amaury; he did not doubt that the new rank to which his father was about to be elevated would smooth out all the difficulties that presented themselves for the moment.

Not wanting to delay informing Sancia of the sentiments she had inspired in him, he flew toward her after the attack without taking the time to allow himself to be disarmed. When he entered her tent he perceived Raymond with her, whose costume announced that he had not taken part in the crusaders' enterprise. The audacious Amaury, carried away by the desire to mortify his rival, pretended to believe that he too had taken part in the attack.

"Prince, he said," after the first compliments that he had addressed to Sancia and Aliénor, "I admire your diligence in quitting the apparatus of combat."

"Seigneur," said Raymond, "it would have difficult for me to be promptly disarmed, for I had no thought of putting on my armor."

---

[40] Amaury, Simon de Monfort's eldest son, was born in 1195, so he would only have been fourteen during the siege of Carcassonne, although he was almost certainly present, having accompanied his father on the crusade.

"It is imprudent to appear in a battle without armor," said Amaury.

"I have not said, Chevelier, that I took part in the assault."

"So, while the valiant crusaders were meriting laurels in fighting for the cause of the holy religion, the brave Raymond, heir to the Comte of Toulouse, preferred to pay court to the ladies, charming them instead with his bellicose stories."

"Seigneur Chevalier," said Raymond, "I can say, without adorning myself with vain chatter, that what I can do is sufficiently well known. One day, perhaps, I shall give proof of that to those who, under fallacious pretexts, are seeking to steal my father's heritage."

"There are, Prince, knights who are unable to repose on their renown."

"Doubtless they do not call the success of an unjust enterprise renown, and above all, they do not boast about it at the very moment when they have just been repelled."

Impelled by anger, Amaury retorted: "Are you referring, Prince, to those who have just fought beneath the walls of Carcassonne?"

"I'm referring to those who count too much on their presumptuous hopes."

At those words, the Princesses and Adémar, seeing the two knights ready to begin a quarrel whose consequences might have become an open rupture, intervened in the conversation. They sought to calm the two proud rivals, who were both seething already to measure their swords.

Addressing Amaury, Sancia spoke to him with so much kindness that she succeeded in making him forget the offense that he thought he had received. Raymond, constrained to respond to his sister, could only dart thunderous glances at Amaury; soon, even he calmed down, and there was no longer anything to be feared from their anger when the crowd of crusader lords came into the tent.

The Comte de Nevers approached Aliénor, laughing. "Madame," he said, "we cannot, like glorious chevaliers, bring the trophies of our valor to your feet; we can only tell you sad tales of our disgrace. The enemy, commanded by one of the bravest princes, has repelled us perfidiously. So, in appearing before you, we do not hide that it is your consolations that we have come to request."

"Can you confess your misadventure so frankly, Comte?" said Aliénor.

"Alas, Madame," said the Comte de Nevers, "this is no longer the century of Charlemagne; we are not Rolands and Renauds. Indomitable, whereas we are sometimes vanquished, those celebrated knights have only transmitted to us their amour for the ladies, whom we cherish as much as they did."

"Is it for them that you have come to seek combats in our homeland?" asked Sancia.

"Princesse, when I set forth, religion alone spoke in my heart," said the Comte de Nevers. "Now, I sense another sentiment awakening, commanding it in its turn."

The gaze with which Léogard—that was the Comte de Nevers' name—accompanied his speech informed Aliénor what new cause was moving that gallant knight's cause. Adémar was not less scornful of him, but, in spite of his extreme affection, he could not decide to hate Léogard as he would have Amaury if, instead of addressing his homages to the sister of the King of Aragon, he had brought them to the feet of the daughter of the Comte de Toulouse.

Aliénor, lowering her beautiful eyes, pretended not to perceive the noble Léogard's intention. Adémar also saw that movement, and I know not what hope slid into his heart.

The princesses having expressed the desire to be alone, the knights hastened to take their leave of them. Adémar and Raymond were excepted, one as a brother, the other as a friend.

Scarcely had the Comte de Montfort's son left than Raymond said to Sancia: "Princess, you have just seen how far the race of Leicester takes insolence; scarcely has Amaury seen you that he already dares speak to you of his amour. He does not believe, I hope, that without my opposition, I will see

155

tranquilly to what point he wants to stand up to me. Let him tremble! I will make him know that Raymond is worthy of the name he bears and the wife he intends to merit."

While glad of young Raymond's sentiments, Sancia feared a violence that might cost him his life. She engaged him to moderate himself, to be able to sacrifice something for the interests of his estates. The union of the legates with the family of Montfort was indubitable; it was, therefore, necessary to avoid a rupture that might be dangerous.

"When one is young, Prince, and in love, one does not calculate the consequences of events very well; one is only occupied with their causes, and never foresees their effects."

While appearing to approve of what his lover said, Raymond made himself a promise to force Amaury to explain himself the first time they were in a place where the Princesses were not.

When Raymond left the tent, Adémar followed him. "Sire Comte," he said, "doubtless I ought not to form the pretention of reading your heart, but I dare to ask you, for the price of your attachment to your august family, not to take any other knight if I am nearby, if you find yourself in a situation in which you need one."

Shaking his hand, Raymond said: "I understand you, valiant Adémar; yes, no other will be preferred to you."

"I shall count on that, Monseigneur."

Chapter VIII: The Mysterious Protector

The siege dragged on. The besieged, always valiant, re-pelled the enterprises of the crusaders. Among the latter there were even seeds of division; several of them, weary of an un-just war, formed desires for peace. A numerous party, sup-ported by the Comte de Toulouse, demanded it loudly. The legates and the Montfort family opposed it incessantly, but, during those debates, the siege made no progress. Several events took place in the meantime, which we shall recount.

You have undoubtedly not forgotten Savary de Mauléon, the amiable troubadour; you know that he left Toulouse on learning the sad news of his beloved's abduction. It was to-ward Foix that he directed his steps. The Comte received him, doubly desolate because of the loss of his daughter and the menace of the legates, who had signified to him that his es-tates would be invaded by the Catholic army, to punish him for the protection that he gave the heretics.

Less afflicted by those threats, which could be repelled with weapons in hand, than by no longer seeing Bélisène, he traveled the entire Pyrenean chain in the hope of finding some clue that might help him discover his plaintive darling. Suc-cess refused to crown his endeavors.

One night, as he was preparing to pass into Spain after a day spent in futile research, sleep, which had not soothed him for a long time, poured the juice of its soporific poppies into him for a few moments.

He seemed to be wandering in a vast plain. His eyes turned toward a forest that he perceived; he penetrated into it without any design. He had been walking there for an hour when a hermitage appeared to him. An individual clad in a long red robe emerged and said to Savary: "Come to Saint-Félix; the Hermit of the Tomb will guide you to your be-loved."

With those words, he disappeared—or, rather, Savary's precipitate awakening terminated the dream.

Moved by what he had just seen, dominated by the superstitious spirit that did so much harm to his century, the troubadour took his dream for a heaven-sent warning; he did not doubt that the hermit who had once given him shelter in the wood of Caillavel could tell him where Bélisène could be found. Without waiting any longer he changed his resolution, and instead of turning toward the kingdom of Léon, as he had initially intended, he took the direction of Carcassonne.

As he approached that city, soldiers that he interrogated told him that the Comtes Raymond, as well as the beautiful Aliénor, were still in the crusaders' camp. He then had the conviction that where the young Comte de Toulouse was, Adémar must be, so he did not turn aside from the road and, coming to the camp, he asked for the Comte's quarters. The banners, on which were the empty golden cross, pommeled, cropped and heightened on a field of gules, indicated it to him. He took a few steps and found himself in Adémar's arms.

A prisoner in her tower, Bélisène, occupied with her amour, suffered with difficulty the fact that Don Juan sometimes dared to penetrate into her retreat. Every day, far from diminishing her distance from them, her hatred only increasing, Don Juan flattered himself in vain; he was always rejected, and his dastardly soul conceived the most frightful projects in his moments of rage.

One evening, after a very hot day, Bélisène, sitting by the window of her large tower, cast a glance over the surrounding countryside and the sky, ornamented at that moment by all the pomp of evening. Before her extended an immense plain covered by rich crops, green grapevines and bushy woods, through which the tranquil waters of the Mayre snaked, its banks covered with gladioli and a thousand other marsh plants...

Still in the same direction, Bélisène's sight discovered the elevated ridge where, several centuries later, a hero issued from one off the foremost French families would be born. On the horizon, the chain of the black mountains appeared, its slopes clad with the fertile marks of vegetation; here, a black rock appeared, there, a clump of oaks stood; not far away, smoke was rising from a woodcutter's hut. Toward the north the gaze descended from the mountains of Castre into an immense and magnificent basin, were towns and villages could be seen, and cultivated lands; there, Sorère and Revel could be made out. In the same direction, on hills arranged in echelons, in a verdant landscape, towns placed in an amphitheater could be admired, including Montgeai, Puilaurens and Caraman. To Bélisène's right, hills formed steps that, over a distance of twenty leagues, rose up to the highest summit in the Pyrenees, the blue crests of which crowned a part of the magnificent tableau.

No, Bélisène thought, as she scanned the various perspectives that charmed her, *there cannot exist a point on the globe where Nature is pleased to show herself with a more imposing pomp!*

At that exclamation, her heart recalled the rich scenery that the land of Foix furnished in great quantity. In thinking about that, Bélisène soon thought about her friend, and, without perceiving it, she started singing the memories of her happiness.

While Bélisène was exhaling in that song the dolor by which she was afflicted, attracted by the charm of her voice, Don Juan had approached. He had penetrated into his captive's chamber without her, entirely occupied by her amour, perceiving that he was nearby; but a sigh that escaped him made her turn around, and a pallor covered her cheeks at the sight of a knight who was so odious to her.

Perceiving that she was trembling, Don Juan tried to reassure her. "Is the sight of me so disagreeable to you, Madame, that I see fear imprinted throughout your person?"

"If Don Juan were not blinded by his presumption," said Bélisène, "he would have perceived a long time ago how displeased I am by his presence."

"You are doubtless forgetting that you are in my power, Madame."

"Take great care to remind me of it, in order to redouble the scorn that you inspire in me."

"So my love has no hope of ever being welcomed?"

"I despise your love. An unworthy knight, a culpable kidnapper, how can you expect to inspire tender sentiments?"

"Well, if I cannot aspire to it," Dion Juan said, "what point is there in my conserving the regard for you that has been your portion thus far?"

"Hasten to plunge me into your dungeon," said Bélisène, "in order that I shall not see you again; then I shall have less to lament."

"It will not be in a cell that you will be imprisoned," said Don Juan, seizing her, "it will be in my arms."

Pulling free from Don Juan, Bélisène cried: "Monster! Leave me alone. Oh, if you want my death, you will endure it by your action. Leave me alone, I implore you."

"No," said Don Juan, "I am no longer listening."

"On my God, come to my aid!"

"Heaven is deaf to your prayers; it has delivered you to my amour."

"No!" cried a formidable voice. "No, the crime shall not be consummated!"

On hearing those words, Don Juan, looked round in surprise, and the pallor that covered Bélisène's face passed over his own when he saw a warrior redoubtably armored, sword in hand, who said to him:

"Stop, Don Juan. Have you forgotten the mountains of Narbonne?"

"Bérenger! Are the dead emerging from the tomb?" cried Don Juan, and remained motionless.

"Yes, you see in me your victim; but fear his fury if you do not go away, and woe betide you if you return to this chamber, entry to which is forbidden to you forever!"

Without response and without resistance, Don Juan withdrew. The warrior followed him with his gaze until he was lost to sight; then, addressing himself to the terrified Bélisène, he said: "Cease to be afraid, daughter of the Comte; henceforth, you will be as safe in this château as you could hope to be in the midst of the battalions your father commands. Adieu. You will see the Chevalier de Mauléon before long."

The warrior had scarcely pronounced those words when he sank into the floor, which opened up to receive him.

During that extraordinary scene, Bélisène's surprise had reached its peak; she could not conceive how, in a place where Don Juan seemed to be the master, there could be someone more powerful than him, and whom he did not know. Nor could she rationalize the sudden disappearance of the warrior protector, how she was known to him, and by what magic words he had suspended the insolent Spaniard's outrages.

A superstitious dread agitated her painfully; she dared not go you of her room nor resolve to remain there alone. Finally, she heard the footsteps of someone approaching the door; soon, it opened, and Germaine appeared, carrying a candle. On approaching Bélisène she noticed the fear that was imprinted in her features.

"Queen of the Angels!" she exclaimed. "The spirits have spread fear today through all the inhabitants of the château."

"What, honest vassal, could have made you form such a conjecture?" Bélisène asked.

"Oh, noble demoiselle," said Germaine, "it doesn't astonish me! During the time I've been in this accursed château. I've been able to accustom myself to everything that frightens us. Just now, Sire Ferdinand was seen coming out of the long gallery; he was marching rapidly, trembling in every limb, and he was heard to say: 'Sinister phantom, will you pursue me incessantly?' I come to you and I find you bearing on your face the imprint of a terror similar to his."

"Is the cause of the extraordinary events that occur in this château unknown to you?"

"God, who is listening to me, knows that I cannot be accused of recounting without need," said Germane, "but I know things that might take me a long way if, to my misfortune, Sire Arembert obtained the certainty that I was informed of them."

Carried away by a surge of curiosity, Bélisène asked: "He has a great interest, then, in their not being divulged?"

"There is his life."

"Are you thinking what you're saying?"

"Truly, yes, I think about it, and that's why I'm discreet. One day, a noble lord said to me: 'Germaine, if you will tell me everything you know about Baron de Saint-Félix. I will make you so rich that you will become a great lady, instead of the serf that you are. But I, who, thanks to the Queen of the Angels, know how to retain myself, said to him: 'Go away, Monseigneur; it always costs to talk too much.' I'll restrict myself to telling you that, since the death of Baron Amanieu, the father of the Chevaliers Arembert and Bérenger, the Devil has taken possession of this castellany."

"Has Seigneur Amanieu been dead for a long time?"

"It will be nineteen years next Saint Martin's Day— please God that we arrive there—since the frightful night when the Baron expired," said Germaine. "There was a tempest so frightful that human memory has never seen one like it, before or since. The next day, when we went into our seigneur's chamber, he was found as cold as marble. His two sons wept for him bitterly. But since that day, lamentable moans have been heard throughout the château; several varlets have seen shadows wandering over the battlements; in sum, desolation was brought to such a point that no one wanted to live in such a place any longer.

"Baron Bérenger got ready to leave for the Holy Land. Before leaving France, he quarreled with his brother, Sire Arembert. He was in Spain, in the house of a great lord of the country, when he learned of the death of the head of his household. We were told that Messire Bérenger had perished at sea; but since then, another rumor has run around."

"What did it say?"

"That the Baron had been murdered during the crossing."

"And who is accused?"

"If I dare tell you, the assassin was named as..."

"Silence!" proclaimed a voice.

Germaine fell to her knees. "Holy Queen of the Angels, protect me!"

"Inconceivable mystery!" exclaimed Bélisène.

"Oh, Demoiselle," said Germaine, "I'm doomed! The spirit is angry with me Monseigneur Revenant, I implore your mercy; don't speak to me, don't show yourself when I traverse the halls and galleries, as you take pleasure in doing when you torment Roberto."

As Germaine was speaking, thus, the door opened with such violence that Bélisène shuddered, while her companion threw herself on the floor, face down.

It was Roberto. "Pardon me Madame," said, addressing Bélisène, "if I enter your room without warning; someone is asking for Germaine, and I've come to fetch her."

Germaine got to her feet. "Why couldn't you have come a moment sooner, Master Roberto? You would have heard the spirit, which seemed to want to enter into our conversation; you accuse me of being talkative, but I swear to you that it didn't find anyone disposed to respond to it."

"Do your stupid fears never abandon you? Go—you have nothing to fear if you're able to cure your mania for talking."

After saying that, and saluting Bélisène, the concierge withdrew, followed by Germaine, who was grumbling excitedly.

Bélisène had not dared to communicate her fears, or what she had seen, to that man; she feared that he might treat her as an insensate. Nevertheless, she trembled at the thought of sending the night in such a dubious place.

As she went to light a second candle that was placed on a marble table, she tripped, which caused her to place her hand forcefully on a panel of the woodwork. She was extremely surprised when she felt the panel give way and withdraw into the wall, offering her access, after its retreat, to a very long and very narrow corridor.

Dreading that someone might introduce themselves into her room by means of that secret passage, she decided to follow it and see where it ended. She took a lamp and, arming herself with courage, she set forth resolutely.

After taking some twenty paces, she encountered a little spiral stairway of extreme steepness; she descended slowly, supporting herself on the wall. At the bottom of the stairway she found a door, which, being unlocked, permitted her to enter a rather large room.

As she scanned it with her eyes, she thought she perceived the warrior who had opposed Don Juan's enterprise a little while before. She shivered, but having drawn a little closer she saw that what had frightened her was only a suit of armor suspended on the wall.

She searched for an exit, and saw a tunnel, less narrow than the one through which she had come, She was about to go into it when she heard the muffled sound of someone walking with precaution. She hastened to hide her lamp under her robe, and looked to see whether there might be a retreat not far away that might hide her from the sight of the person who was advancing. She only discovered a large wooden statue that was placed in a broad recess. She ran to place herself within it.

Scarcely was she there than she perceived, at the extremity of the tunnel, a person clad in a red robe, who was walking slowly. When he passed in front of her she darted a furtive glance in order to see his face by the light of a torch that he was carrying.

Oh, with what terror she was struck when she discovered a death's-head buried under the hood of the robe. At that disgusting sight, Bélisène felt that her strength was ready to abandon her; she made a fervent prayer, and followed the frightful phantom with her gaze. He went into the room where the armor was.

For more than an hour he had not emerged when Bélisène, who had not been able to decide to budge from her hiding place, perceived that the lamp was about to go out. Another fear then came to take possession of her: that of remaining without light in such a place. There was no other way to go than that of returning to her apartment, but it would be necessary to traverse the chamber into which the specter had just passed; she might encounter it, and that thought did not reassure Bélisène. It was, however, necessary to make a decision.

Arming herself with the courage that desperation gives, the daughter of the Comte de Foix decided to retrace her initial steps. On arriving at the fatal door, her heart was beating so rapidly that she was constrained to stop. Hearing no sound, however, she crossed the threshold and looked...

The suit of armor had disappeared, and there was nothing in its place, or in the room.

Bélisène then feared finding the phantom on the stairway or in the corridor, but as there was no longer time to recoil, because the lamp was about to run out of fuel, she steeled herself against the danger and climbed the stairway rapidly.

She saw nothing; nor did the corridor present any disagreeable object. She entered her room precipitately, closed the panel, and, falling to her knees, prayed to Heaven with an entire fervor.

Chapter IX: Treason

Despairing of the length of the siege, the legate Milon and Simon de Montfort feared seeing their prey escape the traps with which they had enveloped him. Already several crusader princes, content with having earned indulgences by serving for forty days, were talking about withdrawing. The Duc de Bourgogne, although a friend of Montfort, was among that number, and the Comte de Nevers was the most eager to effect his retreat since he had seen how much the war displeased Aliénor de Toulouse. The Raymonds supported him in that step, in which they were ready to follow him.

Savary de Mauléon, desiring to see the hermit, whom, he thought, could reassure him as to the fate of his beloved, did not know whether he ought to wait in the camp, where he sometimes appeared, or whether it was necessary to go and search for him in the hermitage. Arembert, for his part, wanted a retreat that might facilitate for him the accomplishment of a project that he had been planning for a long time. In sum, the siege of Carcassonne was a burden on all the crusaders.

In the meantime, a knight who was distantly related to Comte Roger formed the project of bringing him to the crusaders' camp in order to negotiate a peace. Without informing anyone, he departed, escorted by thirty men-at-arms, and, having traversed the ruins of the outlying districts, he arrived at the barriers. As he was not marching as an enemy, the advances sentinels asked him what his intentions were; he replied that he wanted to speak to the Vicomte. Someone was sent to inform the latter, who was close by, and who came to the barrier accompanied by Odon and three other nights.

When the crusader saw him, he went to him, embraced him tenderly, and assured him that, in his quality as a relative, he was suffering from seeing him on the point of succumbing.

"Well, what do you want me to do?" said Roger. "They are obstinate in refusing me the peace I requested."

"But if it were offered to you now," said the knight, "would you refuse it?"

"No, of course not."

"Well, come with me to draw up the articles. Follow me to the camp."

"I would be imprudent to throw myself into the midst of my enemies," said the Vicomte.

"What do you fear? I offer you their word and mine as a safeguard. Don't place an obstacle to the concord that might be reborn by virtue of a mistaken mistrust."

The knight pressed him urgently; he swore to him that all the necessary powers had been given to him. In the end, he succeeded so well that Roger decided to go with him. After handing supreme command over to Odon, he departed as rapidly as possible, fearing that Agnès, informed of his resolution, might hasten to oppose it.

Thus, trusting his perfidious enemies, he marched to his doom of his own will. Odon, on seeing him draw away, uttered a profound sigh, and, his heart full of sadness, he went to see the Vicomtesse.

On learning what her husband had thought he ought to do, Agnès remained motionless. Soon, tears filled her beautiful eyes, and, forgetting Odon's attachment to Roger, she accused him of weakness in his amity. Odon rejected that unjust accusation nobly; he tried to console Agnès, talking to her about the peace that was to be concluded; he made her see the danger to which their common safety was exposed. In the end, if he did not succeed in destroying the Vicomtesse's prejudices, he constrained her to enclose them in her heart.

In the meantime, Roger continued his route. He had intended to go to the tent of the Comte de Toulouse first, but his relative persuaded him to begin by presenting himself to the legate.

At that moment Milon was surrounded by the principal crusaders, with whom he was occupied with the care of defeating Carcassonne, when someone came to announce Comte

Roger. At that name and that unexpected arrival, the astonishment was general.

Roger appeared in the assembly with the modest assurance that courage combined with virtue gives; all the seigneurs stood up at the sight of him. He was welcomed politely, and, charmed by such a reception, he abandoned himself to the most optimistic hopes.

The Comte de Toulouse, having learned of his nephew's arrival, hastened to go to the council, accompanied by his son. On seeing him, the legate and Montfort were disagreeably surprised; it was necessary, however, to listen to the Vicomte. He expressed himself with dignity, speaking in a clear and easy fashion. He asked again for peace, promising to submit to any reasonable conditions that they wanted to impose on him.

After having listened to him, the legate replied: "Your step surprises me, Comte Roger; your speech astonishes me even more. You want peace, you say, you demand reasonable conditions. Have you forgotten those that have been accorded to you? I will repeat them to you, in order that they will not escape your memory again. You, one of thirteen armed..."

"When I consented to appear before you, Seigneur," said the Vicomte, "I did not think it was to hear such dishonorable propositions repeated."

"If it is not to submit," said the legate, "what are you doing here?"

"I came here with the assurance given to me that I would be treated as a Prince."

"No one was charged by me with bringing you to the camp," said the legate. "Perhaps these Ducs, Comtes and Chevaliers have made a resolution in your regard that they have not communicated to me."

The silence of the knights responded negatively to that interrogation of sorts.

"Has a knave abused my good faith, then?" asked the Vicomte.

"No, Sire Vicomte," said the knight, "what I have done was in the conviction I had that my step would not be disavowed."

"Imprudent knight, you are culpable," said the legate. "Vicomte, go away."

"Yes, I shall go," said the Vicomte, "and it will only be under the ruins of Carcassonne that you will find the victory for which you hope,.."

Scarcely had Roger left than the legate said to Simon de Montfort: "Comte, I order you in the name of the power that Innocent III has confided to me, to seize the person of Comte Roger."

Montfort got up and hastened to obey.

On hearing the order given by the legate, a general murmur went up in the hall. The Comte de Toulouse, unable to retain his indignation, rose from his seat and said to Milon: "What have we just heard, Seigneur? Is it in the midst of an assembly of so many worthy knights that the iniquitous order that you have just given has been pronounced? Do you take us for brigands, and is the sacred right of gentlemen unknown to you?"

"What are you complaining about, Comte?" said the legate. "Is your promise being broken? Are we not holding to what we have promised? None of us has answered for Roger; he has presented himself confidently, without being summoned. Ought we to let such an opportunity escape? Do you not see the finger of God in this, which is leading our vanquished enemy to us without it being necessary for us to draw our swords?"

The Comte de Nevers spoke impetuously. "Refrain from speaking of God in committing such a perfidy. The God of truth is the enemy of treason. No, undoubtedly, we shall not suffer that Roger is charged with chains; French knights fight, but do not arrest."

Seeing that the assembly was against him, the legate said: "Well, let the first man to oppose my will tremble; I commit him to the fires of Hell, and I launch the thunderbolt of excommunication upon him."

At those terrible worlds, the most courageous are non-plussed; no one dares stand up to a legate of the Holy See, all of them knowing the danger of such an enterprise; but they have recourse to prayer. The arrogant legate remains inflexible; nothing can change or move him; he rejects the Barons' supplications, and is exciting the souls of the soldiers when Montfort comes back into the hall followed by his prisoner.

Roger had been withdrawing tranquilly when insolent soldiers surrounded him; Montfort appeared before him and signified the will of the legate. Astounded by such cowardice, the generous Roger had drawn his sword in order to defend himself and at least die gloriously: a vain project! The soldiers threw themselves upon him; overwhelmed by numbers, his sword was snatched way; laden with undignified chains he was taken, thus disarmed, to the assembly.

On seeing him appear, the Comte de Toulouse turns away; Raymond hides his face in his hands; the magnanimous Comte de Nevers lowers his eyes; all the knights express by their mute gestures their shame and their consternation.

Roger's speech oppresses the legate. Milon becomes more furious, and, suspending the council, he places the Vicomte under Montfort's guard, no other crusader having wanted to take responsibility for it.

The rumor of the Vicomte's arrest, crossing the boundaries of the besiegers' camp, soon reaches the ramparts of Carcassonne.

On hearing it, Odon could not retain the tears that escaped his eyes. But who could describe faithfully the despair of Agnès, the cries that she uttered, the reproaches that she addressed to all those surrounding her and to Heaven, which betrayed her thus?

"This, then, credulous Odon," she said, "is the peace that the Vicomte was seeking? This is the faith of knights who say that they have taken up arms for the cause of God? Will centuries to come ever believe in the disloyalty of this action? And you, whose beautiful soul is unable to suspect perfidy, unfortunate hero, O my husband, what are you doing far from the one who is weeping for your loss? Irons, shameful irons, shackle your beautiful hands; and I, what am I doing here, why am I not flying in order to share your captivity? Soldiers, if you are faithful to me, do not retain your unfortunate Princesse."

She broke off, the force of her dolor having robbed her of the strength to go on. Then Odon, throwing himself at her knees, implored her to moderate herself, to think about her son, and her husband, whose loss was not assured, and to trust in the valor of his subjects.

While he was speaking, a panic terror took possession of the inhabitants of Carcassonne. Deprived of all appetite for defense by the detention of their sovereign, believing themselves defeated because they were no longer commanded, they thought of fleeing through the tunnels that were known to end several leagues from their city. Odon, Pierre de Courtenay and a few other brave knights tried in vain to dissuade them from their intention. For her part, Agnès was stubborn in not being separated from her husband; she did not what to flee, she wanted to go and join him.

In that situation, overwhelmed by the resolution of the people and that of the Vicomtesse, Odon did not know what to do, when he suddenly saw an individual costumed as a warrior descending from the large tower of the château, who, during the first attack, had put a number of the assailants to flight merely by his appearance. Surprised to see someone emerging from a place that had been uninhabited for a long time, the brave knight could not command his emotion momentarily.

The hermit—for it was him—advanced toward the Vicomtesse. "Madame," he said, "come with me. Heaven, which never abandons the cause of justice, will not let you down at this moment."

"Oh, whoever you are," cried Agnès, "what a time are you choosing to make such a speech to me! Heaven has not forgotten me, you say, but it suffers that my husband..."

171

"Let us not criticize Providence," said the hermit, "when our feeble understanding does not permit us to fathom the profundity of its decrees."

"But what do you want to do, mysterious knight?" said Odon. "What means do you intend to employ to save the wife and son of my friend and master?"

"Do not worry about my resources," said the hermit, "they are immense; all the crusaders united could not raise an obstacle to the retreat that I am offering you."

While they were speaking thus, the impetuous Comte de Montfort, desirous of enabling what he just occurred to be forgotten by means of some great action, had drawn the army toward the city in order to attempt a new assault, hoping to surprise its defenders at a moment when the Vicomte's arrest must have thrown everything into confusion.

As he did not perceive any soldiers on the ramparts, he thought at first that it was a ruse of war, so he ordered the attack with precaution; but when the battlements were crossed, there was no more doubt that Carcassonne had been abandoned. They did not know, however, by what means the inhabitants had been able to withdraw.

As they approached the palace, however, they saw a few soldiers; they were the Vicomtesse's guard, who had not wanted to abandon her.

It was at that moment that Odon perceived that, while he was talking to the warrior, the crusaders were attacking Roger's soldiers.

"Madame," he said to the Vicomtesse, "take refuge in the tower; we will defend you until the last drop of our blood."

Having said that, he went down the steps and ran to where the clamors could be heard.

Agnès, bewildered by the sight of that pressing danger, and fearing for her son the fate of her husband, made no difficulty about following the hermit. Taking young Trencavel in his arms, and guiding the tottering steps of the Vicomtesse, he hastened to regain the keep; they went into it, closing the door.

From that moment on, they were not seen again.

The valiant Odon, inflamed by the courage that amity gives, fought with a bravery by which even he could not help being surprised. The crusaders, indignant that a single man, when all the others had fled or surrendered, was intent on sustaining their combined efforts, redoubled their ardor to overwhelm him. Numbers were finally about to vanquish heroism when a knight with his visor raised appeared in the midst of the battle and marched toward Odon sword in hand.

"Surrender, Chevalier!" he cried

Odon, indignant at that proposition, was about to respond with a thrust of his sword when he looked at the crusader and, far from continuing the combat, he replied: "Chevalier, I am your prisoner."

It was Adémar.

As soon as the latter had saved his brave brother in arms, he said: "Odon, let's go save the Vicomtesse."

With those words, they ran into the palace, which soldiers were already inundating. They ran to the tower; under their redoubled blows, the door yielded; they went in.

The Vicomtesse had disappeared; her son and the hermit had gone with her.

Odon was in despair, but on the basis of the portrait of the warrior that he traced, Adémar reassured him, having no doubt that the hermit had saved the unfortunate Agnès.

The crusades entered Carcassonne from all directions, strangely astonished by the disappearance of the inhabitants of the populous city.

Eventually, the openings of the subterranean tunnels were discovered; they hastened to penetrate them, and succeeded in arresting a large number of citizens who had not yet been able to escape. They perished in the flames.

Chapter X: Odon and the Hermit

Montfort's anger was extreme when he learned that Vicomtesse Agnès could not be found. He ordered that Odon be seized until he had revealed the place of his sovereign's retreat, but Adémar, far from surrendering his prisoner, announced that he would defend him with armed force. The Comte de Toulouse's troops were ranged around him. Montfort feared going to extremities that might have had deadly consequences. He renounced the project of taking possession of Odon, and, more occupied with Vicomte Roger, he ordered that he be transferred to the keep of the château.

Adémar, followed by his friend, was returning to the camp when he perceived Raymond, who was marching at a precipitate pace with every expression of despair. Adémar hastened to catch up with him.

On perceiving him, Raymond cried: "Liberator of my sister Aliénor, will you be that again?"

"Explain Seigneur," said Adémar.

"Heaven has punished us," said Raymond. "While we were fighting for an unjust cause, my sister and Sancia have been treacherously abducted."

"Vengeful God," cried Adémar, "slay the guilty party!"

"It can only be Amaury or his accomplices," said Raymond.

"Let us not lose any time, Monseigneur," said Adémar. "It's necessary to find them or perish."

As he spoke, the Comte de Toulouse, the Comte de Nevers, Savary de Mauléon and a few other knights came running in response to the news of the disastrous event. The legate Milon, fearing that it would be imputed to the Montfort family, was not one of the last to show himself. They were listening to the various accounts of the guards when Amaury appeared.

On seeing him, Raymond's first impulse was to launch himself at him, word in hand. Young Montfort, feigning to be surprised by that attack, up himself on the defensive.

"Traitor!" cried Raymond. "What have you done with my sister and my wife?"

"Is it to me that such a question is addressed?" said Amaury.

"Answer me," said Raymond. "Where have you taken them? For you are only skillful in making arrests."

At those words, which referred to the fact that Amaury had accompanied his father when the latter had taken possession of Roger, Amaury, seething with wrath, fell upon Raymond. The legate, the Archbishop of Bordeaux and the Duc de Bourgogne stopped the two combatants; in spite of their efforts, each of them was taken back to his tent.

The Comte de Nevers, Savary, Adémar and Odon accompanied Raymond to his, and there the noble knights abandoned themselves to regrets in thinking about the persons who were so dear to them, and who had been perfidiously stolen from them. Raymond, Adémar and Savary, above all, were inconsolable; their sentiment was painted throughout their person, and if each of them had not been too occupied with his own dolor, the height to which the simple knight Adémar had dared to raise his pretentions would have been discovered without difficulty. The Comte de Toulouse, desirous of avoiding a further encounter between Amaury and his son, signified to the latter the order to leave for their capital immediately.

"What are you demanding, Seigneur?" said Raymond. "What! I must go away without having punished the odious Montfort and without having been able to liberate the two women dearest to my heart?"

"It seems to me, my son, that it's without very strong proof that you accuse Amaury. In the situation in which misfortune has placed us, we must sometimes lend ourselves to circumstances; let us dissimulate, since we can only defend ourselves by going to the ultimate extremities. You know, in any case, that the roads are covered by our emissaries; we shall be informed before long of the fate of Aliénor and Sancia; but for their sake, let us not doom ourselves by a misplaced outburst. Return to Toulouse, and if your anger has not calmed, carry with you the sad assurance that it will soon be necessary for us to fight those we hate."

Already, a thousand reflections were crowding Raymond's thoughts, but one alone, which presented itself with lightning rapidity, prevented him from refusing his father what the latter demanded. He understood that once outside the camp he would be free to direct his steps toward the place where he wanted to go.

Adémar, prey to the most violent chagrin, had perceived that Arembert had not appeared either in the camp or in Carcassonne. His mind, prompt to connect the circumstances, soon informed him that the Baron de Saint-Félix was the author of Aliénor's abduction; that, in consequence, it had been easy for him to facilitate Sancia's, in order to please Montfort's son, whose interests he had embraced entirely.

The Comte de Toulouse, in haste to see Raymond leave the camp, did not waste a moment; he had his equipment prepared and, after having embraced him tenderly, he sent him away, confining him to the care of Adémar and Savary, who declared that they did not want to be separated from him. Only Odon could not decide to quit the camp; the amity he had for Vicomte Roger did not permit him to abandon him at such a sad moment.

The following morning, the Comte de Toulouse, who believed his son to be in that city, was summoned to the Council by the Legate's orders. For a long time, everything had been secretly prepared; the ruin of the Trencavel family was about to be consummated.

When all the crusader lords were seated, the legate Milon spoke and, congratulating them on the success of the crusade, he decided that it was time to collect the prize. He said that Vicomte Roger, rejected by the Church, was incapable of governing henceforth, and that it was necessary to choose a Prince to rule his estates.

176

At first eyes were cast upon the Duc de Bourgogne, but he, rising to his feet and speaking with nobility, refused the honor that they wished to give him, declaring that, content with his provinces, he did not want to augment them at the expense of an unfortunate. Then they addressed the Comte de Nevers, which went even further; he claimed that it was an odious injustice to want to dispossess Roger of the heritage of his forefathers, and that they did not have the right to do it. The Comte de Saint-Paul, interrogated in his turn, made the same response.

Milon, mortified by those refusals, proposed then that four knights and two bishops be nominated who, combined with him, would choose the person who ought to be invested with the conquests. That proposal having been adopted, the most ambitious of all was chosen; it was Simon de Montfort, Earl of Leicester. Scarcely was he nominated than the custody of the unfortunate was immediately handed over to him.

On learning that news, the Comte de Toulouse and Odon had no doubt that Roger's death had been decided. Odon swore not to survive him.

Then, suddenly, the hermit who was so extraordinary in his conduct came into the Comte de Toulouse's tent and said to him: "Monseigneur, you know that you have no more faithful subject than the one who is speaking to you. I know your new misfortune: your daughter and your son's future spouse have been kidnapped. Hope that fortune will not be contrary to them; you shall see them again before long."

"Mysterious man who has been doing good around me for so long," said the Comte de Toulouse, "I am pleased to believe what you are telling me. Alas, at this moment, another pressing chagrin is afflicting me. My nephew, the unfortunate Vicomte de Carcassonne, is in Montfort's power; I tremble for his life."

"And it is his life that I have come to save," said the hermit.

"Can you do that?" asked Odon.

"Yes, undoubtedly."

"Oh!" said Odon. "You are rendering me my own. But dare I ask you what has become of the Vicomtesse?"

"We shall take her spouse to her. In my turn, allow me to interrogate you. Who are you, to take such a keen interest in Roger's fate?"

"I am his friend of early childhood."

"Are you the child confided with Adémar to the care of the Comtesse, Roger's mother?"

"That's me."

"Brother of Adémar! Come into my arms."

"He is my brother, then?"

"He is, and some day, you will learn more about your common fate."

"My heart had already given to Adémar the title you have just confirmed."

"Pardon me, Sire Comte," said the hermit, "if I still envelop myself in mystery before you; it is necessary to my plan not to make myself known yet. Meanwhile, let us occupy ourselves with Roger. Night is descending over the globe; this is the propitious moment. Come with me, Odon; the Vicomte will soon owe his deliverance to you."

"My impatient amity begs you to hasten the moment," said Odon.

"Come, then; let nothing any longer stop us."

The Comte wished them a fortunate success in their enterprise; he asked them if they needed the assistance of a few knights.

"Thank God," the hermit said to him, "I have with me the wherewithal to confront an entire army." And having knelt down before the Comte, he made a sign to Odon to follow him.

The profound obscurity that reigned then permitted them to depart without being perceived by the secret emissaries of Montfort and the legate, who were incessantly laying siege to the Comte de Toulouse's quarters. Maintaining a profound silence, the hermit and Odon drew away from the camp. At a distance about seven times the range of a stone launched by a vigorously-wielded sling, they reached a place where the Aude rumbled around a mass of rocks as it covered them with its foam.

A small boat, apparently placed there deliberately, allowed them to reach the rocks. After having moored it to a chain at the place of disembarkation, the hermit, hanging on to the stones and plants that were there, followed by Odon, reached an opening into which he prepared to descend.

Having struck brilliant sparks by means of the impact of two stones, he lit a resin torch that he had brought and, making a sign to Odon not to quit him, they went into a tunnel that descended via a shallow slope. Odon perceived that they were under the Aude; then the terrain rose gradually.

After marching for quite a long time they found a broad stone stairway that it was necessary to climb. At the top, after having traversed a gallery in which several iron doors were set, they encountered a second stairway, much narrower than the first; they went up it. As they completed the climb, a rather loud noise reached them; they recognized the Vicomte's voice.

"What do you want of me, wretch?" he said.

"Drink," was the response, "or the cruelest death will be your share."

"Alas," he replied, "shall I perish so miserably? Oh, my dear Odon, oh, my Agnès, oh, my son! Shall I never see you again?"

"You shall see them again!" cried Odon, who could not contain his impatience. "Your liberators have arrived."

As he spoke, he launched himself into the tower, sword in hand; the hermit did likewise.

At the sight of the two armed men, the two assassins panicked; they imagined that they saw a battalion, and without consulting anything but their fear, they fled, dropping the poisoned bowl.

Odon had run into the Vicomte's arms; the latter was only able to hug him in his. After having enjoyed the touching spectacle for a moment, the hermit says: "Let us flee, and not give our enemies time to collect themselves. Come Vicomte, your wife and son await you."

Then took the same route by which they had come.

After learning of the Vicomte's escape, Montfort told all the crusaders that Roger had died after having confessed to the Bishop of Carcassonne. He had a body buried as Roger's, promising himself to treat the latter as an impostor if he ever reappeared.

Chapter IX: The Amorous Expedition

Impatient to snatch their lovers from the kidnappers who had abducted them, Raymond and Adémar, as soon as they were out of sight of the camp, halted the detachment that was escorting them; they commanded them to continue marching toward Toulouse, where they would not take long to reappear, and, only accompanied by Savary—who, like them, was in quest of his beauty—they took a roundabout route to Castelnaudary. Adémar could not distract himself from the idea that the Château de Saint-Félix must be the place in which Sancia and Aliénor were imprisoned.

Savary advised them to remove their military apparel and put on the elegant costume of troubadours in order to attract less suspicion. His advice was followed and they continued their voyage. They had passed the hamlet of Douilles when they saw a large troop of horsemen coming toward them; not wanting to find themselves in the midst of those men-at-arms, the three amorous poursuivants withdrew behind a dense bush, whose vast foliage was sufficient to hide them from the soldiers' view.

Adémar, who examined them attentively, experienced an extreme joy in recognizing the Baron de Saint-Félix's banner and seeing Arembert among them. Then his suspicion changed into certainty; he was convinced that the Baron was the abductor they were pursuing.

When the squadron, which was heading for the crusaders' camp, had drawn away, Adémar communicated his thought to his two valiant companions. The hope of soon delivering their darlings engaged them to continue their course. They did not take long to approach Saint-Félix, of which the steeple and high tower were visible for several leagues. As Adémar was known to everyone, he did not want to enter the town in daylight. Raymond, perhaps more impetuous, did not want to stop.

Then Savary offered advice that was adopted; it was decided that he alone, being entirely unknown to the inhabitants of the town and the château, would seek to introduce himself into the latter by virtue of the costume he was wearing, and that he would try to make sure that the Princesses had been taken to the place. Raymond consented to await the result of Savary's enterprise. Adémar told the latter that they would withdraw to the hermitage in the forest of Caillavel, and that it was necessary to came to join them there the following day.

After having embraced tenderly, they separated, and Savary, playing his guitar as he marched in order to announce himself, did not take long to sing a simple ballad that attracted a number of the inhabitants of the town to gather around him, and a few soldiers who were guarding the first barrier of the château.

> *Bud of amour on your flexible stem*
> *Gently swayed by the zephyr,*
> *To its transports you are sensible,*
> *It is so sweet to be thus caressed,*
>   *Bud of amour!*

> *Bud of amour, the candor of youth*
> *Believes the first of oaths eternal;*
> *But the zephyr is a fickle lover,*
> *And changes all lovers likewise,*
>   *Bud of amour!*[41]

Savary's pleasant voice, and the talent he showed, spread the word instantly within the château that a doubtless-renowned troubadour had just arrived. As people affected an extreme veneration for the children of the Muses in those days, castellan seigneurs would not have those it possible to

---

[41] Author's note: "The music, by the author of the words, is sold by the widow Duhan, in the Boulevard Montmartre, in Paris."

dispense with welcoming a minstrel who would subsequently sing the praises of their bravery and generosity. In spite of his chagrins, Arembert would not have wanted a troubadour to pass through his domain without being pampered; his orders were given in consequence.

Thus, as soon as Savary had been heard, Roberto appeared, engaging him to come in and rest. As that was exactly what Savary wanted, he did not have to be asked twice, and, without further ado, he followed the steward.

Roberto introduced him into a richly decorated room and invited him to sit down. He had him served seasonal fruits, and poured him a few draughts on an excellent villaudrie into an Oriental agate cup.

While he was eating, the worthy Germaine, whose character was not in accord with her surly face, came in, and exclaimed, on seeing him: "The Queen of the Angels be praised! At least we'll have a little amusement, for gaiety accompanies the maker of tensons and God knows how much we need some, as well as those poor demoiselles."

"Shut up, impudent woman!" cried Roberto. "One word more and I'll send you down to the cellar under the keep."

"Mercy!" replied Germaine. "You've no need to recommend me to silence; your threat renders me irredeemably mute."

Savary thought that his costume required that he be introduced to the chatelaine.

"That cannot me, genteel troubadour," Roberto told him. "There is no lady here; we only have demoiselles, who, prey to their dolor, never want to appear."

"Songs, however, have the advantage of distracting chagrin," said Savary, "and troubadours are called the physicians of the soul."

"You're doubtless right, Seigneur," said Roberto, "but it is appropriate, before conducting you to the demoiselles, for me to inform Seigneur Ferdinand."

"Ferdinand!" exclaimed Savary. "Your master is Spanish, then?"

183

"He isn't our master; he's a friend of Baron Arembert."

"Well, tell him that a troubadour is asking to pay his court to the ladies; it's a favor that has never been refused me."

Poor Savary did not know what he was asking; he had not divined that the name of Ferdinand hid the evil Don Juan d'Astorga.

While he finished emptying the flagon that had been served to him, Roberto went to Don Juan. "Sire Chevalier," he said, "A troubadour, noble if one can judge by the escutcheon on his robe, is asking to appear before you and the demoiselles."

"Who can have informed him thus?" asked Don Juan.

"The imprudence of a vassal," said Roberto.

"Does he know their names?"

"He does not."

"Make sure that he does not learn them. You, who have your master's confidence, must know how important it is that no one must ever divine that this château confines the daughters of three powerful sovereigns; our doom would be the certain price of the slightest imprudence. Return to the troubadour, tell him that the demoiselles have refused to see him, but add that I am ready to receive him in their stead."

Roberto hastened to return to Savary. "Troubadour," he said, "the demoiselles want to remain invisible; the lure of sweet songs has not been able to touch them."

"They are not French, then?" said Savary.

Astonished by the simple question, Roberto replied: "What makes you presume that?"

"Vassal," said Avary, "French woman love our songs; they welcome them, and love their praises to be sung by us."

"They have lost persons very dear to them," said Roberto, "so you ought not to be astonished by the retreat to which they want to condemn themselves."

"So my gratitude, if I want to express it, can only be addressed to unknown beauties."

"Sire Ferdinand has charged me to tell you that he will welcome you with pleasure if you wish to appear before him."

"Please take me to him; I'm ready to follow you."

Roberto led him through a long sequence of apartments; they arrived at Don Juan's room.

The latter, having looked at the troubadour, could not retain the exclamation that escaped him, and Savary, having considered him attentively, cried: "Treacherous Don Juan! I've found you at last!"

Throwing his guitar away, he hastened to draw his sharp blade. But Don Juan was unarmed and Savary noticed it. "Coward," he said, "give thanks to my honesty, which does not permit me to take you in treason. I leave you these vile means."

"It ill befits the imprudent Savary to threaten me when he is in my power. You will not get out of the château to which your misfortune has brought you."

"If you command it my fate is decided," said Savary, "but I am not alone; numerous friends accompany me."

"Your life will respond for me to their enterprise."

"What have you done with Bélisène?"

"What does it matter, since you will never see her again?"

"She is in this château."

"She is lost to you."

"What do you mean?"

"Her honor has constrained her to become my wife."

"Monster! And I shall not take your life?"

Carried away by fury, the troubadour threw himself upon Don Juan, but the latter ever cowardly, avoided him by a prompt flight, and returned shortly afterwards surrounded by his men-at-arms, whom he ordered to seize Savary. The brave knight, exasperated by his amour as much as his anger, did not want to surrender without a fight; he backed up against the wall, and threatened the assailants.

Don Juan was urging them on when Bélisène hurtled into the room. As the sight of her, Don Juan, by a spontaneous movement, armed himself with a squire's sword, as if he blushed to be alone without combating while everyone attacked.

The unexpected joy of seeing Bélisène again charmed the amorous Savary to such an extent that he ceased to defend himself, uniquely occupied in contemplating his cherished mistress. Don Juan's satellites, oblivious to the delicacy of sentiments, seized that favorable moment and, before the troubadour could recover from his first surprise, he was seized and disarmed.

At the sight of the sword menacing her lover, Bélisène, braving all consideration, had launched herself to his aid, but that courageous action did not last long; terror prevailed and she fell to the floor, unconscious.

At that new spectacle, Savary, who had paid little heed to the bonds with which he was charged, uttered cries of despair, struggled against the soldiers, and more redoubtable after his defeat, still frightened them.

"Unworthy warrior, do you not feel in your soul any trace of the nobility of valor that animates all knights? Are you only ever able by vile means to dispute the possession of your darling with rivals? Wretch! It is by the aid of your men-at-arms that you triumph, but tremble; I have not yet lost all hope; avengers remain to me..."

Don Juan interrupted him. "It ill befits my prisoner to insult me! Take him away and let a somber cell be his last dwelling."

"Barbarian! If any shadow of generosity still remains in you, do not take me away from here before Bélisène returns to life."

"Obey me!" ordered Don Juan; and, in spite of his vain resistance, poor Savary was taken to the prison designated by Don Juan.

While he was struggling, one of his assailants, whose face he could not see because it was covered with a helmet, took his hand and said: "Have courage!"

Those few words rendered some peace to his irritated soul; he hoped that the sinister château might contain friends, and, more tranquil, he resigned himself to his fate.

He was taken via several detours to a fairly large room that seemed to him to be hollowed out of the rock; he was left alone, and an earthenware lamp was lit by way of illumination. As soon as the soldiers had withdrawn, he examined his fatal dwelling attentively; he saw then that the floor, the ceiling and two sides of the wall had been carved into the living rock, while the other two sides were formed by the union of several immense crudely sculpted stones.

Chapter XII: The Abduction

While the crusaders were scaling the walls of Carcassonne, and, forced to fight against their will, the Raymonds followed the besiegers, Arembert and Amaury de Montfort put into execution a plot that they had been hatching for some time. Equally convinced that, in spite of their power, their merit and their amour, they would never succeed in obtaining the hand of the Princesses—Arembert that of Aliénor and Amaury that of Sancia—they had agreed to choose a favorable moment to abduct them, and to constrain them by violence to form ties to which they would have constantly refused.

Amaury was quite certain that before long, neither the King of Aragon nor the Comte de Toulouse would be in a position to avenge themselves for such an enterprise. However, he did not judge it appropriate to inform Earl de Montfort of what he was about to attempt, convinced that if he succeeded he would be approved, whereas he would be disavowed if success did not crown his audacity.

As we have already said, the moment of the attack appeared to the perverse couple to be the most propitious. In spite of their vain clamors, which constraint immediately repressed, the two Princesses were abducted; Arembert took charge himself of taking them to Saint-Félix, where he thought that no one would divine their presence.

Everything succeeded; Aliénor and the gentle Sancia implored Heaven in vain; Heaven abandoned them for some time to the wickedness of the two villains. When he arrived at the principal seat of his barony, Arembert summoned Roberto and Don Juan; he confided the afflicted beauties to their care, and, without wanting either to listen to them or to pause for a moment, he resumed as quickly as possible the road to Carcassonne, where he hoped to reappear soon enough to avoid any suspicion that might be able to attain him.

Roberto, still eager to obey his sovereign's will, took the Princesses to a chamber situated on the western side of the château. The room was vast, furnished with the Gothic magnificence of the era; some of the window-panes were covered with paintings through which the setting sum launched its colored rays in a thousand fashions. Roberto closed the door carefully. He did not want to confide the service of the ladies to Germaine, for he feared her loquacity, and Arembert had instructed him that, above all, no one must learn that the Princesses of Aragon and Toulouse and the young Princesse de Foix were resident in the same place.

When Aliénor and Sancia found themselves alone, far from allowing themselves to be overwhelmed by dolor, they consoled one another mutually; hope could not be extinguished in their hearts. When they thought of their lovers, they retained the sweet assurance that they would soon attempt to liberate them. Aliénor, however, was even calmer than Sancia; she knew Adémar, she was certain that he would attempt anything in order to merit further gratitude.

Thus the first moments went by, in which others might perhaps have yielded to tears, so much is a brave lover able to inspire confidence in the woman whose tenderness he seeks. Fortunate is the knight made illustrious by success! Rarely will he see the heart of the beauty he idolizes closed.

One arriving at the first enclosure of the cottage, Adémar knocked lightly, although he did not believe that the hermit had returned from Carcassonne. A veiled woman appeared, and it seemed to the warriors that their costume intimidated her; however, in a faint voice, she asked them what they wanted. Adémar replied to her that he was a friend of the hermit, and that they had both come to wait for him in his dwelling. Then the woman, seeing in any case that resistance would be futile, opened the light door and introduced them.

The veil the young woman wore did not permit her face to be perceived; Raymond's helmet, which he had continued to wear, masked his features; only Adémar had removed his.

At the sight of his noble and gracious appearance, the young woman lost her fear. She was about to question him when a richly-clad child came into the room.

At the sight of the boy Raymond, who studied him, could not help asking whether he was not the son of the Vicomte de Carcassonne. At that question the young woman's fear was redoubled to such a point that her knees gave way and were about to let her fall.

Adémar hastened to support her, while Raymond, taking off his helmet, exclaimed: "Have I the good fortune of encountering Vicomtesse Agnès here?"

At those words, all terror was dissipated. Agnès—for it was her—removed her veil; she had recognized her relative, her husband's friend, and no longer felt anything but a mild joy. The memory of Roger, however, came to mingle some regret with the momentary pleasure. The pallor reappeared in Agnès' cheeks. She took her son in her arms and used his blond hair to wipe away the tears that chagrin had drawn from her.

Adémar and Raymond, trying to console her, made her hope for the prompt deliverance of her husband; and, wanting at least to distract her, asked her to tell them by what means she had been saved.

"The crusaders," she told them, "were already masters of the city; my guards were still defending my palace when the hermit, whose conduct is so mysterious, appeared to me, emerging from a room forgotten for many years, in which no one wanted to live, so much were the spirits feared that seemed to have established their abode there.

"The fleshless figure of the hermit, and his singular costume, intimidated me at first. Soon, however, his words reassured me; he did not take long to inspired confidence in me, and I was disposed to go with him. Odon did not want to abandon the Vicomte. The hermit took me into the room from which he had just emerged; he locked the door and then he led me into a corridor and down a stairway.

"Finally, after a long march, during which we traversed subterranean tunnels entirely unknown to me, we found ourselves in the middle of a group of rocks placed on an island formed by the Aude as it flows toward the city; a boat was waiting for us there; the hermit started to row. As soon as we had reached the opposite bank, we were received by several men-at-arms, who served as our escort. The hermit wanted to take me on his horse, but I refused, not wanting to abandon my son; I mounted a palfrey and we departed.

"I noticed that the soldiers who accompanied us were all wearing the crusaders' cross. We passed near the camp, where no one thought of stopping us, and, continuing our route without stopping to rest, we arrived at this hermitage. Scarcely had the hermit deposited me than, after giving me a few necessary instructions, he left again."

Agnès concluded her brief story thus. Raymond assured her that the tempest would calm down, and that a day would finally dawn that would see her sitting on the throne of Carcassonne. The Vicomtesse sighed profoundly, but she dared not yield to that pleasant hope. They had been talking for a little while longer when the sound of horses attracted their attention; they got up and went to the door.

Suddenly, Agnès cried out, and fell into her husband's arms. Having descended precipitately from his horse, the latter responded to his darling's tender caresses. Raymond and Adémar shared their transports; in their turn they were able to embrace Roger, as well as Odon and the hermit. All those various individuals, glad of their reunion, spent moments of joy, but which amour soon came to trouble.

Adémar and Raymond awaited the return of the troubadour Savary with greater impatience, but he did not reappear. The evening passed without their seeing him; night covered the globe, and Savary had not yet descended from the heights of Saint-Felix.

Adémar was quivering with anger; sinister presentiments seemed to announce Savary's arrest. Slumber had fled his eyelids; a thousand thoughts whirled in his head. Finally, he decided to go to the château himself; he had no doubt that the Baron was absent, so he had nothing to fear. In any case, Arembert had only forbidden his presence so long as he was stubborn in following the Raymonds' party, and Adémar was determined to pretend, if necessary, going to that extremity in order to achieve the deliverance of his beauty.

As soon as the sun's first rays had colored the Orient, Adémar leapt out of bed. The hermit was already up; he smiled at the young knight. Soon afterwards, Odon and Raymond came to join them; Roger, less diligent, was forgetting himself with his young spouse.

"Noble hermit," said Adémar, "Suffer that I execute a design that can have no unfortunate consequence. Savary de Mauléon has not come back; we are certain that the Château de Saint-Félix contains the Princesses of Aragon and Toulouse. I want to go into it; I want to make sure myself of what we dread."

"My dear Adémar," said Odon, "beware of falling into the power of that Arembert, who has so promptly passed in your regard from sentiments of amity to those of indifference."

"No, Adémar," said the hermit, "have no fear of the Baron. You can appease his anger with a single word if he appears irritated against you."

"Oh, Seigneur," said Adémar, "if you know the word that can serve me as a talisman, hasten to inform me of it."

"Ask him what he has done with your father," said the hermit, coldly.

"My father!"

"Your father."

"You, who appear not to be a stranger to anything," said Odon to the hermit, "if you do not want us to know the secret of our birth, will you at least tell us whether the bonds of blood, perhaps less strong than those of amity, attach Adémar and Odon together?"

"Amiable brothers, embrace one another," said the hermit, tenderly.

With those words the most touching scene took place. Adémar and Odon could not separate; the sweet names *brother* and *friend* escaped their lips; they wept with joy and, joining their hands, they swore an oath not to quit one another again.

O sweet and pure expansions of fraternal tenderness, how delightful your charms are! What friend, what lover, can replace a brother? Who can share our pleasures and suspend our chagrins better than him? With what other can one prefer to travel the road of life? Who can be a better confidant of one's secrets, and to whom can one testify a greater tenderness? Great God, you know whether, in my eyes, my brother is a half of myself, whether his happiness occupies me incessantly, whether the thought of him mingles with all my happy thoughts, whether his charming face embellishes my hours of chagrin. O my brother, always be my dearest friend; the same sentiments animate you; my fraternal love is shared by your amiable heart, as never changes... Change! Could we? It would require Heaven to take away our hearts, and to give us ice instead.

Odon wanted to depart with Adémar, he begged not to be separated from him; but the hermit opposed that resolution gently. He asserted that Adémar was able to enter the château freely, that his presence could not excite any suspicion, while that of a stranger might give birth to dangerous ones.

It was necessary to yield to the hermit's arguments. It was decided that Adémar would depart for the château alone; desiring to do so, he did not take long to set forth, after Raymond had recommended him urgently to look after interests, Odon his personal safety and the hermit a consummate prudence. They accompanied him to the edge of the forest, and after separating from his companions, he marched toward Saint-Félix. He followed the charming valley crowned by the heights of Clauzades, and climbed the hill on which the town is built by means of the sinuous path on the eastern side.

Chapter XIII: Adémar's Return to Saint-Félix

As soon as Adémar had appeared before the château, the guards, who recognized him, let their joy burst forth. By virtue of his likeable qualities, Adémar had always been able to make those who surrounded him cherish him. The squires, the pages and the varlets ran to met him in order to testify the pleasure they felt on seeing him again. Roberto was not the last to present himself; in spite of his grim appearance, he cherished Adémar, whose childhood he had seen. Above all, however, Germaine was delighted by the young knight's return; Adémar, out of generosity, sometimes listened to the old woman's stories, and Germaine's gratitude had no limits.

"Oh, genteel youth," she exclaimed, on perceiving him, "it's doubtless the Queen of the Angels that is bringing you back; come, come quickly, for since your departure, the Baron's manse has become the thousand times sadder. One can no longer walk there when night has fallen; brigands and phantoms dispute its possession."

"Will you never shut up, wretch?" said Roberto. "Does the fear of the dungeon no longer frighten you?"

"Since the loyal knight has returned, I no longer fear anything," said Germaine.

"Thank you, Germaine for your affection," said Adémar, "but I agree with Roberto; it isn't appropriate to say everything one sees."

"And above all, Monseigneur," Roberto added, "everything one imagines."

"During the Sire Baron's absence, to what knight has command of the château been confided?" Adémar asked.

"A friend of Sire Arembert's governs us," said Roberto.

"Do I know him?"

"No, Monseigneur."

"What is his name?"

"Ferdinand."

"That name is Spanish. But has no one come here during my absence?"

"Except for Don Ferdinand, no knight has appeared?"

"What! You haven't received any troubadour?"

"No," said Roberto.

Adémar did not take his questions any further; he understood that they wanted to make a mystery of Savary's arrival. What had become of the gracious troubadour, though? Adémar promised himself to spare no effort to find out.

Informed of his arrival, knowing how Arembert considered him, Don Juan appeared to receive him. At the sight of him, Adémar could not help being struck by the appearance of falsity that was imprinted on the Spaniard's features; so, far from opening up to him, he maintained a reserve that was far from his character.

Don Juan, knowing that he had come from the crusaders' camp, pretended not to have received any recent news of it; he asked what the army and Baron de Saint-Félix were doing.

"I have not seen him since the attack," Adémar replied. "We were fighting on opposite sides."

"You have doubtless come here to fulfill some mission on his behalf?" asked Don Juan.

"Arembert had not confided one to me. I quit the army of the crusaders because I did not want to follow them to the Comte de Toulouse's lands."

Having said that, Adémar bowed slightly, and, without wanting to prolong a conversation that displeased him, he retired to his apartment.

While Aubin, his squire, aided by a few varlets, were ridding him of his armor, he saw, not without surprise, a piece of paper fall from the ceiling. He did not want to appear to have perceived it while there were witnesses with him, but as soon as the varlets had withdrawn he picked it up and, unfolding it, read these words: *Aliénor and Sancia hope for everything from a brave knight*.

"Yes," exclaimed Adémar, impetuously, without thinking that he might be overheard, "Yes, I shall do everything to steal you from the villains who retain you."

Then someone rapped seven times above his head, and his joy was complete when he realized that the prison of the beautiful Princesse de Toulouse was on the floor above the one on which he resided; he no longer occupied himself with anything but a means of being able to communicate with her.

When he had arrived at the château, Aliénor, standing at her window, had recognized him in spite of the distance. She saw with pleasure that his entrance was not that of a person being dragged; she thought that he must have a reliable means of being tranquil in his enemies' midst. Soon, a confused noise became audible in beneath the princesses' chamber; it was at that moment that Aliénor, discovering a gap in the parquet, had confided to hazard the note that we have reported.

Adémar, for his part, was thinking of his plan of attack. The exterior dispositions of the château were sufficiently familiar to him to know what he had to do in order to reach the door that retained the beautiful prisoners, but that was not all; it was necessary to open that door and find an exit that would permit their escape from the château, which scarcely seemed easy, especially at a time when the war that was rumbling in the vicinity had necessitated a redoubling of precautions, and when a soldier was place on sentry duty in every turret.

The thought of seducing Roberto occurred to him, but Roberto appeared to be attached to his master; it would be dangerous not to succeed in gaining him if it were attempted. Thus, Adémar spent the entire day conversing with the princesses by means of a cord, sometimes turning projects over in his head, forgetting Savary and the friends that were waiting for him in the hermitage in the forest.

Abandoned in his cell to his reflections, Savary deplored his misfortune; he accused fortune of having betrayed him at the moment when he hoped to get closer to Bélisène. Finally, wanting to seek distraction, he played a warrior ballad that he had once composed on the Raymonds' crusades.[42]

The château of his brave ancestors,
Black battlements, ancient towers,
Raymond abandons those places
To fight against the infidels;
He attacks the impure Muslims
To confound their martial valor.
O Sion! Soon above your walls
The white banner will float!

Alix, her eyes bathed with tears
Wants to arrest him still;
The scarf with his green colors
Adorns the hero she adores;
But Raymond sighs in his heart
After an immortal palm.
The French are always victorious
When he is armed by his beauty.

Already the resounding bronze
Has proclaimed the hour of departure;
Raymond draws away, groaning,
And from Alix and his dwelling
He has seized his buckler;
And flown to his noble enterprise.
A gallant and perfect knight,
Amour and honor is his motto.

That ballad and a few others suspended Savary's irritations but did not make them disappear. The rest of the day went by, and his situation was unchanged. It remained the same during the night and all the following day.

---

[42] Author's notes: "The music by the author of the words can be found chez Sieber in Paris."

He was beginning to despair of being aided by Adémar and Raymond; he was afraid that they might have been persuaded that he had left Saint-Félix and had gone elsewhere. Finally, the day having gone by slowly, he saw nightfall arrive with a vague presentiment that it would not pass in silence.

In the evening the door of his cell opened; Don Juan appeared. On seeing him, Savary felt his blood inflamed.

Don Juan approached him and said: "Well, Marquis de Mauléon, does ou captivity seem tolerable to you?"

"Yes," said Savary, "when Don Juan does not come to afflict me with his presence."

"Savary's arrogance proves to me that he has not yet lost all hope of being rescued."

"Don Juan's speech convinces me that he fears that I might be."

"Cease to believe in your deliverance. Your friends have appeared; they have spoken to me, and they will not worry on your account henceforth."

"What have you been able to say to them?"

"That a minstrel came to request hospitality; that he was well received, and departed to go to Toulouse."

"You're lying," Savary said. "They know that I would not have gone away without having rejoined them. They know the motive that brought me to the château."

"What! You knew that Bélisène...?"

Cleverly, Savary said: "...was here; and the friends that accompanied me were knights from her father's court."

"Your life will answer to me for their enterprises!" said Don Juan.

"And your will answer to the Comte de Foix for everything you have undertaken against his daughter or me. Learn, moreover, that you are known at the court of the Comte de Toulouse, and that the battalions of those powerful princes will soon come to besiege these walls in which so many unfortunates are assembled, and where the daughter of the Raymonds is also detained, with that of the King of Aragon."

"They know everything!" said Don Juan, stupefied.

"Nothing is unknown," said Savary, "and vengeance is nigh. Yes, it will soon descend; ramparts and cells cannot defend you against your irritated enemies, powerful and numerous."

Frightened by what Savary had just told him, the vile Don Juan, thinking that he could already see the combined troops of three princes climbing the hill in order to do battle on the ridge that served as a base for the town and the château, withdrew, darting a sideways glance at the man he had come to torment, and who, on the contrary, had thrown dread into his despicable soul.

Left alone, Savary rejoiced in the effect produced by his words; he was now convinced that his friends had not yet presented themselves. In order to reflect on his amour, he threw himself on to his bed fully dressed, after having taken care to pour oil into the lamp that he had been given.

He had been lying down for some time when, on turning his eyes toward the lamp, place on a stone table in the middle of the cell, it seemed to him that the flame was violently agitated, as if a current of air had just struck it. He turned round and, was utterly astonished when he perceived a warrior of the most abundant stature emerge from the wall, traverse his prison, and disappear into the opposite wall.

Fearing that he had been the victim of an illusion, wanting to assure himself as to whether he was really awake, he sat up; but he could no longer see anything; everything was profoundly silent—and yet he was certain that he had not been deceived by his imagination.

The idea of two secret doors immediately came to mind; he picked up his lamp and ran to the side from which the individual he had seen had come. He set about examining the walls more carefully, without being able to find anything, so closely joined were the stones. As he had difficulty in believing in a supernatural apparition, however, he concluded that the doors he could not identify must rotate on pivots sunk into the stone above and below. He tried in vain to agitate the paving stones; the resisted his efforts, which had no more success against the opposite wall.

Then it occurred to him that the warrior might be an assassin set by Don Juan to dispatch him, who, having perceived that he was not asleep, had retired in order to come back later. Troubled by that thought, he promised himself not to go back to sleep.

An hour went by in that situation. Savary was beginning to hope that he would not reappear when, the hidden door having just opened, he perceived the hermit who had welcomed him in the forest of Caillavel, and who had subsequently sought him out in the camp at Carcassonne, still clad in his red robe. On seeing him, Savary lost all dread; he no longer saw him as anything but a liberator and, without waiting advanced toward him.

The hermit, who was carrying a torch, having also recognized the troubadour, set the torch down

"God be praised" he said to him. "He has finally permitted me to find you. For more than an hour I have been searching for you in these immense subterrains."

"What thanks do I not owe you!" said Savary. "Especially at the moment when your presence delivers me from a mortal dread."

"Do you have some danger to fear?" asked the hermit.

"A little while ago I saw a warrior traverse my sad dwelling, and I confess that I feared he might be an emissary of Don Juan."

"That was me."

"Why didn't you stop?"

"I did not know you were here; on the contrary, I thought you were at another extremity. Seeing the light here, I slipped through quietly in order not to be perceived by whoever was in this cell; I have only recently been informed of your arrest, which I suspected. Have courage, Chevalier, your captivity will not last long."

"How is Bélisène?"

"It will not be long before you are with her. Let us quit this cell, however; come to where I want you to spend the rest of the night."

So saying, he picked up his torch, and, followed by Savary, he marched straight toward the wall. When he touched a spring, the paving stone rotated on its pivot, and, after having passed through they entered a spacious tunnel that divided into several branches and in which several staircases ended. They climbed one, at the end of which there were stopped by wooden paneling. The Hermit touched a button and caused a panel to slide in a grove, and they found themselves in a room.

The person who inhabited it, surprised to receive a visit from behind the tapestry, seized his sword and was preparing to fall upon the indiscreet visitors, when, having considered them, he was only able to testify the pleasure he had in seeing them; it was Adémar.

"It is necessary to agree, Sire Chevalier," the hermit said to him, with an uncustomary gaiety, "that our entry into your abode is not at all seemly."

"Seigneur, if I dare call you that, as one always sees you surrounded by mystery," said Adémar, "I would have been more astonished if you had come to see me via the banal route of the door."

"My children, I cannot stay with you long," said the hermit. "It's necessary that I go to where other unfortunates summon me. As for you, Marquis de Mauléon, you must stay here until tomorrow evening; if anyone comes into Adémar's room, withdraw behind that hidden door. And you, my dear Adémar, hope, like Savary, that both of you will soon see your plaintive darlings again. Adieu; I cannot stay any longer."

He embraced them both, still without taking of his vast hood. Then he went to one of the corners of the room and stamped his foot hard; a trap-door opened and engulfed him.

"Everything about that hermit is extraordinary," said Savary. "He alone knows more secret passages than all the Barons of Occitania, and I don't doubt that he could do Sire Arembert the honors of his Château de Saint-Félix."

Abandoning pleasantry then, the two knights recounted their adventures. Adémar learned, not without astonishment, the Comtesse Bélisène had been brought by Don Juan to the same place that also detained the princesses of Aragon and Toulouse.

Chapter XIV: The Declaration

After having hesitated for some time over what he ought to do, the imprudent and cowardly Don Juan, believing that he could already see the triple ensigns of Aragon, Foix and Toulouse floating over Saint-Félix, thought that it was necessary for him to confer with Adémar on the means of defense that it was appropriate to employ in such a circumstance. Having himself preceded by a page destined to announce him, he presented himself in the apartment of Aliénor's lover, who, at that moment, was conversing by turns with his beauty and his friend.

On hearing violent knocking on the door of the room, Adémar and Savary were momentarily troubled; the latter hastened to return to the hidden door while Adémar opened the door. His surprise was not mediocre when he saw Don Juan appear.

The latter, wanting to begin in a solemn manner, asked Adémar whether he was sincerely attached to Baron de Saint-Félix.

"Permit me to represent to you, Seigneur," Adémar said, "that your question is most extraordinary. On what occasion have you come, in the middle of the night, to talk to me about such a subject?"

"We are threatened, Sire Chevalier, by an imminent attack."

"What!" said Adémar. "What enemies could rise up against Sire Arembert? He has been at peace with all his neighbors for years."

"The greatest adversaries are going to attack us."

"What has the friend of the legate Milon and Comte Simon de Montfort to fear?"

"He will have to combat the King of Aragon and the Comtes de Foix and Toulouse."

"Do you think so, Seigneur? By what insult has Baron de Saint-Félix attracted such powerful adversaries? Since when has war been declared? For only two days ago they were all together in the same camp..."

"It is yesterday that his danger commenced."

"In that case, we have all the time necessary to think of the defense. But what can have given birth to that inconceivable discord?"

"Amour."

"Please explain, Seigneur," said Adémar. "I don't understand this mystery."

"The amity that you have for Arembert, and the gratitude that you owe him, engage me not to hide anything from you. You should know that, drawn by his ardor, the Baron has abducted the daughter of the Comte de Toulouse, that young Amaury de Montfort is also the kidnapper of the beautiful Sancia d'Aragon, and that I, who am speaking to you, am that of Bélisène de Foix."

"Chevalier, I beg you to tell me that what you are saying is only a fable with which you want to amuse me."

"How could that serve me?" said Don Juan

"I confess that I really don't know; nevertheless, I would prefer it if your speech were only an imposture. When I left the crusaders' camp, the rumor of the abduction of the two Princesses had spread; everyone was murmuring about the audacity of the discourteous chevaliers capable of committing such an action, and I cannot get over the surprise into which you have cast me in making me this strange confidence, but, in spite of its improbability, what astonishes me even more in all this is that you have yourself abducted the Comtesse de Foix. What ridiculous hope could you have nursed momentarily?"

Proudly, Don Juan said: "The blood of a sovereign Princesse can be allied without difficulty with that of Don Juan d'Astorga, Admiral of Castile."

"Every word that you pronounce, Seigneur, has the gift of adding further to my surprise. You are the Admiral of Castile?"

"I am," said Don Juan.

"You are, and you employ violence for pleasure! What can you be thinking, then? It seems to me that the illustrious Bélisène is promised to the Marquis de Mauléon. Doubtless you have proposed to fight him and he has refused to satisfy you? For how can one imagine that Don Juan d'Astorga, Admiral of Castile, has not sought to meet his rival with arms in hand?"

Without replying to that question, Don Juan said: "You see, Sire Adémar, that it is necessary to put ourselves in a state to meet an imminent attack. At daybreak tomorrow we will engage Arembert to return to us; it is necessary that his return will find us ready to repel the attack."

"I am ready to do everything that is appropriate," said Adémar. "Nevertheless, it seems to me that it will be necessary to let me speak to the Princesses; we can find out from them whether it is necessary to prepare for an imminent attack. I have the honor of having been introduced to them in the camp; I don't doubt that they will experience some satisfaction in seeing me again."

Deceived by the air of candor that Adémar put into his last words, Don Juan agreed to his proposal. He asked him whether he wanted to go to the room they occupied right away.

"Of course," said Adémar. "It's necessary not to lose a minute."

Fearing, however, that his presence might cause a surprise that would cause the scales to fall from Don Juan's credulous eyes, he wanted to warn the princesses that he was about to appear in their room escorted by the Spaniard. He summoned his squire Aubin, and, charging him with the commission, he sent him to Aliénor.

As a skillful valet, who could take a hint, Aubin took great care to acquit his mission in the most adroit fashion. He succeeded marvelously, informing Aliénor in front of the soldiers that accompanied her that Adémar, deceiving the enemies, would not be long in rendering her his homage.

He returned thereafter to his master, who, less agitated, placed himself beside Don Juan, hating him less at that moment, while Savary, emerging from the redoubt that his anger had urged him to quit a hundred times, returned to the room, swearing to himself that he would pay him back dearly for his temporary triumph.

In spite of the desire to dissimulate the secret sentiments by which she was animated, Aliénor could not entire hide in looking at the fortunate Adémar the satisfaction she experienced. He began from that moment on to see hope born in his heart. He was received with a particular distinction, while neither Sancia or Aliénor deigned to cast a glance at Don Juan.

In spite of his pride, the latter was beginning to find his situation painful when a squire arrived in haste to inform him that a host of men-at-arms had appeared at the gates of the château. The Spaniard, fearing that they were the enemies he dreaded immeasurably, launched himself out of the apartment to give his orders, without thinking of taking Adémar with him, As soon as the latter had seen him draw away, he threw himself at Aliénor's knees.

"Divine Princesse," he said, "How sorry I shall be if it is your liberators who are arriving."

Aliénor, seeking to be proud, said: "Are you thinking about what you are saying, Chevalier?"

"Yes, Mademoiselle," said Adémar. "I would like to be the only one who can render you liberty; I would like you to owe happiness and life—everything, in sum—to me. I have so much need of your gratitude in order for you to forgive...O Heaven what am I saying? Unless it is without hope, and in which case I would rather descend into the tomb before having confessed how dear you are to me."

"What am I hearing?" cried Arembert, furiously, suddenly appearing in the room.

PART THREE

Chapter I: Knavery

O Amour, of whom ancient mythology once understood so well how far your power extends; you who, under the appearance of weakness, is able to rule the universe at your whim; you who, in the world submissive to your power, only takes pleasure in tumult, tears of joy; you who, without discernment, strikes the virtuous knight and the ferocious tyrant with the same arrow, why do you toy thus with the mortals you seduce without difficulty? Why do you not respect distances? What pleasure can you savor in seeing the host of unfortunates that you never cease to make? Would it not have been better for the valiant Adémar to sigh for a beauty that he could hope one day to obtain? For Don Juan, Arembert and Amaury to be able to bear their tenderness to demoiselles who would not hold them in horror? And above all, could you not have dispensed with giving birth to a dangerous rivalry between Adémar and Baron de Saint-Félix?

Arembert, whom you did not allow to breathe, and who united in his soul your incendiary flames with the other passions by which he was devoured, could not stay long in the crusaders' camp. A muffled rumor that was circulating reached him, which made him fear that young Raymond, instead of taking the road to Toulouse, as his father had commanded him to do, had plunged into his lands in order to search there for his lover and his sister. Another thought had also tormented him; he feared the fatal hermit. He dared not hope that the individual in question, still occupied in doing good, would remain inactive in such a circumstance. No long-

207

er being able to command his anxiety, he took his leave publicly of the legate and the crusaders, at the moment when they were about to elect a Prince to whom the conquests made and still to make would belong.

In such a circumstance, Amaury could not leave. He promised Arembert to come and join him soon. The Baron pretended that he was going to prepare his château in order to receive the crusaders there when they passed through on their way to attack the town of Lavaur. Followed by his squadrons, charged like him with the legate's benedictions, he departed promptly. In spite of his desire not to suffer any delay on the way, a storm constrained him to rest for a while in Castelnaudary, but as soon as it was possible for Arembert to resume his route he did so, and it was about midnight when he arrived at his dwelling.

A secret terror seized him when the rays of the moon, reflecting from its high turrets, permitted him to perceive it; he recalled all that he had suffered in that château, and his imagination was already making him see a host of phantoms that were flying to meet him, clad in white draperies and holding heavy chains, or carrying candles whose pale light added a further degree to the horror that surrounded them.

Before having the drawbridge lowered, Don Juan, who feared a surprise, took all the precautions necessary for the safety of the château, but which served marvelously to augment Arembert's impatience. Finally, after he had been duly recognized, he was permitted to enter. Don Juan wanted to hug him in his arms, but the Baron, receiving his caresses without much gratitude, immediately asked Roberto whether everything was in order. Roberto replied according to his master's wishes; then it was possible for the Spaniard to communicate his fears.

Arembert was beginning to share them when Don Juan, making him party to the defensive measures he had taken, mentioned Adémar. At the name of the knight, Arembert shuddered; he asked when he had come back; he was told that he had reappeared only that morning. But how great was the

Baron's anger when Don Juan told him that he had thought he ought to confide everything to Adémar, and that he was with the Princesses at that moment!

Stamping on the ground with fury, the Baron, without waiting to reply to his friend, commanded that he be illuminated and taken to Aliénor's apartment. He was obeyed and his anger reached its peak when, on entering the room, he saw Adémar on his knees before the Comtesse de Toulouse, and the latter looking at him with a gaze that was not irritated,

"What do I see?" he cried. "Such audacity, then, can animate the obscure Adémar? And can the proud Aliénor suffer that a simple knight dare to speak to her with so much arrogance?"

"I have much more reason for surprise that the presumptuous Baron de Saint-Félix has dared to abduct me from my father," said Aliénor. "Doubtless Aliénor de Toulouse only owes her sentiments to a sovereign who is worthy of her. But I am in captivity; Adémar wanted to render me the liberty that I have lost, and, whatever his imprudence might be, it does not approach in my eyes the insolence of Arembert."

Thus, by means of ambiguous words, Aliénor, without revealing her secret thoughts, nevertheless gave some hope to her amiable knight. Adémar, in his turn, having quit the respectful position in which amour had placed him before his lover, looking with assurance at the greatly irritated Baron, spoke to him in these terms:

"Yes, powerful Baron, I am without fortune; my existence, until today, has only depended on you, and if gratitude did not speak loudly in my soul, perhaps I would even dare to demand a reckoning for the insulting words that you have just addressed to me."

"You, Adémar?" said Arembert.

"Yes, Sire Baron, me. If my audacity has gone so far as to entertain for Princesse Aliénor the tenderness to which she has given birth, nothing henceforth can be imposed on me. I would confront without shivering the entire crusader army;

thus, a single knight, whatever his valor, cannot intimidate Adémar."

"Young man," said Arembert, "I do not think you doubt my courage, but you are the last person against whom I want to measure myself."

Adémar drew his sword. "That is too much, Seigneur; such an offense cannot be suffered; I demand a reckoning."

"You shall not have one," said Arembert. "Would you want my hand to be steeped in your blood? That final crime is all I lack…! What am I saying? Guards, someone arrest and disarm this reckless fool—but he'll answer for him to me."

"Woe betide the first man who advances!" said Adémar.

"Baron," said Aliénor, "will you, who, until this day have never merited the reproach one makes to cowards, refuse combat?"

"Against him I would refuse it a thousand times," said Arembert.

"Is that scorn or is it indifference?" said Adémar. "Do I not seem worthy of your blows?"

"What does it matter what my motive is?" said Arembert. "Get out, and do not make any reply. Run to shut yourself in your room, and only reappear when I permit you to do so."

"Sire Arembert," said Adémar. "Until this day I have enclosed in my bosom a desire too long hidden; but at the moment when you speak to me with the despotism of a master to his slave, or a father to his son, I can no longer remain silent. Tell me who I am, and *what have you done with my father?*"

"With your father? Your father? Oh, wretch, what word have you pronounced? Into what trap have you led me? Your Father? Well…no, you shall never know the secret of your birth; I will not give it to you thus, armed against me. Blood, treason…oh, how I suffer!"

Then, pursued by his memories, he forgot his jealousy; he abandoned Aliénor and fled at a precipitate pace. Don Juan accompanied him, Roberto did not quit him; and before a minute had gone by, the Princesses were left alone with Adémar.

When everyone had gone, the knight, ceasing to think about the scene that had just passed, only remembered the audacity of his declaration; he trembled that Aliénor might now heap him with her anger; he dared not raise his eyes toward her, and for a second time, he fell to his knees, without proffering a word.

Sancia, softened by the knight's posture, looked at Aliénor with an expression that seemed to intercede on his behalf.

The Princesse de Toulouse herself found no great assistance in her pride; she did not say anything; she was unable to make a move. Finally, making an effort to control herself, while her charming cheeks were covered with a vivid blush, she said: "Great is your presumption, Chevalier; I will consent to forget what you told me just now, but on the promise that you will not speak of it again before your exploits and the services that you have render to my father have given you the right to do so."

Intoxicated by his joy, born of the words that he had just heard, Adémar, still on his knees, dragged himself to the feet of the Princesse and, seizing the hem of her robe in a respectful fashion, he kissed it ecstatically.

Too emotional to recoil, Aliénor was still leaning back in Sancia's arms when a new sound was heard, constraining Adémar to rise to his feet promptly. Roberto appeared in the room and said to Adémar: "Sire Chevalier, Monseigneur Arembert is asking for you; he begs you not to make him wait."

Aliénor, addressing Adémar, who did not seem disposed to obey, engaged him to do as the Baron wished. Not being able to refuse what the lady he adored ordered him to do, Adémar bowed to her and, after darting a languorous glance at her, he went to join the Baron.

The latter was waiting for him in a cabinet that served as an oratory. The walls, up to the height of the birth of the vault, were covered by a magnificent velvet curtain on which a skillful hand had embroidered the Arembert family's arms, which represented silver towers in an azure field, and greyhounds of gules on a silver field. The arcades of the vault were sculpted in the form of Moorish ornaments; and the escutcheon of the suzerain was also on the keystone. The altar that had once sanctified the chamber was no longer there; only the lamps, all lit, were still present.

Arembert was sitting in an armchair ornamented with elegant sculptures; there was a similar one next to it for Adémar. When he saw him come in, he appeared to emerge from a profound torpor caused by the reflections that he had had time to make. Adémar, on examining his face, discovered there an expression of embarrassment and constraint that was not customary, for Arembert's face usually bore either the signs of arrogance of those of suffering.

"Come closer, Adémar," he said, on perceiving him. Come and sit down beside me, and dispose yourself to lend me all your attention. You want to know the name of your father? Well, I shall lift the veil that covers the secret of your birth. Adémar, you are my son."

"Oh, Monseigneur!" exclaimed Adémar. "What are you telling me?"

"That discovery, I see, speaks feebly to your soul, since you are not in my arms. I ought to have expected that; my past conduct must have distanced you from me."

"Sir Baron, I will not hide from you that your confidence seems to me so extraordinary that I fear being the victim of some illusion."

"In summoning you," said Arembert, "and deciding to tell you everything, my intention has been to lift all your doubts in that regard. My father was still alive. Proud of the antiquity of his race, which went back to the advent of Pharamond among the Gauls, it would never have entered his head to contract an alliance that would lose anything of the purity of a blood that had been until then without admixture. Imbued with such sentiments, it was only with indignation that he would have welcomed the prayers of my amour.

"Alas, in the age of passions, my excessively sensitive heart had not been able to defend itself from a tenderness that then embellished the career of life in my eyes. A simple vassal, devoid of titles and birth, had rendered me her lover. Méranie was beautiful; I thought her constant, and, vanquished by her charms, I was unable to combat the impetuous amour that drew me toward her. Méranie soon appeared to share my flame. Can you imagine the days of my happiness, which passed with such inconceivable rapidity? At every instant, I loved Méranie more; at every moment I was able to convince myself that she was necessary to me if I wanted to be happy. Finally, tenderness prevailed over reason; I decided to brave my father's wrath, and to tie before the altar the knot of which he could only disapprove.

"Méranie also had a father, a simple squire, but bearing in his soul a great elevation of character, an art for bringing to a conclusion anything he cared to undertake, an unparalleled skill in enlacing those he wanted to deceived. It was not thus that I saw him; it was only when the scales had fallen from my eyes that I saw what he was capable of doing. Far from bringing obstacles to my union with his daughter, he trembled that his weakness might give rise to insurmountable ones. His fears were in vain; Méranie, whether out of love or skill, was able to guide herself to the altar at which our two destinies were linked irrevocably.

"Hiding my young spouse in the hamlet of Saint-Pierre, I went to forget in her arms the difficulties attached to the splendor of my rank; I hoped that one day I would be able to recognize Méranie; in sum, my dreams were pleasant. One night, my father died; rumors rose regarding his death; I still owe it to you to be silent in their regard, the one who gave birth to them is no more. It was at that moment that you were born, you and the handsome Odon, for the same day saw your eyes open to the light. At the summit of my desires, I was only waiting for the consent of my brother to enable you take the place that you merited, when…how can I tell you…?

"I discovered that your mother, forgetting her oaths, the love that I had for her, everything that I had done for her, had dared to abandon herself to a culpable flame. And for whom? Great God, for my own brother, for the seducer Bérenger. That discovery, in throwing despair into my soul, gave birth there at the same time to an insurmountable need for vengeance. I learned that for three months, Méranie had been secretly receiving Bérenger; I finally learned no longer be able to doubt my shame. Prey to fury, I was ready to do anything, when Bérenger, doubtless pursued by remorse, departed for the Holy Land.

"In learning of his departure, the odious Méranie could no longer retain any control; she ran away, and wanted to go with my brother. I pursued her. Not far from Narbonne, I caught up with her; Bérenger tried in vain to defend her. Pity me, my son; she died by my hand."

"O crime!" exclaimed Adémar.

After having remained silent for some time, Arembert continued.

"Bérenger, furious, wanted to fight me; I refused that execrable combat. He left. The sea completed my vengeance; Bérenger was swallowed by the waves. I returned in all haste to the two of you, but you had disappeared; Méranie's father had stolen my sons. For a long time to I did not know where you were hidden; finally, I discovered that the squire had confided you to the Vicomtesse de Carcassonne. It was to snatch you from those who retained you that I undertook the war of which I recently recounted the outcome to you. I succeeded in seizing you, but I have never been able to obtain since, either by pleas or menaces, that Odon could be returned to me.

"At that time the squire disappeared; several years went by without him coming to torment me again. Doubtless that state of calm did not suit him; he reappeared, or rather I believe so; for it seems to me that the mysterious hermit, so determined for my doom, cannot be anyone but the father of my spouse. That is why he has sought to embitter you against me; he has never forgiven me for the sin that my jealousy caused me to commit. Alas, my son, I deplore it every day in tears of blood. By night the shade of Méranie troubles my dreams, and to complete my torture, I see myself in horror of my own children."

Adémar took his hand. "Father!"

"Come, Adémar, come, that I may render you all my tenderness." They embraced. "If the hermit, my enemy, had not provoked that explanation, I would have delayed it until my death-bed, and you would only have learned of it via the act by which the domains of which I am sovereign would have been divided between you and Odon."

Fatigued by all that he had just said, Arembert went for some time before speaking again. Finally, he addressed his son again, and, wanting to break off a conversation that he was no longer in a condition to sustain, he advised him to go to bed.

Adémar, equally pressed to go away, retired without saying a word, and, returning to his room, he delivered himself to all his despair. In vain, Savary, whom he found there, tried to console him; everything was futile. Adémar could not bear the idea that he owed the light of day to a man from whom he felt an invincible estrangement; it was repugnant to him to be the son of Arembert, and he thought within himself that, whatever his mother's sins might have been, he could never love the man who had killed her. On the other hand, though, he did not form any doubt as to the revelation that the Baron had made to him; his story coincided too well with the hints that the hermit had pronounced a thousand times; he did not doubt that the latter, fearing for Adémar the anger of Arembert, had wanted to suspend it by forcing him to recognize his son.

Savary, to whom he confided his sad story, could not help saying, with his customary frankness: "Adémar merits a better father." They conversed for a long time on that subject, until the moment when, involuntarily, slumber closed their weary eyes.

Chapter II: Sooner or Later the Murderer is Punished

As soon as Adémar had retired, Arembert had Don Juan come in, and asked him how he had been informed that the Comtes de Toulouse and de Foix and the King of Aragon knew the place where their daughter were imprisoned. Don Juan told him about Savary, whom he said was being held in one of the château's prisons. Arembert, whom sleep fled and who feared finding himself alone, proposed to the Spanish seigneur that they go to interrogate Savary without waiting any longer Don Juan accepted the proposition and, each carrying a lamp, they went down into the vast subterrains that extended for several leagues.

After some research they found the door of the one where he troubadour ought to be, and, putting the key in the lock, they prepared to go into it. At that moment, a muffled moan was heard; the sound, rumbling under the vaults, was prolonged for several seconds. Arembert was intimidated by it, and stopped without any longer making the slightest movement. Don Juan, also astonished, could not help saying to his friend: "Let's go back; these galleries are unsafe; death doubtless inhabits this place."

"The voice of some detainee has reached us," said Arembert. "That, Chevalier is the sole cause of the noise we heard."

As he spoke, he opened the door; he pushed it and they went in.

O new terror! Instead of Savary, who had disappeared, they saw the hermit sitting at the table. Bewildered, they stopped.

The hermit, astonished to hear the sound, rose to his feet precipitately, thus deploying his colossal stature, which, to the fearful eyes of the two knights, appeared even more gigantic.

"What are you seeking here?" cried a formidable voice. "Do you think that I do not retain the power to steal all your

216

victims from you? And you, Arembert, has the advice of Heaven not corrected you? Will you always be the same? Will it be necessary for me to show myself before you?"

Arembert turned his head away. "No, no, supernatural being, I do not pretend to dispute the empire of my château with you. Hide yourself, that I may not perceive you; that is all that I ask."

"Do you consent to render liberty to the Princesses you have abducted?"

"You're asking too much of me."

"Be just," said the hermit, "overcome your passions, and fine days might yet shine for you; but if you persist in your blindness, your doom is decided, and from this moment on, I declare a war upon you that will only finish with your execution."

"What are you saying?" demanded Arembert.

"You blush to hear it, but you do not fear to merit it! And you, Don Juan, who do not even have the bravery with which a scoundrel ought to adorn himself, before long, you shall pay for your crimes."

"Hermit," said Don Juan, "who counts on our weakness, I shall put an end to your audacity as to Arembert's despair."

"What do you intend?" said he hermit.

"Your death," replied Don Juan, drawing his sword.

"Advance," said the hermit.

As he spoke, a blue-tinted flame surrounded him. He touched Don Juan's arm with a long wand; scarcely had the latter been lightly touched than, experiencing an unbearable pain, the Spaniard dropped his weapon. In the meantime, a dense cloud enveloped the hermit; a loud detonation was heard, and flaming streaks formed the words: DEATH TO THE GUILTY!

Arembert was on his knees; Don Juan scarcely existed.

Finally, calm was reestablished. The hermit had disappeared; the two knights were alone with their dread.

Not daring to remain in the subterrains any longer, they hastened to go back up the stairway that led to their apartment;

there they separated, and each went into his room, reflecting on what he had seen.

After Adémar had set forth for the Château de Saint-Félix, the hermit had told Raymond that his darling and Alienor were imprisoned within its lugubrious walls; he promised him that before two days had gone by, his lover and his sister would be returned to him. Suspending the knight's impetuous impatience by means of those words, he left him in the company of Vicomte Roger and the tender Agnès. As for him, having resumed the secret routes that led him to the château, he played there the various scenes that we have just recounted.

Scarcely had authority been devolved to Simon de Montfort than he showed all his ambition. The Comte de Toulouse was constrained to quit the camp in order to go and prepare to defend himself. Léogard, Comte de Nevers, did not stay thereafter; in spite of the entreaties of Simon de Montfort and the legate; he left with the Comte de Toulouse, animated by the desire to find the beautiful Aliénor.

As soon as Raymond found himself alone, he could not suffer the idea that he was idle while people were occupied elsewhere with the deliverance of the princesses; he greatly regretted not having kept his squadron, in order to attack the town of Saint-Félix immediately. Animated by those ideas he left the hermitage, accompanied by Odon, in spite of the representations of Roger and Agnès. He took the road to Castelnaudary, where he hoped to find soldiers ready to follow him.

As soon as daylight had appeared, Adémar got up in order to go see Arembert again. The latter, in the calm of the night, having reflected on what he ought to do, welcomed him gladly. Then, taking him aside, he said: "My son, yes, I admit, I have committed a great fault in bringing the Princesse de Toulouse here; but there is still time and I hope to repair everything. Hasten to depart, go to Carcassonne, intercede for me with the Comte de Toulouse; tell him to come and that I will return his daughter. Let him hurry, however, for the Princesses will be lost irredeemably if his troops do not get here before those of Simon de Montfort."

Adémar's heart, incapable of falsity, did not permit him to see the trap that was being set for him; he believed that the Baron was acting in good faith, and, glad of the service that he was going to render to the Raymonds' family, he went to prepare for his journey.

When he got back to his room he found Savary, who told him that he had to make him the confidence of a visit he had just had from the hermit: he had come to warn Adémar about the precipitate departure of Raymond and Odon for Carcassonne. Adémar did not want to delay his own departure for that reason; he proposed that Savary go with him.

"No, replied the latter, "I cannot leave the place inhabited by my Bélisène. I shall await your return, trusting the hermit to take care of my subsistence."

Seeing that he would not change his sentiment, Adémar bid him adieu.

Arembert accompanied his son as far as the barriers of the château, and there, having wished him bon voyage, he quit him and went back in.

First, Adémar took the route to the forest of Caillavel. In spite of his impatience he could not help going to see in passing the hermit, Vicomte Roger and his wife. Before arriving at the hermitage, he met the hermit, who was coming toward him.

"How glad I am to encounter you, my dear Adémar!" he said. "I already know the purpose of your journey; I wanted to turn you away from the mission you are about to undertake."

"And why, if you please," said Adémar, "do you not want me to render the daughter of the Comte de Toulouse to her unfortunate father?"

"Credulous Adémar," said the hermit, "you are going to consummate the doom of Sancia and Aliénor."

"What do you mean?"

"That the villainous Arembert is sill deceiving you."

"Stop, Seigneur," said Adémar. "It is not permissible for me to hear such talk of my father."

"Great God! Him, your father! What a scoundrel! What a detestable lie! No, Adémar, you are not his son."

"Deceived on all sides," complained Adémar, "shall I ever know the truth?"

"It will soon make itself known, but, I repeat, you do not owe your birth to the perfidious Baron."

"Can I at least know for what reason you do not want me to fulfill the mission confided to me?"

"Know that Arembert has conceived the hope of becoming Princesse Aliénor's husband during your absence."

"Him?"

"Yes, him. He wanted to get rid of you. It is necessary that his plan is thwarted. Follow me; I will enable you to see everything that he is meditating."

As he spoke, the hermit approached the tomb that rose up in his dwelling; he opened the door and, taking Adémar in with him, he took him along a subterranean tunnel into the château that he had recently quit.

Arembert's project was conceived with an ingenuity worthy of a perfidious heart, and, as soon as he saw Adémar on the road to Carcassonne, he prepared everything for the accomplishment of his odious plot. First, he sent word to Aliénor that he intended to talk to her and that she ought to be ready to receive him. He appeared soon afterwards, and began with a host of compliments, whose intention Aliénor did not perceive; but it did not take long for her to be informed.

"Madame," Arembert said to her, "the excess of my amour has been clearly demonstrated by the action that it has caused me to commit; I dare to ask you now for the recompense."

"I believed that all the Baron de Saint-Félix could demand was that the action he has committed, and of which he dares to boast, might be forgotten."

"You are in my power, Madame," said Arembert, "and I declare to you that I will use violence, if necessary, to obtain your hand."

"It is not by threats that one can intimidate the daughter of the Comte de Toulouse, and I despise you too much to fear you."

"I see, Madame, that a simple knight has stolen your heart from me; but tremble for the object of your amour, if you fear nothing for yourself."

"What more can you do?" said Aliénor, troubled.

"I can take the life of the man you prefer."

"You?"

"Yes, me, Madame; my passion renders me capable of anything."

"Think, Chevalier!" said Sancia. "Even if the Princesse consented to accord you her hand, can you think that such a marriage would obtain her father's consent?"

"Oh," said Arembert, "if I obtain that of the beautiful Aliénor, the others appear to me to be of scant importance."

"Lose all hope," said Aliénor.

"Lose, in your turn, that of seeing Adémar again."

"Monster! Disloyal knight! Unworthy of the name you dishonor, are those the great deeds with which you would like to signal yourself?"

"Just one word, Madame," said Arembert. "Follow me to the altar, or I will drag you there, after having Adémar killed before your eyes."

"O Arembert!" said Aliénor. "Resume the noble sentiments that ought never to have ceased to animate you. Renounce designs that can only attract my hatred to you; content yourself with my friendship, for my amour you can never hope to attain."

"I merit it, Madame. But time is being wasted in vain discourse. Let's go!"

"No; never."

"Soldiers," said Arembert, "kill Adémar."

"Stop, cruel men, stop!" cried Aliénor. "Yes, Arembert, I will follow you to the altar. Oh my God, what have I done to you? By what crime have I merited your wrath?"

"Unfortunate Alienor!" said Sancia. "Arembert, have pity on her tears."

"Has she pity for my amour?" said Arembert. "What, Madam! You remain immobile! Is your promise fallacious?"

At the peak of despair, Aliénor said: "Let's go!"

Thus vanquished by the rascality of Arembert, and by the fear of Adémar's demise, the daughter of the Comte de Tou-louse consented to the most odious of marriages; but she did not explain all her thoughts; she promised herself death at the foot of the altar at which the cunning Baron de Saint-Félix dared to hope for happiness,

Allowing herself to be led by the sad Sancia, who shared her tears, surrounded by an importunate crowd that redoubled her despair, Aliénor went to sacrifice herself in order to save the man to whom she had not yet entirely admitted her tender-ness.

Arembert, on the contrary, proud of obtaining what he had not longer dared to promise himself, forgot the dangers that would be the consequence of his action. Trusting in his bravery as well as the amity of Simon de Montfort, he thought himself powerful enough to brave the anger of the Comte de Toulouse, whom the crusaders would not take long to embroil in troublesome affairs.

Meanwhile, the Baron's orders having been given, the chapel of the château is being made ready in haste; the prepa-rations are being made for the fatal marriage that was about to be consummated.

Everything is done; the Seigneur's minister is already at the altar; the two spouses, bearing very different sentiments in their souls, approach the sanctuary.

Then Aliénor, addressing the Baron, says: "Arembert, you are a stranger to honor to this point, what will answer to me for the life of the unfortunate Adémar?"

"My word, Madame."

"Can I trust it?" says Aliénor.

"I swear to you," says Arembert. "I, Baron de Saint-Félix."

Then a voice says: "Who dares name himself Baron de Saint-Félix?"

"What do I hear?" cries Arembert.

"What voice is that!" cry the members of the crowd.

"Is there any other Baron de Saint-Félix than Sire Bérenger?" demands the voice.

"Bérenger!" exclaims Arembert.

"You know that, Arembert," says the voice. "Dare you deny it?"

With those words, a secret door placed behind the altar opens, and the mysterious hermit appears, followed by Adémar, who, forgetting his conductor's orders, hurls himself toward Aliénor as if to defend her.

At the sight of him, Count Raymond's daughter utters a cry of joy; she ceases to fear Arembert, while the latter, bewildered on perceiving the hermit, does not dare either to advance or to open his mouth to respond.

"Arembert!" cried the hermit. "Some time ago, I gave you a rendezvous in the mountains of Narbonne. I hoped then that your conscience would give birth in your heart to remorse; but, far from repenting your past crimes, you want to complete the measure. Well, it is before these warriors, who serve under your orders with regret, that I accuse you of the murder of your father, that of Loïse de Toulouse, and that of Bérenger."

Seeking to collect himself, Arembert speaks. "Impostor! Tremble! You will not have in this place the resource of your tricks to impose on those who surround us. I see with you that young Adémar, whom you have tried to make my mortal enemy, and to whom I have admitted that I was his father."

"You, wretch!" said the hermit. "You, his father! What have you done with the sons of Bérenger and Loïse?"

"By what right do you interrogate me!"

"I shall tell you that soon, but I repeat to you: What have you done with Bérenger's children?"

"Bérenger, my brother, never submitted to the laws of marriage."

"Was he not united with the beautiful Loïse de Toulouse?"

"No."

"Well, I declare that Adémar and Odon are the secret but legitimate fruits of that marriage."

"You're lying."

"I swear it."

"Where are the proofs?"

"I will give them to you."

"When?"

"Now."

"You cannot."

"It will be sufficient to show myself to you."

"Make yourself known; but do not put on that odious face..."

"I shall show my own," the hermit declares.

"What is it?" demands Arembert.

The hermit, letting his robe fall, appears fully armored, but without a helmet. "That of your brother Bérenger," he says.

Arembert hides his face with his hands. "Vengeful Heaven!"

"Bérenger!" cry the warriors.

"My father!" cries Adémar.

"Yes, Adémar!" declares Bérenger. "Yes, you are my son, and there before you is the assassin of all my family: the ingrate brother who, in order to slake his fatal amour and his perfidious ambition, immolated his father and my wife, and believed that he had sacrificed me. Speak, Arembert. Can you belie me? Will you say now that I am seeking to impose on you? Am I not your brother? Am I not your sovereign?"

Bérenger could have spoken for longer; Arembert would not have thought of interrupting him. Torn by a thousand sen-

224

timents, crushed by the tableau of his sins, he sensed that death was the only refuge that could hide him from the shame by which he was menaced.

"Bérenger!" he cried. "Adémar, Aliénor, all of you who are listening to me: yes, I am guilty; yes, I have heaped up crimes in order to satisfy my passions; but there are degrees in my crimes. I caused Loïse to perish; I believed that I had caused my brother to perish; but my father is still alive, imprisoned in the subterrains of my château."

"For four years," said Bérenger, coldly, "he has been no more, and the tomb of the hermitage contains his mortal remains."

Arembert struck himself with his sword. "Well then, it is to him that I immolate myself. Forgive me, Bérenger."

At that unexpected action, a general clamor rose up. Arembert's victims, forgetting their misfortunes, hastened to lavish their tender cares upon him. It was in vain; death had already claimed its bloody prey.

The rapidity of the solemn scene that I have just described had suspended the faculties of the souls of the actors. Adémar, torn between amour and nature, ran from Bérenger's arms to Aliénor's knees. The latter, happy to have escaped Arembert and happier still to have learned the illustrious birth of her lover, was already smiling at a gracious future. The knights and the inhabitants of Saint-Félix, charmed to rediscover their worthy Baron, strove by their acclamations to prove their delight to him. He showed them Roberto and said: "That is the man to whom I owe life."

Chapter III: The Price of Courage

While everyone was thus occupied within the château, war cries were suddenly heard resounding under the ramparts: the combined cries of "Toulouse!" and "Raymond!" rose into the air. A few squires ran into the chapel and announced that a numerous detachment of Toulousan troops had unexpectedly attacked the town of Saint-Félix and, having taken possession of it, were marching toward the château.

"Oh!" cried Alienor. "Seigneur, it's my brother, who is coming to liberate me."

Bérenger ordered that the gates should be opened, and, followed by the Princesses Aliénor and Sancia, and his son Adémar, he went to met young Raymond in order to receive him as a friend in the walls that the latter had believed he would enter by force of arms.

In the vicinity of Monfleur, Raymond had rallied his father's squadrons and, wanting to punish the presumptuous Baron Arembert himself, he had pressed his march in order to surround and surprise the insolent individual who had dared to abduct his sister and her noble friend. How astonished he was when he saw that, far from thinking of opposing any resistance to him, the drawbridge was lowered and he was able to recognize Aliénor, Sancia and Adémar. They lavished the most tender caresses on one another; they returned to the château, where the flags of Toulouse and Saint-Félix were mingled.

But who was the man whose joy was boundless? It was you, brave and sensitive Odon; you rediscovered your father; you were able to raise your head, proud of your high birth. Oh, what was the delirium of your joy! How your transports intoxicated your father, who, from that moment on, forgot his past misfortunes.

With what rapidity that happy day went by! But with what impatience they awaited the following one, when Bérenger promised to recount the story of his life.

(In order not to hinder the march of events, we have judged it appropriate to postpone that story until the end of the volume.)

After the first moments of general delight had passed, Bérenger and Adémar shared two concerns; the first was to render the unfortunate Arembert the last duties; the second, which Adémar fulfilled, was to run to his apartment in order to liberate the troubadour Savary de Mauléon, who must have been anxious about the tumult of whose causes he was undoubtedly unaware...

But what a spectacle struck Adémar's eyes! He perceived Savary lying on the floor, pierced by several sword-thrusts and ready to yield his last sigh. Next to him, Don Juan was lying, stone dead, while a young beauty—that was Bélisène—seemed deprived of sense.

At that disastrous sight, Adémar commanded the squire that had followed him to lavish the cares on Savary that the situation seemed to demand; for himself, picking up Bélisène, he tried to bring her to her senses.

The news of the catastrophe having spread immediately, the Princesses came running, and did not take long to recognize the daughter of the Comte de Foix. That recognition added to the interest that they took in Bélisène, but they could not conceive by what fatality the Château de Saint-Félix had been the rendezvous of so many unfortunates.

In a few words, Roberto made it known who Don Juan was, and it was not without some joy that they ascertained his death.

The first apparel having been removed from Savary's wounds, he did not take long to open his eyes. His strength increased, and, as soon as he was able to speak, the name of Bélisène emerged from his lips. She was beside him, occupied in watching his movements and anticipating his desires, and, on her knees beside the troubadour's bed, she was imploring Heaven, which had finally ceased to be favorable to him.

Bérenger, profiting from the knowledge that he had acquired from the old Arab, promptly composed a sovereign balm, which, in a short while, rendered Savary his exhausted strength. It was then that he was able to tell his friends by what accident he had almost been the victim of the cowardly Don Juan.

"I was in Adémar's room," he said, when there was a loud noise. I listened, and did not take long to realize that it was coming from a room next door to the one I was occupying. Soon, a voice reached me, and what a sentiment overwhelmed me when I recognized the tones of Bélisène! I launched myself forth and, without calculating the danger, I presented myself to the gaze of Don Juan.

"At the sight of me, Bélisène threw herself into my arms. Don Juan called his two men-at-arms and all three of them attacked me. I retreated drawing my beloved with me. With a thrust of my sword I struck the Spaniard; he fell, but there was an item of furniture beneath my foot; I tripped, and accompanied him in his fall; it was then that his satellites pierced me with thrusts. I don't know the rest, having lost consciousness."

That brief report by Savary increased further, if that were possible, the hatred that they had for the perfidious Spaniard, but he was dead, and the generous hearts that he had persecuted did not think of pursuing his remains by refusing him the last duties that he did not merit.

While the members of the illustrious assembly were gathered around the troubadour de Mauléon in order to hear the end of his adventure, the squire Aubin entered the room precipitately.

"To arms!" he cried. "From the height of the ramparts, squadrons can be seen in the plain carrying the blazons of the Montforts on their banners."

At that name, odious to all those who were in the Château de Saint-Félix, everyone became agitated, and got ready to defend it. The timid Sancia, by virtue of an involuntary movement, drew nearer to the valiant Raymond; Aliénor looked at Adémar; while Bélisène sighed, thinking that perhaps Savary would not be able to share the dangers of the defense.

While the young heroes were preparing for the battle, the prudent Bérenger recalled that the Vicomte de Carcassonne, as well as his wife and son, were still in the hermitage, and that the crusaders might perhaps have surprised them there. He hastened to take the subterranean route that led to his former dwelling once again, and, hastening his steps, he emerged from the tomb that contained the ashes of Loïse and Amanieu at the very moment when the barrier of the hermitage was about to be forced by Amaury de Montfort's soldiers.

Amaury, not having received any news of Arembert for some days, nor of Sancia, whom he believed to be in his power, had decided to send a messenger to the Baron de Saint-Félix. The squire, on arriving in the town, learned of the events that had recently occurred in the suzerain family. He had not tried to enter the château, but had returned to Amaury and told him everything he knew.

Amaury, rendered desperate by such a misfortune, had had no trouble in engaging his father to permit him to besiege a town in which the elite of his enemies was to be found. The legate Milon, who was consulted, approved young Montfort's designs, and it was resolved in the Council that before attacking Lavaur, the army of crusaders would begin by taking possession of the town of Saint-Félix.

Tranquil in his retreat, Roger, Vicomte de Carcassonne, had not wanted to quit it when he learned of the death of Arembert. He did not think that, in his situation, it was appropriate to show himself. He only wanted to reappear when, or if, the combats permitted him to resume his titles,

Bérenger, by his appearance in the hermitage, saved the life of the unfortunate couple for a second time.

"Hasten to follow me," he cried to them, "Comes into the midst of your friends. Lave this humble abode to the soldiers who have come to profane it."

Roger and Agnès followed him; they entered the tomb, which closed again, and the Abbot of Bonnecombre, who had flattered himself with taking possession of the hermit's person, only found uninhabited walls.

That first contretemps afflicted Amaury, who had hoped to obtain precious information from the hermit. Not allowing himself to be downcast, however, he marched, followed by his squadrons, toward the town that contained so many individuals interesting by virtue of their misfortunates or commendable by their bravery.

At the first news of his arrival, Raymond, Adémar, Odon and even Savary had hastened to run to the ramparts; they had garnished them with a sufficient number of troops, and all of them, only respiring dangers, challenged the enemy battalions while agitating their swords. Soon, Roger and Bérenger came to join them, and all of them, confident in one another, answered to one another for their success.

In spite of the preponderance of the legate, as well as Simon de Montfort, the rest of the crusader lords did not share their sentiment. Several rose up against the action of Amaury, who, without any aggression, was about to attack knights who had not participated in the errors of the Albigensians. But the discontent took another turn when the Comte de Toulouse, informed of Montfort's enterprise, declared that he would give his daughter to the man who delivered her from the pursuits of the superb Amaury.

A large number of knights, on hearing that proclamation, and desiring to merit Aliénor's hand, separated their ensigns from those of the leader of the crusaders. The most impetuous, and undoubtedly the most ardent to embrace the defense of the daughter of the Comte de Toulouse, was the hot-heated Léogard, Comte de Nevers. Forgetting the amity that linked him to Montfort, he only thought of the charming prize that he might merit. In vain the legate employed in his regard the weapons of persuasion and threats; Léogard braved the latter and was insensible to the others. He said that if the Château de Saint-Félix was attacked, he would fall upon the assailants, determined to sustain the cause of the ladies, as well as the honor that commanded imperiously all noble French knights.

Before the Comte de Toulouse could be informed of the danger to which his family was exposed, however, and had said what we have just reported, Amaury, as impetuous as his father, had already attempted a first assault. His troops had scarcely arrived at the foot of the hill on which the town stood than he disposed them in battle order, and, encouraging them with his voice and by example, he scaled the rock with them and came to plant his banner outside the southern gate.

Raymond, impatient to measure himself against that impetuous adversary, could not consent to remain behind the walls when his proud rival was challenging him with loud cries. He demanded that a sortie be effected. Adémar, Odon, Roger and Savary supported him vigorously with regard to Bérenger, but he, being more prudent, refused their pleas for a long time.

His representations were in vain, however; he was constrained to open the gates of the town, and the young warriors, followed by a good number of men-at-arms, fell upon the crusaders abruptly. The latter, who had not expected such a prompt attack, lost their footing at the first impact. Perceiving their disarray, Amaury flew to their aid, accompanied by the Sire de Voisin, Gui de Lévis and Giraud de Lavallette, noble knights whose great deeds renown was pleased to celebrate.

Like a rock that, detached by a thunderbolt from the crest of the hill from which it is suspended, falls rebounding into the plain without being stopped by the barriers that nature opposes to it, Raymond, fighting for his beloved, descends into the midst of soldiers, whom he strikes down, all the way to the bottom of the valley formed by the environs of the village of Escascs; everything disperses before him.

Giraud de Lavellette, who sees him, think that the knight is worthy of his courage. He drives toward him; it is to find death; Raymond's blade, striking Giraud to the default of his breastplate, penetrates by six inches into his body and leaves that noble warrior devoid of life. The Vicomte de Saint-Pol, who tries to avenge him, experiences the same fate. Matignon, the lover of beauties, succumbs similarly. Richard de Livri, Henri d'Escar and Pierre de Montesquiou also perish at Raymond's hands. Adémar, his worthy rival, fells Sancerre,

231

Crussol, Rigaud, Basas, the Marquis d'Aubenas and the Baron de Bauselle. Odon signals himself by saving the life of Mauléon, who, already vanquished by his lack of strength, was about to be slain by the bellicose Lévis; Odon wounds that knight.

In sum, victory smiles on the Toulousan heroes. Amaury launches himself into the melee in vain; in vain he lavishes the valor that often merited him the title of the Brave; he cannot repel the knights, who, after having brought terror all the way to the crusaders' tents, withdraw tranquilly, insulting the enemies that had flattered themselves on surprising them.

The young Princesses were waiting for their lovers, and took pleasure in lavishing upon them the praise that they had so richly merited. The rest of the day was only spent in rejoicing; it was spent at table or dancing. The French always combine the fatigues of war with the relaxations of peace.

After the banquet, Savary, from whom a song was demanded, wanted to recite one that could add to the general gaiety, and, remembering the exploits and the character of the famous Marquis Olivier, the nephew of Charlemagne, he sang an adventure of that illustrious paladin.[43]

> *On the harp with flexible strings,*
> *Let us attempt amorous songs.*
> *Listen, sensible beauties,*
> *I will sing of the love of knights.*
> *Made for love and victory,*
> *He collected a double laurel:*
> *It is thus that history speaks*
>   *Of the Marquis Olivier.*
>
> *Valiant warrior, fickle lover,*
> *His fires only lasted a day;*
> *He was prompt in his homage,*
> *And prompter still in his amour.*

---

[43] Author's note: "Music by Dalvimare."

Next to a genteel damsel
He liked to forget himself.
Beauties, I wish you still
   A Marquis Olivier.

One evening, in his castellany
Appeared, with eyes bathed in tears,
A dwarf who had come to recount
The misfortunes of young Alie.
She has fallen into the power
Of d'Ambure, a felonious knight,
But she awaits her deliverance
   By the Marquis Olivier.

Let's depart, he said, without delay;
Dwarf, guide my steps toward her;
When a damsel requires defending,
A knight takes up his arms.
But is she young and pretty?
At her feet can I cry:
Oh deign to be the darling
   Of Marquis Olivier?

Sire Marquis, she is naïve;
She is aged, it is said, fifteen.
She is as white as a lily
As fresh as a flower of the fields
Her figure is as delicate and slender
As an elegant poplar;
She is occupied in her thoughts
   With the Marquis Olivier.

Inspired by that depiction
(Vanity is always seductive),
The Marquis, of Ambure's castle
Sees the towers the next day.
He seizes his horn and summons

The tyrant he wishes to challenge.
The dwarf run to speak to the beauty
   Of the Marquis Olivier.

On the battlements the genteel Alie
Appears, a handkerchief in hand.
The warrior, who sees her, cries:
Of the Moor, the inhumane oppressor,
Of the valiant paladin of France.
In vain d'Ambure has fled the steel;
He will succumb to the valor
   Of the Marquis Olivier.

Alie, as adroit as she is sage
Gives irons to her vanquisher
What prodigy of that inconstancy
Could change humor to that degree?
It's because the clever beauty
Far from trusting oaths
Is able to desire incessantly
   The Marquis Olivier.

You who desire every day
The gift of a faithful lover;
Trust me, take for a model.
The one praised by my song.
The desires of an amiable lover
Know always to distrust.
For every Frenchman is like
   The Marquis Olivier.

Chapter IV: The Generous Rival

In spite of his anger, Amaury was obliged to rest his troops, whom he had seen so cruelly repelled by the besieged. It was then that the news of the Comte de Toulouse's proclamation penetrated both the crusaders' camp and the town of Saint-Félix. Adémar, on learning it, let his joy burst forth, for he thought that he would suffice for Aliénor's defense. The delight that was painted on his face told Raymond what the latter was beginning to suspect; it was without difficulty that he convinced himself of the tenderness of Adémar, his cousin, for his charming sister Aliénor; but at the same time, politically adroit and submissive to the will of his father, he hid it from the two lovers that he had discovered their secret, not wanting, by to marked a preference, to distance other competitors irrevocably, of whom he might have need for the success of his cause.

It was not without a keen displeasure that Aliénor was informed of her father's promise; while she had sought externally to hide her amour from the man was its object, she had abandoned herself to it in her soul, and now she feared that the success of arms might not respond to the desires of her heart. Occupied with these various sentiments, she was dreaming at the top of the high tower that she had climbed when she heard a sigh nearby.

She had no need to turn round to be convinced of the presence of Adémar; that amiable knight had followed the lady of his thoughts in order to enjoy her conversation and, standing close by, he abandoned himself to the pleasure of contemplating her.

"Yes," he exclaimed, enthusiastically, "it is the most beautiful prize that can ever be offered to courage; and if I did not obtain it by victory, I would not think myself worthy of possessing it."

"Sire Adémar," said Aliénor, "my father seems very unjust to me, in wanting my hand to be the recompense for valor."

"Demoiselle," said Adémar, "it is doubtless appropriate for a vulgar beauty to love a lover and to be cherished by him; and at the whim of their desire they can marry in obscurity; but the splendid Aliénor, the daughter of the powerful Comte de Toulouse, ought to obtain a husband worthy of her, and it is not in the games of tourneys that he ought to signal himself, but in punishing the enemies of his lover's father. It is in delivering her from the pursuits of a tyrant, and in overwhelming his own rivals with the weight of his glory, that he can succeed in meriting worthily the one who should make his happiness."

"Generous Adémar," said Aliénor, "Oh, how worthy you are of your birth! Well, it is at the moment when I can be conquered that I take pleasure in confessing to you without indirection all that you have been able to inspire in me. Yes, Chevalier, I love you, I beg you and I command you to surpass all your rivals; but I swear to you that if fortune deceives your great heart, the candles of marriage will never be lit for me."

Adémar fell to his knees. "O lady! Do not make oaths; they are not necessary for you. What your lips have said, answers for my victory, and if I had to combat alone all those knights whose banners are floating in that immense plain. I would not doubt being victorious."

Having spoken, he rose to his feet; he pressed his inflamed lips five times to the hand that Aliénor deigned to abandon to him.

However, it was necessary that effects responded to words; more than one warrior promised himself the deliverance of Aliénor. Léogard de Nevers, the Comte de Beaumont, the Sire d'Allais and a number of others arranged themselves under the ensigns of Toulouse. Amaury, fearing to see the number increase, did not want to delay the assault he was preparing any longer

As soon as the vermilion Aurora, mounting her luminous chariot, opened the gates of the Orient and commenced her customary career, when the sound of military instruments, the noise of bells and the clamors of the combatants announced the triple combat that was about to take place. The army of the crusaders, arranged in battle order, was divided into two corps by Amaury de Montfort, one destined to attack the château, the other to oppose the attempts of the Comte de Nevers and the seigneurs united with him.

Léogard, fully armored, placing a helmet of pure gold on his head, surmounted by three crimson plumes, shows himself before the crusaders followed by his brave battalions, assured of Aliénor's heart.

Adémar, who is wearing in his bosom a lock of that beauty's hair, does not hesitate to promise himself a joyful success.

Raymond, who is fighting for Sancia, is even more audacious; he hopes to overturn forever this day the projects of the crusaders, the enemies of his family. Savary goes with that same idea to sustain the impact of the assailants.

Roger wants to reconquer his domains; unfortunate and alone, he will not succeed.

Bérenger is forced by his sons to remain in the town in order to prepare a retreat if fate disappoints their endeavors; but he, who knows what he blood can do, does not doubt an entire victory.

At the moment when Amaury commanded his men to furnish themselves with ladders in order to scale the ramparts, the three gates of the town opened simultaneously, and three battalions, guided by the bravest leaders, fell upon those who believed that they would anticipate them.

It was you, handsome Odon, who struck the first blows. Baron Conrad, one of the most powerful lords of Swabia, had followed the crusaders in order to acquire a great renown in the combats whose necessity he foresaw; he merited the palms of glory, but he served to heighten that of Bérenger's son.

Adémar, spurred on by what he had just see his brother do, precipitated himself into the midst of the squadron that was commanded by Créqui, one of the scions of that illustrious family, the pride of Picardy. Raoul Créqui might have been able to balance the success, but he was not fighting for an Aliénor; Adémar tipped him into the ditches of the town, pierced by two sword-thrusts. Du Rourai tried to avenge him, but the same destiny was his share. Potou, Gamache and d'Aulnay perished similarly in challenging the knight favored by the daughter of the Comte de Toulouse.

The soldiers frightened by the blows he struck, were fleeing in all directions when Enguerrand de Boucicaut stopped them. For a long time, Enguerrand had not found an adversary worthy of him; he yearned to fight a warrior made to dispute with him the glory of arms; Adémar appeared, and Boucicaut thought that he had found what he had sought in vain.

Like two rival clouds each bearing lightning, coming together with equal force, the two knights precipitated themselves against one another. Their stature, their skill and their bravery were the same; the same desire to signal themselves excited then; they struck one another with the rudest blows, they threatened one another, they evaded one another, and drew together; and the combat would doubtless have been prolonged if the cries of triumph that proclaimed the great deeds of Léogard had not reached Odon's brother. Rendered desperate by what he heard, the impetuous Adémar struck the proud Boucicaut furiously; in vain the latter tried to stiffen himself against his adversary's blows; in the end, he ceded, and, wounded in the head, the body and the arm, he was constrained to abandon the battlefield.

As soon as the Comte de Nevers had seen the crusader troops in movement, he had hastened to make his own take up arms, and like a vulture swooping on its prey, he had attacked Amaury's soldiers. His valor, sustained by the hope of obtaining Aliénor, guided him to a certain victory; the other seigneurs, his rivals, followed him, with the thought of sharing the honor of the day with him.

While they were advancing from the direction of Vaus, Amaury formed an attack against the château, where Bérenger was alone. Montfort's son, having expelled the Toulousans who opposed his efforts, did not take long to reach the foot of the platform; then, seizing a ladder and standing it up against the wall, he climbed up, followed by his most intrepid chiefs.

The valorous Bérenger, rediscovering all his courage, sought to defend himself against such an assailant, but numbers triumphed over his ardor. The crusaders had already scaled the ramparts in several places. Amaury, like a brave man, was the first who had crossed the battlements; he hastened to run, followed by a party of his men-at-arms, toward the apartments of the château; he had reached the threshold when, like the impetuous winds that running from Antarctic lands, drives vessels before it noisily. Adémar, to whom the news of Amaury's success had been brought, hastened to oppose obstacles to it.

It was within the sight of the Princesses that those two knights attacked one another twice, struck one another twice; the incessantly moving crowd separated them; the crusaders were penetrating the château from all directions.

In vain, magnanimous Adémar, you tried to repel them; those attempts would have been futile if Raymond, Léogard, Odon, Savary and a few others had not run to support you. Their presence reanimated the combat.

It was at that moment, with an equal advantage, that Adémar and the Comte de Nevers disputed by their heroic actions the lady of their thoughts. Adémar snatched his darling from the hands of a few soldiers who were trying to take her prisoner, but then the Comte de Nevers, at the peril of his days, defended those of young Raymond, who was hard pressed by the Sire de Voisin.

Meanwhile, Raymond, impatient to repair the insult the thought he had received in having need of Léogard to come to his aid, sought out Amaury in the midst of the melee; he perceived him, but that was the moment when, having overcome all obstacles, the son of the ambitious Simon de Montfort was dragging in his steps the beautiful Sancia, whom he had just taken prisoner.

239

"Stop, Amaury!" cried Raymond, furiously. "Stop, knight who only has courage enough to abduct a timid woman! Come, it's against me that you ought to fight; it's in taking my life that you can hope to conserve your own."

"Raymond," replied Amaury, "I did not think that you could doubt my bravery. Well, since you dare to insult it, advance. I'll teach you to know it, and let us see whether you merit, more than me, the beauty for whom I'm fighting this day."

As he finished speaking, Amaury dealt Raymond a terrible blow, which the latter parried with his buckler; in his turn he responded to his rival by shattering his breastplate with the flat of his redoubtable sword.

Their combat had lasted for some time when the legate of the Holy See was seen advancing through the ranks of the soldiers, clad in his priestly garb. Raymond, understanding without difficulty that victory was about to be snatched from him, hastened to strike Amaury; he did so with such success that young Montfort fell in the arena, spilling his blood through a double wound that left great fear for his life.[44]

"In the name of Heaven," cried the legate, "Toulousan crusaders, I command you to cease this combat, which is compromising the interests of the sacred cause. What! The weapons that ought to be turned against the enemies of the religion, you are turning against one another! Comte de Nevers, do you not shiver at the excesses of which a blind passion has brought you? Have you not sworn in my hands never to deliver battle except to the Albigensians? Comte Raymond, Comte Amaury, if your woes permit you to hear me, do not pursue enterprises that Heaven can only detest, and

---

[44] Unnecessary fear, presumably, as the historical Amaury succeeded his father as Earl of Leicester and—temporarily— as Comte of Toulouse. He subsequently became Constable of France but died in 1241 in the aftermath of his captivity during the so-called Barons' Crusade of 1239.

think that I am menacing with the lightning of the Church anyone who does not sheathe his sword."

Thos spoke Milon.

O power of religion! Those knights, who the entire world could not have caused to recoil, ceded to the voice of a single man who spoke to them in the name of God. The crusaders retired to their camp, followed by the legate, who had not wanted to abandon young Amaury.

In the meantime, Bérenger had the gates of the town closed for a second time. He ordered further works that might serve to defend it if it were attacked again; but, in order to distance the war entirely from the vassal town, he advised the young knights to take the three princesses to Toulouse. His proposal was accepted, especially by Adémar and the Comte de Nevers, who intended to have their causes judged by the Comte de Toulouse, Aliénor's father.

The beautiful Aliénor, Sancia and Bélisène, under the escort of their lovers' squadrons, departed the following day, desirous of getting away from a place that had almost been the theater of their misfortune.

Old Raymond was awaiting his daughter and his son impatiently. It was with an extreme joy that he took them in his arms, and he experienced a sentiment of mingled pleasure and sadness in recognizing, in Odon and Adémar, the two sons of a cherished sister. Deceived by the knavery of Arembert and the anxious amity of the Vicomtesse de Carcassonne, he had believed that his two nephews were dead, but he alone knew that Bérenger had not ceased to exist. In order not to displease his brother-in-law, he had pretended not to know who the mysterious hermit was. It was the Comte de Toulouse who had secretly furnished Bérenger with the gold and the soldiers necessary for his various enterprises.

On arriving in Toulouse, Bélisène found the Comte de Foix there, who had come in response to a courier whom his daughter had sent to him as soon as Adémar had rendered her to liberty.

All those various individuals delivered themselves to the joy of seeing one another again, and that charm suspended the Raymonds' just anxieties for a while, who could not doubt that the storm that had already rumbled under the walls of Saint-Félix would soon come to burst under the ramparts of Toulouse itself.

Léogard, unaware of the love that Aliénor had for Adémar, did not hide his pretentions and the hope that he had of possessing that beautiful person. Raymond, whose life he had saved, could not help remaining neutral in spite of his predilection for his cousin. The sovereign Comte, for reasons that he concealed, was in no hurry to chose a husband for his daughter, and by virtue of that adroit maneuver, retained around him a large number of knights who might have quit him if he they had not been excited by the lure of such a charming recompense.

Only Aliénor was suffering; she was ready to make a confession of her sentiments to her father when, one evening, after an exceedingly hot day, she went down into the gardens of the palace with Sancia. They walked for a while; finally, they went to rest beside a branch of the river, and there, sitting at the foot of a willow that the crusaders had brought back from the Orient, they confided their secret thoughts to one another.

The naïve Sancia explained herself first; she did not hide from her friend how anxious she was for the course of events to permit her to be united forever by the most tender bonds to the Prince for whom she experienced such an ardent amour.

"My dear Sancia," Aliénor said to her, "how fortunate you are; you love my brother, he adores you, you are assured that he will be your husband; but I, alas, who have loved for so long a knight worthy of my flame, see myself on the point of being separated from him forever. It is permitted for you to repel the homages of the presumptuous Amaury; your refusal is approved by your father, while mine might perhaps seek to influence my choice.

"What am I saying, my choice? I have not been left free to make one; my hand has been promised without anyone even thinking of consulting me, and what redoubles my pain is seeing Adémar given the most redoubtable rival who could be opposed to him. It is not an ordinary knight who sighs for my feeble attractions, to whom arms have given some right; it is the amiable and valiant Comte de Nevers. Oh, if only I could offer him the heart of a beauty worthier of him, who would be able to appreciate his tenderness. O Léogard, you would have mine if Adémar had not already merited it!"

"The confession I have just overheard is enough, Madame, for my heart," exclaimed Léogard, appearing before Aliénor. "I am as happy as it is permissible for me to be, since you have given some regret for my amour. Yes, undoubtedly, I shall bear all my life the chains that I have taken voluntarily, but I shall cease to pretend to obtain a hand that is already promised. Adieu, noble Aliénor; let Adémar make your happiness; it will not be Léogard who would want to raise obstacles to it. I renounce my rights, if it is possible to have any without your consent; and, if I cannot aspire to your amour, let your amity compensate me for the sacrifice I am making to honor."

"O brave Chevalier!" the young Comtesse replied. "How worthy you are of the name that you bear!"

She put so much fire into the expressions of her gratitude that Léogard sighed more than once, in depicting for himself what happiness would have been his if he had been able to please Aliénor.

He did not take long to put his promises into effect. He hastened to go to find the Comte de Toulouse, confided to him that his duty recalled him to his estates and that he was preparing to leave before the end of the following day.

Old Raymond was surprised by such a sudden resolution; he could not help asking the Comte de Nevers whether he had received dome displeasure in his court that could command him to go away so rapidly.

"Prince," Léogard replied, "if I am fleeing you, only blame me; I adore your charming daughter; combats have given me some rights to her hand, but it is not sufficient to merit it, it is necessary for her to give it to me herself."

"Have you encountered her refusal?" said he Comte.

"I could not be refused, since her heart was already given."

"What are you telling me? Has my daughter made a choice?"

"Yes, Comte; but that choice cannot be disavowed by you; he is worthy of your daughter."

"Can you not tell me who it is?"

To merit your approval," said Léogard, "it is sufficient from me to name Adémar."

"The son of Baron de Saint-Félix? Oh, why have my children kept that secret from their father for so long?"

Old Raymond hastened to summon his son, his daughter and Adémar; he gave them his blessing, and promised to unite them in a few days. Oh, what were the transports of the two lovers! How many times Adémar swore to his young lover an endless and unweakening tenderness! How many oaths he received in return!

Then, informed of the generosity of the valiant Léogard, he ran to him. "Comte," he said, shaking his hand, "you have just acquired a friend who will only cease to be when the icy hand of death weighs upon my heart."

"And by what dolor would I not have been afflicted," said Léogard, "if I had caused the torments of an amiable Chevalier?"

In spite of the solicitations of the Toulouse family, however, he did not want to prolong his sojourn in that city. The genteel Comte de Nevers knew that amour can only be cured by absence. Having taken his leave of his friends, promising them his help if it were necessary against the attacks of the crusaders, he took the road to his states, and only ceased to think about Aliénor when another beauty that he cherished replaced the daughter of the Comte de Toulouse in his heart. His memory always remained dear to those whose happiness he had ensured, and when Aliénor and Adémar thought of a friend, it was the name of Léogard that they pronounced together.

A courier was sent to Bérenger, who hastened to me to Toulouse in order to witness the marriage to his son, and 28 April 1208 saw the triple union of Raymond and Sancia, Adémar and Aliénor, and Savary and Bélisène.[45] Only Odon was not yet bound by sacred bonds. His amiable but light character seemed to reject constancy; a long time passed without him being able to fix his affections; his adventures were numerous and varied; he recorded them himself, along with those of his brother, which we are finished retracing. Perhaps one day we shall occupy ourselves with Odon's.

Adémar and his wife lived together for many years; the shared the fortune of their father and their brother; like the Raymonds, they were persecuted by the ambitious Comte de Montfort, but finally, Heaven wearied of being contrary to them, and the death of Simon de Montfort delivered them from that ardent enemy, terminating their troubles. Aliénor had the glory of giving death to that vindictive prince herself, when he tried to reenter Toulouse, which had revolted against his unjust domination.

Savary was similarly, with Bélisène, the companion of the Princes of Toulouse. In their reverses as well as their successes he never abandoned them, and when destiny rendered to that noble family the estates that had been stolen from them, Mauléon received marks of munificence and amity.

Bérenger, renouncing forever his profession of hermit, returned to combats; he heaped benefits upon the majordomo Roberto, who, thinking himself worthy of celestial punishments for the crimes in which he had taken part, retired in his turn to the abandoned hermitage and spent the rest of his life praying for the soul of Arembert.

---

[45] This is a blatant falsification of chronology, the cited date being more than a year before the massacre of the inhabitants of Béziers and the siege of Carcassonne, and prior to the launching of the crusade.

Vicomte Roger, pursued by misfortune, did not survive his reverses for long. He perished in the famous battle of Muret, which overturned Raymond's throne for some time. The tender Agnès, his wife, remained inconsolable, but conserved herself for the son who remained to her, and to whom she succeeded in having a part of the heritage of his ancestors returned by the Kings of France.

THE HERMIT'S STORY

The day of my birth was not marked by those sinister presages that announce the misfortunes of those who were commencing the career of life. On the contrary, everything seemed to promise me a brilliant future; the joy of the Baron, my father, that of my dear mother, and the delight of our vassals combined to make that day the most beautiful that Saint-Félix had ever seen. Over the fonts of regeneration, I received the name of Bérenger.

Soon afterwards, my brother was born. Should I give that title to someone who, almost from infancy, was only occupied in working for my doom? We grew up together, me cherishing him while he hid the hatred he bore for me under a deceitful exterior.

I shall pass rapidly over the early years of my life. They went by in the exercises appropriate to the young nobility; I learned to bear arms, to handle a horse, to love God and to respect ladies. When I had reached my fifteenth year, my father took me to the Court of Toulouse, where he wanted me to establish my abode for some time. We took the road to that great city after having embraced my tender mother, whom I was never to see again; she perished shortly thereafter, the victim of the cruel malady that the crusaders had brought back from Araby. I shed tears at her loss. Alas, she was fortunate in perishing; she avoided the sight of the crimes that ambition led my brother Arembert to commit.

We departed from Saint-Félix accompanied by an escort worthy of my father's rank. Toulouse did not take long to receive us within its walls. The great Alphonse Jourdain reigned then in the city of the Tectosages;[46] he welcomed my father with a very particular distinction; he testified to me an amity of which I sought to render myself worthy, and he promised the author of my days to treat me with a particular generosity.

I was admitted at that moment to the number of the young pages who were attached to his august person; he preferred my service to that of my companions and often, on his orders, I was summoned to the interior of the palace, where I shared he games of the princes, his children. One among then, in particular, inspired in me more than the others the fraternity of soul so common among our knights; that was Comte Raymond VI, who reigns today, and whose valor holds in suspense the arms for France entire. I felt myself borne to love him; he matched my sentiments, and I swore a fidelity to him from which nothing could make me depart.

I cannot help admitting that amour counted for a great deal in that which bore me to cherish the family of Toulouse. Yes, my sons. At the age of fifteen I dared to love the daughter of Comte Alphonse, the beautiful and virtuous Loïse.[47] She was my age; accustomed to seeing me, perceiving the predilection that her father testified toward me, she regarded me with more attention; for myself, struck by the splendor of her charms, I promised myself to adore her until the tomb.

From that moment on I employed all my faculties to rendering myself worthy of the hand to which I dared to aspire; always with arms in hand, I tried every day to merit the palms of victory, in order to enlace them in the cherished tree of the god of tenderness. I was also extremely assiduous to the lessons of celebrated troubadours; I took pleasure in listening to

---

[46] This is incompatible with the chronology of the main story; the hermit's story, like Savary's, is presumably based on an independent story, but other details therein suggest that it was originally set considerably earlier than the twelfth century.
[47] Neither Alphonse Jourdain (1103-1148) nor Raymond V (1134-1194), the actual father of Raymond VI, had a daughter name Loïse; Raymond VI's only sister was named Adélaïde.

them; taking them for examples, I sought to extract sounds from the guitar to company the songs that I composed; I carried everything back to Loïse, and without mentioning my flame to her, without asking her for the gift of amorous thanks, I was assured of her heart, as she knew, similarly, the empire that she had over my soul.

I was entering my eighteenth year when the Comte de Barcelona sent envoys to request help from the Comte de Toulouse.[48] The Moors were threatening his estates with a formidable army, and in the name of generosity and religion, he solicited Christian princes to send him reinforcements that would enable him to repel the enemies of the Holy Gospel.

All the young nobility of Alphonse's court, glad to find an opportunity to signal themselves, asked the sovereign for permission to go to Barcelona. In spite of my amour for Loïse, I was not the last to show myself. Prince Raymond also wanted to share the perils of the enterprise, and his father, thinking that he would not find a more propitious circumstance for enabling his son to appear with splendor, permitted him to take up arms in favor of the Comte de Barcelona.

The day of our departure was fixed for the day after the festival of Easter. On the day before I was walking in the gardens of the palace, which descend in an amphitheater all the way to the bank of the Garonne. There, immersed in my reveries, I was imagining the glory that as in preparation for me in Spain, and, at the same time, the regrets that my heart was experiencing in quitting the demoiselle that I cherished; that double sentiment agitating my heart simultaneously inspired the ballad of the departure.

I was concluding my song when Loïse appeared before me. She had heard my ballad; an amiable blush covered her face, but a smile of bounty embellished her vermilion mouth.

---

[48] Alphonse II of Aragon, who was Count of Barcelona and King of Aragon from 1162-1196 was usually at war with the Comtes de Toulouse, as his father had been before him, and suffered little aggression from is Moorish neighbors..

"Sire Bérenger," she said to me, it seems that you are quitting Toulouse without regret?"

"Oh, noble Princesse," I exclaimed, vehemently. "What can have given birth in you to that false belief?"

"One does not sing when one is suffering."

"Do not think so, Demoiselle; dolor also has its song."

"You must teach it to me, Sire; today I could not even sing the sad ballad of Mélusine."

"Can it be that this day is causing you some pain?"

"Does it not precede that of tomorrow? Is my brother not departing, and are you not going with him?"

"The interest that you testify to me touches me, but doubtless I merit it. My attachment to the noble Raymond, and for the Comte, your father, for your illustrious house, for yourself..."

"I am pleased to see brave chevaliers professing such sentiments," said Loïse.

"Oh, Madame, they dare not allow all those they experience to burst forth."

"One does not hide that which does not offend honor."

"No, doubtless, honor cannot be offended by the sentiments with which my heart is filled; that is what gave birth to them, after you had inspired them."

"Chevalier!"

"Even if I appear very audacious in your eyes, I must tell you all that my respect had forced me to keep silent thus far. Yes, Madame, I burn for you; it is for you that I am flying to the walls of Barcelona; it is there that, by means of my exploits, I hope to conquer the right to maintain you in my tenderness; it is for you that I shall combat, it is your memory that, in the dangers, will be the talisman whose influence will render me invincible. I save said everything. Now, beautiful Loïse, transport me, intoxicate me with joy by your response, or plunge my soul into despair; it is at your knees that I will hear the expressions of your indulgence or the accents of our wrath."

"Get up, friend of my brother," said Loïse. "Be victorious over the Moors; it is the last victory that remains for you to win."

As she spoke thus, Loïse hid her face behind her silver veil. As for me, incapable of getting up, I had remained at her feet, devoured by amour and overwhelmed by the excess of my good fortune. O, my sons! What a moment for an ardent soul like mine! With what delights was I intoxicated! I was loved by the one for whom I would have given my existence; it was her lips that had made me he seductive confession; it was still echoing in my charmed ear; it overwhelmed me; it transported me.

Oh, it is necessary to have loved like me to appreciate all that that moment had of enchantment! And Loïse, trembling and timid, contemplating me with those eyes in which the azure of the sky was shining, as beautiful as the perfect being, and as tender, could neither flee me nor impose silence on her own heart. Yes, we were soon convinced of the reciprocity of our tenderness; we promised one another that it would be eternal; and with her beautiful hands, the daughter of the Comte de Toulouse made me a present of a long purple veil that served her as a waistband she had embroidered a cross and her family's arms on it, as well as a motto: LONG LIVE THE COMTES RAYMOND, TOULOUSE AND SAINT-SERNIN. I received it humbly, on my knees, and when she placed it over my heart, I sensed, with emotion, how redoubtable I would be to the followers of Mohammed.

Eventually, it was necessary to separate. In order not to arouse suspicions, we agreed a means of establishing a correspondence between us that could aid us to endure the irritations of absence.

I went back to the palace transported by joy; I trembled that the cause that had given birth to it might be legible in my face, and imagine my fear when it was announced to me that Comte Alphonse wanted to see me in private. I went to his cabinet; I was truly anxious about what he might want with me, when, on going in, I saw my father with my brother

Arembert. I flew into their arms. My father, applauding the journey that I was about to make, announced to me that he had brought my brother to take my place with the Comte de Toulouse.

At that news, I felt an unknown secret emotion within me to which I could not assign a cause. Alas, my sons, it was a sad presage of what my brother destined for me. I saw Arembert with all his graces; I feared for myself his presence near Loïse; knowing the lightness of the women of Toulouse, I feared that my lover might be similar to them. However, it would have been inappropriate for me to make Loïse party to my reflections; I was constrained to hide them in my soul, and to present externally a joy that I no longer felt.

My father occupied the rest of the day in giving me the instructions of his tenderness as well as his experience. He also took care to furnish me abundantly with equipment; he augmented the number of the men-at-arms that were to follow me; in sum, he treated me as the cherished son who was to succeed him in the rich barony of Saint-Félix.

I spent the night in a perpetual agitation; it seemed to me that Loïse was betraying me; the name of Arembert resounded in my ear; I thought I saw floods of blood flowing; I was wandering in somber cells. Oh, how painful my dreams were! Heaven surely sent them to me to teach me to mistrust a brother who would not take long to become my mortal enemy.

I leapt out of bed at the instant that the steeple of La Dalbade was colored by the first light of day. I went to see my father; he was already dressed. We marched toward the meeting place, where I had the pleasure of seeing my lover again. Taking for a pretext accompanying her brother Raymond for a few leagues from Toulouse, she went with us, mounted on a white palfrey, surrounded by her women. After we had made our last adieux with our eyes, the knights and I rode rapidly along the road to Carcassonne, which was to see us within its walls before the end of the following day. We headed toward Narbonne, and Perpignan was the last place where we stopped.

The Comte de Barcelona received us with the loyalty and nobility that characterizes the house of Lara; he heaped us with the marks of his magnificence, and young Raymond received from him the honors that he merited by his virtues as well as his birth. But we did not remain inactive for long; couriers came to announce the approach of Moorish troops, which were advancing, menacing the Christian princes. We ran to arms. I placed the rich scarf given to me by Loïse over my breastplate and, drawing near to her brother, prepared to charge with him the enemies of the holy religion.

Uttering frightful clamors, invoking their false prophet, the Moors appeared on the ridges of the hills, from which they descended into the plain like devastating torrents. Abderame was commanding them; a valiant knight, he combined his natural bravery with civility, the amiable prerogative of French paladins.[49] The hope of measuring himself against them had led him to declare war on the Barcelonnais. His hope was not disappointed. We spurred our horses as soon as the signal had been given, and we launched ourselves against our adversaries, invoking our ladies.

The standard of Toulouse, surrounded by a valiant elite, found itself at the heart of the battle. Raymond, Sicard, Gérard, and Pestillac surrounded it. I was with them, and, by our combined efforts, we sought to make fortune incline toward the Spanish side; but our adversaries were worthy of us. Abderame, armed with his large scimitar, escorted by the valiant Muley, the impetuous Abdalla, the superb Mohammed, Tarif, Osmanar, Ismael and Zerfar, a bellicose troop, opposed

---

[49] Abderame was the name given by French chroniclers to the Islamic leader, Abudul Rahman al Ghafiqi, who confronted Charles Martel at the battle of Tours in 732, which was later seen as crucial in halting the Islamic advance into France. Langon appears to have borrowed the prestige of the name to ornament a fictitious character, just as he subsequently appropriates the name of Ferragus (or Ferragut) from Carolingian romance.

our efforts everywhere. His sword felled the young Baron de Castelnaud d'Entrefonds, it cut off the head of the Sire de Revel, and it defeated the squadron of the Carcassonnais, while Comte Raymond caused the Arab Mohammed to bite the dust and the ferocious Alamar, who ornamented himself with his enemies' bloody remains.

I shall not detail for you here, my sons, the noble feats of arms by which I signaled myself on that memorable day. Let it suffice for you to know that the frightened Moors recoiled before me more than once. My lance first pierced Ferragus, whose pride gave him for an ancestor the famous Ferragus who was an antagonist of the likes of Roland and Renaud. Then I attained Emiraud, a presumptuous African who, proud of his gigantic stature and supernatural strength, found in me a double adversary in those two undesirable qualities.

The battle, however, went on with an equal advantage. Burning to distinguish myself by means of some extraordinary feat, which would permit the celestial Loïse to be proud of her choice, I searched with my eyes for the place where the danger appeared to me to be most pressing. I perceived the squadron emerged from the walls of Carcassonne, which, as I have already told you, was fleeing before the supernatural valor of the celebrated Abderame. I did not hesitate to run to place an obstacle to his rapid success.

"Why are you fleeing, cowards?" I shouted at Trencavel's soldiers. "Is it thus that you sustain the honor of the provinces of Occitania? Feeble warriors, unworthy of that fine name, will you recoil before a single man? Oh, cease to cover your renown, once so famous, with that humiliating affront. Come, follow me; perhaps I have bravery enough to guide you to the road of victory."

My words, my reproaches, the blade that I caused to flash, and with which I menaced the most timid, al rendered them a new vigor. We returned to the battle uttering howls of wrath. Abderame stopped, surprised by seeing battalions he thought were in complete rout retracing their steps. Soon, however, he recognized the cause of that change, in perceiving me in the first rank, sword in hand and holding in my left hand the banner of my suzerain. He pushed his charger toward me.

I knew by his manner, even more than his blows, that I had found a worthy assailant. We attacked one another with an unparalleled ferocity; he could not suffer that I would snatch the victory; I was indignant that he dared to dispute it with me. We had pressed one another for some time with an equal advantage, when, gathering al my strength, I dealt my enemy a blow so terrible that I broke his scimitar, and my sword, descending on the head of his horse, sent it rolling over the arena.

The valiant Moor, dragged by the fall of his destrier, fell with it. I leapt from my horse and, pushing away the soldiers who wanted to finish Abderame off, I extended my hand to him.

"Noble Abderame," I said, "get up. A French knight does not fight his enemy when he is not in a state to defend himself."

"I recognize there," he replied, "that character of your great nation. Chevalier, whoever you are, learn what Abderame wants to do. From his moment on, if the Comte de Barcelona approves, I will cease the war that is desolating his estates; I will order my troops to withdraw and I will sign a peace with him of which you will be the guarantee."

"Flattered by the discourse of the magnanimous cherif, I extended my hand to him as a sign of amity. He mounted a horse that I had given to him, and, faithful to his promise, he rode into the heart of the battle to stop the carnage.

At his voice, and is orders, which reached all of them, his phalanges withdrew to some distance from the battlefield; those of the Comte followed their example; the swords were sheathed. Finally, after a few minutes, the two armies that had been slaughtering one another ceased all attacks; the knights of the various parties came together. By my intermediation, Abderame and the sovereign of Barcelona conferred. They did not take long to conclude a treaty that closed the temple of war for a long time.

They wanted to give me all honors; I refrained from accepting them. I was young but, in spite of my age, I knew how difficult it is to conserve the amity of a prince who might imagine that he is thought to be your inferior.

My adroit modesty served me beyond my hopes; everyone proclaimed, multiplying it a hundredfold, the part that I had played on that memorable day. The rumor reached all the way to Toulouse, and a letter from the sensitive Loïse appeared to my amorous heart to be the most beautiful recompense that I had a right to expect.

Meanwhile, Abderame desired to have me with him. I could not refuse his entreaties, and, some time after the ratification of the peace, I left Barcelona in order to go to Toledo, which was the abode of the prince whose amity I had been able to conquer. I had several adventures on the way from which I extracted myself with glory, and the renown of which, preceding me to Toledo, gave birth in the Moorish knights the desire to see me. Abderame, when I appeared before him, came to embrace me.

"Noble Frenchman," he said, "I yearn to see you near me; my heart is anxious to recognize before all my warriors the important service you rendered me. I owe you life, and I am proud to say so; it is only a coward who blushes to acknowledge such an action."

"King," I replied, "You praise an ordinary action too highly. No, you do not owe me life; I am unable to kill a man whom fate has left without defense. Your fall might have been mine, and you would have done for me what destiny permitted me to do."

A flattering murmur that rose up round me told me how my speech had been able to please. Abderame took me to his private apartments, and we spent the day agreeably.

During my sojourn at the court of Toledo I made the acquaintance of an old Arab who had been Abderame's tutor; Zalostal was his name. A skillful physician, he had spent part of his life traveling in Asia, Africa, Spain and the islands of the Mediterranean. He had acquired vast knowledge, of which he was able to make use for the god of humanity. Although a Moor, he was tolerant; he believed that a Christian could be saved, and although far from resembling the imams and mullahs, he only preached peace and indulgence for various religions. I did not take long to merit his amity; he attached himself to me immediately, in recognition of my conduct toward the Prince of Toledo.

One day, when we were walking in the gardens of the castle, we were talking about the marvels of nature. "Chevalier," Zalostal said to me, "you cannot know it in its entirety, nature, so beautiful, so rich and so varied. Arms and your youth have not permitted you to devote yourself to that attractive study, but there are things that your profession as a man of war renders it indispensable for you to know; there are simples that, cleverly combined, arrest life that is ready to flee, calm dolors and cause the most profound wounds to disappear in a short time; it only depends on you to know them. There are others that, in these centuries, also have their real utility. They can subjugate men, they can aid in doing good, as they can become the instruments of crime in the hands of vicious individuals."

"Oh, my gratitude would be great," I said, "if you would deign to confide those important secrets to me."

"I will not hesitate to initiate you into our mysteries," said Zalostal, "for, my dear Bérenger, in Spain I am the principal chief of a secret association that corresponds with the one that hides its useful works in the depths of Egyptian pyramids; it is in silence and in the dark that we study nature. Fortunate to surprise her sometimes, we seek incessantly to divine her."

"Before going any further, Seigneur Zalostal," I said, "will you tell me whether our association demands oaths and things incompatible with my double quality as a knight and a Christian?"

"My son," he replied, "permit me to give you that name, our institution, perhaps more enlightened than the rest of peoples, has taken for its motto the sublime word *Tolerance*. We welcome Muslims, Christians, Jews and idolaters. Are you faithful to the religion you follow, we say; if you are, you might be our brother, for the man who follows his religion exactly cannot be a dishonest man; only woe betide the man who has none!"

"That is sufficient for me, Seigneur," I said. "Now, I solicit you not to delay in initiating me into your assembly."

"Tomorrow, Chevalier, when the shadow covers the globe," Zalostal said, "I will come to fetch you from your apartment in order to take you to the place where the sages meet."

Our conversation ended there. I returned to Abderame, and I continued to take part in the feasts that succeeded one another without interruption among those gallant and brave people.

At the appointed hour, Zalostal appeared before me. He was carrying a lamp in his left hand; his robe was red; embroidered thereon were the planets, the signs of the zodiac, animals and flowers; his turban was white, ornamented with a long black plume.

"Come, Bérenger," the Arab said to me, "the moment has come to witness our ceremonies."

I answered him with the expressions of my joy, and prepared to follow him. We went down the great stairway of the palace; we then found a low door through which we went and entered a room formed as a long rectangle, at the end of which was a statue representing a Visigoth warrior. Zalostal tapped it lightly and it moved, allowing us to see a little spiral stairway...

(*Here Bérenger's manuscript is torn, but a few words that can still be read inform us that he was initiated into the mysteries of a society skilled in the art of phantasmagoria, and in those of chemistry and physics. In brief, he learned in Toledo the tricks that he used following his return to Saint-Félix to frighten his brother, and which scientists have rediscovered in our day.*)

While I was avidly studying the sciences that presented so many charms to me, a monster, whom it is necessary for me to call my brother, was working to destroy the edifice of my happiness. Arembert did not take long to feel for Loïse the same sentiments that I had experienced, but amour cannot be virtuous in such a soul; it was necessary that it was signaled by a few sins. Loïse saw in Arembert the brother of the man she adored; that title engaged her to treat him with a marked distinction; the kindness she showed him nourished hope in that presumptuous heart.

For some time she had not received my news; my silence made her desperate, and she often drew away from her importunate court to go and bury her sad reflection along the banks of the Aquitanian river, There she appealed to me, sometimes criticizing the events that separated us, sometimes criticizing me, and every new days found her suffering more. But I was not culpable; exact in writing to the daughter of the Comte de Toulouse, I thought of nothing but her, and it was not my inconstancy that she had to fear; it was the perfidy of Arembert, of which neither she nor I had any suspicion.

He had discovered, I don't know how, the secret correspondence transmitted between Loïse and me, the assurances of our mutual ardor. What was his rage at that moment! He understood how redoubtable a rival I was; however, far from renouncing his projects, he swore on the altar of jealousy to make every effort to disunite two lovers whose tenderness was an obstacle to his happiness. He seduced the page to whom I had my letters sent; that wretch sacrificed us to his vile interest. From that moment on, Loïse and I were prey to the torments of anguish and the sharpest anxieties.

Loïse, as I have already told you, my children, did not know to what cause to attribute my silence, which was breaking her heart. She shed bitter tears, and, without being able to sing, engraved the ballad that her love inspired in the bark of a plane tree.

She had ceased to write those regrets when Arembert, emerging from the wood, approached Loïse affecting a cheerful attitude, which he suddenly repressed at the sight of the chagrin with which the face of the young Princesse was covered.

"Noble demoiselle," he said, bowing respectfully, "can it be that a dark cloud veils to this extent your eyes, in which contentment alone ought to shine? Is it necessary for me not to allow the pleasure that I am experiencing in having received news of a brother who is very dear to me?"

The pallor that covered Loïse's cheeks was replaced by a vivid blush. "Don't deceive me, Sire Arembert," she said. "Bérenger has written to you? Doubtless he speaks to you about my father, about me; he gives you details of the actions of my brother, for we know the attachment he has to the house of Toulouse."

"Entirely given over to his amour," said Arembert, "he never ceases to talk to me about it."

"His amour!"

"Keenly smitten by the charms of young Zuleïma, the sister of the Prince of Toledo..."

"Oh, Seigneur, what are you telling me? Could he...no, Sire, you are imposing upon me; your brother is not a disloyal knight."

"Pardon me, you who are the daughter of my suzerain! I did not know that my brother..."

"Yes, Sire Arembert, I have given him my heart. He had promised me an inviolable fidelity, and your speech..."

"Has brought despair into your sensitive soul. Oh, Madame, how frightful it is for me to afflict you! But how painful it is for me to be the brother of a perjurer who must no longer love you!"

"Can Bérenger be culpable?"

"Unfortunate Princesse, he is unworthy of you."

"Give me proof."

"I accuse him with regret, but read his letter; it will convince you of his perfidy."

"Give it to me," said Loïse. She read a letter in which Arembert had imitated my handwriting. "Oh God! It is over; there is no more happiness on earth for Loïse."

"Princesse," said Arembert, "forget an ingrate; let a just pride expel him from your heart, and banish him to distant memory."

"Arembert," said Loïse, "you have not loved if you think our will is sufficient to steal us from amour."

"No," said Arembert, "I cannot get over my astonishment. What! My brother obtains your tenderness and he dares to renounce it! No, he's no more than an unworthy warrior who ought to bear the punishment of his offense. I will go to him; I will remind him of all that he has lost."

"You will go to Toledo?"

"If you order me to do so."

"Oh, good Arembert! Leave immediately; carry my despair to the fickle Bérenger; tell him that he has made me very unhappy, bring him back…what am I saying? No, I never want to see him again."

After having reflected, Arembert said: "Princesse, suffer my zeal to become manifest at this moment. Yes, I will go to Bérenger, and heap him with my indignation, if he is guilty, or help him, if he has only gone astray. But, either to punish him, for his infidelity or his weakness, give me two letters; let the first respire anger, speak to him about a new lover, tell him that you are breaking with him irrevocably; let the second repair the harm that the first will have done."

Thus spoke the knavish Arembert. Seduced by his fallacious devotion, the credulous Loïse hastened to write the letter that was to cost me so many tears. She gave the two dispatches to my brother, not without uttering deep sighs; and, wishing for my innocence, she did not forget anything in writing it that could convince me of her perfidy.

Furnished with a letter so favorable to his projects, Arembert did not want to delay setting forth. He obtained permission easily from the Comte de Toulouse to come and join me, and two days after that scene, in which confidence had been the dupe of malevolence, Arembert took the road to Barcelona.

I had just quit Toledo, sufficiently instructed in the art of the mages. Yearning to see my homeland, and above all my Loïse, I had gone to Barcelona, where I solicited Prince Raymond to return to Toulouse, but he, retained in Catalonia by the charms of the beautiful Elvire d'Aragon, was in no hurry to yield to my entreaties.

Arembert experienced some displeasure in finding me already so close to Occitania; he hoped that the further I was plunged in Spain, the less easy it would be for me to disconcert his plans.

I was with Raymond when one of my squires came to announce the arrival of my brother to me. I took my leave of the Prince immediately and ran to my lodgings, where my brother had arrived. As soon as he perceived me he hugged me, even shed a few tears, and lavished the most tender caresses upon me; I believed that I was loved. It was very pleasant for me to experience such a pure and celestial sentiment: the love of a brother.

After the first compliments, I said: "Arembert, how have you left the court of Toulouse? Have the Comte and his daughter forgotten me?"

"You have nothing of which to complain in their regard; they never cease talking about their Bérenger—that is how they name you—and if Princesse Loïse did not feel a tender amour for the son of the Vicomte de Lille en Jourdain,[50] I would not hesitate to proclaim you her preferred knight."

---

[50] This character is fictitious, but the historical Jourdain II, who became Seigneur de Lille-Jourdain in 1191, and who also held to title Vicomte de Gimoes (mentioned briefly in the main story in a different context) later became a significant figure in Napoléon Peyrat's fantasized account of the Albigensian crusade as the husband of Esclarmonde de Foix, the daughter of the Comte de Foix replaced in the present story by the fictitious Bélisène.

"Arembert!" I exclaimed. "What are you saying? Are you talking to me about the tenderness of Loïse for the arrogant Godefroi?"

"I have reason, my brother, to be surprised by your astonishment. Can it be that you do not know what is public knowledge in Toulouse?"

"Arembert! You're doubtless mistaken."

"I would like to be, if that displeases you. But at least, if you doubt what I say, perhaps you will learn more in reading this letter, which Princesse Loïse gave me for you."

"Wretch!" I said. "Why not give it to me promptly, that desired letter? It would have immediately put an end to the bitter anxiety that is devouring me."

Having said that, I took the letter me brother handed me, and prepared avidly to read it with a delicious pleasure—but, oh my sons, what became of me when I read those fatal pages in which, speaking to me with the most offensive indifference, Loïse admitted that she was abandoning me for a new lover, whose name she did not reveal.

I have suffered a great deal since, but I do not think that I have ever experienced anything comparable to all that struck me at that fatal moment. Rage, furious amour, anger, despair, all those various sentiments, divided my soul, all lacerating it at the same time. In how many reckless exclamations I exhaled my fury! With what odious names did I not charge the pure Louise? In an instant, the daylight was in horror for me; I detested human beings, and life seemed to me too frightful to bear.

Yes, doubtless, if I had only listened to my ardor, I would have extracted myself from life, but the need to punish the man I believed to be my rival retained my hand, already turned toward myself; I sensed that I could only die in immolating the fortunate Godefroi, and it was without a second's delay that I wanted to leave Barcelona in order to fly to the place where I believed that vengeance summoned me.

Strangely annoyed by that sudden resolution, Arembert tried by a thousand means to give another direction to my ideas; he was wasting his time, and, far from yielding to his arguments, I felt driven to get away from him; I hated him, as the price of the letter he had brought me. I did not want to bid adieu to the Comte de Barcelona or to young Raymond, for fear that they might raise obstacles to a departure of which I did not want to tell them the cause.

Arembert, convinced that he could not retain me, did not seek to calm my despair by showing me Loïse's second letter; no, he thought that I would go to challenge Godefroi de Lille en Jourdain, that perhaps I would be killed, and that, whatever the issue of the combat, it would raise great obstacles to my rapprochement with the young Comtesse de Toulouse.

As soon as I had gone, Arembert thought of devoting himself to pleasure, and to seeking combats, for which he was avid; for, far from resembling the perfidious in their cowardice, he had all the courage of a loyal knight. At the court of Aragon, to which he went some time thereafter, he encountered a man illustrious by his birth but debased in his sentiments; that was Don Juan d'Astorga, who, born for crime, completed the inoculation my brother's heart with it. They soon became worthy of one another. They were associated in their enterprises, and the misfortune of a large number of virtuous young women was born of their union.

I shall leave that perverse couple for a while, who would not take long to play too great a role in the story of my life, and return to an adventure that occurred during my journey from Barcelona to Toulouse.

Night was showing in the Orient, but the Occident was still brilliant with all the pomp of evening; followed by my squires, I was descending from the crest of a rather high ridge that was part of the chain of the Pyrenees. Buried in my reflections, I let myself drift into a vague reverie that soon animated in my head a vague poeticism, the impulse of which I sometimes felt. Wanting to compose a song that depicted my dolorous situation, I dismounted and, desiring not to have the men of my retinue as witnesses to my delirium, I engaged them to continue their course, assuring them that I would catch up with them before long. They drew away; I remained alone, and I then composed a ballad that I entitled "The Troubadour's Last Song."[51]

By this linden, mute and desolate,
Repose, harp of the troubadour.
No more joy for his bewildered soul;
The one he loves has betrayed his amour.

Repose, my redoubtable sword;
Corrosive time can tarnish your gleam.
When pleasure flees me like a vain dream,
Should I seek the palms of combat?

Pass on, jongleur; I no longer want to hear
Your pleasant chords, your gracious concerts.
If the sensitive and tender lover is betrayed
Sing no more, form no more verses.

A frightful woe agitates and devours me!
I die, alas, a victim of amour.
O my friends, come to hear again
The last song of the plaintive troubadour.

The shadow had finished covering the sky when I concluded my plaintive ballad. The air was calm and the silence of nature reined around me. Collecting myself, I thought that it was time to go to the place where my retinue was doubtless waiting for me. I was already on my feet when I perceived a dozen brigands around me, who called upon me to surrender. As a knight only surrenders when his strength no longer per-

---

[51] Author's note: "Music by the author of the words. There is another music composed by M. le Chevalier Achille de Lamothe." Achille de Lamothe is recorded in Lamothe-Langon's *Biographie-Toulousaine* as his younger brother, and the second son of Joseph de Lamothe

mits him to fight, far from yielding to the insolent appeal that was made to me I did not hesitate to draw my sword.

My resolution imposed itself upon my cowardly adversaries for a moment; soon, however, they rallied and fell upon me. I defended myself vigorously; three assassins thrown by me into the dust attested to my courage; but the fury of my enemies increased, while the lassitude by which I was afflicted fought for them.

Then, a knight of tall stature, accompanied by four squires, doubtless attracted by the noise, ran to my defense. His first thrusts dispatched two of the brigands; the other, frightened, hastened to seek their salvation in flight. We did not bother to pursue them.

"Chevalier," I said to my liberator, "my life belongs to you; you can employ it in your service."

"Valiant unknown," he said to me, "far be it from me to refuse such an offer, and if you care to follow me, I will take you to a place where your assistance will be very necessary to me."

"There is no place to which I will not follow you," I replied.

In the meantime, we were rejoined by my men-at-arms.

"Who are these?" the knight asked me.

"They are the men of my retinue, Monseigneur," I replied. "They are all devoted to me."

"So much the better; they can be useful to us."

Not wanting to fatigue the knight with my questions, I rode beside him for about an hour. We then arrived before a château situated on the summit of a rock.

"This," said my liberator, "is the goal of our journey. It is from here that it is necessary to deliver Yolande de Valiech, whom the brutal Montorban is holding prisoner, contrary to the law of men. I have an intelligence in the château, and we shall only fight in the last extremity."

As he finished speaking, my conductor stopped before a postern, which did not take long to open in response to a signal that he made.

We all went in together, observing the most profound silence. The varlet who had introduced us guided us, via a secret stairway, to a large room, in which we perceived a young woman whose portrait I cannot help myself painting for you. Yolande de Valiech, for it was her, seduced at first glance by a pleasant combination of vivacity and the most admirable restraint. Her figure was slender, like the elegant poplars that rise on the banks of the impetuous Eridan; her dark eyes, in which the fires of youth gleamed, were adorned with two magnificent eyebrows; the freshest colors shone incessantly in her mobile features; her physiognomy, sometimes piquant, playful, naïve, impish, sulky, serious or melancholy, incessantly lent her new charms. Such was, in her springtime, that angel of beauty and candor.

As soon as we appeared to her eyes, far from being frightened, she uttered a cry of joy and, launching herself into the arms of the knight, my liberator, she said: "Oh, dear Godefroi! I have ceased to be unhappy, then!"

At the name of Godefroi I felt a sudden emotion; I trembled at having obligations to the man I regarded as my rival. "Chevalier," I cried, without reflecting on how unjust I was, since the lover of Loïse could not be Yolande's. "Are you the son of the Vicomte de Lille en Jourdain?"

"Yes, Monseigneur," he replied, surprised by the eccentricity of my demand.

"Well, then," I said to him. "I shall forget what I owe you and I challenge you to single combat."

"Chevalier!" said Godefroi. "Do you doubt my courage?"

"You have insulted me," I said.

"Suffer that, without responding immediately to your inconceivable challenge, I ask you in my turn what reason can have animated you against me?"

I drew nearer to him in order not to be overheard by my retinue. "Are you not the favored lover of Loïse de Toulouse?"

Hotly, Godefroi replied: "The man who burns for Yolande cannot bear other chains."

"Can my brother have imposed upon me, then?"

"What, Chevalier!" said Yolande. "Can you accuse Godefroi of an attachment that would render him despicable?"

"Oh, Demoiselle," I cried, "how painful it is to be deceived by one's brother or the one to whom one owes the light of day!"

"Chevalier," said Godefroi, candidly, "if it were not for the amour that I have for my lady, I would descend with you into the lists, but God forbid that I poison such sweet moments. I swear to you by honor and by my Yolande that I have never addressed my prayers to the daughter of Comte Alphonse de Toulouse."

I put my hand in Godefroi's. "Forgive me, Chevalier; excuse Bérenger, Sire de Saint-Félix."

Scarcely had I finished speaking than a noise was heard; clamors burst forth in all directions, and voices that we distinguished were crying treason; we did not doubt that we had been discovered, and no longer thought of anything but facing up to the enemies that were about to attack us.

We were not mistaken in our conjectures; the reckless Montorban, awakened by his remorse, had perceived us; he had hastened to assemble his soldiers, and it was at their head that he fell upon us; but he had not expected to find such a large number of men-at-arms to fight, for my squires, united with Godefroi's, formed a detachment capable of revising a troop more numerous than the one Montorban opposed to us. We did not hesitate to attack, and prompt to anticipate him, we stopped him at the moment when he thought he only had to seize his rival.

Here I had a moment of good fortune, since I was able to render to the son of the Vicomte de Lille the signal service that he had rendered me; I saved his life and that of Yolande, whom two soldiers were about to immolate; I felled Montorban beneath my blows, and victory crowned the efforts of recognition.

After Godefroi and I had sworn an eternal amity, I left him happy with his lover, and I hastened to resume my route toward Toulouse. It was no longer with a broken heart that I continued that voyage; no, I no longer feared Loïse's inconstancy; I thought that the letter was false, and that it had been traced by my culpable brother, whose veracity I justly suspected. However, I was not entirely tranquil, for a veritably smitten heart always fears displeasing the one it cherishes. My impatience made me hasten the pace of our chargers, and it was toward the end of the day that I entered the capital of Comte Alphonse's estates.

The extreme desire that I had to see Loïse did not permit me to put it off until the next day. Not wanting to appear before her unexpectedly, I sent my principal squire to make my compliments to the sovereign of Toulouse and asked him for permission to come myself to bring him news of Comte Raymond, his son.

On learning that I was nearby, Loïse needed all the strength of her soul to dissimulate her secret sentiments. Wanting to see me, not doubting that my return was a proof of my innocence, she had wanted her father not to refuse me the honor of being admitted to his presence. Far from rejecting my request, my messenger came to tell me that I was awaited immediately at the Château Narbonnais. I went there without further delay.

The Comte's welcome was bound to flatter my pride, but I was only occupied with that of his daughter. Constrained to dissimulate before the strangers that surrounded us, her eyes alone could speak to my heart. In spite of the impression of severity with which she sought to fill them, I read in them nevertheless the assurance that I was still preferred.

"Sire Bérenger," said Alphonse, "have combats alone occupied you during your absence?"

"Monseigneur Comte," I replied, "it is not beyond the Pyrenees that I have sought to relax in the arms of amour from the fatigues inseparable from war."

Those few words sufficed for Loïse; the constraint disappeared, and her charming eyes no longer showed me anything but tenderness. This passed our first meeting. The next day we had the facility to stroll in the gardens and speak to one another without witnesses. There we opened our hearts, we reached an understanding, and we fell into accord that we had been the victim of the perfidious Arembert. We promised one another not to listen to his culpable insinuations henceforth, and to seek to explain ourselves every time anyone tried to disunite us.

We did not have that trouble, however; several years passed without Arembert reappearing in Toulouse. In the meantime, he lived in Spain, where he signaled himself by a thousand acts of high valor, while I fought in France for the cause of Comte Alphonse. My name was surrounded by some brightness of glory. Every day, Loïse cherished me more; every day, I learned to cherish her even more. Her brother showed a frank amity for me; my father treated me as a son worthy to inherit his name. I was able to hope for happiness; but I had a brother, and it was him who was to cause me to drain the bitter cup of misfortune.

Weary of his distance, Arembert, unable to free himself from the passion that Loïse had inspired in him, decided to return among us in order to transport his sins there. On arrival he asked me for a private meeting. There, far from seeking to palliate his misdeeds, he augmented them, but it was in confessing to me his attachment for Loïse.

"My brother," he said to me, "you know as well as I do that one is never the master of one's heart. But finally, absence and the sight of new objects have changed my sentiments. I have endeavored no longer to see in Loïse anything but a cherished sister. Cease to fear me and render me a tenderness that is necessary to me."

Seduced by his words, and being unable to resolve always to mistrust a person whom nature commanded me to love, I pressed Arembert to my bosom and all was forgotten. But he, more adroit in his maneuvers, employed the strongest means to doom me. He got around Comte Alphonse, he gave birth to doubts about my fidelity. Alphonse, blinded, commenced by no longer showing me as much amity.

I had no suspicion as yet of the storm that was about to burst over my head when, one day, carried away by amour with my Loïse, in one of the islands formed by the arms of the river flowing from the high Pyrenees, adjacent to the gardens of the palace, we forgot our duties...

Oh, what was my lover's despair when the delirium had calmed down! With what odious names did she not lavish me? What reproaches did she not make to herself?

"Flee me," she said to me. "Go, cruel Bérenger, far from one who can no longer look at you without blushing. Oh, my friend, what have we done?"

I sought to calm her bitter dolor with my words.

"No," she replied, "there is no longer happiness for me if the bonds of marriage do not legitimate the sins of amour. Bérenger, you are of a rank that gives you the right to aspire to my hand; go find my father, obtain his consent, and may we be less culpable."

"Yes," I said to her in my turn, "I will fulfill a sacred duty; but suffer that before addressing myself to the Comte, I try to prejudice the Prince your brother in your favor."

Loïse did not oppose that project; she even wanted us also to inform her sister, Princesse Jeanne, who was subsequently to marry the Vicomte de Carcassonne, Roger Trencavel, of our tenderness. We did not take long to make that double confidence.

"Bérenger," the noble Raymond said, as he embraced me, "It was pleasant for me to have you as a friend; it will be even more pleasant for me to have you as a brother."

Assured of his consent, I only occupied myself with securing that of Comte Alphonse. At the moment when everything gave me hope of obtaining it without any obstacle, I received a message on the part of the sovereign, sent to me via a page, ordering me to appear before him immediately. Astonished by such a command, not knowing whether Raymond has spoken to him of my love for his daughter, I hastened to obey, determined to take advantage of the circumstance to open my heart to him.

As soon as I appeared before him, he said: "Sire Bérenger, it is necessary that you go to the Court of France."

"What, Monseigneur!" I said. "You want to send me away? Have my services displeased you?"

"If you want to please me," Alphonse said, "You will obey me immediately."

"Once more, Sire Comte, suffer that I ask you whether someone has done me a disservice in your regard."

"You will do yourself a disservice if you disobey me any longer."

"Is it necessary, Monseigneur that I go away without having consulted the will of my father?"

"Oh well, depart for Saint-Félix; it is sufficient for me that you leave my court."

As he finished speaking he turned his back on me, and left me in a state difficult to describe. How disappointed I was in my hopes! Could I ask him for the hand of his daughter at the moment when he was signifying my disgrace? I withdrew, heartbroken with dolor, and returned to Raymond and his sisters, abandoning myself to my despair.

I threw them into an inexpressible astonishment in telling them of my conversation with their father. They did not hesitate to believe that someone had done me a disservice with him. Raymond wanted to go and find him immediately, but he could not change the Comte's mind, and was instructed not to see me again.

In the meantime, I had withdrawn. Loïse had remained alone with her sister, and there, though a thousand sobs, she told her how necessary our marriage was. Raymond came back equally consternated; Loïse and I implored his assistance, and, vanquished by our pleas, he consented to a secret union between his sister and me.

In order not to give rise to suspicions in the mind of Comte Alphonse, it was decided that I would depart for Saint-Félix, but that on a fixed day I would go to Rabastens, where I would enchain my destiny to that of Loïse. I therefore left the Court of Toulouse, dissimulating my chagrin, or, rather, charming it with the flattering hope of soon being the husband of the woman I idolized.

Arembert, over whom I did not extend my suspicions, proposed to accompany me; I refused that mark of amity and begged him not to remove himself from Toulouse, but, on the contrary, to remain in order to serve me there with regard to the Comte, if ever he adopted a less unfavorable opinion of me. Arembert did not insist; he pretended to share my views; content to see me separated from Loïse, he asked for nothing more, but his joy was not of long duration.

When he learned that the Princesses de Toulouse and young Raymond were going to spend a part of the summer at the Château de Rabastens, in spite of his maleficent genius, he did not divine the motive for that journey, and thus could not raise any obstacle to it.

For my part, as soon as I learned that the moment was favorable, I escaped from Saint-Félix, giving my father the pretext that I was going to visit the Marquis d'Escalquers. I went by night to the château at which amity, amour, marriage and duty awaited me. I shall not describe for you, my sons, the simple ceremony that took place; suffice it for you to know that Loïse became my legitimate wife, and that you are the fruit of that bond.

The two princesses found several pretexts to dispense with returning to Toulouse before the moment when Loïse was to give birth to you. Fate came to her aid in that conjuncture. War flared up in Aquitaine. Comte Alphonse devoted all his cares to it, and was not displeased that in his absence, his two daughters were secure in one of his best fortresses. As for me, hiding in the ranks of the soldiers that my brother commanded during my absence, I fought secretly for my father-in-law, only making myself known to Raymond and Arembert.

Finally, I received a message from Loïse; she told me that the moment that would render me a father had arrived; she had brought into the world two twins: that was you, Adémar and Odon. A mysterious obscurity enveloped your birth; it was only known to Arnaud, my squire of confidence, who,

273

taking you away from the Château de Rabastens, gave you to his wife Paulette; she alimented you with her milk.

The pleasure that I experienced in receiving that happy news was so visible that Arembert could not help asking me the cause of my joy. Unforgivable weakness! I was sufficiently abandoned by wisdom to want to tell my brother what I had so much interest in hiding from him. Skilled in hiding his sentiments, he contained within himself the rage by which he was devoured; he heaped me with caresses, congratulated me on the splendor of such an alliance. His heart, he told me, tranquil for a long time, allowed him to share my happiness. I went to sleep on those words with a dangerous security.

Two days went by. I was asleep in a tent next to Arembert's when I was woken up by four soldiers who, throwing themselves upon my simultaneously, sought to neutralize the resistance that I strove to oppose to them. The one who was in command ordered me, in the name of Comte Alphonse, to render me his prisoner. At the name of the Comte I did not doubt that my arrest originated from the discovery he might have made of my marriage to his daughter; not wanting, by a longer defense, to embitter my sovereign against me, I then allowed myself to be charged with chains, content to request that I be permitted to speak to Prince Raymond.

That favor was refused me; I was placed on a horse and, all night long, I was drawn toward the Pyrenees. After a day and a half of travel, we arrived at the entrance to a gorge at the end of which was an immense château that I assumed to be the end of my journey. I was not mistaken. At the sight of us the drawbridge was lowered. I was taken to a vaulted chamber, the window of which was barred; there my irons were removed. I was left alone with my despair and my reflections.

It was not the Comte de Toulouse who had had me abducted; again I was the victim of Arembert's villainy, and the place that was to be my dwelling belonged to Don Juan d'Astorga, my culpable brother's friend.

After having stolen my liberty, Arembert hastened to quit the army and go to Toulouse, where Loïse had returned after giving birth, in order to witness the wedding of her sister to the Vicomte de Béziers.

My sudden and inconceivable disappearance had brought the sharpest dolor into the souls of my father, my wife and my friends; they lost themselves in vain conjectures; no one knew where I might be, but they did not divine the author of my misfortune. Arembert, taking part in the general dolor, seemed to be my good brother, when he was my enemy. His regrets, however, did not make any impression on Loïse; suspicion returned to reside in her soul; she conceived doubts about the sincerity of Arembert's tears, and, far from giving him the slightest part of her confidence, she rendered him suspect to Comte Raymond.

Meanwhile, Arembert employed all the resources of his evil imagination to discover where my two children were. It was important to him to cause those two innocent creatures to perish, who seemed to be insurmountable obstacles to the atrocious project that he had formed some time before. His measures were futile; Heaven, which never abandons anything entirely to misfortune, conserved my two children. It was in vain that Arembert lavished gold, that he filled the environs of Toulouse with intelligent emissaries; Paulette's dwelling was shielded from his gaze. He was in despair at that, but he promised to avenge himself on me for the lack of success of his enterprise.

Locked in my prison, I sought to avoid the distress that overwhelmed me. It came to my mind to occupy myself with the secrets that I had learned from the Arab Zarostal; soon, my ideas were magnified; I thought that it might be possible to owe my deliverance to those marvelous secrets. Materials were lacking; I thought that it would be very difficult for me to procure them, but I was agreeably disabused in that regard. My jailers, who had not been ordered to refuse me anything, hastened to furnish me with all I asked of them. From then on my liberty appeared certain. I labored with the activity that hope gives; the success surpassed what I had dared to expect.

One night, when two soldiers came to bring me my provisions for the week, scarcely had they entered my room than they were surrounded by black smoke, and they saw fiery death's-heads floating over their heads.

"Wretches!" I cried to them, vomiting flames from my mouth and touching them with a wand that numbed their arms, "you are dead if you do not open the door that you have dared to close upon me."

I could have demanded much more of them; they would have been unable to refuse me anything, so much fear was agitating their souls. Redoubling my illusions, I passed before them; they hastened to facilitate all the means of escape for me, so eager were they to rid themselves of a magician as redoubtable as I appeared to them to be.

As soon as I had crossed the drawbridge I hastened to take the road that would take me to Toulouse and, borne by the wings of hope, I did not stop for a single instant. At the first town I procured a complete suit of armor in order better to disguise myself, and, sure henceforth of not being recognized, I continued my journey.

Arembert, impatient to complete my misfortune, desperate not to be able to discover my children's refuge, decided to steal my wife from me, hoping to succeed in that abduction as he had succeeded in mine.

The night always favorable to the wicked, was the time that Arembert chose to consummate that new crime. All was tranquil in the palace of the Comtes de Toulouse when the page that my brother had previously corrupted entered Loïse's apartment.

"Madame," he said to her, "you noble friend Sire Bérenger has just arrived at the gates of the château."

"What are you telling me, page?"

"The truth, Madame. The young Baron has succeeded in escaping from the prison where Monseigneur le Comte, your father, was keeping him; he does not want to introduce himself within these walls, where his safety would be compromised, but he is waiting for you at my father's house; he has arrived there secretly. 'My friend,' he said to me, 'run to find the Comtesse, my wife; tell her that I am waiting for her and that I cannot wait long.'"

"Page, I'll follow you," said Loïse.

With those words, my unfortunate wife, not suspecting that she was going to her doom, hastened to take off her rich garments; she put on a modest costume, and, taking roundabout ways that were known to her, she left the palace that she was never to enter again.

Scarcely was she in the street than the abductors threw themselves upon her and dragged her away. Her terror and indignation robbed her of the use of her senses at first, but as she went through the Montolieu Gate she came round and started uttering screams that ought to have brought liberators to her.

It was me who presented myself. At the first sounds uttered by Loïse I recognized her beloved voice; I launched myself forward promptly.

"Stop, scoundrels!" I cried. "The Princesse still has defenders."

At the sight of me, the furious Arembert hurled himself upon me, and we commenced the most horrible of all combats. Our equal valor rendered it indecisive. Loïse, wanting to end it, placed herself between us, and—O dolor! O despair! O my sons!—she succumbed to the thrusts of the brother of the one who gave you life. O, dear Loïse, from the celestial vaults that you now inhabit, cast a tender glace upon your spouse; remember my tears, my cries, my distress, and the fury that all animated me at the same time. You know, Loïse, that I fell beside you, without thinking of defending myself; I demanded the end of an existence that could not offer me any happiness henceforth. Alas, you perished, and I remained to deplore your loss.

In spite of his ardent desire to fight me. Arembert could not see the blade of his sword stained with the blood of the daughter of the Comte de Toulouse, whom he pretended to adore, without experiencing a sentiment of horror and regret.

Far from seeking to continue our frightful combat, he recoiled two paces, and confounding his cause with mine, he sought to render existence to the woman he had immolated; but there was no longer time, the beautiful soul of Loïse had quit her mortal remains, and nothing any longer remained of that model of perfections than a body deprived of warmth and life.

Meanwhile, the noise of our attack and the number of the men-at-arms who accompanied Arembert had attracted the attention of the soldiers charged with watching over the security of the city. They advanced toward the gate, demanding in loud voices whence came the tumult they had just heard. At their approach, my brother's squires, justly fearing for their safety, hastened to drag him away by force from the place he no longer wanted to quit. He was placed on his horse and they rapidly took the road to Saint-Félix.

I remained alone, despairing of the life of my wife; I was ready to take my own when the concierges of the Montolieu Gate, escorted by soldiers, arrived unfortunately, in time to raise an obstacle to the execution of my project.

The tumor immediately spread through the city that someone had murdered the Comte's daughter, and that I had been wounded trying to defend her.

Oh, what an awakening for a father when he learned of the disastrous event that had brought desolation to his family! Young Raymond, followed by Comte Alphonse, ran precipitately to the place that had witnessed the most frightful of crimes, but, before they had crossed the barriers of their palace, the body of the unfortunate Loïse was brought there by a tearful crowd that was making the air resound with moans. I was carried there myself, for in the excess of my dolor I had lost the sentiment of my existence.

Raymond and Alphonse threw themselves on the remains of my beloved; they shared the despair of the people and they sought to lighten my regrets. The Comte de Toulouse believed that they originated from my attachment to his family, but his son, better informed, gave me the cares that nature commanded for a cherished brother.

For a long time, I was unable to appreciate his cares. I only asked for death; I could not support the idea that I must share the light of day with a man such as my brother. No, my sons, I will never be able to describe for you the horrible state in which I found myself; not only did I have to regret the loss of a cherished spouse, but it was necessary for me to keep silent about the name of her murderer.

Adémar, Odon, however enormous Arembert's crimes were, I could not decide to charge him with Loïse's murder. That thought was far from me, which, in my eyes, would have rendered me equally culpable. When they tried to extract some enlightenment from me on that abominable action, I only spoke of unknown brigands, and I even hid from Raymond what I could have confided to him. He appeared to me to be convinced that my brother was at least the author of the abduction, if not the murder, but the young Prince still believed that his sister had been the victim of her haste to throw herself between the abductors and me.

More than a year passed before I was able to form a reason that diminished my chagrin. Throughout that time, my sons, you were left in the refuge that hid you from all gazes. Raymond and I agreed to keep the secret of your birth from everyone until the death of the noble Amanieu, my father, and that of the Comte de Toulouse. Prudence dictated that conduct to us.

When my strength as sufficiently reestablished, my father, who had come to see me, advised me to travel, in order to distract myself from the somber melancholy that had not abandoned me. I followed his advice; I drew away from the fields of Occitania; I traveled through France, I went to Paris, the abode of the sovereign. I was the witness to the celebrations held there for the marriage of the heir to the crown. Alas, splendor, pomp and dissipation did not bring any relief to my pain. I resolved to change conduct and, far from appearing at the court, I shut myself way in my dwelling and delivered myself to the study of the occult sciences.

I studied Nature with care, I admired her in her effects; I spied on her in her march and surprised her in her causes; eventually, I attained a degree of knowledge that, I dare to believe, no one before me had had any idea, to the extent that I was in a state to produce such astonishing illusions that it was impossible for anyone but me to be able to attribute them to illusion. It was necessary to agree that I could produce prodigies at will, although I was only able to draw upon a part of the resources that Nature offers us.

I do not know what evil spirit breathed malice into Arembert's gangrenous heart; it had seemed natural that the murder of his beloved ought to recall him, by overwhelming him with bitter despair, to sentiments more worthy of him; I had thought that remorse must be pursuing him. Well, far from deploring his crimes and abandoning society, far from retiring to a holy monastery, he delivered himself more than ever to atrocious thoughts.

The first moment, after the fatal death of Loïse, was witness to Arembert's repentance, but when a few days had calmed his first emotion, he ceased to reproach his actions and prepared to pursue me again. The blood that had been shed extinguished his amour but, at the same time, it gave birth to ambition, and it was at that point that the new series of crimes began in which my brother engaged.

He had, as I have already told you, retired to the town of Saint-Félix, where his worthy accomplice, Don Juan d'Astorga did not take long to join him. There, they hatched together a plot to steal my father's heritage from me and to precipitate me, by all sorts of means, into the extremes of misfortune.

Arembert, like almost all the culpable, combined a strong determination for crime with an extreme weakness of imagination; he allowed himself to be taken by the idea of consulting with regard to his future destiny a woman who had been living under the stones of Naurouse for years. The voices of the people rose up against her from all sides; if a storm ravaged the crops, the old woman of Naurouse, as she was called, as blamed; if some destructive scourge depopulated a hamlet, it was her again who was rendered responsible. In sum, feared and hated, everyone believed that it depended on her to evoke the dead, to direct the course of the clouds, to summon mortal exhalations and spread at her whim abundance or calamities in the neighboring regions. It was her that my burgher wanted to consult as to his future destiny.

Dressed in the simple costume of a squire, accompanied by Don Juan, similarly clad, Arembert left Saint-Félix to go to the stones of Naurouse and seek to learn from the old witch the events that Heaven had prepared for him. Alas, it was crime that was about to find a being even more criminal. Sold to Hell, the old woman of Naurouse did not pronounce a single word that evil did not command. She divined my brother under his modest garments and, in order to encourage him to commit new sins, she pretended to believe what he told her.

After a host of hideous, ridiculous and sacrilegious ceremonies, that living demon, having taken care to disturb my brother's head by means of fallacious apparitions, said to him: "Son of a Baron, Baron you will be, when the Baron is no longer."

"What?" cried Arembert. "Am I to succeed my father?"

"If you are able to forestall your father's successor."

"What do you mean by that ambiguous speech?"

"You have committed one murder; no one knows, but all will be discovered. I see the husband advancing; he wants your death, and he is teaching his sons to curse you."

"His sons! What are you saying, woman? Bérenger has sons?"[52]

---

[52] Arembert knew full well that Bérenger had children a few paragraphs ago; the parts of this narrative might not have been written in the order in which they appear in the printed text, and might have incorporated, in a rather careless manner, text from more than one entirely different story, introducing several inconsistencies.

"I do not know the name of the husband; but I assure you that the woman who was your victim has left twin sons."

"Woe betide those children!" said Arembert. "They will follow their family."

"Receive as a present this beverage," said the witch. "It will bear death into the veins of the one who drinks it, and believe me, hasten to make use of it to serve for your own security."

"Is my security menaced, then?"

"Before the moon has shown its ruddy crescent three times," said the witch, "the subterrains of your château will enclose you forever."

Thus spoke the culpable woman. She ignited dread and wrath in Arembert's heart. A thousand passions agitated him when he had learned that Loïse, in expiring, had left two avengers summoned sooner or later to repay him for the death of their mother. He swore to discover the place of their retreat and to make them share the fate of my wife, and mine; for that ingrate and unnatural brother saw no limits to his crimes.

He returned to Saint-Felix prey to the most culpable ideas; it was tremulously that he approached his father; he seemed to hear Amanieu giving him the order to stop; he saw nothing but enemies everywhere. Every day he familiarized himself more with the horrible idea of parricide. Finally, after long combats, Hell prevailed and my brother decided to be its prey. Yes, my sons, you will doubtless have difficulty believing it, so repugnant is such a thought to your beautiful souls, but, alas, it is only too true that Arembert resolved to destroy the author of his days.

In spite of his amity for Don Juan, he dared not confide to him the action he intended to commit, he carried it out alone.

It was night. After having feasted with his vassals, Baron Amanieu desired to yield to slumber. There is, as you know, my sons, an ancient custom that is practiced everywhere; when one wanted to rest one's weary limbs, one takes what is called a bedtime drink. Well, it was into that beverage that

Arembert slipped the poison that the witch had given him. Ambition guided his hand; he immolated his father.

It seemed that Nature, informed of that horrible catastrophe, wanted to show the extent to which it was odious to her; that night was witness to the most frightful tempest that had every roared on earth; the elements battled with one another, jagged lightning streaked the clouds.

Far from the theater of the crime, I was devoting myself to my peaceful studies when, all of a sudden, the lamp only yielded a faint light. My surprise caused me to look up. How astounded I was when I saw, on the other side of my room, through a light cloud, a vaporous shade! It was my father! It approached me. I was frozen by terror. It showed me the cup that it held, it pronounced the words *poison* and *parricide*, and soon vanished, leaving me in a state impossible to describe. I tried in vain to blame my fascinated senses for the vision that had frightened me; the more I sought to doubt its verity, the more its evidence overwhelmed me.

I delivered myself to the most sinister thoughts; I feared the death of the author of my days, and I trembled that he might have perished by a crime, so much did the idea of Arembert persecute me. Ought I to believe that that thought, which I rejected obstinately, was true? Well, I was not mistaken; Amanieu, as you know, had perished by his son's hand.

As soon as the crime had been concluded, the infernal powers took possession of the château of my ancestors. Arembert was pursued by vengeful spirits and, unable to inhabit Saint-Félix, he withdrew to the terrain of Saint-Julia, which had been given to him for his prerogative, and he sent a messenger to inform me of the death of our father, in order that I could take possession of the domains that I was to inherit.

I left Paris promptly, overwhelmed by new regrets, but hoping to see my sons, whom young Raymond had sometimes mentioned to me in the dispatches that he sent me. Their existence was the only thing that could enable me to conserve my own. I feared abandoning them to the enterprises of my brother, who might extend to them the hatred that he bore to their father.

I was not mistaken; Arembert had had the certainty that the marriage formed between Loïse and me had born fruit that closed to him forever the hope of taking possession of my barony. During my absence he spared no efforts and trouble to discover their retreat, but in vain. The Vicomtesse de Carcassonne, who served you as a mother, my sons, was always able to preserve you from the malevolence of Arembert, who was furious at not seeing success respond to his attempts.

I finally reached Toulouse: I presented myself before the Comte and rendered him homage for my lands. Raymond took me secretly to the place where my children were being raised. I lavished the proofs of my tenderness upon them, and removed myself from their presence without suspecting that I would not see them again for a very long time, when Heaven had exhausted all its wrath upon me.

Arembert did not ask to see me when I went to Saint-Félix; he did not leave Saint-Julia, and I did not ask him for exterior demonstrations that would have displeased us both.

However, I could not bear the idea of remaining in a country in which everything depicted my misfortunes, where I had to mourn my wife and my father, and where I might encounter a brother who was the author of my pains. I resolved to go away for a time and travel in the Holy Land, fighting the enemies of the faith. After having taken a roll call of my soldiers I ordered them to take the road to Aigue-Morte, to embark there and disembark in Tripoli, where I would go after spending some time at the court of the Comte de Toulouse, whom I appointed as the agent of my domains. I also confided the education of my children to him, Alphonse having died and Raymond having succeeded him.

I departed, impatient to go, in the midst of dangers, to extinguish the woe of my memories. Followed by two squires, I did not stop in Saint-Félix; it was to Carcassonne that I went in order to savor some repose. The Vicomtesse welcomed me kindly; she shed tears for the fate of her sister and, at that moment, I was less unhappy, for I found a sensible being who shared my tears. The next day I left, after having recommended my children to her a thousand times. I traveled all day.

At the moment when the shadow was disputing the empire of the air with the light, my two squires and I went into a narrow defile formed by the mountains of Narbonne. We had been riding for some time when a whistle blast sounded close by. I stopped and, fearing an ambush, drew my sword. My fears did not take long to be realized; we were surrounded by a numerous troop of armed men, who fell upon us impetuously, without calling upon us to surrender.

I disposed myself to receive them, and combat was engaged in spite of the numerical disadvantage. We defended ourselves for some time; I split the helmet of a knight with my sword and was then able to recognize Don Juan; from that moment on I did not doubt that the enemies surrounding us were directed by my brother. Soon, I perceived him, some way off, but giving his orders.

One of my squires fell from his horse; men threw themselves on him and he was tightly bound. The rage that animated me lent me new strength; I shouted to Arembert in a loud voice, I lavished on him the names that his villainy merited. Alarmed at having been recognized, he advanced to fight me, but at the moment when, for the second time, we were about to soil ourselves with a fratricide, I was pierced by three lance-thrusts, which brought me down.

I felt the chill of death gliding through my veins; my eyes closed, and, murmuring the names of those dear to my heart, I lost consciousness, believing that I was losing my life.

At the moment when I appeared to have succumbed, Arembert drew away precipitately, followed by his troop, only leaving Roberto with the order to give me a sepulcher, as well as the second of my squires, who had remained on the battle-field.

I don't know how long I remained in that state; in the end, I was brought out of it by the generous pity of Roberto, the concierge of the Château de Saint-Félix. That brave vassal, concealing a heart of fire under the appearances of vulgarity, took me, dying, to the Abbaye de Saint-Polycarpe, where I spent several years, so long did it take me to recover from my dangerous wounds. Eventually, he quit me, having remained behind under a specious pretext, but not wanting to awaken my brother's suspicions by too long a sojourn.

Oh, how great my fury was! I swore in the first instance to take a striking vengeance; I promise myself to accuse Arembert loudly of the crimes by which he was soiled, and I did not recoil from the idea of a fratricidal combat. Those thoughts agitated me constantly. Heaven doubtless delayed my recovery in order to give me the means of making more salutary reflections. The saintly Abbot of the monastery, from whom I concealed neither my name nor my projects, tried to touch my heart, to make me understand the horrible excess to which anger was about to take me; he made me see the hand of God directing all human actions, and he proved to me that I had come to equal my brother, by virtue of my insensate fury, in all his black deeds.

Alas, what can I tell you? He was able to touch my heart and change it entirely. I asked him to reconcile me with Heaven; he consented to that. After having undertaken a long penance, I was able to approach the sacred table. There I swore to the venerable monk to forget the world forever, to renounce the rank to which I was born, to take the monastic habit and to wait in silence for the moment when the Supreme Being wanted to strike Arembert, who promised himself impunity.

I kept the solemn engagement that I had made for as long as I could. I struggled against the desire to approach the place of my birth, but in the end, the Abbot of Saint Polycarpe having died, it became impossible for me to remain in the convent, Yielding to the desire by which I was devoured, I took my leave of the good monks and, disguising my name under that of Brother Étienne, I established my dwelling in a hermitage that I built in one of the crossroads of the forest of Caillavel.

Several motives had led me to choose that place in preference to any other. I know that secret passages existed in the Château de Saint-Félix ending on the one hand in various rooms, and on the other communicating with immense subterrains hollowed out in the rock, which led to profound caverns formed by the hands of Nature. One issue was prolonged through the countryside all the way to the somber forest; there, one entered it via a door masked by a large stone. On looking at it, it seemed impossible to move because of its enormous volume, but it was set on a pivot, and a weak hand was sufficient to disturb it.

That subterranean route had been formed in order to be able to get out of the château in the event of a siege, and I was the only one who knew of it, my father not having wanted to show it to his son Arembert, who was not destined to possess his rich barony.

The indications that I had of that place were precise, so I had no difficulty finding it. I established myself there. Wanting to keep the curious away from my dwelling, which they might have approached during my frequent absences, I sought to surround myself with a system of mystery and terror appropriate to repel indiscreet gazes. In consequence, I commenced by edifying a monument n which I engraved the sinister word *vengeance*. I dressed in a bizarre costume, the red color of which was combined with my unusual stature, which I was able to increase further by wearing thick-soled boots, giving myself the appearance of a supernatural being.

I did not stop at those precautions; I added physical procedures of which I had learned the secret in my voyage to Spain. I caused blue flames of appear, of frightening form; I imitated lightning and thunderclaps during the night; I traveled the vicinity of my hermitage enveloped in light flames; I dragged heavy chains, the clinking of which could be heard from afar. Eventually, I succeeded in my objective; fear filled the hearts of the inhabitants of the hamlets surrounding the forest; brigands, and even warriors, would not have dared to cross the barriers that I had placed, so much did they dread the vengeance that I might draw down upon the reckless.

After having thought of my security, however, I wanted to work for the wellbeing of my former vassals. The secret treasure of my family was at my disposal, for I was the only one who knew where it was deposited, so I made use of it to lighten the sufferings of the unfortunate. My cares were blessed, and in the surrounding area, the hermit Étienne was venerated. A zealous servant of the Comte de Toulouse, I sought to render him the services that were within my scope. He was soon informed of it; he wanted to see me…

(*Here there is a lacuna in the manuscript.*)

I went to the château every night and, hidden in the secret chamber that it concealed, I was witness to the scenes that happened there. I took pleasure in importing terror to Arembert's soul by multiplying illusions around him. Sometimes my thunderous voice mingled with his conversations and made him tremble in the midst of his guards. But, always in haste to watch over Adémar, whom I had so much interest in cherishing, I kept away from him everything that might frighten him. Fortunate to have him under my eyes, as well as his brother, the sensible Odon, I was also able to get closer to the latter. The hidden issues from the palace of Carcassonne were known to me, as well as those of the Château de Saint-Félix.

I redoubled my vigilance in the epoch when Princesse Aliénor de Toulouse came to my hermitage, when Arembert embraced the party of the crusaders, drawn by the Abbot of Boncombre, who also wanted to engage me under the same flags. He thought himself well disguised under his pilgrim's costume, but I had seen him in society and I had no difficulty in recognizing him and confounding him. I even had a visit from Arembert once. It was the first time he had thought about me since I had been living in the forest.

His presence excited my indignation; I reproached him for his crimes; in particular, I spoke to him about most horrible with which he was soiled, and of which I had been in-

288

formed by the faithful Roberto. Sire Amanieu, our father, had not terminated his career in the epoch when we had mourned his loss. The barbaric Arembert, pursuing the course of his audacious enterprises by all means, had procured the author of his days a lethargic sleep. He was thought to be dead, and preparations were made for his burial. He was transported, in accordance with custom, to the crypt where he ancestors sleepy; there he recovered life to curse the unnatural son who had conserved him there. He lived for twelve more years in a round dungeon, where he expired about a month before my arrival in the region.

Roberto, solely informed of that horrible story, had done everything he could to lighten the old man's fate. Certain that Arembert would not dare to visit him under those obscure vaults, he had taken him out in order to hide him in an apartment, where he procured the means of sustaining his feeble existence; he only took him back to his prison when Don Juan came to visit his friend.

In order to be more certain that Arembert would not have the curiosity to go to see his father, he talked about Amanieu's anger, the curses that he lavished on his parricidal son; he assured him in addition, that his eyes were witness to the most sinister apparitions; in sum, he succeeded completely in his project, but he went even further. When death had delivered our father from such a painful existence, he hid that end from Arembert, wanting to retain him by fear. Roberto would have told me about my brother's crime before I reappeared in Saint-Félix, but for a long time he believed that I was dead. He had returned to the Abbaye de Saint-Polycarpe a few months after I had been transported there; the monk to whom he addressed himself told him that I had died, fearing that he might be an emissary of Baron Arembert.

Having no motive for doubting what he had been told, he went away, heartbroken. It was, therefore, with an intense surprise that he recognized me in the subterrains of the château when I showed myself to him for the first time. He wanted to flee; I called him back and his joy was extreme in having found me again. But I had come too late; my father was no more.

At least I avenged his memory by means of the terrors that I inflicted upon my unworthy brother. Sometimes in the costume of the hermit, sometimes that of a warrior, and sometimes placing a pellicle under my helmet that gave me the terrible appearance of a death's-head, I showed myself appropriately, either to frighten Arembert, or to protect his victims. It was in that manner that I appeared before the Comtesse de Foix in order console her and deliver her from the pursuits of the unworthy Don Juan to whom I had only mentioned the mountains of Narbonne in order to inspire in him a fear that my brother shared.

When the crusaders besieged Carcassonne, I watched over the days of Vicomte Trencavel and his family. Driven by my warrior ardor, which revealed itself involuntarily, I even appeared on the rampart one day, where my presence alone repelled Arembert, who was ready to climb over.

Eventually, I was fortunate enough to be able to snatch the noble Roger from the death that threatened him, and take him outside his palace, as well as the Vicomtesse, by the routes that we know. Soon afterwards...

(*Here the manuscript in completely lost; several more pages have been torn out, and the end of the hermit's story is unknown to us. The intelligent reader who has read* The Mysteries of Udolpho, The Italian, The Subterrains of Mazzini,[53] The Tomb,[54] etc., *can substitute for the text.*)

---

[53] *Julia, ou les souterrains de Mazzini* is the title of the 1798 French translation of Ann Radcliffe's *A Sicilian Romance* (1790).

[54] *Le Tombeau, ouvrage posthume d'Anne Radcliffe* (1799) is the imitation signed "Hector-Chaussier et Bizet" to which reference is made in the introduction.

SF & FANTASY

Adolphe Alhaiza. *Cybele*
Alphonse Allais. *The Adventures of Captain Cap*
Henri Allorge. *The Great Cataclysm*
Guy d'Armen. *Doc Ardan: The City of Gold and Lepers; The Troglodytes of Mount Everest/The Giants of Black Lake; The Abominable Snowman*
G.-J. Arnaud. *The Ice Company*
André Arnyvelde. *The Ark; The Mutilated Bacchus*
Charles Asselineau. *The Double Life*
Henri Austruy. *The Eupantophone; The Olotelepan; The Petitpaon Era*
Barillet-Lagargousse. *The Final War*
Barbot de Villeneuve.*The Naiads/Beauty & The Beast*
Cyprien Bérard. *The Vampire Lord Ruthwen*
S. Henry Berthoud. *Martyrs of Science; The Angel Asrael*
Aloysius Bertrand. *Gaspard de la Nuit*
Richard Bessière. *The Gardens of the Apocalypse; The Masters of Silence*
Chevalier de Béthune. *The World of Mercury*
Albert Bleunard. *Ever Smaller*
Félix Bodin. *The Novel of the Future*
Pierre Boitard. *Journey to the Sun*
Louis Boussenard. *Monsieur Synthesis*
Alphonse Brown. *City of Glass; The Conquest of the Air*
Émile Calvet. *In a Thousand Years*
André Caroff. *The Terror of Madame Atomos; Miss Atomos; The Return of Madame Atomos; The Mistake of Madame Atomos; The Monsters of Madame Atomos; The Revenge of Madame Atomos; The Resurrection of Madame Atomos; The Mark of Madame Atomos; The Spheres of Madame Atomos; The Wrath of Madame Atomos* (w/M. & Sylvie Stéphan); *The Sins of Madame Atomos* (w/M. & Sylvie Stéphan)
Jean Carrère. *The End of Atlantis*

Félicien Champsaur. *Homo-Deus; The Human Arrow; Nora, The Ape-Woman; Ouha, King of the Apes; Pharaoh's Wife*
Didier de Chousy. *Ignis*
Jules Clarétie. *Obsession*
Jacques Collin de Plancy. *Voyage to the Center of the Earth*
Michel Corday. *The Eternal Flame; The Lynx* (w/André Couvreur)
André Couvreur. *Caresco, Superman; The Exploits of Professor Tornada* (3 vols.); *The Necessary Evil*
Gaston Danville. *The Perfume of Lust*
Camille Debans. *The Misfortunes of John Bull*
Captain Danrit. *Undersea Odyssey*
C. I. Defontenay. *Star (Psi Cassiopeia)*
Charles Derennes. *The People of the Pole*
Georges Dodds (anthologist). *The Missing Link*
Charles Dodeman. *The Silent Bomb*
Harry Dickson. *The Heir of Dracula; Harry Dickson vs. The Spider*
Jules Dornay. *Lord Ruthven Begins*
Alfred Driou. *The Adventures of a Parisian Aeronaut*
Odette Dulac. *The War of the Sexes*
Alexandre Dumas. *The Return of Lord Ruthven; The Man who Married a Mermaid* (w/P. Lacroix)
Renée Dunan. *Baal; The Ultimate Pleasure*
J.-C. Dunyach. *The Night Orchid; The Thieves of Silence*
Henri Duvernois. *The Man Who Found Himself*
Achille Eyraud. *Voyage to Venus*
Henri Falk. *The Age of Lead*
Paul Féval. *Anne of the Isles; Knightshade; Revenants; Vampire City; The Vampire Countess; The Wandering Jew's Daughter*
Paul Féval, *fils. Felifax, the Tiger-Man*
Charles de Fieux. *Lamékis*
Fernand Fleuret. *Jim Click*
Charles-Marie Flor O'Squarr. *Phantoms*
Louis Forest. *Someone is Stealing Children in Paris*

Arnould Galopin. *Doctor Omega*; *Doctor Omega and the Shadowmen* (anthology)

Judith Gautier. *Isoline and the Serpent-Flower*

H. Gayar. *The Marvelous Adventures of Serge Myrandhal on Mars*

Louis Geoffroy. *The Apocryphal Napoleon*

G.L. Gick. *Harry Dickson and the Werewolf of Rutherford Grange*

Raoul Gineste. *The Second Life of Doctor Albin*

Delphine de Girardin. *Balzac's Cane*

Emmanuel Gorlier. *The Nyctalope and the Tower of Babel*

Léon Gozlan. *The Vampire of the Val-de-Grâce*

Jules Gros. *The Fossil Man*

Jimmy Guieu. *The Polarian-Denebian War* (2 vols.)

Edmond Haraucourt. *Daah, the First Human; Illusions of Immortality*

Nathalie Henneberg. *The Green Gods*

Eugène Hennebert. *The Enchanted City*

Jules Hoche. *The Maker of Men and His Formula*

V. Hugo, P. Foucher & P. Meurice. *The Hunchback of Notre-Dame*

Romain d'Huissier. *Hexagon: Dark Matter*

Jules Janin. *The Magnetized Corpse*

Gustave Kahn. *The Tale of Gold and Silence*

Gérard Klein. *The Mote in Time's Eye; Starmasters*

Fernand Kolney. *Love in 5000 Years*

Paul Lacroix. *Danse Macabre; The Man who Married a Mermaid* (w/Alexandre Dumas)

Louis-Guillaume de La Follie. *The Unpretentious Philosopher*

Jean de La Hire. *The Fiery Wheel; Enter the Nyctalope; The Nyctalope on Mars; The Nyctalope vs. Lucifer; The Nyctalope Steps In; Night of the Nyctalope; Return of the Nyctalope; The Nyctalope and the Tower of Babel*

Etienne-Léon de Lamothe-Langon. *The Virgin Vampire*

André Laurie. *Spiridon*

Gabriel de Lautrec. *The Vengeance of the Oval Portrait*

Alain le Drimeur. *The Future City*

Georges Le Faure & Henri de Graffigny. *The Extraordinary Adventures of a Russian Scientist Across the Solar System* (2 vols.)

Gustave Le Rouge. *The Dominion of the World* (w/G. Guitton) (4 vols.); *The Mysterious Doctor Cornelius* (3 vols.); *The Vampires of Mars*

Jules Lermina. *The Battle of Strasbourg; Mysteryville; Panic in Paris; The Secret of Zippelius; To-Ho and the Gold Destroyers*

Maurice Level. *The Gates of Hell*

M.-J. L'Héritier de Villandon. *The Robe of Sincerity*

André Lichtenberger. *The Centaurs; The Children of the Crab*

Maurice Limat. *Mephista*

Listonai. *The Philosophical Voyager*

Jean-Marc & Randy Lofficier. *Edgar Allan Poe on Mars; The Katrina Protocol; Pacifica 1, 2; Robonocchio; Return of the Nyctalope;* (anthologists) *Tales of the Shadowmen 1-14; The Vampire Almanac* (2 vols.)

Ch. Lomon & P.-B. Gheuzi. *The Last Days of Atlantis*

Charles Malato. *Lost!*

Maurice Magre. *The Marvelous Story of Claire d'Amour; The Call of the Beast; Priscilla of Alexandria; The Angel of Lust; The Mystery of the Tiger; The Poison of Goa; Lucifer; The Blood of Toulouse; The Albigensian Treasure; Jean de Fodoas; Melusine; The Brothers of the Virgin Gold*

Victor Margueritte. *The Bacheloress; The Companion; The Couple*

Camille Mauclair. *The Virgin Orient*

Xavier Mauméjean. *The League of Heroes*

Joseph Méry. *The Tower of Destiny*

Hippolyte Mettais. *Paris Before the Deluge; The Year 5865*

Louise Michel. *The Human Microbes; The New World*

Tony Moilin. *Paris in the Year 2000*

Michael Moorcock's *Legends of the Multiverse*

José Moselli. *Illa's End*

John-Antoine Nau. *Enemy Force*

Marie Nizet. *Captain Vampire*

Charles Nodier. *Trilby and The Crumb Fairy*
C. Nodier, A. Beraud & Toussaint-Merle. *Frankenstein*
Oksana & Gil Prou. *Outre-Blanc*
Henri de Parville. *An Inhabitant of the Planet Mars*
Gaston de Pawlowski. *Journey to the Land of the 4th Dimension*
Georges Pellerin. *The World in 2000 Years*
Ernest Pérochon. *The Frenetic People*
Pierre Pelot. *The Child Who Walked on the Sky*
Jean Petithuguenin. *An International Mission to the Moon*
J. Polidori, C. Nodier, E. Scribe. *Lord Ruthven the Vampire*
P.-A. Ponson du Terrail. *The Immortal Woman; The Vampire and the Devil's Son; The Police Agent*
Georges Price. *The Missing Men of the* Sirius
René Pujol. *The Chimerical Quest*
Edgar Quinet. *Ahasuerus; The Enchanter Merlin*
Jean Rameau. *Arrival; in the Stars*
Henri de Régnier. *A Surfeit of Mirrors*
Maurice Renard. *The Blue Peril; Doctor Lerne; The Doctored Man; A Man Among the Microbes; The Master of Light*
Restif de la Bretonne. *The Discovery of the Austral Continent by a Flying Man; Posthumous Correspondence* (3 vols.); *The Fay Ouroucoucou* (2 vols.)
Jean Richepin. *The Crazy Corner; The Wing*
Albert Robida. *The Adventures of Saturnin Farandoul; Chalet in the Sky; The Clock of the Centuries; The Electric Life; The Engineer Von Satanas; In 1965*
J.-H. Rosny Aîné. *Helgvor of the Blue River; The Givreuse Enigma; The Mysterious Force; The Navigators of Space; Vamireh; The World of the Variants; The Young Vampire*
Marcel Rouff. *Journey to the Inverted World*
Marie-Anne de Roumier-Robert. *The Voyage of Lord Seaton to the Seven Planets*
Léonie Rouzade. *The World Turned Upside Down*
Han Ryner. *The Human Ant; The Superhumans*
Henri de Saint-Georges. *The Green Eyes*
Louis-Claude de Saint-Martin. *The Crocodile*

Frank Schildiner. *The Quest of Frankenstein; The Triumph of Frankenstein; Napoleon's Vampire Hunters*
Nicolas Ségur. *The Human Paradise; Penelope's Secret*
Pierre de Selenes: *An Unknown World*
Norbert Sevestre. *Sâr Dubnotal: Vs. Jack the Ripper; The Astral Trail*
Angelo de Sorr. *The Vampires of London*
Brian Stableford. *The Empire of the Necromancers (1. The Shadow of Frankenstein; 2. Frankenstein and the Vampire Countess; 3. Frankenstein in London); The Wayward Muse; Eurydice's Lament; The Mirror of Dionysius; The Pool of Mnemosyne; The New Faust at the Tragicomique; Sherlock Holmes and The Vampires of Eternity; The Stones of Camelot* (anthologist) *News from the Moon; The Germans on Venus; The Supreme Progress; The World Above the World; Nemoville; Investigations of the Future; The Conqueror of Death; The Revolt of the Machines; The Man With the Blue Face; The Aerial Valley; The New Moon; The Nickel Man; On the Brink of the World's End; The Mirror of Present Events; The Humanisphere*
Jacques Spitz. *The Eye of Purgatory*
Kurt Steiner. *Ortog*
Michel & Sylvie Stéphan. *The Wrath of Madame Atomos* (w/André Caroff); *The Sins of Madame Atomos* (w/André Caroff)
Eugène Thébault. *Radio-Terror*
Edmond Thiaudière. *Singular amours*
C.-F. Tiphaigne de La Roche. *Amilec*
Simon Tyssot de Patot. *The Strange Voyages of Jacques Massé and Pierre de Mésange*
Louis Ulbach. *Prince Bonifacio*
Théo Varlet. *The Castaways of Eros; The Golden Rock.; The Martian Epic* (w/Octave Joncquel); *Timeslip Troopers* (w/André Blandin); *The Xenobiotic Invasion*
Pierre Véron. *The Merchants of Health*
Paul Vibert. *The Mysterious Fluid*
Villiers de l'Isle-Adam. *The Scaffold; The Vampire Soul*

Gaston de Wailly. *The Murderer of the World*
Philippe Ward. *Artahe; Manhattan Ghost* (w/Mickael Laguerre); *The Song of Montségur* (w/Sylvie Miller)

MYSTERIES & THRILLERS

M. Allain & P. Souvestre. *The Daughter of Fantômas; The Death of Fantômas*
A. Anicet-Bourgeois & Lucien Dabril. *Rocambole* (stage plays)
Guy d'Armen. *Doc Ardan: The City of Gold and Lepers; The Troglodytes of Mount Everest/The Giants of Black Lake; The Abominable Snowman*
A. Bernède. *Belphegor*; *Judex* (w/Louis Feuillade); *The Return of Judex* (w/Louis Feuillade); *The Shadow of Judex* (anthology)
A. Bisson & G. Livet. *Nick Carter vs. Fantômas* (stage play)
André Caroff. *The Terror of Madame Atomos; Miss Atomos; The Return of Madame Atomos; The Mistake of Madame Atomos; The Monsters of Madame Atomos; The Revenge of Madame Atomos; The Resurrection of Madame Atomos; The Mark of Madame Atomos; The Spheres of Madame Atomos; The Wrath of Madame Atomos* (w/M. & Sylvie Stéphan); *The Sins of Madame Atomos* (w/M. & Sylvie Stéphan)
Félicien Champsaur. *Homo-Deus; Nora, The Ape-Woman; Ouha, King of the Apes*
Jules Clarétie. *Obsession*
V. Darlay & H. de Gorsse. *Arsène Lupin vs. Sherlock Holmes: The Stage Play* (stage play)
Harry Dickson. *Harry Dickson: The Heir of Dracula; Harry Dickson vs. The Spider*
Séamas Duffy. *Sherlock Holmes in Paris*
Paul Féval. *The Black Coats (The Parisian Jungle; Heart of Steel; The Sword-Swallower; 'Salem Street; The Invisible Weapon; The Companions of the Treasure; The Cadet Gang); Bel Demonio; The Companions of the Silence; Gentlemen of the Night; John Devil*

Paul Féval, *fils. Felifax, the Tiger-Man*
Louis Forest. *Someone is Stealing Children in Paris*
Fortuné du Boisgobey: *Two Crimes*
Émile Gaboriau. *Monsieur Lecoq; The Casebook of Monsieur Lecoq*
Arnould Galopin: *Harry Dickson: The Man in Grey; Tenebras*
Goron & Émile Gautier. *Spawn of the Penitentiary*
G.L. Gick. *Harry Dickson: The Werewolf of Rutherford Grange*
Léon Gozlan. *The Vampire of the Val-de-Grâce*
Georges Grison. *The Heads that fell in Paris* (non-fiction)
Paul d'Ivoi. *Around the World on Five Sous* (w/Henri Chabrillat)
Paul Lacroix. *Danse Macabre*
Jean de La Hire. *Enter the Nyctalope; The Nyctalope on Mars; The Nyctalope vs. Lucifer; The Nyctalope Steps In; Night of the Nyctalope; Return of the Nyctalope*
Rick Lai. *Shadows of the Opera: Retribution in Blood; Sisters of the Shadows: The Curse of Cagliostro*
Etienne-Léon de Lamothe-Langon. *The Virgin Vampire*
Steve Leadley. *Sherlock Holmes and The Circle of Blood*
Maurice Leblanc. *Arsène Lupin vs. Countess Cagliostro; Arsène Lupin vs. Sherlock Holmes: 1. The Blonde Phantom; 2. The Hollow Needle; The Island of the Thirty Coffin; 813; The Many Faces of Arsène Lupin* (anthology)
Gustave Lerouge: *The Mysterious Doctor Cornelius* (3 vols.)
Gaston Leroux. *Chéri-Bibi* (stage play)*; The Phantom of the Opera; Rouletabille & the Mystery of the Yellow Room; Rouletabille at Krupp's*
Maurice Limat. *Mephista*
Jean-Marc & Randy Lofficier. *The Katrina Protocol;* (anthologists) *Tales of the Shadowmen 1-13; The Vampire Almanac* (2 vols.)
Charles Malato. *Lost!*
Richard Marsh. *The Complete Adventures of Judith Lee*
William Patrick Maynard. *The Terror of Fu Manchu; The Destiny of Fu Manchu*

Frank J. Morlok. *Sherlock Holmes: The Grand Horizontals* (stage play); *Sherlock Holmes vs Jack the Ripper* (stage play); *Sherlock Holmes, Fantômas, Lupin, Raffles and More: The Spanish Plays* (stage plays)

Jean Petithuguenin. *The Adventures of Ethel King, The Female Nick Carter*

P.-A. Ponson du Terrail. *The Immortal Woman; The Vampire and the Devil's Son; The Police Agent*

Georges Price. *The Missing Men of the* Sirius

Charles Rabou: *The Secret Bureau: The Secret Bureau: The Brothers of Death*

Antonin Reschal. *The Adventures of Miss Boston, The First Female Detective*

Henri de Saint-Georges. *The Green Eyes*

Norbert Sevestre. *Sâr Dubnotal: Jack the Ripper; The Astral Trail*

Eugène Thébault. *Radio-Terror*

P. de Wattyne & Y. Walter. *Sherlock Holmes vs. Fantômas* (stage play)

David White. *Fantômas in America*

Pierre Yrondy. *The Adventures of Thérèse Arnaud of the French Secret Service; The Adventures of Marius Pégomas, Marseille Detective*